His Excellency,
The Ambassador

Erico Verissimo

HIS EXCELLENCY,
THE AMBASSADOR

TRANSLATED BY

Linton Lomas Barrett

and Marie McDavid Barrett

THE MACMILLAN COMPANY : *New York*

COLLIER-MACMILLAN LIMITED : *London*

The Macmillan Company, New York
Collier-Macmillan Canada Ltd., Toronto, Ontario

Designed by Guy Fleming

PRINTED IN THE UNITED STATES OF AMERICA

Contents

I

Washington

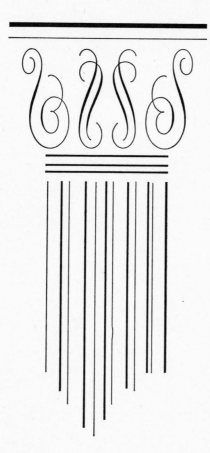

1

O N THE DAY that William B. Godkin completed
thirty-five years' service with Amalgamated Press
as correspondent and specialist in Latin American affairs, his colleagues gave a luncheon in his honor
at the National Press Club in Washington. The toastmas-
ter, in his speech, tempered biography with humor, and
took care to add a touch of sentiment to the mixture. He
recalled incidents, some dramatic, others anecdotal, of
Godkin's long career. Among other things, he said, "To
us, Bill, you are more than a good friend and a loyal
colleague. You are a symbol and—if I may say so—already
a sort of monument."

At the close of his speech he presented to the guest of
honor, as souvenirs of the Amalpress boys, a Swiss wristwatch and an English pipe.

At first Bill Godkin figured that he could wriggle out
of the affair by saying a general "thank you" and making a
sweeping gesture that would include the twenty-odd
friends around him. He detested all types of oratory, especially the kind customarily produced after banquets. However, as cries of "Speech! Come on, Bill! Speech!" rose from
around the table, there was nothing else to do but get up
and talk.

He did not put down the old pipe, still burning, he
had in his hand, and he did not vary his tone of voice,
ordinarily drawling, monotonous and with no dramatic in-
flection. Even when he was not gripping the pipe between
his teeth, he mumbled his words indistinctly, barely moving his lips.

He spoke more than he intended to, revealing

thoughts and feelings he would have preferred to keep secret. Pointing with the stem of his pipe at the master of ceremonies, he said, "When I was the age of that youngster, I took pride in possessing the essential quality of a reporter, that of reporting only facts. Today, in the adolescence of old age (*You can't be ignorant of the fact that I am reluctantly traveling the last mile that separates me from sixty.*) I am beginning to have my doubts . . ." He paused to puff at his pipe, and went on. "The thing we call a fact, isn't it really a kind of iceberg—I mean, something whose visible part is hardly a tenth of the whole? Because the invisible part of the fact is submerged in a turbulent sea of national and individual political and economic interests, egoisms and appetites, not to mention other motives and mysteries of human nature deeper than the depths of the ocean.

"When they split the atom, the scientists of our century also disintegrated semantics and even ethics. Who knows nowadays with absolute certainty the meaning of words that we use so lightly and so often as *liberty, peace, right* and *justice*? As for that terrible word *truth,* what sort of animal is that? How many truths exist in our world of today? I know a lot of them—the truth of the White House. The Kremlin. The Vatican. Wall Street. Broadway. The truth of the U.S. Steel Corporation. The AFL–CIO. Yes, and we mustn't forget the truth of Madison Avenue, perhaps the most fantastic of them all."

He had a slight spell of coughing, cleared his throat, sipped some water, and resumed.

"The young speaker said that I am a symbol. A symbol of what? Perhaps of a type of journalism in process of liquidation. I belong to an era in which correspondents wrote about events. You moderns want to compete with God Himself. You not only try to give tomorrow's facts today, you also arrogate to yourselves the right, when news is lacking, to create events in order to write about them."

He was silent for an instant, and stood staring at the tablecloth, as if the text of his speech were written there.

"As for being a monument, well, maybe what my esteemed colleague meant was that I'm already a wax figure
of myself about to be retired to the dustheap of a city
museum of journalism."

There were voices of protest: "Objection!" "What's the
matter with you, man?" "Nonsense!" Godkin raised his
hand asking for silence, and wound up his speech:

"Be that as it may, don't think I don't appreciate your
gesture—this luncheon, the speaker's words, the handsome
presents. All right, I'm going to shut up so I won't utter
any more idiocies. Thanks, boys."

He sat down amid applause, but was annoyed at himself. He had got up to make a brief, jocular talk befitting
the occasion, and yet he had ended by talking seriously
and, what was worse, making a ridiculous self-pitying
spectacle of himself. Irritated, he knocked out the bowl of
his pipe against the edge of an ashtray, harder than necessary.

He returned to the Amalpress office, where he sat for
a few moments at his desk, examining the papers in front
of him with vague hands and eyes. Then he lifted his head
and gazed at the calendar on the opposite wall. Monday,
April 6. There was only one decent thing to do, he decided. He summoned his secretary. Miss Kay entered,
notebook in hand, a yellow pencil stuck through her
bleached hair above her ear. She was a smallish woman of
uncertain age, sharp profile, and steely eyes.

"Anything important?"

"No, Mr. Godkin."

"Fine. Tell the boys I'm going out and won't be back
today."

"Very well, Mr. Godkin."

Admirable Miss Kay! Exact as a chronometer. Efficient as a machine. During work hours she never allowed
herself any observation or gesture of a personal nature.

"I've just made a great discovery," the newspaperman
muttered as he put on his topcoat and picked up his hat.

"Yes, Mr. Godkin?"

"The most important thing in Washington is not the White House. Or the Department of State. Or the Treasury. Or the FBI. Or the Smithsonian Institution."

Her face impassive, the secretary waited, at attention. At the door Bill completed his thought. "It's the cherry trees along the Potomac in the first week of April. If the papers don't lie, they should be completely covered with flowers today."

He stole a glance at his secretary, hoping for a smile or some other human reaction from her. But Miss Kay remained serious, still at attention. She refused to enter into the joke, maintaining her metallic, machinelike indifference. Does a teletype tremble with pleasure or indignation at the news that it receives or transmits?

"See you tomorrow, Miss Kay."

"Good-by, Mr. Godkin."

Out on the street Bill Godkin felt on his face the almost chill breath of springtime, redolent of humid, green distances. He decided to walk to the Tidal Basin. Hands thrust into the pockets of his topcoat, he turned southward along Sixteenth Street. He thought of his friend Pablo Ortega, First Secretary of the Embassy of the Republic of Sacramento. One day when the sky was as clean and luminous as it was now, the younger man had looked upward and exclaimed, "I'll bet God gave Fra Angelico the job of painting the sky today. Only he knows the secret of that pure blue." Curious, Bill reflected, it was precisely on such beautiful days that he felt his loneliness most poignantly. He had no children, and he had lost his wife to leukemia only two years before. And that gentle creature, who looked liked a pastel portrait, had gradually faded away without ever complaining, without losing even for an instant the joy and hope of living, or her affectionate interest in people, animals, and things. "God knows what He's doing . . ." was her favorite sentence. "The truly mature man is the one who understands the symbolic language of his Creator."

Still thinking of his deceased wife, Bill Godkin approached Lafayette Square. He caught sight of the White

House beyond the park. In his opinion it was the most beautiful building in Washington, a happy combination of dignity and grace, simplicity and harmony. In some room of that mansion the President at that hour was undoubtedly meditating apprehensively over problems of the moment: the outcome of the Cuban revolution, and more serious yet, the drama of the Secretary of State, who was in a hospital with an abdominal cancer, his days numbered.

Bill prepared to cross H Street. Ruth's image, accompanied by the ghost of her voice, popped into his mind: "Darling, never cross a street without first looking both ways, will you?" Bill obeyed her recommendation, but in a merely mechanical way, for he had no clear awareness of whether he could or could not cross without danger. He stepped forward in his slow, habitual stride, but he had to quicken his pace when a black Cadillac of funereal aspect suddenly loomed up close at his right. He finally made it to the sidewalk. (A car like that had carried Ruth's body to the cemetery.) Yonder in the center of the square rose the equestrian statue of Andrew Jackson—the horse with his forelegs in the air, the rider with his right arm raised, his hand holding his cocked hat. According to the experts, the position of the horse, balancing on his hind legs, had presented a difficult mechanical problem which the sculptor had solved brilliantly. (Orlando Gonzaga, his Brazilian friend, had told him once, "You Americans confuse art with artisanry.")

Godkin had no enthusiasm for the statues in the capital. The great majority of them were conventional and lacked grandeur and beauty. The most admirable monuments of Washington were the trees and parks, he concluded, as he walked in the shade of the elms along the sidewalk of Jackson Place. Those tall, slender trees, of noble aspect, evoked for him the figure of Abraham Lincoln.

Bill stopped an instant to watch a flock of starlings, with dark, iridescent plumage and yellow beaks, which were warbling and chattering excitedly in the branches of a magnolia. Ruth used to say that the trees, the flowers, the birds, the babies, and the other beautiful things in life are words scattered from a message that God repeatedly sends to men, a message of hope in the midst of this cruel, sordid, absurd world. Sordid and absurd . . . Godkin remembered that, some years before (Five? Six? Maybe seven?), early on an August morning, humid and oppressive in the heat, after a particularly tiring evening in the Amalpress offices, he had come to relax there in the square, and had stood for some moments under that same tree. The sweetish fragrance of the magnolia flowers in the stagnant air was like a warm physical presence, as disturbing as a carnal caress. Bill had never forgotten that night and that place because of what had happened then and there. A homosexual had accosted him, bluntly making an obscene proposition. He had merely cast a quick glance at the stranger—blond, slender, well dressed, presumably about thirty-odd years old—and had started walking without responding to the invitation or even getting indignant. What he had felt was a certain constraint mingled with pity. The man had followed him, repeating his proposition more and more insistently. He was breathing hard, and his contralto voice was painfully grotesque. When he grabbed his arm, Bill thrust him away, threatening to beat him up. The pervert halted, recoiled a step or two, and said, "If you came strolling along here at this time of night it's because you've unconscious *tendencies*."

Bill Godkin could not understand the reason—if reason entered into the story—why the sexual deviates of Washington had chosen that square, so close to the Executive Mansion, for their amorous encounters.

He stopped at a corner on Pennsylvania Avenue. After the traffic light opposite one of the White House gates had turned green, he crossed the avenue and continued along the opposite sidewalk, past the mastodonic edifice, the color of old bones and designed in French neoclassic style, in which the Department of State had formerly been located. He thought again of the Secretary of State. He was a man of courage and integrity, but prejudiced by his

calvinistic view of the world. How could a puritan statesman understand Latin America? And what was going to
happen in Cuba now? Fulgencio Batista's partisans responsible for atrocities and various other crimes were still
being shot. The revolutionary government had taken over,
"provisionally," the Cuban Telephone Company, a sub-
sidiary of the U. S. Telephone & Telegraph Company. The
nationalization of other American enterprises, Godkin reflected, would inevitably follow sooner or later. How
would the government of the United States act in that
case? Bill knew that eventually some congressman or
other, invoking human rights, would make a speech in the
Capitol protesting against the shootings in Havana, but
the members of Congress would get really indignant, moving heaven and earth, only when Fidel Castro started con-
fiscating the property of North American citizens. Bill
Godkin stopped short and recalled that Machiavelli had
counseled the prince to have his subjects murdered when
necessary, but to avoid touching their property, because a
man more easily forgets his father's death than the loss of
his patrimony.

But how could anyone think cynical thoughts on a
spring afternoon like this, Godkin asked himself as he
started diagonally across the Ellipse toward the Washington Monument. In the air was an idle, luminous holiday
contentment. Hundreds of persons (or could it be thousands?) were strolling over the grass and along the walks:
men, women, and children, multicolored blots in motion
that suggested to Bill a modern parody of a painting by
Brueghel, *The Country Wedding,* which he and Ruth had
seen in a Vienna museum. (Poor Ruth! In spite of knowing
that she would have barely a year to live, with what child-
like gaiety she had enjoyed her first and last trip to Europe.) All these people were heading for the cherry trees
on the banks of the Potomac or coming back from there.
The Greyhound buses, blue and silver, bedecked with flags
and filled with tourists, rolled down Constitution Avenue,
where traffic was thick. On one of the sidewalks of South
Executive Avenue many people were taking pictures or

simply gazing through the iron fences at the gardens and
the south façade of the White House.

The scent of new grass rising to Bill's nostrils brought
to mind a landscape from his childhood: Kansas pastures
in April. He began whistling between his teeth a tune
which he always associated with the idea of leisure and
holiday time. He stopped for an instant to toss some bread
crumbs to three squirrels, two gray and one black, which
had drawn near. During the luncheon at the Press Club he
had taken care to stick a few lumps of bread into his
pocket, thinking specifically of these "customers."

He gazed at the obelisk of the monument on the top
of its green hillock, surrounded by national flags fluttering
in the breeze. Again the voice of Orlando Gonzaga came to
mind: "The obelisk? Obviously this federal town needed
an imposing artificial stone phallus as a compensation for
its castration complex." Bill, smiling at his friend's observation, had asked him, "Why castration?" The reply was
prompt. "Well, to begin with, it's a conglomeration of government officials and diplomats, some of them of doubtful
sex, and elderly retired people. And besides that, my dear
fellow, this enclave squeezed between Maryland and Virginia hasn't even the right to vote."

As he slowly climbed the hill toward the monument,
Bill kept up the imaginary dialogue with the first secretary
of the Brazilian Embassy. "Look there, Gonzaga. How can
you people call us a materialistic nation, concerned only
with the dollar, when those little Japanese trees which
flower in April have the power to attract thousands of citizens from all over the country every year to this city?"

Now halfway up, Bill Godkin glimpsed the tops of the
cherry trees surrounding the Tidal Basin. He paused,
breathing heavily, whether from the effort of the ascent or
from pure emotion caused by the view he could not tell.
Before him was a sight so lovely and at the same time so
fragile that the mere attempt to describe it in words, to
paint it or even to photograph it, might break its spell. He
must approach the blossoming cherry grove with the
greatest caution, treading and breathing lightly.

He thought of his dead wife, and sadness dimmed his glance. Poor Ruth! She was right. God was a poet, the greatest of them all. Unfortunately, men, obtuse and illiterate, could not read the poems written by the Creator. "Obtuse and illiterate," murmured Bill, walking on toward the cherry trees, "all of them. Even I. Especially I."

2

W HEN, HOURS LATER, he reached the little bar on Connecticut Avenue where he had an appointment to meet his two diplomat friends, Orlando Gonzaga was already there, ensconced at his usual table, his back to the rear wall of the room. The Brazilian used to say that he was like his maternal grandfather, the swaggering political boss in the interior of Minas Gerais, lord of vast lands and numerous enemies—he felt secure only when he had the solidity of a wall at his back for protection.

"Bill, old man!" Gonzaga exclaimed, gripping the hand held out to him by the newspaperman. "You're late. I've been here nearly half an hour waiting for Godkin. If only it were for Godot!"

Bill, who was no addict of either the theater or literature, did not catch the allusion or ask for an explanation. He sat down and mentioned where he had been.

"The cherry blossoms!" the diplomat exclaimed. "The great botanical commonplace of Washington."

"Don't be snobbish. I can't believe you don't appreciate the sight like everyone else."

Gonzaga smiled. "What are you going to have?"

"A Campari."

"Keep your voice down, or someone may denounce you to Congress for un-American activities. Have you quit bourbon entirely?"

"A Campari," the newspaperman confirmed his order, lighting his pipe and loosening the knot of his bilious green tie.

Gonzaga, who was finishing his second martini, summoned the waiter and gave him the order.

"If I had any sense," Godkin grumbled, "what I'd have would be hemlock."

"Why, Socrates?"

"I came to the conclusion today that no man ought to consent to his own aging. I was comparing the annual re-flowering of the cherry trees with the progressive, irreversible hardening of my arteries."

"Nonsense. I don't believe what you're saying. I consider you a solid citizen."

"Today I feel hollow," Bill confessed. (And lonely, he thought.)

The waiter set the glass of Campari on the table in front of him. Godkin proposed a toast. "As you say in Brazil, 'Here's to our good qualities!' "

"Which are not few," the other added, also raising his glass.

Godkin observed that his friend's eyes were fixed on something, or rather someone—probably a woman—at the other end of the room. It was a gaze so thick with sensuality, Bill thought, that it seemed to leave a viscous trail in the air.

He resisted the temptation to turn his head, and sat studying his friend with the eye of the reporter. Orlando Gonzaga had a fleshy face, all but verging on fat, with slightly protuberant chestnut eyes and purplish eyelids. A carefully trimmed mustache, as black as his hair, crowned his well-shaped lips. His voice, deep, soft, and persuasive, was the kind appropriate to dimly lighted boudoirs. A man of medium height, the diplomat had the athletic bearing that Godkin habitually associated with judo practitioners. He dressed with a discreet elegance (gray and blue were his favorite colors), wore only custom-tailored shirts, and showed a decided predilection for Italian ties and shoes and English suits. When he was with this man, always well-dressed, well-kept, well-shaven, well-brushed, Bill Godkin was most keenly aware of his own untidiness. Not long before, in a contest jestingly held by his colleagues, his name had appeared among the ten worst-dressed corre- spondents in Washington. He could put on a brand-new suit one day and by the next it would be looking old: the trousers would lose their creases, the jacket its shape, and the pockets came to look pregnant, filling up with papers, bread crumbs, postage stamps, coins, stubs of pencils, books, and frequently whole newspapers.

"And what about our friend Pablo?" Bill asked.

Without taking his eyes off the "vision," Gonzaga re- plied, "He telephoned just now to say he couldn't come. He's busy with his new ambassador, who is to present his credentials to the President tomorrow."

"Poor fellow! I'd hate to be in his shoes."

"So would I. These ambassadors who, besides not being career officers, are bosom friends of the President, make a hell of a lot of work. But, Bill, changing the sub- ject, don't look now, but take a glance at that lovely lady in the back of the room. I've been giving her the eye for hours, but there's no way to make her look at me."

Godkin smiled, waited a few seconds, then turned his head and saw, sitting at a table against the opposite wall, an attractive woman smoking and drinking alone.

"What do you think of her?"

"Beautiful, brightly made-up, and unreal as a multi- color illustration for a story in *The Saturday Evening Post.*"

"Right! Perfect! You've just given a marvelous defini- tion of this country's pretty women. Brighter in colors than those of any other country in the world. Odorless because they take a bath every day and are obsessed with deodor- ants. But they have no flavor, no taste, just like American food."

"No taste?"

"Listen, Bill. Take one of those magazine advertise- ments illustrated with wonderful reproductions of dishes and foods. What colors! What realism! What beauty! They make our mouths water. But you might as well eat the very pages of the magazine as eat the food, because the flavor of the printed page is as tasty as that of the food itself."

"Don't tell me that it's all the same whether you take an American woman or her color portrait to bed with you."

"Nearly."

"Don't exaggerate."

Gonzaga frowned.

"You needn't look behind you, Bill, because I'm going to describe what's happening with our beauty. A fellow about six-feet-six has just come in, blond, fullback type, face like a dolt, maybe a hero of the Korean War. He bent over and kissed her, the so-and-so. She smiles. He sits down. They talk. Can they be married? Well, the kiss looked matrimonial to me. Let's assume they are married. They probably have sexual relations once a month, because he, as an efficient junior executive in a prosperous firm, has social and business worries that make him a little negligent in the fulfillment of his marital duties."

Godkin smoked, smiled, and listened. Gonzaga leaned over the table as if he were going to disclose a state secret.

"Since you Americans settled the West, you've been constantly seeking new frontiers to conquer. You climb mountains, you go hunting under the water, you set new speed records on land and in the air, you cultivate the giddiest and most dangerous sports just to prove to yourselves and to the world that you are enterprising, skillful, and, principally, male. And yet you haven't seen that the most important internal frontier in this country is still virgin and unconquered. The American woman, Bill! Lay aside for a moment your electronic toys and try to use your virility better than you use a baseball bat."

"You Latins know it all, don't you?"

"I'll tell you one thing, old man—at least we know how to use our bodies without inhibitions. Wait! The full-

back is paying the waiter. The goddess has got up. Wow!
What a lovely *derrière* she has!"

Like so many other Brazilians of his acquaintance,
Bill reflected, Gonzaga seemed to feel a special attraction
for that part of the female anatomy.

"Another Campari?"

"No. I had wine with lunch, something I rarely do."

"Ah! How did the anniversary party go?"

"Oh, the usual stuff. Wisecracks, kidding, speeches."

Bill looked around the room. Shaded lights gave the
atmosphere a crepuscular intimacy. A fragrance of gar-
denia floated in the air (Could it be coming from that
sturdy blonde at the next table?), blended with whiskey.
An invisible loudspeaker was softly spilling a sad, sultry
blues melody into the room.

"Mr. Godkin, you're a real hero. Thirty-five years with
the same firm. One year longer than my own existence in
this vale of tears."

"And you want me to feel happy today? I've been
totting up a balance of my life's accounts, sitting on a
bench on the bank of the Tidal Basin. Soon I'll be starting
on my sixties. I am neither rich nor famous. By American
standards, I ought to regard myself as a failure."

"Send those standards to the devil, Bill. Who are
Americans to set up absolute standards for humanity?
Supermen? Gods?"

"I don't know, but even so . . ."

Gonzaga leaned back against the leather upholstery of
his seat and abstractedly eyed his third martini, which the
waiter in response to his signal was now setting before
him.

"You've never told me how you fell into the talons of
the Amalpress."

"You really want to know?"

"Of course."

Bill looked at the diplomat in indecision. He was
doubtful about the other's sincerity. He knew that Gonzaga, like the majority of Latins, was a poor listener. He
liked to talk, but he did not know how to listen.

"Among my scanty academic achievements in City College of New York, the most notable was a thesis I wrote under the pretentious title of *Latin American Dictatorships Under the X Ray*."

"Pretentious? Why?"

"Why, because I was a greenhorn of not quite twenty-four, and had never set foot in Latin America. I knew a bit of Spanish, I nourished a romantic admiration for figures such as Bolívar, Zapata, Juárez . . . and I had devoured scores of books in the public library on Latin America. As you see, my X-ray machine was nothing more than a secondhand binocular—"

"Prescott wrote his *Conquest of Mexico* without ever having visited Mexico."

Bill smiled, displaying his yellowed teeth.

"I don't remember how or why, but one of the directors of Amalpress read my thesis, thought I had the qualities of a reporter, and offered me a job in his agency. I accepted. I was sent to one of those little Central American republics where they expected excitement on the eve of a presidential election. I spent a really rough month in that tropical hell. The correspondent for another agency, my roommate in the hotel and victim of the same mosquitoes, contracted malaria. I was luckier. I came out of the adventure with amebic dysentery, which took five years to cure."

"How about the revolution?"

"There wasn't any. No election, either. The usual story. But . . ."

He stopped, seeing that Gonzaga was no longer paying any attention to what he was saying.

"Bill, old man, a subversive brunette has just come in. She must be a Latin. Oh, I know who she is now. Daughter of the ambassador from El Salvador. What eyes! But go on, Bill, go on."

"I know that young lady, Gonzaga. She is married, and no nonsense about it. Abandon hope."

"I know. But is it a sin to look? Go on with your story,

Bill. Don't be jealous. My eyes may be on the brunette, but my ears are with you."

"It's not worth bothering with."

"All right, if you insist, I'll look at your face, even though freckled blond men in the late fifties are not my type. . . . Waiter! More olives. On with it, Bill."

"My big chance came at the end of 1925. In the Republic of El Sacramento, where Don Antonio María Chamorro had been dictator for nearly twenty-five years, a young lieutenant, Juventino Carrera, led an army battalion in revolt at the barracks in the city of Los Plátanos, and took refuge with his soldiers in the Sierra de la Calavera, from which he initiated an implacable guerrilla war against the federals."

Bill Godkin took a sip of Campari and went on. "One day I determined to get a personal interview with Lieutenant Carrera in his burrow, or rather, in his eagle's nest. My chief thought the notion a little visionary. El Sacramento was an unimportant country. Everybody regarded the young revolutionary's cause as lost. Don Antonio Chamorro was solidly entrenched in power. The peasants who aided the revolutionaries were summarily shot. Besides everything else, "El Chacal del Caribe," as his enemies called the dictator, had the moral support of Don Herminio Ormazábal, the archbishop primate of El Sacramento."

"And probably the protection of the United Plantations Company," added Gonzaga.

"Yes, and of the Caribbean Sugar Emporium. In short, Chamorro's administration looked about as firm as the Andes. But the fact is that nobody could get the idea out of my head. I was in sympathy with the rebel cause. And, just between us, being a man of the plains, I have always felt the fascination of mountains. All right. I got in touch with the U.S. Embassy in Cerro Hermoso. The ambassador tried to dissuade me, and only with the greatest reluctance did he use his good offices with the Chamorro government to get me what I wanted. To cut the story short, I got a safe-conduct, swore before the Sacramentan authorities that I would not take advantage of the opportunity to lend any service whatever to the revolutionaries, and promised to submit my interview with Carrera to the censor before publishing it."

The Brazilian now seemed interested in the narrative.

"You don't know El Sacramento, Gonzaga. The Sierra de la Calavera stands at the eastern end of the Cordillera de los Indios, which cuts the island from east to west." Bill took out his fountain pen and sketched the map of the Republic of El Sacramento on a paper napkin. "Here at some twenty-odd kilometers from the spurs of the Sierra lies the town of Soledad del Mar. It was there that I began the climb. You can't imagine the trouble I had to find a native who would guide me to Carrera's hideout."

"Of course they all distrusted you."

"Naturally. The authorities were afraid that I might be taking some message to the rebels. The peasants suspected that I was a secret agent of the dictatorship sent to assassinate Carrera. Finally Padre Catalino, the young parish priest of Soledad del Mar, came to my aid. It was rumored that he had already been reprimanded several times by the archbishop for giving comfort to the revolutionaries. Well, the good padre secretly fixed me up with a guide whom he trusted and who promised to take me as far as Carrera's first sentry. And off I went up the mountains, mounted on a burro, with a camera slung round my neck."

"What sort of man was this Juventino Carrera?"

"Physically, very much like Simón Bolívar. He knew it, and turned the likeness to good account."

"In your climb up the Sierra you ran the risk of getting shot from both sides."

"Isn't that the eternal position of the liberal? A man always caught in a crossfire."

"When you came back down, naturally you were questioned by Chamorro's men."

"Yes, interrogated, frisked, sniffed over. . . . I prepared

expressly for the Sacramentan authorities a fictitious news story in which I described the revolutionaries as a band of undisciplined adventurers, ill-armed, ill-supplied, with extremely low morale and on the verge of total collapse. I managed to hide the roll of films I had taken, and I memorized the conversations I had with Carrera. Back in Washington I wrote a series of illustrated articles favorable to the revolutionaries and against Chamorro's dictatorship."

"And those articles, published throughtout the world, naturally aided the cause of the rebels."

"I have good reasons to think so."

"They could have awarded you the Pulitzer Prize for Journalism for 1925," Gonzaga observed.

Godkin shook his head, picked up his pipe, and began to fill it with tobacco.

"Hardly. I don't deny that my articles contained facts set forth objectively, but they lacked what critics call 'literary distinction.' I know my limitations, my friend. I am not a brilliant writer. My superiors consider me a 'competent professional.' My colleagues are in the habit of saying that I have a toad's prismatic eyes—which is no disadvantage to a reporter, certainly. I know I have a photographic memory." He touched his forehead with the stem of his pipe. "But, as it happens, this camera photographs only in black and white. Believe me, Gonzaga, I'm a man of little imagination."

"But to get on with your story . . . what happened after the publication of those articles?"

"My situation in Amalpress improved enormously. In 1926 Juventino Carrera overthrew the dictator and was elected president of the republic. He invited me to his inauguration and granted me an exclusive interview, as he had promised me in the Sierra."

"And your superiors then began to look on you with more respect."

"Worse than that. They went so far as to consider me a specialist in Latin American affairs. In 1928 they appointed me correspondent-at-large, with my base of operations first in Mexico City and then in Rio. I was one of the first foreign newspapermen to interview Vargas in October of 1930 when he arrived from the south, heading the revolutionary troops which had just taken over the government."

"At that time—let me see—that year I was starting kindergarten."

"I think I was the last correspondent to interview General Augusto César Sandino, in Nicaragua, a few weeks before he was assassinated."

"What kind of man was he?"

"The official press made him out a bandit. But Sandino, a mining engineer and agriculturist, was a patriot, a liberal. He took up arms against his country's dictatorship and fought for six years, opposing not only the government soldiers but also the United States Marines. He was never captured. When the Marines withdrew from Nicaragua, Sandino agreed to lay down his arms, and he devoted himself peacefully to the realization of a plan of farm cooperatives. One day he went to visit President Moncada, and when he was coming out of the Government Palace, one of the guards took him unawares and murdered him."

"There are some pretty sordid chapters in the history of this America of ours, aren't there, Bill?"

"And speaking of sordid chapters, at the beginning of 1935 Amalpress sent me to the Chaco Boreal to cover one of the most senseless wars in history. In that arid, desolate region Paraguayan and Bolivian soldiers, most of them Indians and mestizos, had been killing each other for years *por la patria*."

"And for the interests of American oil."

"Exactly. The Amalpress editors generally cut out of my stories each and every reference to that company. I was attached to the Paraguayan forces, and had the opportunity to examine some of the weapons captured from the Bolivians. They were of American manufacture, and everything indicated that they had been used by the U.S. Army in the First World War."

For some seconds Bill sat smoking and drinking in silence, and then broke out in an inaudible but visible laugh, his shoulders shaking and his face wrinkling in a comic expression.

"Once upon a time," he said, "in Buenos Aires I got a memorable beating that nearly cost me my life."

"Why, you never told me that."

"In 1943 Amalpress sent me to Argentina to write a series of articles on the political situation there. Castillo's government had been thrown out by a coup inspired by the GOU, the Group of United Officers, whose leading spirit, as you must remember, was Colonel Juan Perón. In the first article I revealed the connection of that gang with Nazi espionage. In the second, I gave as my opinion that our Department of State should not recognize the revolutionary government of General Pedro Ramírez because he had Hitlerian leanings and would inevitably sabotage the program of hemisphere defense. *La Nación* published those articles. The nationalistic papers naturally hurled the most virulent insults at me and demanded that the government expel me immediately from the country."

Godkin paused, and for a moment doodled concentric circles with his pen on his paper napkin.

"One night, quite late," he continued, "I was returning to my hotel in Buenos Aires when three strangers came up, seized me without a word, and dragged me into a deserted street. Ah, Gonzaga, why is it that a man's ashamed to cry out for help? I could have yelled loud enough. To this day I don't understand why I clamped my mouth shut and got ready for the worst."

The Brazilian smiled. "It must have been because you subconsciously thought you deserved punishment."

"I don't know. I took the first blow, which broke my nose. It left my face looking like a retired prizefighter's. I hit back and landed a punch on my attacker's chin. One of the hoods then got a strangle hold on me, another gripped my arms and legs so I couldn't move, and the third then really went to work on me. By the size of the man and the impact of his fists, I could tell that he must have been an athlete. A blow in the pit of my stomach knocked the wind out of me. A kick on another, still more sensitive, part of

my body made me faint from the pain. While I lay unconscious on the ground, I don't know for sure how long, they
stamped on my face, my chest, my kidneys. When I came
to, I found myself in a hospital bed with the United States
ambassador sitting by it. I had several teeth and ribs
broken, abrasions over my whole body, hematomas around
both eyes. . . . In short, from my head to my feet I was one
solid ache. I was under sedation for days."

"And what action did the police take?"

"None. They faked an investigation in which it was
ascertained that I had been attacked by parties unknown
with the purpose of robbery. But it was quite clear that
my assailants were nationalists. When they discharged me
from hospital, I was declared *persona non grata* by the
Ramírez government and invited to leave the country."

"What an honor, Bill!"

"When I got back to Washington, Amalgamated Press
gave me a bonus and sent me to San Juan on a paid vacation. It was there I met the girl I finally married at the end
of 1944." He paused, and then added with a resigned sadness, "And who I lost two years ago."

"What did you do during the last world war?"

Godkin was on the verge of confessing that, inter-
mingled with newspaper chores, he had done "a few special services" for the FBI, but he thought it best to keep
quiet about that.

"Well," he grumbled, puffing out a smoke screen, "I
went from pillar to post. In '45 I was in Rio when the
Brazilian generals deposed Getúlio Vargas. I'm not going
to relate my adventures in the *bogotazo,* that uprising in
Bogotá in '48, because it's too long a tale. But, just to
round out this cloak-and-dagger short story, in 1952 my
chief summoned me to tell me that I had been promoted—
get that, *promoted*—and chained me to a desk in Washington with the pompous title of Chief of the Latin American
Bureau. End of career, you understand."

Gonzaga gave his friend an affectionate glance. "But,
getting back to Juventino Carrera, what a nasty piece of

goods that hero of the Sierra de la Calavera turned out to be!"

Bill shrugged his shoulders. "He has followed the general rule of Latin America. He overthrew the tyrant and wound up becoming a tyrant too. Do you know the first thing he did after he took up lodgings in the Government Palace? He signed a decree promoting himself to *generalissimo,* like Trujillo, whose friend, *compadre,* and ally he later became. And as he wanted a title, too, like that of the Dominican dictator, there was a scribe to propose one to the people—'El Libertador'—which caught on immediately."

"Have another Campari?"

"No, thanks."

"Hemlock?"

"No hemlock, either. I feel better now. I think it did me good to recall all those stories."

"After Carrera's inauguration ceremonies you saw him again sometimes, of course."

"Many times. Whenever there was some trouble in El Sacramento, Amalpress would dispatch me to Cerro Hermoso."

"Then you must know the ambassador personally, the one that the generalissimo has just sent here, don't you?"

"Don Gabriel Heliodoro Alvarado? Sure I know him. The first time I saw him, he was with Juventino Carrera, up in the Sierra de la Calavera. He was one of Carrera's youngest and bravest comrades. He must have been around twenty-five, at the outside."

"What type of man is he?"

"Physically? Six feet, three inches tall, more or less. A coppery face whose features remind you a little of certain Mayan sculptures. Lively, dark eyes, expressive of a compelling personality. Of all the men I met in the *cordillera* with Carrera, the face most deeply engraved on my memory has been Gabriel Heliodoro's. The surname he uses is adopted, but it suits him."

Orlando Gonzaga picked up the newspaper lying beside him on the banquette, and spread it out on the table.

"The *News* today carries an item about his 'Mayan sculpture' face, with a photograph. Look at this picture. The rascal does have an attractive face. The biographic note says he was born in 1903, so he must be fifty-six now. This must be an old picture, because it shows a man of forty-five to forty-eight years old, at most."

Bill took out his glasses, mounted them on his nose, and leaned over the paper. "No, the photo is a recent one. Those Indian faces don't show their ages."

"The paper also tells a tale of heroism which strikes me as being fabricated by our ineffable Titito Villalba in his zealous little efforts to publicize his new ambassador—for whom he must be burning with passion."

Bill Godkin grinned. "The affair of the hand grenade? I assure you that it's true, Gonzaga. I was the first to publish it, in my 1925 news stories. I had it direct from the mouth of Juventino Carrera himself. It happened at the start of the campaign. One day, to evade an ambush, the revolutionaries had to take refuge in a cave. One of the federals succeeded in throwing a grenade into the hideout, and it rolled to Carrera's feet. Our Gabriel Heliodoro did not hesitate a second. He leaped forward, snatched up the grenade, ran to the mouth of the cave, and hurled it back toward the enemy. The grenade exploded in the air, and a splinter wounded Gabriel Heliodoro on his forehead. In the picture you can plainly see the scar, shaped like a lightning flash."

"What a fire-eater!"

"That explains everything that Carrera did for Gabriel Heliodoro after he established himself firmly in the government. They became intimate friends, *compadres* . . . and partners. And our hero has had a spectacular career, socially and financially. And now we have him as the representative of his country to the White House and to the Organization of American States."

"It's fantastic. Pablo told me that Gabriel Heliodoro never even finished high school."

"But El Libertador is counting on the shrewdness and the personal attractiveness of his *compadre* to arrange a delicate matter with the U.S. government. You probably recall that the Vice President visited the Republic of El Sacramento last year, and was booed in the streets of Cerro Hermoso by the common people and students, who hurled stones, tomatoes, and rotten eggs at the official car in which he was riding. Well, one of those eggs hit full on target and smashed against his chest."

Gonzaga laughed. "And now Don Gabriel Heliodoro is going to try, with the cleaning fluid of his personal charm, to remove the eggstain from the Vice President's clothes and from the American flag."

"Yes, and as was to be expected, he also has the mission of preparing Uncle Sam's mind to pry another substantial loan out of him."

Gonzaga looked at the picture again. "Well, the scoundrel is undeniably attractive."

"He may turn out to be a good ambassador."

"Is he pure Indian, I wonder?"

"On his mother's side, without the slightest doubt."

"And on his father's?"

The newspaperman shrugged. "Only God knows. Gabriel Heliodoro's mother never had a husband. She was a whore."

3

WHY SO MUCH HEAT on the mountaintop? Surely because the sun was so close. But why so quiet and deserted? Why, the war was over. He was happy, he was going to be received by the king of Spain. He had bet the padre that he could climb as far as the Pico de la Calavera. He was climbing half blindly. Where was the sun? Maybe it was night. Yes, it was night. He must not be late for the audience with the king. He had lost his watch on the way. The darkness was so great that he could not manage to avoid the corpses that were covering the slope; he trod on them, his bare feet were getting tangled up in their intestines. He could not understand—he had given orders to bury the dead, both friends and enemies. But the corpses were still there, decomposed, stinking. He had won the bet, but how could he present himself before the king with that evil smell permeating his skin? Suddenly he felt completely naked, with blood and feces running down his legs. Where could his companions have gone? Why had they abandoned him? He put his hand to his waist. Neither belt nor holster nor pistol. Unarmed, on the heights of the Sierra. Was he going in the right direction? His compass was broken. But he kept on climbing, *seeing* through the soles of his feet the things on which he was stepping: skulls, ribs, entrails, scrota. He was filthy, he needed to take a bath, he could not come into the presence of the "Great Man" in such a state? But which king was he going to see? Felipe? Fernando? Carlos? One of the many sovereigns out of the vicar's history lessons? A crusading king? He had to take a bath as quickly as possible, had to find a river. The heat was getting worse. He was going to see the king. What a victory! But he was naked. He could not understand. He remembered putting on his best suit. What would the king think when he saw him? "Your Majesty, I have the honor of presenting to your Highness my *cojones*. I am the ambassador of the Republic of El Excremento." The courtiers were going to laugh at him, murmur that an Indian doesn't know how to walk with shoes on. A disgrace! Suddenly he had a presentiment of danger. He had walked into an ambush. Enemies were going to leap on him, knife him in the back. He uttered a cry and turned swiftly to defend himself.

The guerrilla fighter was the first to awake. He propped himself up in bed and stared, half-dazed, at the dim light of early dawn, while his hands automatically groped around him for the weapon that always lay beside him in sleep. But it took only a few seconds for Gabriel Heliodoro Alvarado to orient himself in space and time;

the ghost of the guerrilla fighter returned to the land of dreams, and then the ambassador of the Republic of El Sacramento to the United States, amused at his own fright, burst into a low laugh. Of the dream nothing was left now in his mind but the shadow of an indefinable sense of peril and the half-extinguished recollection that he had returned to his youth and was wandering once more in the high, bleak paramos of the Sierra.

He jumped out of bed, turned on the lamp closest to hand, and looked at his watch on the night table. Exactly five o'clock in the morning. Five was a constant number in his life. He had been born on January 5 at five in the morning. It had been at five on another morning, in the year 1915, that a platoon of soldiers of the 5th Infantry Regiment at Soledad del Mar had shot Juan Balsa, the revolutionary leader he admired so much. It was said that five bullets had pierced the hero's chest.

The stifling heat of the room was causing a leaden unease in him. He was wearing only his pajama pants, and sweat was running down his half-naked torso. How on earth could Americans stand these overheated houses?

He began wandering aimlessly around the room, turning on lamps as he found them in his path. He went over to the thermostat and squinted at it, trying unsuccessfully to see what temperature it indicated. Whatever it was, he had not yet learned how to cope with the gadget.

He had detested the decor of the room ever since he had slept there the first time, some four or five days before. Ernesto Villalba, his second secretary of embassy, had explained that the furniture in the ambassador's rooms was pure Empire. "I can assure you, Excellency, that this is a faithful copy of the bed of Napoleon Bonaparte." "But, Titito, you must understand that Napoleon was a pygmy and I'm six-three." Gabriel Heliodoro gave a hostile glare at the bed. He thought it ugly, pretentious, and uncomfortable, and unsuitable for certain activities. He had had proof of this that same night, a few hours earlier. Rosalía had undoubtedly been lovely, lying there naked in the Napoleonic bed, but they had ended by making love on the white bearskin rug. The solution was to move into the apartments reserved for honored guests.

He headed for the bathroom, relieved his bladder, drank some water from the faucet, using his hands as a cup just as he had done so many times in the brooks and waterfalls in the Sierra. He went back into the bedroom and opened one of the windows that overlooked the street. The cold night air enveloped him. Through the mist he could make out the trees on the embassy lawn. The street lamps, blurred in the fog, gave him the impression of festering eyes. Rubbing his hands over his chest, he stood for a moment staring into the night. A solitary taxi was coming down Massachusetts Avenue, passing the embassy of Great Britain, a structure of bare brick, solid and sober as the British Empire itself. Inside—Gabriel Heliodoro imagined—at this hour the English ambassador, Sir Somebody-or-Other, must be sleeping respectably with his lawful wife, Lady Something-or-Other. How many ambassadors in Washington had, as he, Gabriel Heliodoro, had, a beautiful, healthy, twenty-five-year-old mistress with erect breasts and generous haunches? What he could not understand was how a girl like that could have married Pancho Vivanco, that greasy, repellent fat slug.

He felt a sudden shiver. And from some region as remote and vague as that of his dream came a voice: "Shut that window, Gabiliodoro, or you'll catch pneumonia." There was a time when his mother's eyes were constantly festering. What bit of earth, or what birds of ill omen had eaten those great, dark eyes? His mother had died during one of his many absences from Soledad del Mar, and he had never been able, nor for that matter had he seriously tried, to locate the burial place of the *chingada*. Some said that the corpse had been tossed into a common grave. Others whispered that it had remained unburied in the country and had been devoured by vultures. Gabriel Heliodoro closed the window, leaving the maternal specter outside.

He took a few steps, and then, feeling chilled, sat down at the writing desk, crossed his arms to warm his chest, and stared abstractedly at his toes. Titito's sprightly voice came back to him: "This escritoire, Excellency, is a masterpiece of French marquetry of the beginning of the past century." Gabriel Heliodoro smiled. *Maricones* were generally quite knowledgeable about art and furniture.

On the escritoire beside his glasses, he saw the letter that he had begun to write that night, a little after Rosalía had left the embassy. He smelled it to see whether his hands had transmitted his mistress' perfume to the paper. He put on his glasses, gazed affectionately at his own handwriting, and re-read what he had written:

"My adored Francisquita; Things are going well here in the embassy. It is an enormous house, with great luxury and comfort. We have a battalion of servants, and they all treat me with attention and respect. Next Friday I am giving a great reception to the diplomatic corps and the representatives of the national and foreign press. It's too bad that you are not here to do the honors of the house. On the other hand, I think it is a very good thing for you to stay for the time being in Cerro Hermoso with our daughters and grandchildren, for they say that the Washington summer is terrible, and I know how much you suffer from heat and humidity. I shall have to go on enduring your absence until September or October, when you will be able to come fulfil your functions as wife of the Ambassador. Don't worry because . . ."

He thought of Francisquita. Not even in her twenties had his wife ever had youth, grace, or beauty. A practicing Catholic, goddaughter of the archbishop, she was convinced that God had invented the sexual act solely for the purpose of guaranteeing the propagation of the human race, and that therefore it was sinful for anyone to derive any physical pleasure from carnal intercourse. Since she had entered the menopause she had deemed herself exempt from her functions as a wife. It was as though she had rubber-stamped her sexual organs with the words MISSION FULFILLED.

Poor Francisquita! An exemplary wife. A great soul. Her eyes always grew damp when she thought about the poor. A real lady of charity, she was ever busy heading charitable campaigns. She had an excellent education, she had brought up her children well, she was a first-rate candymaker, she could paint porcelain, and she could even speak a bit of French.

On his way back to bed, Gabriel Heliodoro turned out the lamps, one by one. He lay down, the room again in semidarkness. He needed more sleep; he wanted to get up in the morning looking rested. He still caught the scent of perfume from Rosalía's body on the pillow and the sheets. Lying on his stomach, his thoughts turned to his mistress, ruminating the pleasures that she had given him. Suddenly he burst into laughter. The story had come into his head that he had read one day about the exiguity of Napoleon's virile member, responsible for his amorous failures and his military conquests. And he reflected, I have to thank God for the generosity with which He treated me. And, as he did every night before going to sleep, he kissed the little medal bearing the image of the Virgin de la Soledad which hung from a silver chain around his neck.

He was awakened hours later by Monsieur Michel, who combined the duties of butler and *valet de chambre* in the embassy residence. Dressed in his impeccable, gray, medium-weight suit, the Frenchman stood indecisively for some time at the foot of the bed, not daring to speak aloud or to touch his new boss, confining himself to coughing timidly at intervals. Finally Gabriel Heliodoro opened his eyes, fixed them on the stranger, wrinkled his forehead in a scowl, and for the fraction of a second his face froze in an expression of questioning surprise.

"Good morning, Mr. Ambassador. It is eight o'clock, the hour at which Your Excellency requested me to wake you."

Gabriel Heliodoro sat up in bed, wrapped his arms around his knees, remained in that position several moments blinking and yawning, and abruptly, startling the butler, he stood up and leaped to the carpet with the agility of a puma. A youthful gaiety ignited his whole body.

The great day had dawned! He went over to one of the windows and ran back the drapes. The morning light struck full on his face. The trees in the park seemed to say a green "Good morning" to him. Gabriel Heliodoro began walking up and down, now scratching his chest, now stretching his arms, and yawning musically all the while. Suddenly he stopped short two paces from the butler and examined him from head to foot.

"Now, what is your name?"

"Michel Michel."

"Why twice Michel? Wouldn't one do?"

The butler, serious, made a little bow, and his arms sketched a gesture of apology. "Well, Mr. Ambassador . . ."

He was a man of indefinite age, of medium height, and lean of flesh. He had an oblong head, an angular face, as thin as his nose, which recalled that of Francis I, from whom—as rumor had it—he descended in bastard line. His mouth was so small, and was always so wet, that it was reminiscent of a rosebud wet with dew. Gabriel Heliodoro continued to analyze his butler with the curiosity of a man inspecting some rare animal. Gradually to his memory came the data given him by Ernesto Villalba about this man. Michel Michel, a native of Avignon, was a devoted servant of the embassy to which he had come in 1931, brought by Don Alfonso Bustamante when the latter had been transferred from Paris to Washington. Gabriel Heliodoro had thought the Frenchman's face comical from the first day he saw it. "He has the sour look of one who's forever sucking limes," he told his first secretary of embassy, Pablo Ortega. The latter, in his turn, had informed the ambassador that Michel had literary propensities, was a voracious reader, familiar with the works of Camus and Sartre, besides knowing by heart Rimbaud's *Le Bateau Ivre*. Don Alfonso, it was said, was in the habit of spending long hours discussing Spanish and French literature with his valet.

"Does Your Excellency wish me to prepare a warm bath? Or perhaps a shower?"

"I hope you don't think you are also under obligation

to bathe me," the ambassador responded, dropping his pajama pants to the floor and kicking them away.

Michel Michel cleared his throat and quoted a sentence from Cervantes. He spoke Spanish fluently but with a heavy accent full of throat-scratching *r*'s that made Gabriel Heliodoro think of the French prostitutes in the bordellos of Puerto Esmeralda.

"What does Your Excellency desire for breakfast?"

"Black coffee and dry toast. None of that gringo food, eggs, sausages, ham, and stuff, hear me? Ah, a large glass of orange juice without sugar."

"Very good, Mr. Ambassador."

Gabriel Heliodoro stepped into the bathroom, looked at himself in the mirror over the basin, saw with satisfaction that his eyes were clear and the pouches no more accentuated than usual. He started brushing his teeth with his customary enthusiasm, which made his gums bleed a little. He rinsed out his mouth then in a prolonged gargling that sounded more like a vocal exercise. Then he tried to shave with the electric shaver, and failed once again. (That's not for a man's beard!) He lathered his face, fitted a blade into his safety razor, and passed the edge over his cheeks. He got under the shower, opened the faucet, uttered a howl, and began to dance about when the stream of cold water fell on his body. "How do you do, Mr. President?" He gripped the great man's hand, smiled at him, seeking to captivate him from the first minute. A pity, not knowing English . . .

He soaped himself vigorously, proud of his narrow waist and the hardness of his muscles. He felt his flat belly, on which he prided himself. Another thing that gladdened him was not having those dark blotches that old age generally paints on the hands. "Ha-oo doo yoo doo, mees-ter Pre-ssi-den-te?" he repeated, this time in a deep voice that reverberated in the bathroom. He surrendered then to the rapture of drying himself with a thick towel, of rubbing his body with eau de cologne, of massaging brilliantine into his hair, of combing it.

When he re-entered the bedroom, the towel wrapped

about his waist like a sarong, Michel was still there, putting two well-bred fingers to his little mouth every time he cleared his throat.

"What's the matter with you, man?" Gabriel Heliodoro asked. "Spit it out."

"Mr. Ambassador," the butler said, after a brief hesitancy, "if you will allow me, I suggest your wearing striped trousers, a double-breasted dark gray coat, and gray silk tie."

"I'll wear what I think best. If I take the notion, I'll go to the White House in pajamas. Or in the raw."

"Very good, Mr. Ambassador."

"Ah, Michel! Don't look like that. I'm going to put on a navy-blue suit, white shirt, dark tie. And black shoes, of course. Is that very much of a departure from protocol?"

Michel made a little bow and the rosebud that adorned his face spread in the imitation of a smile. "No, Mr. Ambassador. The President in all probability will be dressed the same way."

"Well, then, there's no problem, my friend."

Moments later, his underwear on, the ambassador sat down on the bed to pull on his socks and shoes. "You must be missing Don Alfonso a lot."

"Dr. Bustamante was a perfect gentleman."

"Which I'm not, am I, Michel?"

"I did not mean to insinuate that, Mr. Ambassador."

"But I know I'm not. I am not a career diplomat. I don't kiss ladies' hands. I kiss them elsewhere. (*When I can, of course.*) I'm not up on literature and I don't give a damn for that protocol hooey."

Michel kept his eyes lowered. His ears had turned as red as a cock's comb.

Gabriel Heliodoro put on his trousers. "How many ambassadors have you served in this house?"

"Your Excellency is the fifth."

Five—again the magic number.

"Are you superstitious, Michel?"

"I am a skeptic, Excellency."

"I forgot that skepticism is the national sport of

France. But, returning to those ambassadors, they were all a little difficult, weren't they?"

"Begging Your Excellency's pardon, I prefer not to comment."

"Certainly. You are a gentleman. And that being so, I hope you didn't see the girl who came into the embassy residence at eight o'clock and left after midnight."

"I remember nothing of the matter, Excellency. Or, rather, I saw nothing."

Gabriel Heliodoro knotted his tie in front of the mirror, in which he could also see the image of the butler, who was holding the coat to the blue suit as a bullfighter holds the cape with which he is going to excite the bull.

"I presume that after you retire you will go back to France."

"That is precisely my intention, Excellency."

"And naturally you will write your memoirs."

"It is a possibility."

The rogue is ironic, thought the *compadre* of Juventino Carrera, stepping back to see himself better in the mirror. The butler came closer.

"I should like to know how I am going to be handled in those memoirs," the ambassador said jokingly as he put on his coat.

"In the light of the strictest truth," murmured Michel, clearing his throat in apology for the boldness of the phrase.

Gabriel Heliodoro turned to the butler. *"Truth?* But what is the truth? Write the book with passion, man! Because passion is the truth of every one of us."

The small room where Gabriel Heliodoro was now drinking his Colombian coffee prepared in an Italian machine was one of the pleasantest in the embassy. Its unpretentious furniture, the light tone of the walls and rugs, the presence of some oil paintings in vivid colors and simple design, the work of Sacramentan primitive painters, all contributed to lend to the room a festive, youthful air which the morning light accentuated. Gabriel Heliodoro was alone; he had sent away the servant who brought his breakfast, for he detested being watched while he ate.

From where he was sitting he could see, through the panes of the broad window, a segment of the park, with its oaks and lindens rising thick-leaved above the flowering tops of the Judas trees and the forsythias, and beyond them the grove in the ravine of Normanstone Park. But of all the trees surrounding the mansion the ambassador's favorite ("Love at first sight, Pablo!") was a Japanese red maple beside the fountain. Gabriel Heliodoro had never seen a plant like it; it looked more like a delicate bronze sculpture than a real tree. He sat gazing at it for a long time, lovingly, while he absent-mindedly chewed his toast and drank his coffee.

Subtle and silent as a shadow, Michel entered the room and, with a respectful throat-clearing full of implications, laid a folded newspaper on the table beside his employer.

"Señor Villalba asks you to examine the marked page in this paper, Mr. Ambassador." He sketched a smile, did an almost military about-face, and retired.

As he knew no English, Gabriel Heliodoro knew American newspapers and magazines only "by sight." On page six of the daily he was holding he saw his picture and under it a paragraph circled with a blue pencil. For some moments the ambassador had eyes only for his photograph. The dalliance, however, was interrupted by his curiosity to find out what had been written about him in those columns. ("Diplomatic Merry-Go-Round," by Miss Potomac.) Titito had taken care to staple to the page a piece of paper containing the translation of the marked text.

The Republic of El Sacramento now has a new ambassador in Washington. He is Mr. Gabriel Heliodoro Alvarado, who will today hand his credentials to the President. His Excellency, who arrived a few days ago, seems to have made a great number of friends already. Tall, dark, and attractive, a fine figure of a man and, as I am told, endowed with a disconcert-

ing frankness, he is a personal friend of the President
of El Sacramento, at whose side he fought bravely in
the Revolution of 1925, which freed his country from
the dictatorship of Don Antonio María Chamorro.
It is said that His Excellency Mr. Alvarado is a great
admirer of Abraham Lincoln, with whose life he is
more familiar than most. Welcome, then, Mr. Ambassador, to the "Diplomatic Merry-Go-Round!"

Hardly had Gabriel Heliodoro finished reading the
translation when Michel re-entered the room, this time
with telephone in hand. "A call for Your Excellency."

"From whom?"

"From Señor Villalba."

"What does that fairy want?"

"*Pardon, monsieur?*"

"Never mind. Give me that thing." He snatched the
phone and put it to his ear. "Hello!"

The fluting voice of Ernesto Villalba came over the
wire. "Good morning, Mr. Ambassador!"

"Ah, Titito. What is it?"

"I am calling to congratulate you."

"What for, man?"

"Haven't you seen the paper I sent you with a page
marked?"

"I have, but what of it?"

"Your Excellency may not know that merely to have
your name mentioned in Miss Potomac's column, which is
read all over this country by fifty million people, is a sure
sign of social success. Now, to get more than ten lines in
the 'Diplomatic Merry-Go-Round' as you did is positively
an enshrinement. Congratulations!"

Gabriel Heliodoro did not know how to interpret his
second secretary's words. Could the *maricón* be making
fun of him—or was he really taking the thing seriously?

"Who is this Miss Potomac?"

"That is the pseudonym of one of the sacred cows of
Washington, Señor Ambassador. One of the most adulated,
respected women in this country."

"Pretty?"

"Hardly, Señor Ambassador! A good sixty. Ugly as necessity and fat as a hippopotamus."

"Then have the witch thrown into the river of the same name. Listen, Titito. Speaking seriously, did you people send that gringo woman an invitation to my party?"

"Excellency, her name was on the first envelope that we addressed!"

"*Bueno*. Tell Pablo not to be late. The President expects me at eleven sharp."

4

WHEN THE LEGATION of El Sacramento in Washington was raised to the category of embassy in 1930, Generalissimo Juventino Carrera's government authorized the foreign minister to buy, for the seat of its diplomatic mission, a residence located on Massachusetts Avenue nearly opposite the Embassy of Great Britain and belonging to an old family of the Virginia aristocracy. Investigations carried out twenty years later, when Dr. Julio Moreno, candidate of the opposition, was elected President of the Republic, and El Libertador was in exile in the Dominican Republic, revealed the fraudulent nature of that transaction, which had yielded for the *caudillo* and his minister a personal, illicit profit of nearly a hundred thousand dollars.

The mansion, in Georgian style, rises with discreet colonial grace in the midst of a park of lindens, ash trees, yews, and maples. The severity of its bare brick walls, of the color of clotted blood, is broken by the white-enameled frames of many windows, tall and narrow, with double-hung sashes, aligned symmetrically on the four faces of the house.

With a pediment of plain molding crowning the central part of the façade over the projecting portico, supported by four Doric columns, the present residence of the ambassadors of El Sacramento has a strong resemblance to the historic Dunbarton House in Georgetown.

For some time the chancellery operated in a rented house on 30th Street. To Dr. Alfonso Bustamante—the first ambassador chosen by Juventino Carrera to represent his government in Washington—fell the task of planning and supervising the construction of a building especially intended for the chancellery. As El Libertador, his personal friend and admirer, had given him *carte blanche,* the old diplomat, a humanist educated in Europe and deeply fond of the men and things of the Renaissance, did not hesitate to have built, beside the residential mansion, an edifice that Ernesto Villalba now keeps saying *sotto voce* is nothing but a ridiculous pastiche of several Italian *palazzi.* It is a rectangular structure of light granite, two stories high. The lower floor, of rusticated masonry, has the bristling, defensive air of a fortress, softened, it is true by a central loggia with two arcades garnished with Ionic pilasters. The façade of the second, where among its fifteen windows is repeated the motif of the pilasters, is reminiscent of the Palazzo Rucellai in Florence, where Don Alfonso served in his youth as consul of his country.

A staircase of five steps, also of granite, leads directly from the sidewalk of Massachusetts Avenue to the loggia of the chancellery. Set into one of the pilasters between the two arches gleams the coat of arms of the Republic of El Sacramento. On the upper part of the escutcheon, just under the Phrygian cap and against a red background, the figure of a golden puma holds proudly an ancient sword, which divides the shield into two fields. In one of these is a rising sun, symbolizing the day; in the other, a star, representing the night. On the lower part, in gilt letters, the motto of the Republic stands out: LIBERTAD Y HONOR.

As one enters the chancellery vestibule he is received by a taciturn man, of indeterminable nationality and accent, usually seated at a table facing a white telephone. On the ground floor are the library, the archives, the storeroom, and the rooms for the stenographers and other minor functionaries. In the center of the upper floor is the

ample office of the ambassador, flanked by a reception
room and by another, larger, room in the middle of which
stands a mahogany table surrounded by ten chairs. The
other rooms of the main floor are occupied by the minister-
counselor of embassy, the secretaries, and the military attaché and his aides.

According to the oral folklore of the embassy, the
most important figure of the Sacramentan representation
in Washington was never the ambassador, no matter who
he might be, but the American citizen Miss Clare Ogilvy,
an employee on contract. Ambassadors would arrive, sign
papers, make speeches, give lectures, hold press confer-
ences, strut about, absorb many dinners, drink uncounta-
ble cocktails, and one day be transferred to another post;
in short, they passed. Miss Ogilvy, on the contrary, remained. No one ever discovered a title that could de-
scriptively encompass her multiple duties. The American
combined the functions of a private secretary to the ambassador with those of a translator of documents, dispatches,
and letters from Spanish to English and vice versa. It was
she who prepared or revised speeches written in her
mother tongue, both for the ambassador and for the minister-counselor and the secretaries of embassy. It was also
her job to watch over her chief's privacy, keeping him
from being unnecessarily bothered. There was a saying in
the chancellery that anyone who wanted to get as far as
the ambassador would first have to pass over his secretary's dead body.

A veritable living manual of encyclopedic knowledge,
Clare Ogilvy held on deposit in her photographic memory
the most varied data about universities, libraries, museums, embassies, questions of protocol, industrial patents,
customs duties, income tax, and so on. She knew by heart
not only the charters of the UN and the OAS but also the
Constitution of El Sacramento. The schedules of trains,
buses, planes? The height of Mount Everest? The name of
that historic figure who said such-and-such on this-or-that
occasion? The pound sterling quotation at the moment?
Ask Miss Ogilvy.

When someone compared this prodigious American woman with an electronic computer, there was always some colleague to add, "But with a soul!" Because Miss Ogilvy also exercised two functions that did not appear on her work sheet: those of a wailing wall and a bank. When one of her colleagues had some problem of a personal nature (sentimental affairs and hurts to recount, or complaints to formulate), it was on the shoulder of this American friend that he came to weep. Miss Ogilvy would listen with fraternal, sometimes maternal, patience and, at the end of the jeremiad, would murmur, "It's not all that bad, boy. It could be much worse." And immediately she would give advice and consolation. If the problem was of a financial kind, Clare Ogilvy was always there with purse open, ready to lend her dollars without interest or any set date for payment.

Tall, of a sturdy leanness (five-nine in her bare feet), this cordial, extroverted spinster, whom her chiefs and colleagues called affectionately "La Ogilvita," was so attractively ugly that it was fascinating. Her huge, protuberant teeth lent her elongated face an equine touch. Her wide mouth, with heavy lips, was endowed with the plasticity of modeling clay. And her cold gray eyes did not disclose —on the contrary, they denied—the warmth of her heart. She had a deep, rather hoarse voice, and her laughter, which broke out with spontaneous frequency, nearly always degenerated into the bronchitic cough of the heavy smoker. La Ogilvita chain-smoked, and was invariably to be seen with a lighted cigarette in the corner of her mouth.

Of her earlier life little was known other than that she belonged to a rich Connecticut family ruined by the crash of 1929, and that, on completing her college degree at Vassar in 1930, she had then found a position in the Legation of El Sacramento. In general the persons who had most to do with her accepted her as an act of God, and seemed to think that to explain Clare Ogilvy's existence not merely a biography but a whole cosmogony would be necessary.

"My first salary," she used to say in amusement,

"barely permitted me to keep body and soul together. And even today, after nearly thirty years, I find that I have not achieved a very solid union between them."

When she felt inclined to reminiscences, La Ogilvita used to say that, firm at her post, she had survived dozens of Sacramentan crises, one revolution, a coup d'état, four ambassadors, and several ministers and secretaries. Her discretion was exemplary as regards what she said about chancellery matters. But now and again, in intimate circles, she allowed herself to make certain confidences, usually after the first glass of whiskey. "One day I'm going to publish my White Paper," she declared one night at a gathering of old friends. "But I can let you in on a few chapters in advance. When I was admitted to the Embassy of El Sacramento I was a fresh young damsel of twenty-four, just out of college. The first job they gave me was to compose and type strange and mysterious letters addressed to a gentleman with an Italian name who lived in Virginia. The correspondent referred to something always designated as 'the merchandise,' without it's being clear just what it was. Prices, places, and dates of delivery were discussed. This was still in prohibition days, a little before the election of F.D.R. Well, friends, one day the American authorities discovered the whole scheme and the scandal burst like a bomb. The secretary of embassy who signed, with a false name, of course, the letters that I composed and typed, was using his diplomatic privileges to import cases of rum from his own country and sell them to American bootleggers who operated in Washington and environs. Thanks to the good offices of the Department of State the *chargé d'affaires* of El Sacramento managed to suppress the scandal and shipped the smuggler back to Cerro Hermoso. As for me, boy! Only by a miracle did I escape the clutches of the federal agents. Imagine, I used to put my initials proudly on all those compromising letters!"

La Ogilvita chortled. Another round of whiskey came, and she continued.

"The first ambassador I served under came to Washington in 1931. Don Alfonso Bustamante was a nice old fellow, short, stout, a widower, and sad. He had the air of a trained tapir. He loved to read, was an amateur of the arts, a real intellectual. Every time his superior, the minister of foreign affairs, sent him orders that he thought absurd, he would start pacing up and down his office, grumbling, 'I'm going to resign from this post. I will not carry out orders from uncivilized men. I am a civilized man. A man of the Renaissance. A Florentine!' But he didn't resign, he liked the post too well. He was crazy about honorary titles and decorations. Every time he received a decoration in a formal ceremony and had to make and listen to speeches, he had dizzy spells and pains in his chest, and his heart ran away with him. After the ceremony the little man would throw himself into bed and urgently summon his doctor."

La Ogilvita was interrupted by a fit of coughing. She took a swallow of whiskey and went on, refreshed.

"But that didn't stop our ambassador from continuing to want, to win new decorations. That poor little Don Alfonso! In the ten years that he spent in this federal town, which he hated with all the ardor of his Florentine soul, he did little beyond trot from party to party, complaining of a chronic sinusitis, the official disease of Washington, you know, and sighing for the post of ambassador to Rome, which he always called 'the Eternal City.' "

Seeing that her friends were entertained by her narrative, Clare Ogilvy paused theatrically before finishing the story of her first ambassador.

"On December 7, 1941, after hearing over the radio the news that Japanese planes had bombed Pearl Harbor, Don Alfonso, livid, locked himself in the bathroom. As he was still bolted in after two hours, Michel, the butler, knocked the door down and found his employer sitting on the toilet, dead of a cardiac collapse. God bless him! As you see, an inglorious death for a Florentine of the Renaissance."

"Another whiskey, Clare?"

"Why not?" she exclaimed. After all she was the life of the party. She shook her glass to listen to the tinkling of

the ice cubes swirling and colliding, which was music to
her ears. And as her friends were silent, their eyes fixed on
her, she went on to the story of her second ambassador. He
was the brother-in-law of President Carrera, and had
paranoiac deliriums. Shut up in his office, he would argue
in loud roars with imaginary interlocutors (always important personages), uttering the nastiest words in the Castilian language. La Ogilvita could never forget that gray
winter afternoon in 1942 when, from her room, she heard
the chief yell, "Mr. Cordell Hull! I had you summoned to
my presence to present a protest. My government does not
approve of using Puerto Esmeralda as an American naval
base. I'll have you know that we are no colony of the
United States, you scum! We are a free and sovereign nation, you ass! Read the motto of our Republic: *Libertad y
Honor*. And tell President Roosevelt to . . . himself." At this
point Clare Ogilvy swallowed the four-letter word in the
certainty that her hearers knew what was meant.

The fourth round of whiskey stirred her to the tale of
the third ambassador.

"That one belonged to the period of Dr. Julio Moreno's administration. He was a frail, saffron-colored little
bachelor who suffered from gastric ulcers and wore dark
glasses behind which he sought to hide his timidity. He
was a cultured, introspective, very scrupulous man, and
reached his decisions only after much meditating. He
spoke little, practiced yoga, and admired oriental philosophy, which he knew intimately. He didn't last long in the
job. When Dr. Moreno was deposed, he requested asylum
in the United States and went to live in Miami, where he
died two years later. Perforated ulcer, complicated by
homesickness for his native land."

Clare paused. "It was that ambassador who decorated
me with the Order of the Silver Puma—the gold is conferred only on foreign statesmen and national heroes—he
was the one, too, who gave me the title of honorary citizen
of El Sacramento."

"What about the fourth ambassador?"

"He was a sex maniac, in spite of being in his sixties.

He was always running after the typists. A real faun. One day that degenerate actually had the gall to slap me on the fanny, with the most innocent face in the world. Believe it or not. All that, however, didn't stop one of our minor colleges from bestowing on him the degree of Doctor of Laws, *honoris causa*."

If anyone ever asked Clare Ogilvy's opinion on the character and habits of the current embassy personnel, she would assume an Olympic silence, her lips pressed together and her chin stuck out stiffly in an expression of stubborn, offended refusal. A well of secrets, her discretion was protection for everyone. Naturally, for her private use she had a kind of mental file in which she set down her impressions of both superiors and colleagues—things that she observed through daily contact with them, added to the stories she heard about this one or that, generally told by the irrepressible, indiscreet Titito Villalba. If she were to reduce those impressions to written expression, this is what she would probably write:

"*Gen. Hugo Ugarte.* Military attaché. Now close to seventy. Short, fat Indian, with bowed legs and dull, slimy, crocodile eyes. They say he was the cruelest chief of police that El Sacramento has ever known. He used to submit his prisoners to exquisite tortures, some of them of his own invention, like the famous electric needle, which he made a police dentist touch to the tooth nerves of the victim, who in many cases confessed even things he didn't know— when he did not pass out from the pain. (And yet, whenever the monster has an appointment with the dentist here in Washington, he has to take tranquilizers.) He got his present post in the embassy as a reward for his good services to President Carrera. Besides his pay of $3000 a month, free of taxes, he is making a fortune by buying refrigerators, radios, and other electric appliances at a discount and shipping them to El Sacramento, where he sells them at a profit of 70 percent. The merchandise enters the country at Puerto Esmeralda without paying duty, for the customs officers are part of the gang.

"According to Titito, in the 'good old days' Ugarte gave himself up to sexual orgies with girls of school age. My private title for that fellow is 'the Satyr of the Caribbean.' He has a little giggle like splitting bamboo. He is personally as disgusting to me as a great toad drolling poisonous saliva.

"*Sra. de Ugarte.* Doña Ninfa is well along in her forties. The general's second wife. Physically she resembles the odalisque in that Renoir picture in the National Gallery of Art. Fat, dark, with Arabic eyes. Like the majority of Latin American women I know, she suffers from acquisitive mania. Gluttonous, she particularly loves chocolate candy, cakes, whipped cream—in short, all the fattening things. Ever since I've known her she has been announcing that she is going to start dieting 'next Monday.' (Her interest in the young Italian chauffeur for the embassy, Aldo Borelli, is becoming the talk of the town.)

"*Pancho Vivanco.* A sad little guy deceived by his wife, who is the new ambassador's mistress. A month before his arrival in Washington (information of the 'Titito Press') Don Gabriel Heliodoro requested Vivanco's transfer to this chancellery, in which he was made head of the consular service. A sad little guy! It is not surprising that he is a neurotic full of nervous tics and facial twitches. One day I went into his office and was struck smack on the nose by one of the little paper planes—he calls them 'birds' —that now and then the consul sails into space. Unsure of himself, he has the habit of rolling a new dollar bill in his fingers, a banknote rolled into a cylinder thinner than a cigarette—a kind of psychological cane. I feel sorry for the poor guy and try to be nice to him. I sense that he is trying to muster up the courage to come and confide in me, but he backs off at the last minute. Everybody in the embassy knows about the love triangle.

"*Sra. de Vivanco.* Olé! Olé! Rosalía is sailing, pleased with herself, over the blue sea of the twenties. Maybe it would be more accurate to say that she is flying, since with her streamlined, firm breasts she looks more like a bi-motored plane. A girl of humble origins, she must have married Pancho for selfish reasons. She has a face and a body that cannot inspire pure thoughts in men. Titito puts it this way: 'She's so good-looking that if I were a woman I would fall madly in love with her.'

"*Ernesto Villalba.* Titito is an epicene type, which is the most euphemistic classification I can give him. He loves pastel-toned shirts, he adores the ballet, he is knowledgeable about matters of art, and he does have good taste. Second secretary of embassy. He has served in Athens and in Ankara, where his behavior was shocking. He considers Turkey the most civilized country in the world because there, he says, homosexuality is accepted as a natural thing. Not a day passes but Titito comes to me with some new tittle-tattle about his colleagues or about the 'sacred cows' of Washington. Age? He will not confess it. He must be wandering through the forties. His face sometimes reminds me of a boy's face that has suddenly withered. Short, slender, sinuous. I like him. I think he likes me.

"*Dr. Jorge Molina.* Minister-counselor. He is already beginning to descry the gray entrance to the fifties. I haven't yet deciphered this sphinx's enigma. A reserved, introspective man of few words. He walks without looking to right or left. Actually, he has a handsome face, for those who like the type. But what type is it? Well, it's an ascetic face like that of the monks to be seen in the pictures of certain Spanish painters of long ago—a long face, fleshless, beard always shadowing blue even when freshly shaved, thin lips, high forehead, dark, intense eyes. He studied for several years in the Seminario Mayor de Páramo, but abandoned his career before being ordained. I don't know why. Maybe not even God knows. No one takes liberties with the minister-counselor. And yet he is a polished gentleman who never raises his voice to anyone. He reads a great deal, he knows things. But he is a closed garden. A sterile garden, in my opinion. Either I am much mistaken or he despises Ugarte. I don't think he's a friend of Don Gabriel Heliodoro, either. I have never seen him smile. He is unmarried, lives alone, and has never been seen in the

company of women. Titito swears that the man is chaste.
Or castrated, he adds with a malicious smile.

"*Mercedes Batista.* Merceditas, a stenographer-typist,
looks like an owl, not only because of her enormous glasses
and her nocturnal air, but also the shape of her head,
broad on top and thin at the chin, with a beak of a nose.
Short, chubby, and melancholy, she constantly nurses a
feeling that she is the victim of injustice; she is easily
moved to tears, and she speaks a soft pneumatic kind of
Spanish like that of the majority of the Sacramentans. She
is a sort of scapegoat for Rosalía's husband, who apparently takes pleasure or finds relief in making her suffer.
Merceditas is one of my most assiduous confidantes.

"*Pablo Ortega.* This one is my favorite. Barely thirty.
Dark face, extremely attractive, clean-cut mouth, with an
expression in which gentleness and energy are combined.
Unlike nearly all his compatriots, he has the good taste not
to use hair oil. He is an intellectual, although he doesn't
like being classified as such. He has published one book of
poems and another of essays. He despises them both. He
considers himself frustrated as a writer. He paints, too, but
is not satisfied with what he does. Bachelor. I note that
women fall for him easily, and, say what they will, I'm a
woman myself. Titito declares that, as far as my relationship with Pablo is concerned, I must fit squarely into the
Jocasta complex, since I am old enough to be his mother.
Ortega has been having a few inconsequential sexual adventures here in Washington, but he is too conscientious to
be satisfied with things of that sort. A man of rather reserved nature, he does not unburden himself spontane-
ously; I have to drag his confidences out of him. His father
is of the famous Ortega y Murat family, rich lords of lands,
plantations, and sugar mills, one of the most influential
families of El Sacramento. The young man seems to be
going through a serious crisis, which the arrival of Don
Gabriel Heliodoro can only aggravate. He is tormented by
a keen sense of guilt for serving a government that he
considers corrupt.

"And the rest of the chancellery personnel? Well, the

minor functionaries, colorless people—good, even interesting when we get to know them better, but two-dimen-
sional and vague when we merely see them in these rooms
and corridors in the pursuit of their routine activities.

"Oh, yes, there are still the aides to the military attaché: a dyspeptic colonel, a major addicted to gambling
at cards, a captain who collects stamps, and about three
lieutenants with a lot of brilliantine on their black hair
and, so to speak, in their lubricous eyes. They spend their
time smoking and chatting in the halls, without much to
do; or else they sit at their desks looking at pictures of
nude women in back numbers of *Playboy*. Nearly all these
aides of Ugarte's have big cars and try to pretend that they
are constantly involved in love affairs—which may or may
not be true, a point that matters little to me.

"And what of the new ambassador? Too early to form
any opinion. What I can say now is that Don Gabriel
Heliodoro is quite a man. He radiates a powerful animal
magnetism. If on the one hand the scar on his forehead
gives him the disreputable look of a gangster, on the other
hand it constitutes a kind of piquant spiciness that
enhances the sexual curiosity which women must feel for
him. Many stories are told of this man—some of them
dark, but all of them interesting. It isn't surprising that
Rosalía takes pleasure in going to bed with a type like
that. Titito has made a remark about Don Gabriel Heliodoro that is at once grotesque and terrible: 'Oh, Clare!
He must have a phallus of stone!'"

5

AMONG THE MANY preoccupations that clamored for
Clare Ogilvy's attention that April morning, the
greatest was making sure that the new ambassador reached the White House at the appointed time.

Michel had telephoned her shortly before, informing her that his employer wished to leave the residence at ten-thirty sharp.

She looked at her wristwatch, and decided to go see Pablo Ortega. First she powdered her face, touched up her lipstick, and then looked at herself in the mirror of her purse. She was wearing her wool salt-and-pepper suit, and displayed on the left breast of her jacket a silver brooch in the form of an Inca deity, the present of a Peruvian friend. She took an aspirin tablet from her purse, filled a paper cup with water, and, with almost an air of contrition, as if she were going to take communion to a dying man, she went out, marching along the chancellery hall, enveloped in an atmosphere redolent of L'Heure Bleue.

As usual, she entered without knocking on Pablo's office door, and found her friend sitting at his desk gazing pensively at the papers before him.

"How does the first secretary feel today?"

"Rotten. Got a splitting headache."

"Just as I imagined. Here."

She thrust the tablet into his mouth and handed him the cup, which Pablo drained in a long swallow. Clare stepped back.

"You look good in that navy-blue suit. Gray is becoming to you too. Never wear green or brown. They don't go well with the dark tone of your skin."

Ortega tasted the sour bitterness of the aspirin in his mouth. He had chewed the tablet before swallowing. "I'm worried about Dr. Molina," he said.

"Why?"

"You know as well as I do that it's his job, not mine, to go with the ambassador to the White House. The minister-counselor must feel offended."

"If Don Gabriel Heliodoro preferred you as his interpreter, my boy, it isn't your fault."

"I know Dr. Molina. He's an extremely proud man, quite uncompromising in matters of precedence."

Clare said nothing. She did nothing beyond glancing at the day's mail on the table. She picked up one of the empty envelopes and smelled it: essence of jasmine. "Another *haikai?*" she asked.

Pablo nodded.

"How is that romance going to turn out?"

"There isn't any romance."

"No? You are introduced one day at a reception to Miss Kimiko Hirota, an employee of the Japanese Embassy. You both sit down in a corner and talk for more than an hour about poets, *samurais*, butterflies, painting on silk, and the art of arranging flowers—in short, you discover that you are twin souls, you become friends, she starts sending you a *haikai* every week and you respond with another. What is that but a romance?"

"To have erotic thoughts of Miss Hirota, Clare, would be as absurd as to want to sleep with a porcelain doll."

"Don't forget that the Japanese transistor radio is small and delicate, but it works as well as any occidental radio."

Pablo smiled. "Be that as it may, our relationship is purely spiritual."

Clare made a skeptical grimace.

"At heart you're an incorrigible racist," Pablo said.

"I, a racist? If I were, I wouldn't put up with you Sacramento Indians for a minute." She paused, and finally, in a conciliating tone, asked, "What was today's *haikai?*"

Pablo picked up a sheet of letter paper the color of a dry leaf, and read what Miss Hirota had written on it in her round, ingenuous schoolgirl's hand:

SPRING
Butterflies? Not at all!
Blossoms from a cherry tree
In the April wind.

Clare put her head on one side and half closed her eyes, not quite sure whether she liked the little poem or not.

"Have you answered yet?"

"No. Today I feel more inclined to *harikiri* than to a *haikai.*"

The secretary laughed. Both lighted cigarettes and sat for some seconds in a kind of dialogue of smoke puffs. Clare pointed to a cardboard folder containing a bundle of typed sheets.

"That thing any good?"

They were the originals of a thesis, "The Republic of El Sacramento," by Glenda Doremus, an American student at Georgetown University, who two weeks before had hunted up Pablo at the chancellery to ask him to read and criticize her work.

"The author is more interesting than the work."

"That I've noticed. And I've also noticed in your eyes, Pablo, that you liked the girl. I'll warrant she has not remained indifferent to your Latin charm."

He frowned. "You think so?"

"My instinct never deceives me. The things I said just now about the little Japanese were just joking. But the American girl, my boy, set off all my alarm bells. Stop, thief!"

"Jealousy, Clare?"

She folded her arms and looked squarely at her friend. "If I were twenty-five years younger, I'd enter the competition myself."

"There's no competition."

Clare changed the subject. "Come on, get ready for the sacrifice. The chief is waiting."

"Let the chief go to hell!"

"Don Gabriel Heliodoro likes you, Pablo. He told me so himself yesterday. He praised you to the skies. And you know something? To him you represent the son that God has denied him. The man has a brood of females, five, I think, but no male. I am very sorry, but, like it or not, you've gained a second father."

"One father's enough. Sometimes too much."

Clare aimed an accusing finger at the envelope edged with oblique red and yellow stripes lying in the incoming basket. "What's the matter with you, boy? I brought you that letter from your mother two days ago and you haven't even opened it."

Pablo hesitated an instant. "I held the envelope up against the light and saw what looked to me like the shadow of a check in it."

"Well!"

He got up, went to the window, hands thrust into his trouser pockets, and stared out. "I'm tired of this farce, Clare, this masquerade. Tired of smiling at a scoundrel like Ugarte and pretending I don't know that he is a lecher, a murderer, and a common thief. I am fed up with tolerating the conceit of some of those officers who think that *uniform* is a qualifying adjective and not a common noun. Tired of forever selecting words and gestures in order not to wound the sensibilities of the Señor Minister-Counselor or bruise the sores of that poor fellow Vivanco. And the worst of all—you know about this—are these lectures of mine at clubs and universities in which I am obliged to tell half-truths or whole lies about my country to maintain the fiction that we are a democracy. All that demeans me in my own eyes."

La Ogilvita sat down and crossed her thick, ill-shaped legs, so disproportionate to the rest of her body. Ortega turned to her.

"What is the solution? Tell me. What is it?"

"How should I know if you have never furnished me all the data of the problem?"

"Very well, I'll give you the rest right now."

He picked up the copy of the Washington *Post* on top of the steel filing cabinet and brandished it before Clare. "Have you read the letter from Dr. Gris published in this paper today?"

She nodded. Dr. Leonardo Gris, ex-minister of education in Dr. Julio Moreno's administration, exiled in Washington for the last two years, had not only given lectures against the Sacramentan government in clubs and colleges ever since he arrived, but had also written letters to the editors of the most important dailies denouncing Juventino Carrera as a cruel and corrupt tyrant. Today's letter contained a direct attack on Gabriel Heliodoro Alvarado, whom he accused of "complicity in the crimes of the dictator, his *compadre*."

"All right, now I'm going to tell you a story, and you will have some basis for understanding why I am lost in this labyrinth without finding a way out."

The secretary's gray eyes were fixed on him, and, as always occurred when she was moved, at intervals she drew a long breath and at the same time twisted her mouth and nose to one side.

"Toward the end of 1951," Pablo Ortega began, "on the day the mercenary soldiers of Juventino Carrera entered Cerro Hermoso and invaded the Palace of Government, Dr. Leonardo Gris was the only minister who stayed to the end beside Dr. Moreno, with a handful of loyal soldiers and a few students. You undoubtedly know that Don Gabriel Heliodoro was the one who personally commanded the forces attacking the palace. The rest of the drama is known. Dr. Moreno preferred to commit suicide to falling into the hands of his enemies. Dr. Gris succeeded in escaping abroad."

"I am well acquainted with the history of your country, Pablo."

"But there is one detail you don't know. Where do you think Gris took refuge on the famous Tragic Night? I'll tell you—in my house. I was alone. My parents were in Soledad del Mar. Don't forget that I admired and esteemed, as I still admire and esteem, Dr. Leonardo Gris, who was my professor in the Federal University. Right. The man put himself in my hands. I knew that if he should be captured by the revolutionaries he would be summarily shot."

Clare Ogilvy, troubled, was listening.

"I didn't hesitate a minute. I had to save my friend, make him take asylum in an embassy. We decided that it would be the Mexican. It was eleven o'clock at night. Shooting and explosions could be heard coming from various parts of the city. The invaders and the soldiers who had joined the revolution were beginning the slaughter, the looting, and depredations. I put my friend in the luggage compartment of my car and headed for the Embassy of Mexico. The revolutionaries were pursuing Moreno's partisans, hunting them down as if they were animals. Many of the residences of members of the deposed government were going up in flames. I had to take the craziest twists and turns to avoid the intersections guarded by patrols. At one corner, unexpectedly, three men armed with carbines appeared in front of me and signaled me to halt. If I stop, we are sunk, I thought. I clenched my teeth, put my head down, and stepped hard on the accelerator. The bandits made way yelling and waving their arms, and then opened fire on us. One bullet whizzed close by my ear and smashed the windshield. To cut the story short, I drove the car diagonally across a plaza, by-passing flowerbeds, benches, trees. Finally, several minutes and frights later, we came in sight of the Embassy of Mexico, which stands in a residential suburb. The silence of a cemetery prevailed throughout the neighborhood. The streets were deserted. I jumped out of the car and tried to open the gate. Locked! I opened the car trunk, helped Dr. Gris to get out, and told him, 'We have to climb the grillwork, Professor. No help for it. Quick!' It was less difficult than I imagined. Gris surprised me with his vigor and agility. When we were crossing the embassy garden, we were pinned by the glare of car headlights. We heard shouts. A car pulled up next to mine. We threw ourselves to the ground, and rolling and crawling, protected by the shadows of trees and shrubs, we managed to get around the corner of the embassy building and knock at a window in the rear. The butler, after an anxious dialogue, opened the door to us. We did not answer his questions and went on in. Gris wanted to talk immediately to the ambassador, who was his particular friend. I threw myself, panting, into a chair, the sweat pouring down, dust all over me, my heart thumping irregularly, my mouth dry. The request for asylum was formalized. The Mexican ambassador, considering that I would be running grave risks if I left the em-

bassy, offered me lodging. I accepted, but I spent a sleepless night, listening to distant, intermittent shots and
howls of sirens and excited voices. At nightfall of the next
day my parents appeared at the embassy. My father re-
proved me harshly for what I had done. I rejected his
recrimination, retorting angrily that I was not repentant.
My mother took me aside. 'Do you want to kill your poor
father? Don't you know he has a weak heart?' I shut up. It
was the same old blackmail they had been using against
me since my childhood—my father's illnesses. As you
know, I enjoy the privilege of being an only child."

Pablo crushed out the stub of his cigarette in the bottom of the ashtray.

"Señor D. Dionisio Ortega y Murat conferred in private with the ambassador of Mexico, and later, taking me
by the arm, he led me to a corner and whispered, 'Your
automobile was identified, but we have succeeded in keeping the newspapers from publishing anything about your
act, the gravity of which you stubbornly refuse to understand. The archbishop and I had a talk this afternoon with
the Generalissimo, and he stated that he is ready to pardon
you, but he feels it would be best for you to leave the
country for a while, until the new government is consoli-
dated and the incident forgotten."

Pablo stuck his hand in his pocket, fished out another
aspirin tablet, tucked it in his mouth, and chewed it in a
kind of fine fury.

"Days later they sent me off to Paris. After negotiations that lasted nearly a month, Dr. Leonardo Gris finally
got a safe-conduct and embarked for Mexico City, and
from there, much later, he moved here." Ortega drank the
rest of the water in the paper cup. "Can you imagine a boy
of twenty-three, with artistic and literary fancies, loose in
Paris with a fat monthly allowance? I accepted the paternal checks without too many scruples. The city dazzled
me. I frequented the cafes on the Rive Gauche, where I
rubbed elbows with celebrities. I painted pictures in the
little *place* in Montmartre. I attended lectures at the

Sorbonne. I took in so much of the Louvre that I got cultural indigestion. I wrote verses, and I had my amorous
adventures, of course. One day, this was in 1955, I had a
letter from my mother. She informed me that not only had
the incident been forgotten but the Generalissimo,
through the archbishop's intercession, had had the generosity to appoint me secretary of his embassy in Paris.
Imagine! That was the last straw. I refused the job. But
there came another letter. 'Your father has not been well
since the heart attack he had last year. He wishes you to accept the post in the embassy, for that is the surest and
safest way to your return to Cerro Hermoso. Do what he
asks of you. It is for your good, my son. Think only of one
thing—the health of the author of your days lies in your
hands.' "

Pablo perched on the edge of the desk, and sat in
silence for some moments.

"Note this, Clare. I had in my hands, according to my
mother, the power of life and death over the author of my
days. The blackmail was continuing. I accepted the job. I
won't deny that I ended by accommodating myself to the
new situation. My parents paid me two visits during the
two years and a bit that I spent in Paris as a secretary of
embassy. Whenever they turned up, the three of us went
on a kind of honeymoon. We would visit museums, go to
concerts and theaters, eat in the finest restaurants, stroll
along the Seine, buying books and engravings from the
bouquinistes, but going very slowly and with frequent
stops because of Don Dionisio's heart. No one touched on
the incident. Now and then my father would discreetly
refer to El Libertador. He was running a moderate government, my father said. The country had a legally elected
Congress, and a liberal constitution. Poor man! It was
touching and at the same time distressing, the effort he
was making to believe his own words."

Clare Ogilvy listened to her friend, but without losing
sight of the movement of the hands on her watch.

"My parents are militant Catholics. I haven't the

slightest doubt about their sincerity. One night the three of us went to a concert in Sainte-Chapelle. The Pamplona Chorus gave a program of ancient music of mystic inspiration. Don Dionisio sat with arms folded and head down, as if he were praying, during a good part of the performance. As if the singing and the exquisite beauty of the historic chapel, with its illuminated glass, were not sufficient. In one of the intermissions the Papal Nuncio entered, followed by the Prince de Bourbon, by the Grand Prieur de la Lieutenance de France, and by dignitaries, knights, and ladies of the Order of the Holy Sepulcher, all wearing their traditional costumes. The prince was carrying in his pale hands nothing less than the Savior's crown of thorns, brought from the Holy Land by Saint Louis IX, King of France. Clare, my father's face was transfigured when he saw the relic, and tears came into his eyes. When we came out of the chapel, he took my arm affectionately, and, giving vent to his feeling, murmured in my ear, 'Can it be necessary for me to tell you that when I am obliged to approach the Generalissimo I turn red with shame and feel like holding my nose? I hope you will not deem me so ingenuous or dishonest as to support that man politically because I consider him an ideal president. Know one thing, my son. If I tolerate him it is because at the moment he is the lesser of two evils. Unfortunately, the alternative to the situation we now have in El Sacramento would be communism, and that would mean the end of all the spiritual values we prize, in short, an atheistic regime that would expel our priests from the country, burn our temples, depriving us of the right to worship God in our own way and to bring up our children and grandchildren as good Christians and not like soulless robots in the service of a totalitarian state.' Don Dionisio paused significantly, and then added, 'We should also be despoiled of the lands which our ancestors, since the seventeenth century, have irrigated with their sweat, their tears, and their blood.' "

Clare Ogilvy stood up and cast a quick glance at the dial of her watch.

"Less than a year after that last visit," Pablo continued, "I received notice that I had been transferred to this embassy. And here I am, still playing the diplomatic comedy, in the pay of a tyrant surrounded by thieves and bandits. As if the thousand dollars a month I earn were not enough, my father from time to time supplements them with generous checks. And every time I make an attempt to put my foot down and get out of all this—I don't really know where or how—there comes another letter from Doña Isabel with the external question, 'Do you want to kill your poor father?'"

"Just how real is the old man's illness?"

"I have the opinion of a doctor whom I trust. My father's health is genuinely precarious. He has already had two serious heart attacks. He is a cracked glass that demands special care."

Ortega pointed to the letter which he had not yet opened.

"I can imagine what is written in that letter. My parents are not ignorant of the fact that I am in the habit of seeing Dr. Leonardo Gris frequently. In her last letter, Doña Isabel wrote, 'I beg of you, don't continue cultivating that dangerous friendship. Sooner or later you will be discovered and denounced, the old incident will be disinterred, you will lose your post, and, what is worse, perhaps you may never again be able to return to your country.'"

Clare went up to her friend and straightened his tie. "Now I understand that you are really in a bad situation. But it could be worse. And, be that as it may, what you have to do *now* is to escort His Excellency the Ambassador of El Sacramento on his visit to the White House. Come on. It's time."

She kissed her friend's cheek and started for the door. "God go with you, son!" she exclaimed.

And when Pablo was out in the corridor, La Ogilvita wiped her eyes and blew her nose on a facial tissue. Then, still sniffling, she lit another cigarette.

6

ICHEL, who opened the door of the ambassador's residence to Pablo, murmured that His Excellency awaited him in the library.

Gabriel Heliodoro received the first secretary with open arms. "Pablo, man!"

He wrapped his muscular arms around him, clasping him to his chest. A strong scent of lavender struck Pablo's nostrils.

"How do I look?" the ambassador asked, spinning around.

"Fine. But you went too heavy on the perfume."

Gabriel Heliodoro smelled his own hands, his lapels, his handkerchief. "Do you really think so?"

"Yes. In this country men don't wear perfume."

"Well, I'm not from this country. I'm an Indian from Soledad del Mar," the dictator's *compadre* exclaimed in a mixture of playfulness and pride.

The Indians of Soledad del Mar, thought the secretary, smell of soot and dried urine. I know very well what you are—a scoundrel and a traitor. Like me.

"Let's be off, Pablo."

"Why, you can go from here to the White House in ten minutes. We still have half an hour."

"Yes, but before seeing the President I have an appointment with another President." He paused, and his face lighted up like a Maya sun. "I am going to visit the monument to Lincoln, to keep a promise I made to myself when I was a boy."

You humbug! Pablo exclaimed to himself.

"You probably don't know it, but Lincoln is one of the two objects of my greatest devotion. The greatest of all, after the Virgin de la Soledad."

Humbug! Faker! Pablo was doing his best, though in vain, to dislike the ambassador.

Gabriel Heliodoro drew himself up, took three steps toward Ortega, made a little bow, and held out his hand, which the secretary, with some constraint, had to take, lending himself to the comedy.

"How do you do, Mr. President? Ha, ha! how's that?"

"Very good. But pronounce it préz-i-dent, not pre-ssi-dén-te. And before I forget, the name of this city is Uá-chin-ton, not Guá-ssin-ton."

"What will the ceremony be like?"

"Very short. It will last hardly more than five minutes. The presentation of the credentials is a mere formality. There is no necessity to say anything special. It is sufficient to express your pleasure in being appointed to this post and your desire that our countries continue to maintain the best relations. But don't worry, I'll take care to translate everything."

Gabriel Heliodoro looked at his watch. "Let's go."

In the vestibule, Michel gave him a fresh, unperfumed handkerchief and assisted him in putting on his overcoat. The ambassador stood for a moment in front of the mirror, adjusting his Homburg.

"*Bonne chance,* Monsieur l' Ambassadeur!" the butler said.

The two went out. Tall and slender in his navy-blue uniform, Aldo Borelli was standing at attention beside the black Mercedes-Benz, holding the door open. He was a shrewd-faced Roman in his twenties.

"Good morning, Señor Ambassador."

"Good morning, Aldo. We are going first to the Lincoln Memorial."

After the two diplomats had settled themselves on the back seat and Aldo had started the car, Gabriel Heliodoro burst into a guffaw that shook him all over. Pablo thought, If he thinks I'm going to ask him why he's laughing, he's wasting his time. But the other quickly explained.

"Do you know what I find funny? When the American Marines, at the request of the dictator Chamorro, landed in El Sacramento in 1915 to capture Juan Balsa and his guerrillas, I, who was about twelve at the time, spat on the United States flag one day. Hidden behind trees, I threw a lot of stones at patrols of gringo soldiers. With these very hands I wrote in charcoal on many a wall AMERICANS DIRTY DOGS. And now, Pablo, here I am, the ambassador of my country, on my way to the White House. Isn't it fantastic?"

Ortega limited his reply to a nod.

Gabriel Heliodoro gave him an oblique glance. What can this boy have against me? Can it be that he has taken a dislike to me? Let him wait. In less than two weeks I'll win him over, or I'm not the son of my father.

But who was my father? he thought, bitterly. And suddenly the image of his mother returned, clear and plain, to his mind, and a shadow darkened his face.

The automobile was rolling along Massachusetts Avenue. As they passed in front of the Embassy of Brazil, Pablo thought of his friend Orlando Gonzaga and the many things he would have to tell him that afternoon in the Connecticut Avenue bar. Bill Godkin would certainly be there, curious likewise to learn how the ceremony went.

"What tower is that?" Gabriel Heliodoro asked as the car was crossing a bridge over Rock Creek Parkway.

"It is the minaret of a Moslem mosque, Excellency," Aldo Borelli hastened to inform him, in his Italianate Spanish.

"Moslem?" the ambassador asked, surprised, looking at Pablo. The latter confirmed the fact with a nod.

The Mercedes entered Rock Creek Park. Along the bank of the stream which gave the park its name, the Judas trees and the forsythias were covered with flowers. Gabriel Heliodoro saw a cemetery which began on the other bank of the *arroyo*, with its simple gravestones, gray or brownish, climbing a slope of dark earth and extending in several terraces to the top of the hill.

"That is Oak Hill Cemetery," Pablo remarked.

"How different from ours! The headstones on the

graves look more like the kind that mark kilometers on the
highways at home. Flat tombs. No statues. No angels. I
prefer ours, Pablo, a thousand times over. In this country,
even death seems less tragic than in ours."

In Gabriel Heliodoro's mind the cemetery walls of his
home town gleamed white on the top of a green hill overlooking the sea. He turned his head toward his first secretary and gave him a quick, cordial pat on the knee.

"*Chico*, what I'm going to tell you now, I'll bet you
didn't read in your schoolbooks. The year 1913 went down
in history as the Tragic Year. The tyrant Antonio María
Chamorro was ruling El Sacramento with an iron hand.
Juan Balsa was in the Sierra with his guerrillas, fighting to
free the people from tyranny. Early one summer morning
the revolutionaries made a surprise descent on Soledad del
Mar and wiped out an army patrol in the streets. While
half the attackers held the soldiers of the 5th Infantry shut
up in their barracks, on the defensive, the other half was
going through the streets of the town, collecting food,
medicines, arms, munitions, and new volunteers."

Against his will, Pablo Ortega found himself interested. The ambassador was talking fluently, and he had a
voice of pleasant metallic timbre.

"When day broke," Gabriel Heliodoro went on, "the
revolutionaries had returned to the Sierra and all the doors
and windows in Soledad del Mar were shut. In the street
only those who had fallen in combat were to be seen.
Bueno. The commander of the federal garrison came out
of the barracks and counted his casualties. The guerrillas
had killed ten federals and wounded about thirty. Do you
know what that swine of a commander did? In that same
hour he picked fifty able-bodied men from among the inhabitants of the town and announced that he was going
to have them shot. Worse than that, he forced nearly the
whole population, men, women and even children, to climb
up to the cemetery to witness the shootings."

Gabriel Heliodoro looked at Pablo to see the effect
that his story was causing.

"I remember that day as if it had been yesterday. I

must have been about ten. I was barefoot, wore a shirt and
trousers of soiled white cotton, and a straw hat on my
head. Juan Balsa was my idol and I hated the federals."

Pablo perceived that Aldo Borelli, too, was attentive
to his employer's narrative.

"The commander ordered those condemned to death
to bury the corpses of the government soldiers first. Then
he made the poor doomed men dig a long trench outside
the walls of the cemetery, and throw into it the bodies of
Balsa's guerrillas killed in the fighting. The shootings
started a little after eleven o'clock. It was one of those
sultry days, and the sky was like a red-hot coal covered
with ash. Crying with grief and gritting my teeth with
rage, I saw and heard it all, perched in a tree.

"The condemned men were placed in groups of four
against the cemetery wall, their hands tied behind their
backs. The firing squad would fire . . . *Tr-r-r-r-á!* . . . and
the dead would topple over. The wall got spattered with
blood, and bits of brains and bones. *Tr-r-r-r-á!* Before he
died the town shoemaker yelled, 'Viva Juan Balsa! Death
to the tyrant!' There was one Indian who fell laughing.
Another man, I don't remember who he was, had a fit of
weeping, threw himself on the ground, and lay there huddled up, shaking, his legs doubled with his knees against
his chest, just like a foetus in its mother's womb. The lieutenant commanding the firing squad had no alternative
but to put a bullet in his ear. The man flopped around and
then lay there as though stretched out and pegged down.
The earth sucked up his blood. And the worst of it all were
the screams and cries and tears of the poor people who
witnessed the massacre. Holy Virgin! If I live a thousand
years I'll never forget that picture—the women in black,
weeping and praying a chaplet in chorus. Some were faint-
ing. Others had attacks of hysteria. Others rolled, moaning
on the ground. The sun was enough to melt a Christian's
brains. On my face sweat and tears mingled, running into
my mouth like streams of brine. I didn't want to look at the
wall, but I did. In the common grave the corpses were
beginning to stink. The vultures alighted, attracted by the

slaughter, and the soldiers shooed them off, first with stones and then with shots. And do you know, *chico*, what impressed me the most? It was the men who died resigned, in silence, their eyes still, as if they were seeing a vision. Padre Catalino was there with them, sobbing. Before dying, the condemned men kissed the crucifix that the vicar was holding in his hand. And so, Pablo, I saw friends of mine, people I knew, people I respected, go down in groups of four. A gruesome pool of blood soiled the wall and the ground. I went days without being able to get rid of that smell of rotting human flesh, of hot blood, of gun-powder and of dust. Things like that mark a man for the rest of his life."

Gabriel Heliodoro fell silent. The end of the story of that unforgettable day he would not relate. On reaching home that night he had found his mother in the bedroom with a sergeant of the infantry regiment. In the other room several soldiers were playing cards and smoking, awaiting their turn with the mistress of the house. Anyone who had two lunas could use her body.

He had wandered in a daze through the streets, had stepped into the church to beg for consolation from his patroness, the Virgin de la Soledad, and then had gone like a sleepwalker through the streets and neighboring fields until he had seen a new day dawn. On returning home, with the sun almost straight overhead, he saw that someone had written three words with pitch on one of the walls of the house: LETRINA DEL REGIMIENTO (Regimental Outhouse).

Gabriel Heliodoro sank into a morose silence. The car was coming out of the park. Ortega glimpsed the waters of the Potomac and the gray roofs of Georgetown University. He thought of Glenda Doremus. The Memorial Bridge, with its plain arches, reminded him of one of the bridges that cross the Seine in Paris.

He looked at the ambassador, whose eyes were closed and whose shoulders were slumped as though over-whelmed by the story he had just told. "Are you ill?" he asked, despising himself a little for being so solicitous.

The ambassador opened his eyes, smiled, and straightened up. "No. I was only thinking of some sad things."

A few minutes later the Mercedes came to a stop in front of the monument.

"I'll wait for you here, Señor Ambassador," Pablo murmured.

"All right. I shan't be long."

Aldo Borelli opened the door and the ambassador jumped out on the sidewalk, took a deep breath of the morning air, thrust his hands into his overcoat pockets, raised his eyes, and his face broadened in a smile as he saw, between two columns of the temple, the statue of Abraham Lincoln. The patriarch was seated, and, with his great, noble, woodcutter's hands gripping the arms of his chair, he gave the impression that he was about to rise to his feet to receive his visitor.

Gabriel Heliodoro climbed the steps slowly, the better to enjoy the moment. Here I am, Mr. Lincoln. I'm that dirty little Indian from Soledad del Mar, remember? At the White House the President is expecting me. I've showed all those sons of bitches that I've got guts.

He continued to climb toward the illuminated figure.

7

SINCE TEN O'CLOCK that morning Pancho Vivanco had been going every other minute to the window of his office, overlooking the park. He did not want to miss seeing Gabriel Heliodoro at the moment when he was emerging from his residence to go to the White House. When he saw the Mercedes-Benz stop in front of the mansion, his pulse leaped, a shiver ran over his body. He was like a murderer lying in ambush waiting for his victim. A cold sweat dampened his hands and his forehead. Yes, with a carbine fitted with a telescopic sight, from his window he could make, with a well-aimed shot, a target of the ambassador. He toyed with the idea, which was at once pleasant and impossible to him, as a boy makes believe that he is a cowboy waiting for the redskin to fall into the ambush set for him. And when Gabriel Heliodoro came out of the door, imposing in his black overcoat, Pancho Vivanco, tremulous with an emotion which he wished were simply hatred, leaned his forehead against the glass pane and stood contemplating his wife's lover. He knew that his colleagues in the chancellery were aware of the whole story. And they were not ignorant of the fact that he, Vivanco, also knew that he was being betrayed by his wife. How could he expect others to respect or esteem him? The best they might feel for him was contempt or pity.

Gabriel Heliodoro stopped for an instant in the portico before getting into the car. Mentally Pancho saw himself with the carbine in hand, taking aim. *Pow!* The man would fall on the flagstones. And then he, Pancho, would immediately present himself to the minister-counselor. "Dr. Molina, I have just assassinated the ambassador." He would be tried in Cerro Hermoso. He could not allege temporary insanity. The prosecutor would insist on premeditation, and he would be right. Thirty years. The Mercedes-Benz circled around the garden, entered the avenue, and passed slowly in front of the chancellery.

Pancho Vivanco went back to his desk, sat down, and stared at the passports, letters, and consular invoices that he had to dispatch that morning. Miss Clare Ogilvy had remarked to him one day, "Vivanco, you have the soul of a bureaucrat." As a matter of fact, dealing with papers, examining them, stamping them, initialing them, annotating them, ransacking files, classifying documents—all this constituted for him a fascinating game. It was with an almost carnal pleasure that he handled papers. Where the service was concerned he was a perfectionist. He had a horror of erasures, ink blots, stains of any kind. His handwriting was tiny, but clearly and meticulously set down. Nothing upset him more than to be caught in an error, however minor.

He looked at the photograph of his wife which he kept under the glass top of his desk. Rosalía! Rosalía! His wife had never been amorous with him, even on their honeymoon. At first she was at least submissive, patient. But now, ever since they had arrived in Washington, Rosalía seemed to feel an ever-increasing repugnance for him. On certain nights she would lock herself in the bedroom and refuse to let him in, alleging as pretexts her migraine or fatigue; and he would have to sleep on the sofa in the living room, often burning with desire for her.

Vivanco again looked at the documents piled before him, and, as always happened, he was taken by a singular inhibition that came to him every morning and that he could not manage to explain to himself. To gain courage and disposition to begin his work, he had to give himself over first to a kind of ritual. He picked up a sheet of blank paper, and with his trained fingers—he was a skilled prestidigitator, and often performed tricks of parlor magic at family parties—folded it into the shape of a bird. He shot it into the air, using the index fingers of both hands like a catapult, and sat watching delightedly the graceful curve that the bird described in the air before it fell. A gull squawked in his memory.

Ah! His honeymoon in that hotel in Puerto Esmeralda. The dinners on the terrace overlooking the sea. The orchestra of marimbas and maracas. That happiness that filled his whole being, in spite of his knowing that Rosalía did not truly love him. To get to the beach, they had only to cross the asphalted avenue. They would start out, hand-in-hand, walking over the pale sand. Sometimes he would let go of his wife's hand and fall back a pace or two in order to gaze at her figure, her long, well-turned thighs, her lovely hips, her slender waist, her walk like that of a goddess. He had taken hundreds of color snapshots of her. He observed that other men devoured her with their eyes when they saw her pass. That did not provoke him to indignation or jealousy; on the contrary, it gave him a sort of ferocious pride to be the husband of a female so coveted. At times he would get actually irritated when some vacationing male passed them without staring at Rosalía from head to toe with lustful eye. And at night, when they made love with the window open to the breeze and the sound of the sea, he would think of all the males who had desired his wife during the day, imagine them gathered there in the room to watch him in the sexual act, and would find the pleasure of the orgasm exquisitely increased.

Vivanco now gazed sadly at the little paper bird lying on the green carpet—a dead gull on the surface of the sea. But he had to work! He took off his glasses, breathed on both lenses, wiped them methodically with his silk handkerchief, replaced them on his nose, and cast a satisfied glance over the crowded desk, covered by a collection of objects that he, when a boy, had desired but had never been able in his poverty to buy: fountain pens of the most varied types, a pottery jar full of pencils of different colors, pencil sharpeners, staplers, plastic rulers, a magnifying glass, paper cutters, notebooks. The United States was a paradise for anybody who liked such things. Vivanco could not pass a drugstore or a stationer's without going in and buying some article for his desk, even knowing that he would never use it.

The ritual, however, was not yet over. The consul opened one of his desk drawers, where he kept dozens of wax color crayons, took out a few of them, and for some minutes scribbled and doodled on his memo pad of lined yellow paper. It was funny how, after filling a page with geometric designs, he felt so relieved of anxiety and stimulated to begin working.

He pulled out his handkerchief again and wiped his face. He thought of Gabriel Heliodoro's hands—strong as talons, of an earthy brown, with prominent veins. Just yesterday, when the ambassador was signing papers in his presence, he had stood examining the hands that, with every certainty, had been caressing Rosalía's body the night before. He had felt a strong desire to bite them,

lacerate them. And then he had contemplated the ambassador's face with equal fascination. It looked like a sculpture carved out of sandstone. He caught a whiff of lavender mingled with the scent of a good Havana cigar. His
eyes had focused next on the back of his chief's neck. He
thought, If we should grapple with each other, he would
crush me in his giant arms. But I could bite his jugular. . . .
He imagined him rolling on the carpet, both hands to his
neck, from which the blood was spurting. The fancy occupied his mind for a fraction of a second. How many things
can be contained in a tenth, a hundredth, a thousandth of
a second! A whole life. A whole death.

Vivanco heaved a sigh, replaced the crayons in the
drawer, tore off the sheet of doodling from the memo pad,
crumpled it, and threw it in the wastebasket beside the
desk. Then he picked up the first paper with a certain
reverence, whistling under his breath, in a kind of self-
satisfaction, all but forgetful of the things that had perturbed him shortly before. This was a letter that he had
composed by hand, in Spanish, which Miss Ogilvy had
translated to English and Señorita Mercedes had typed.
Suddenly his inner sky clouded over again. He had discovered a poorly done erasure in the text. He pressed a button. Mercedes appeared a moment later in the door of the
office. Pancho Vivanco drew himself up and presented the
paper to her.

"This letter was typed like your face! Do it over."

"Excuse me, Señor Vivanco," the young woman
began, whimpering.

"I accept no excuses. Pay more attention to your
work. Give less thought to men. Work with your fingers
and your head, not with your uterus."

Merceditas took the paper and went out of the office
with her eyes full of tears. Pancho Vivanco sat down,
rubbed his hands, and went on to the next paper.

The minister-counselor's office was next to the consul's. It was, however, more ample and furnished with a
less bureaucratic taste. Clare Ogilvy used to put fresh

flowers in a vase on the little round table opposite the leather sofa. Dr. Jorge Molina, though, had asked her not to do so any more, and to take the vase out of the office. On the faded rose walls there was not even a picture. Compared with Vivanco's desk, Dr. Jorge Molina's was of a monastic sobriety.

At that hour the minister-counselor was sitting at his desk, his hands folded in an attitude of prayer, thumbs under his chin, the tips of his index fingers touching the tip of his nose. He had been in that posture for minutes, his eyes as though hypnotized by the newspaper open on the desk.

Two things were worrying him that morning. The first was the resentment he felt, despite himself, at not having been invited by Don Gabriel Heliodoro to accompany him to the White House. The other was the letter from Dr. Leonardo Gris which the *Post* had published. Dr. Molina was doing his best to convince himself that neither of these things was of capital importance. They were not going to affect his inner life. They did not really wound him deeply; they were superficial scratches. But the mere fact that he *felt* these injuries displeased him, as a sign that he was not as immune to them as he hoped and wished.

Gabriel Heliodoro was an uncouth fellow. He ignored or scorned protocol. He, Molina, would simply have to get himself accustomed to these irregularities. Others, worse, would come. He must arm himself with patience. And willy-nilly, Gabriel Heliodoro would have to lean on him if in the exercise of his ambassadorship he did not wish to commit gross blunders, exposing himself to ridicule.

He consulted his watch. At that moment the ambassador was possibly climbing the steps from the porte-cochere of the White House, where the President was awaiting him. The head of the most powerful nation in the world was going to shake hands with that "parody of an ambassador" from that "parody of a country"—yes, one had to recognize the sorry, ridiculous truth, for El Sacramento was an island in the Caribbean Sea, governed by a common, ignorant, dishonest dictator—"whom you are

serving," said someone in the minister-counselor's mind. It
was the voice of Leonardo Gris.

Jorge Molina got up, and with hands behind his back
began to pace up and down. The image of Gris habitually
pursued him like the implacable personification of a guilty
conscience. The fact was that the minister of foreign
affairs of his country had sent him to Washington for the
purpose of, among other things, keeping an eye on Leonardo Gris and replying to the attacks that he made on the
government of El Sacramento—in short, to neutralize the
actions of the exiled refugee.

A reader of Plato, Molina loved dialogue, which he
considered the clearest, most succinct form for the exchange or the discussion of ideas. Unmarried and solitary,
he was in the habit of debating his problems with himself,
verbalizing them aloud or mentally. Among his imaginary
interlocutors his favorite was Don Pánfilo Arango y Aragón, the archbishop primate of El Sacramento, his personal friend, a man whom he admired and esteemed
deeply, and whose biography he was writing with loving
care. And, incredible as it might seem, another of his
most assiduous phantom interlocutors was Leonardo Gris
himself, his old colleague at the university and his present
political enemy.

Molina was now imagining Gris sitting there on the
sofa, legs crossed, his handsome, silvered head erect, his
eyes fixed on him with that keenness of his which on some
occasions actually became disconcerting.

Gris lit a cigarette. Molina had never smoked in his
life. He detested any habit that might tend to enslave his
will.

"I read your letter in today's *Post*," the minister-
counselor said in his thoughts. He imagined the other's
reply:

"Be honest and confess that my article does not contain a single false statement."

"I admit that it contains no lies. What I do argue
against is its timeliness. I condemn your conduct on the
ethical side. Dirty clothes are washed at home."

"I, too, have serious objections to your ethics, Jorge. If you accept in principle my criticism of your government, your president, and your ambassador, how can you explain your being here in the service of all three?"

"One moment!" And as he thought these words, Molina halted in the middle of the office and looked at the sofa. "What I am serving is my country, which will continue to exist many centuries after I disappear, and my Church, which is eternal."

Gris's deep, sonorous laugh, which could poke fun without malice and even be satirical without losing its tone of cordiality, that famous laugh so beloved of the university students of El Sacramento, sounded in the minister-counselor's memory.

"Your Church? How can you say that, Jorge, when it is no secret that you abandoned the seminary because you had lost faith in the existence of God? Do you deny that?"

"I do not. But we have a subtle point there. You are an atheist, and your atheism makes you happy. I have lost God and I suffer because of it, and I never cease seeking Him, and I have the hope of finding Him one day. And more, I *love* the idea of God's existence, while you scorn it and ridicule it as something childish and inferior. You want to destroy the Church to whose defense I devote myself passionately."

"From whom are you defending it? I think you're attacking windmills."

"I defend it from communism, Leonardo, from materialism, from despair, from general disintegration, from chaos. And from men like you!"

"Don't commit the injustice of considering me a Communist."

"No. You are worse than that. As much as I detest the idea of Marxism-Leninism, I cannot help admiring the Communists for their fidelity to an ideology and for the coherence of their ratiocination and of their conduct within its limits. What I despise and detest are the so-called liberals like you, men without definite political program, without the shelter of a body of doctrine. You limit yourselves to criticizing governments of the right and of the left, without offering them a plan of constructive action. You are against what you frivolously call the *obscurantism* of the Church, you constantly clamor for freedom of thought, you are, in short, a bunch of *nice boys*— like that Pablo Ortega, your pupil—who take refuge in a skin-deep, diffuse humanism. At bottom what you seek is to evade definite commitments which both the Catholics and the Communists—and the Fascists, yes, even the Fascists!—have assumed."

"Don't make me laugh, Jorge. There is nothing vaguer and more absurd than your own attitude. If you have no certainty that God exists, what use is it to maintain His Church?"

"I could reply by saying that it is because I love that Church, do you understand? I love its tradition, its pomp, its ritual, the history of its saints and martyrs—in short, its mystic body. What other force in the world can oppose the materialistic wave of Marxism and nihilism? We need something more than an intestinal philosophy, a digestive interpretation of history, Leonardo."

Molina heard steps in the hall. He waited for someone to knock at his door. Seconds passed, and the steps went away. Now Gris was over by the window. The minister-counselor felt a certain pleasure in imagining his ex-colleague standing, for Gris was a short man, while he, Molina, was nearly six feet.

"I accuse you, Leonardo Gris, of having, by ideas and actions, by omission or commission, aided the cause of communism in El Sacramento in the days when you were minister of education and culture."

The other's face remained serene. His clear glance intimidated Molina a little.

"Make specific accusations."

"You ordered the crucifixes withdrawn from public schools, you abolished the custom of morning prayers in them, and you eliminated the teaching of religion from their curriculum. You also transformed a secular university into a nest of free-thinkers, Communists, and pragmatists.

You not only permitted but encouraged, and all but made
obligatory, the teaching of the theory of evolution in secondary schools and even in the primary ones. And you will
do me the justice of recognizing that I criticized and
combated all those measures through the press, unequivo-
cally, during Moreno's administration."

"And do you know why that was possible for you?
Because in Moreno's administration there was always the
most absolute freedom of thought and speech throughout
the country. No newspaper was ever censored."

Molina approached the desk and cast a swift glance at
the *Post* page on which the exile's letter was printed. "I am
going to retort to your attack immediately."

"Do you deny that Gabriel Heliodoro is a sharper and
a thief? That he is a partner in the shady deals of his
compadre Carrera? Are you going to attempt to convince
the American public that the Republic of El Sacramento is
really a democracy?"

"No. I am going to prove that when you were in the
government of your country, you played, consciously or
unconsciously—it does not matter which—the game of the
leftists. You wanted for your country a type of government
similar to that of Colonel Arbenz in Guatemala. Your administration's agrarian reform project was plainly com-
munistic. You and your colleagues were, in short, innocent,
useful tools. Perhaps more useful than innocent."

Molina pressed a button. Moments later there was a
knock on the door. "Come in." Merceditas entered.

"You rang, Señor Minister?"

Molina had an impulse to shout, "If the bell at your
desk rang, lighting number two disk, of course it was I
who rang." But he restrained himself, merely nodding.

"Sit down. I am going to dictate a letter, which you
will then take to Miss Ogilvy for her to translate into English."

He perceived that the secretary's eyes were inflamed.

"Why have you been crying?" he asked, immediately
regretting the query, since he did not like to meddle in

others' private affairs, so that no one might feel he had the
right to meddle in his.

"Oh, Señor Minister! It was nothing."

"Vivanco again?"

She bowed her head and murmured an almost inaudible "Yes." Molina felt like summoning the consul to his
presence and slapping him. That despicable little fellow,
not having courage enough to attack the ambassador, was
avenging himself on the lowliest of the clerk-typists in the
chancellery.

Silence fell. The secretary waited, pencil and steno-
graphic notebook in hand. Jorge Molina glanced swiftly
out of the corners of his eyes at the girl. Mercedes Batista
was ugly. Her torso and head promised a tall woman, but
her short legs grotesquely belied the promise. The minister-
counselor thought it providential to have a secretary of her
type in the chancellery. The others—pretty, young, perfumed, with exuberant breasts and excessively painted
faces—were the ones preferred by Ugarte and his aides. If
by chance one of them came into his office, Molina felt an
uneasiness which gradually turned into something closely
resembling panic. He did not have much practice in dealing with women. He never had had. Since he left the seminary he had preserved the habit of chastity. Why? he
sometimes asked himself. The old monastic notion that
sexual desire is sinful? Repugnance? Fear of failing as a
man? He regarded himself as a normal person; desire visited him frequently and he fought it off with cold baths
and spiritual exercises. Prayers were of great aid to him in
those hours of the devil. ("Devil?" Gris asked. "You don't
believe in God, and yet you accept the idea of the devil?")
At times he had nocturnal emissions that he was never
able—he did not try—to link to any definite dream. He
came in contact with women only socially at dinners, receptions, lectures. ("The truth," Gris butted in, "is that
when a woman faces you, you turn your eyes away.")
Nonsense! Women never laid siege to him. Perhaps he
maintained his chastity out of sheer convenience. Or pride.

He felt strong because he did not yield to lust. His solitude was a citadel. His celibacy a cuirass.

"Ready, señorita?"

"Yes, Señor Minister."

"Address the letter to the editor in chief of the Washington *Post*. Miss Ogilvy knows the formula."

Molina joined his hands together as if he were going to pray, rested his thumbs on his lean chin, pressed the tips of his index fingers to the sides of the tip of his nose, and began dictating.

8

AT THAT MOMENT Ernesto Villalba was passing the door of the minister-counselor's office. In his loafers he walked with the light step of a dancer, and in a falsetto voice was crooning a fragment from *Pelléas et Mélisande*. He came to a halt in front of one of the many doors in the long corridor and gave two short raps. A half-choked voice came; "*Adelante!*" and he made a stage entrance into the office of General Hugo Ugarte. He drew himself to attention before the military attaché, clicked his heels inaudibly, bowed slightly, saluted, and said, "*À vos ordres, mon général!*"

At his desk, which was bare as usual, Ugarte sat staring at a voluminous book as thick as a telephone directory, which Villalba recognized as the latest Sears catalogue.

"Titito, I called you to get your help. I want you to put this business into Christian language. Look."

The secretary of embassy went around behind the old man's back and looked at the page at which his thick, knotty index finger was pointing.

"Don't tell me you're going to buy a toupee, General!"

"Don't be stupid. Translate this stuff. I haven't decided yet."

Titito stepped back a couple of paces and contemplated Ugarte's baldness. Seen from the rear, it gave the impression of an enormous shiny egg projecting from a nest of black feathers. (The general dyed his hair.)

"Well," the secretary said, after reading the indicated text to himself, "the ad is addressed to the fifteen million bald men of the United States.

"Fifteen millions? *Caramba!*"

"See this detachable paper pattern? It's to measure the shape of the client's head. The general sends his measure along with a lock of his hair for them to see the exact color for the toupee. Everything can be done by mail. If the general does not want to use his own name, use mine. Oh yes! The ad says that the firm has false hair in fifteen different shades. How lovely!"

Ugarte began to produce deep in his throat a noise that sounded like the caw of a crow. He leaned back in his swivel chair and raised his eyes to Villalba.

"What will they say about me if I turn up in Cerro Hermoso with a false hairpiece?"

"You'll be a success."

"And suppose some s.o.b. laughs in my face?"

"Shoot him in the mouth!"

Hugo Ugarte got up, plucked at the seat of his trousers, which had worked in between his fat buttocks, opened the metal jug standing on a small side table, pured out a little water into a glass, and drank a gulp. He looked obliquely at the catalogue.

"No. I won't risk it. Ninfa would be the first to make fun of me."

The general was in civilian clothes, a suit the color of lead, poorly cut and too tight. He examined Titito critically from head to foot.

"What have you been up to these last two days?" he asked, adding with a provocative sarcasm, "Have you taken on a new lover?"

"Now, General, what is this? You know that I'm a model of conjugal fidelity."

Ugarte put up with such impertinences of the fairy

because he did for him services of every kind, including fixing him up with women. Moreover, the secretary's cynical humor amused him.

"I can explain my absence, *mon général*. I went to New York especially to buy a ticket for the opening night of the Bolshoi Theatre of Moscow. And do you know how much I paid for it? One hundred and fifty dollars!"

"You're stark, raving crazy! I wouldn't pay fifty cents to see those shitty Communists dance. Our Indians from Páramo dance better and cost a lot less. You don't need to pay them more than a round of *aguardiente*."

He sat down again at the desk.

"Another thing, Titito. Write a letter for me to General Electric and ask what is the maximum discount they can give me on those big refrigerators, the largest ones. You know? Tell them that if the discount is good, I'll buy ten at a time, and on sight draft."

Ernesto Villalba made a note on a slip of paper. Then he looked at his platinum wristwatch. "At this time our ambassador must be with the President."

The military attaché's telepone rang. Titito picked up the phone helpfully, and after listening to the chancellery operator's message, handed the instrument to the general, murmuring, "It's your wife."

"*Hola*, Ninfita, what is it?"

"Everything is all right, Hugo. Look, we had agreed to lunch together, but it isn't going to be possible now. I've been held up with my shopping."

"Where are you?"

"At Hecht's, with Rosalía."

"*Bueno*, we'll see each other at home at five-thirty. But you needn't buy out the whole stock at Hecht's."

From the other end of the wire came a naughty word. The general burst out laughing.

Ninfa Ugarte replaced the phone and left the booth with the feeling that she was going to faint. This always occurred when she stayed long in a close, overheated atmosphere. For nearly two hours she had been in the great

store, going through its innumerable departments gazing
at things and asking, "How much?" She had started with
the top floor and had come down the escalator, as she
always did, with the blissfulness of a provincial woman.
Há-oo-mó-che? Her head was weary from calculating, mentally changing dollars into lunas. And now she was visited
by a touch of dizziness, similar to the kind of seasickness
one feels more in his head than in his stomach. The dizziness was aggravated by the jumble and shuffle, before her
eyes, of the variegated colors of the merchandise displayed
and of the faces and clothes of the numerous, constantly
shuttling customers, and, further, by the splendor of the
special glittering decorations with which the store was
celebrating the entry of spring. Added to all this were the
fluorescent light and the incessant sound of voices, cut by
those sounds of a little bell—*ting! ting!*—which she heard
every other instant, with the regularity of clockwork, and
of which she had not yet succeeded in discovering the
source or the purpose. And the worst was that she was
wearing woolen clothes that made her itch as with heat
rash, making streaks of fire on her skin. *Dios mío!*

She stopped a moment, closed her eyes, and spread
her fat, stubby hand on her bosom, over her heart. Could it
be palpitations? No. It was nothing. She would feel better.
But where could Rosalía have got to? She caught sight of
her near the escalator and headed for her. She could not
resist the temptation, however, of examining the kitchen
utensils all around her.

She stopped at a counter where Pyrex dishes were
lined up, for she had a special predilection for them. Now
colored ones with designs were available: turquoise blue,
rose coral, red. . . . She had already bought, since her
arrival in Washington, more than a dozen of the lovely
things. She could imagine the success they would have
when she exhibited them before her Sacramentan friends.

A saleswoman approached her and asked, with a
smile, in English, whether she could help her. Doña Ninfa
smiled also and replied with her customary phrase, "I em
jos' loó-king-e." The saleswoman withdrew. It was just

then that the general's wife had a bright idea. Why not
buy a lot of those Pyrex dishes in a wide assortment of
colors and sizes, send them to Cerro Hermoso, and sell
them to persons of her acquaintance? She could make two
dollars apiece. She would send the dishes along with the
merchandise that Hugo was always shipping to El Sacramento. Two dollars' profit. Who knows, maybe three. She
was daydreaming about it when Rosalía took her arm.

"Ah!" Ninfa exclaimed. "Let's eat something, love. It's
eleven-forty, but my stomach has already struck noon. It's
a good idea to get to the restaurant early so as to find a
place."

She cast a last greedy glance at the kitchen items—
pots and pans and kettles of aluminum, objects of copper
and nickel, dish cloths—oh, how nice!—and a whole
arsenal of knives—things to drive a woman crazy with
delight—and went off with her companion toward the escalator.

"Don't you think that's enough shopping for today?"
Pancho Vivanco's wife asked. "My feet are simply aching."

"First let's line our stomachs, dearie, and then we can
take a look around the *basimento*," Señora de Ugarte replied, enriching her language with a neologism.

They got a table in the restaurant and began studying
the menu. When the waitress came over—blonde, clean,
vividly made-up—each woman chose a dish by the appropriate number.

The general's wife pulled off her shoes and heaved a
sigh of relief. Sitting down at last! She picked up the glass
in front of her, in which there was more crushed ice than
water, and drank avidly. Rosalía smiled.

Natural teeth, thought Ninfa with a certain nationalistic pride, and not capped like the American beauties of
the theater, the movies, and television.

When the food came, Señora de Ugarte looked at
Rosalía's lunch with an envy in which there was a touch of
rancor: lettuce, slices of boiled egg, carrots and beets, half
of a canned apricot and a scoop of cottage cheese. Nothing

more. Nothing fattening. It wasn't surprising that the little bitch kept her figure—and what a figure, *Neustra Señora!* She looked at her own plate on which the pork chops glistened with grease, swimming in thick gravy, surrounded by a miniature mountain range of mashed potatoes.

They began to eat. Live models, slender and elegant, were strolling between the tables, exhibiting spring fashions to the sound of soft music emanating from loudspeakers which Ninfa could not locate. In the air floated the scent of apple-blossom cologne.

The general's wife, from time to time, raised her eyes to examine her companion. Rosalía was pecking at her food like a bird. She was pretty, too—like a bird? No. Like a thoroughbred animal. She talked with an almost imperceptible lisp which went very well with her slightly snub nose. Her eyes, with some curious golden flecks in the iris, were chestnut brown, tender on the surface; sensuality hid in their depths, the older woman guessed, and came to the surface only when her male was handling her appropriately.

Ninfa felt for the ambassador's mistress that tenderness tempered with hostility which the mother still filled with youthful delusions feels toward the daughter who has become a woman and, besides the threat of making her a grandmother, is becoming likewise a serious competitor in the contest for men's attention.

Rosalía in her turn glanced furtively at the matron. Her feelings toward the latter were ambivalent. Ninfa sometimes caused in her a discomfort hard to explain. She was authoritarian, disagreeable, and—worse than all else —had led her around by the nose ever since the day they had met. She wanted to run her life even in the least things. "Don't buy this, buy that. . . . The blue is not becoming to you, choose the gray one. . . . Today you must go shopping with me." And yet there were moments when she found the creature attractive, with that goodhearted, outspoken air of hers. She came out with the funniest sallies as often as she did coarse and vulgar expressions. Her fingers were always full of rings, and brooches of dubious

taste decorated her full bosom. There were days when
Ninfa Ugarte wore so many gewgaws, medals, pins, and
brooches that she looked rather like Marshal Goering in
his days of glory. Now, for example, Rosalía reflected,
chewing a piece of carrot, her lipstick went beyond the
limits of those fleshy lips smeared with the grease from the
pork chops—and the grease was streaking her chin. And
why didn't she have the hair removed from her upper lip?
Ay, Jesús! Suddenly Rosalía realized that the mustache
made Doña Ninfa look like Aunt Micaela, of whom she,
Rosalía, had the worst kind of memories. Tia Micaela was
harsh, incapable of affection, and she had constantly reminded the girl of her status as a poor orphan. ("You think
you're some princess or other? You want to marry the son
of the president of the Republic? Grab that fellow Vivanco. He's no movie star, but he's a nice boy, a diplomat,
and they even say he's going to be sent to Paris.")

"Love," murmured Ninfa, "I'm rather worried."

"Why?"

"Things in El Sacramento are not going well. This is
election year, and the constitution prohibits the Generalissimo from being a candidate again."

"I don't understand politics, Doña Ninfa."

"It's not a matter of politics, dearie, but our lives. If
the opposition wins the election, we're *jodidos.*"

Rosalía flushed. Ninfa noticed it and thought, She's
ashamed of words but not of decorating her husband's
head with horns.

When the waitress brought the dessert—apple pie á la
mode for the matron and currant gelantine for the young
woman—the conversation took the course most feared by
the wife of Pancho Vivanco.

"Let's start the game, love," Ninfa said, fixing her
pornographic eyes on the other woman. "Frankness never
hurt anyone. I know about your affair with Don Gabriel
Heliodoro."

"What affair?" the other parried automatically.

"It will get you nowhere to deny it. It's common
knowledge. In Cerro Hermoso everybody knows, except

Don Gabriel Heliodoro's wife, of course. Doña Francisquita always has her head in the clouds."

Rosalía's lips were trembling like the rosy bit of gelatine she was balancing on her spoon, en route to her mouth.

"Now don't get upset," Ninfa soothed her. "I'm not criticizing you. In your place I'd have done the same. Don Gabriel Heliodoro is quite a man. Your husband is a nasty piece of garbage."

Eyes cast down, Rosalía was playing with her dessert, cutting it with her spoon into many tiny pieces which she wound up by mashing, without eating them.

"Come now!" the other woman encouraged her. "Are we friends or not? Last night Pancho telephoned to my house asking whether you were still with us. Hugo, the old monkey, caught on right off and lied, saying that you and I had gone to a movie together. Rosalía, little silly, you can count on us. We're all on Don Gabriel Heliodoro's side. We're all on *your* side."

The younger woman continued staring in embarrassment at the rose-red mush she now had in her dish.

"Look, sweetie, you're going to need a . . . a . . . what's that thing one always sees in a detective film, when a fellow wants to prove that he was in another place at the time somebody was murdered? Alibili?"

"Alibi," Rosalía murmured.

"That's it. You're going to need a lot of them, often. From now on you can dine unworried with the ambassador and—and so forth. I'll call Pancho on the phone and say that you and I have something special to do. You fix it all up with Don Gabriel Heliodoro and ask him to send the embassy car to pick me up at my house. With Aldo driving, naturally. We can start today. You stay with your man and I'll take a ride around . . . Arlington, Mount Vernon, Bethesda. . . ." She winked. "Can there be a more perfect alibi?"

Rosalía screwed up her courage and said, "For us both, eh?"

Ninfa giggled. "Of course for us both. You're an intel-

ligent girl. We must be allies. Life is short and men are all
dogs. All of 'em. And now, my dear, changing the topic,
look what a pretty suit that is. *Ay, Dios mío!* If I had your
body, Rosalía, I'd buy a suit like that. And I'd do other
things, a lot of other things."

She signaled the waitress, calling for the bill. "I'll pay
today," she declared, winking again.

At that moment Rosalía hated her. And she wished
she could vanish from sight.

9

THAT AFTERNOON Pablo Ortega felt the need to see
Dr. Leonardo Gris. He telephoned him from a public booth. "What do you say to our having dinner
together in one of those Georgetown restaurants?"

"I think it's a fine idea," the exile responded. "But are
you certain that it isn't going to put you in a compromising
position?"

"Are you speaking seriously, Professor?"

It was a pleasure to hear the warm, clear laugh of his
friend.

"Well, there is *some* seriousness in my question, but
not much. At seven, then, at the Carriage House."

"Perfect."

Five minutes before that hour, Pablo Ortega parked
his car in one of the side streets off Wisconsin Avenue and
walked toward the restaurant. Curious, the façade of the
Carriage House, with its wood portico painted black and
adorned with carriage lamps from colonial times, always
reminded him of a funeral home.

He entered the restaurant and did not have to look
long for his friend. Leonardo Gris was sitting at a table in
a corner of the main room, which was filled at that hour
to capacity.

"What a relief," Pablo exclaimed as he sat down, "to have someone to talk to, unburden myself. I've had an awful day, with a tremendous headache."

"How did the ceremony go?"

"Better than could be expected. Much better. It seems incredible, but our ambassador cut quite an impressive figure. He conducted himself like an experienced diplomat."

'That he has *le physique du rôle*, nobody can deny."

"More than that, he radiates a kind of magnetism. I haven't the slightest doubt about it, the President liked our wild Indian. It isn't surprising. Up to now I have never met a rascal who wasn't attractive."

When they were finishing their cocktails, Gris said, "When I asked you today whether you weren't afraid of compromising yourself, the question was not wholly gratuitous. What will Gabriel Heliodoro say when he finds out that you are still keeping up your friendship with this renegade?"

"He must know about it already."

Gris nodded slowly in assent. "It is possible and it is probable. These last two weeks, a stranger has been following me like a shadow. I have seen him on the university campus. When I come home, he accompanies me in his blue car. At times I peek through the window of my apartment and see the fellow standing on the nearest corner."

"Are you certain it is always the same man?"

"Positive. I am certain, too, that he is going to appear in a very short time in the doorway of this room, making sure that I see him. That insistence on being noticed leads me to believe that the person who orders him to follow me intends nothing but intimidation."

"I only hope that is all. But take care." Pablo chewed the olive from his martini. "What does he look like? A Latin type?"

"No. He is a tall man, stout and blond. I don't know why, but he looks to be of Irish origin. But let's talk of pleasant things. What are we going to eat? I suggest broiled lobster."

"Excellent."

"Wine?"

"That's for you to choose. But don't forget it was I who invited you to dinner."

"We'll fight over that when it's time to pay."

While the professor went over the wine list, Pablo studied him. At fifty-seven Leonardo Gris retained the physical and intellectual vigor of the days when, more than a decade past, he taught literature in the Universidad Federal in Cerro Hermoso. After being widowed at forty-odd, he had never married again. As he had no children, he had, so to speak, adopted his students, for whom he held, beyond the interest of a teacher, the affection of a father. The capacity for expression in his eyes was surprising. They could be alternately (or at the same time?) tender and forceful, serious and jesting, full of faith and skepticism. His skin, the color of old ivory, was still smooth and firm, and his eyebrows, completely black, contrasted with his hair, graying with silvery lights. His voice, deep and rich in modulations, constituted what could be called a precision instrument, which Gris knew how to use masterfully as professor and as lecturer. This man, Pablo thought, is one of the exceedingly few people in the world in whose presence I feel completely at ease, so at ease that I feel impelled to turn on my confessional faucet and let my problems, doubts, and perplexities pour forth.

"Last night," Gris said, when, after several minutes, the food came, "I had a strange dream about Dr. Julio Moreno. We met in a deserted and somber street. I ran to him, tried to embrace him, but on seeing me he ran, giving me to understand by gestures of his head and hands that he refused to speak to me. I woke up in anguish. Analyzing the dream, I concluded that it was inspired by a sense of guilt."

"I don't see why you have to feel guilty in connection with your old companion. Because he is dead and you are alive?"

Gris made a gesture of doubt. "Consciously, I reject the guilt. I tried to stay with Moreno up to the end. It was he who insisted that I escape. He not only insisted, he *ordered.*"

Pablo looked at the scarlet carapace of the lobster on the other's plate, and suddenly through his mind passed the abstract painting he had left unfinished on the easel, months before.

"That night, in the Embassy of Mexico," he said gently, still gazing at the vivid red, "we could not talk freely, remember? After your asylum was formalized, the ambassador confined you to your apartments on the upper floor, incommunicado. I confess that, on the many occasions we have met here in Washington, I've had a desire to touch on that subject, but I felt some scruples."

"You see?" Gris laughed. "It is because, at heart, you think I ought not to feel very proud of having survived the *Noche Trágica.*"

"Come, Professor! I just didn't want to revive sad memories. And do you want to know what I think of the problem, in all frankness? . . . All right. This exile of yours is pleasant for you, your moral and material position in this country is excellent, your colleagues and students in the university admire and esteem you, you live in reasonable comfort, you frequent the Library of Congress, you visit art galleries, you have the opportunity of attending good concerts, of seeing good theater. Now, all this can cause that execrable, or admirable, phantom inhabiting the depths of our inner caverns to take advantage of your sleep and whisper in your ear the accusation which both you and I fear so much. Yes, because according to mythological syntax the adjective that modifies the word exile must of necessity be *bitter.*"

"You may be right."

There was a short silence in which Pablo Ortega occupied himself in stripping the meat from his lobster with his fork. When he raised his eyes to his friend, the latter remarked:

"I am certain that Dr. Julio Moreno did *not* commit suicide."

"What!" Ortega exclaimed in astonishment, frowning.

"I knew Moreno better than anyone else. He had a tremendous reverence for life, not only for that of others but also for his own. He never carried a weapon. He hadn't even a pocket knife on him that night. You remember the situation. It was hopeless. Gabriel Heliodoro was marching on the palace with his mercenaries. There were some two hundred of us ready to resist to the death. Moreno summoned us and said, 'I do not want the sacrifice of anybody. I hate the idea of useless death. Lay down your arms and then do what you think best—surrender or flee. I absolve you from all commitment to my government. Thank you. And God bless you!' When I objected that he would be shot if he should be taken prisoner, Moreno replied, 'In any case, dead or alive, I shall be a problem for them.' "

Gris took a sip of wine, glanced toward the door of the restaurant, and then faced his friend again.

"Fifteen minutes before the palace was invaded, I was still arguing with Moreno. We two were alone in the building. He was livid, cold sweat on his face, and he was breathing with difficulty. I insisted on staying with him, but the man ordered me away. He succeeded in convincing me with one argument, that I could carry on the revolution abroad, for he considered his government a white revolution. 'I am too old and too sick to go with you,' he said. And he practically shoved me out of the deserted palace. To abandon my friend in that situation was the hardest decision I have had to make in all my life. Minutes later, Pablo, I was knocking at your door. And the rest you know."

"But why did Carrera and his bandits create that fiction of his suicide?"

"The fact is that, if they had spared Moreno's life, a man so respected not only in the country but abroad, they would be left with a hot potato in their hands. If they shot him openly, world opinion would be aroused against them, causing them tremendous harm. Inventing the story of the suicide, the ruffians not only got rid of the problem but laid the foundation for an even greater infamy—the lie that Moreno had committed suicide because he feared that

an official investigation of his administration would be
made and all the so-called illicit deals he had made for his
own profit would be revealed. Do you understand now?"

Ortega was astounded.

"Then Dr. Julio Moreno may have been murdered—
by Gabriel Heliodoro himself?"

Gris shrugged.

"As to that I cannot say. I imagine they took him, still
alive, out of the Palace of Government to some prison outside the city and only later decided to kill him secretly.
The fact is that no journalist, no foreign correspondent,
ever got permission to see the corpse. The Sacramentan
papers limited themselves to giving a succinct notice of
the suicide. No photograph of the body was published. No
one knows to this day where they buried him."

Gris paused, and then repeated, "I am quite certain
that Dr. Julio Moreno did not commit suicide." Perceiving
that his revelation had left Pablo deeply upset, he changed
the subject. "What news of Don Dionisio have you had?"

"Two days ago I had a letter from home—but I
haven't opened it. The inhibition continues."

"And to think it was I who got you into that jam." Gris
touched Pablo's arm cordially. "From time to time I look
back on our dramatic ride that night. I don't know how to
thank you for what you did for me."

"Don't talk of that, Professor. The help I gave you
may have been the most useful, decent thing I've done in
all my life."

"Believe me, it was not in vain, my friend," Gris replied, looking furtively around. "We know that Carrera is
not going to allow elections to be held this year as the
constitution provides. Not even with a puppet candidate of
his own choosing. Fidel Castro's victory in Cuba came to
aid our cause enormously. I can assure you that the revolution is under way."

"Please!" Pablo interrupted him. "Tell me nothing."

Gris smiled. "I have the most absolute confidence in
you."

"But I don't want to know anything, either facts or

names. Knowledge of all those things can only confuse me more."

"Don't think that I myself know all the details of the movement. But I understand your situation, Pablo. Let's talk of other matters, then. Have you been writing? Painting?"

Ortega shook his head in a disheartened negative. "I've been doing nothing. I feel empty. I am restless, distrustful of words. I take aspirin and tranquilizers as if such drugs could solve my problems. As for the rest, I continue to obey a remote control managed by an extremely able operator, Doña Isabel Ortega y Murat, who uses an apparatus as old as life, but very efficient—the human heart, which in this case happens to be my own father's."

"And so now you feel like a satellite in orbit," Gris said.

"And the worst of it, Professor, is that I gravitate around a low-grade sun. Isn't it shameful?"

Leonardo Gris tapped his forefinger on his own chest over his heart. "To use an old euphemism, how goes your noble viscera?"

"Love? Women? Nothing serious. I pick up a semi-prostitute today, another three or four days later. Everything with me remains on the tepid plane of the *semi*. I'm a semipoet, a semipainter. I sleep with semiprostitutes. I am semisatisfied sexually. And the worst of it all is that I feel only semiashamed of the whole situation."

"Yonder is my shadow! The fellow in the light raincoat."

Pablo turned his head and looked for the man indicated. "The blond one, with his hat in his hand?"

"That's the one. See, he is looking hard in our direction."

Pablo got up, determined to approach the stranger to question him, but Gris pulled resolutely at the tail of his coat, forcing him to sit down again, while the man in the pale raincoat abruptly turned on his heel and went out.

"Take it easy, Pablo. I am sure that they merely want to frighten me. I don't pretend not to understand. This

morning I had a telephone call apropos of my letter to the
editor of the *Post,* published today. Have you read it?
Good. The voice said, in English without the shadow of an
accent. 'Listen, brother, if you have any regard for your
skin, don't write any more letters to the newspapers.' But
let's talk about something else. You have at least been
listening to music lately?"

"Yes. I always do. It is what saves me from becoming
completely coarsened. The quartets of Béla Bartók bring
to mind so strongly the smashing up of our world that I no
longer have the courage to listen to them. They hurt me. I
prefer the Italian primitives. They speak to me of an
angelic world, fictitious perhaps, but beautiful. Yes, and
there is always old Johann Sebastian, the man who speaks
and understands the language of God. Such people make
me believe that life and the world can be simple and love
possible. And speaking of music, professor, how goes the
cello?"

"Badly. Gathering dust in a corner. For weeks I have
not touched it."

"I haven't forgotten the evening when you played that
Bach *partita* for Gonzaga and me. Do you·remember? The
room was in shadow, the window open, there was a full
moon, and it was October. Everything perfect."

Gris smiled with a touch of sadness. And Pablo
thought, I wish this man were my father. The idea struck
him as intellectually so maudlin that his face and ears felt
as if on fire. He took a big swallow of wine, in an automatic gesture.

When the coffee came, Gris asked, "Do you think it
possible for a man to be playing Bach on his cello, let's say
a *passacaglia,* and at the same time be plotting a revolution, wondering where to buy weapons and ammunition,
how to smuggle them into El Sacramento, what military
contacts to establish, what strategic bridges to blow up,
etc., etc.? And further, do you think it possible for that
same man to be at heart a pacifist who rejects violence and
whose ideal is to stay put in his little corner, reading Plato
or writing an essay on Góngora?"

Pablo hesitated an instant.

"I find it possible. And that is what startles me." He took up a morsel of bread, rolled it in his fingers, and thought of his friend Bill Godkin, who always carried provisions in his pockets for the birds and the squirrels. Then he asked, "In your opinion, Dr. Gris, what makes a good revolutionary?"

"As that Malraux character said, the good revolutionary is a Manichaeist with a taste for action."

"And how do you appraise yourself as a revolutionary?"

"Third-rate at best, Pablo. The truth is that we so-called intellectuals will always be very poor men of action. With good reason Stalin detested that type of man. We reject political and philosophical absolutes. We do not accept the idea that things can only be black or white. We believe in the shadings, in the complexities of men and of their problems. All these amount to stumbling blocks in the path of revolution, things that infuriate the men of pure revolutionary action. It is still another personage in Malraux, I believe, who says that many people seek to find in the Apocalypse the solution for their individual problems."

Pablo toyed pensively with the ball of bread.

Gris disclosed confidentially, "Look at my situation. I am no Manichaeist nor do I love action. I consider myself more of a contemplative. If I remain indifferent to the fate of my land, my conscience condemns me. If I involve myself in the revolutionary conspiracy, the man of the cello, the reader of Plato, and Góngora eyes me distrustfully and condemns me likewise, in his way. And it is quite possible that if the revolution triumphs, one day I may be condemned by my own companions. In short, the intellectual is a condemned man by definition!"

"There must be a way out."

"Be that as it may, I have to keep my word, given to a friend who died. I closed my eyes and entered into the conspiracy. I shall go on to the end."

When the waiter was on the point of handing the

check to Gris, Ortega intercepted it over his friend's protests.

When they came out of the restaurant and took a few steps in the direction of Q Street, Gris caught sight of the man in the light raincoat standing at a corner. Ortega saw him too and growled a threat.

"Pay no attention," the professor said.

Pablo, however, quickened his step, leaving him behind, and approached the stranger to ask him point-blank, "What do you want with my friend?"

The other took a step backward as if to defend himself from physical aggression. "I don't know what you're talking about," he retorted.

Fists clenched, facial muscles taut, Ortega had to contain himself in order not to hit him, even knowing that he would be at considerable disadvantage in a physical struggle.

"You know very well! But you're wasting your time. Dr. Gris cannot be terrorized. Tell that to whoever is paying you for this filthy job."

"You're nuts," the other said with a forced smile. He turned on his heel and marched off. Gris approached his friend.

"Pablo, you risked getting a real drubbing. The man has all the appearance of a prizefighter."

Ortega was shaking with indignation. The dead cigarette stuck to his lips. The two walked on for a while in silence. Pablo was thinking of the face of the man in the light raincoat: ruddy, square-jawed, with a hard, cruel mouth. Who could be paying him for the job? Ugarte? Yes, it would be the old police dog.

He spat out the cigarette.

Gris took his former student by the arm and tried to take his mind off the incident.

"I am invited to give a lecture at American University in May. I am going to tell a few truths about our government."

"I'll be there, you may be sure."

"No, Pablo, I beg you not to come. You are taking unnecessary risks."

They walked on in silence as far as Q Street, where they turned west. The building in which Dr. Gris had his small apartment was in the block where the Russian Embassy was located in the days of the Czar.

"Will you come up, Pablo?"

"Of course. I shall not rest until after I see you safely locked in at home."

The professor's apartment was on the third floor. Only after making sure that no one was concealed inside did Pablo agree to leave. The profesor smiled. "You are seeing ghosts. No matter, many thanks anyway . . . once again. Will you stay for a cognac? Or for a dose of Bach or Vivaldi?"

"No. I must get to sleep early tonight. It has been a hard day."

They shook hands. Back on the sidewalk, Pablo looked all around but saw no suspicious person in the vicinity. He started walking toward the spot where he had left his car.

Q Street. Q Street? Suddenly he remembered. That was the street where Glenda Doremus lived. The girl had left her address written with blue pencil on the cardboard cover of her thesis. 3050 Q Street. He had only to take a few steps more to find the building with that number. What floor was Glenda's apartment on? That detail he could not recall. He stopped an instant and stood looking at the several lighted windows in the building.

10

L YING ON THE SOFA fully dressed except for her shoes, Glenda Doremus was staring at the television screen where figures were moving, but every effort to concentrate her attention on their words and actions was in

vain. All day long, during working hours, she had managed
to forget that she had a stomach. Hardly had she got
home, however, when the unpleasant sensation, that
species of hunger pangs mingled with a nauseated feeling,
had recommenced. She suspected that she had a gastric
ulcer, or something worse. Her last X ray, taken less
than a week before, had disclosed nothing abnormal in
her digestive system. The doctor persisted in declaring
that everything she felt was psychosomatic in origin. He
had advised her to find an analyst. Not that! Never!

That evening Glenda had declined the invitation of a
colleague in the Pan American Union to dine together at
Aldo's. Now, just thinking of food made her queasy. And
yet she knew that only with some nourishment could she
alleviate that feeling of painful emptiness in her stomach.

On the television screen cowboys were exchanging
shots. Glenda got up, turned off the set, went to the
kitchen, took out a bottle of milk, poured a little of it into a
glass, and took a swallow, with some trepidation. Nothing
evoked memories of her home more than the smell and the
taste of milk. She returned to the living room, thinking of
her father and her mother. She stood for a moment gazing
at their portrait on the slant-top desk, beside a vase of
flowers. From one of the desk drawers she took the letter
she had received from her father that morning, sat down in
an armchair, and re-read it.

Dear Daughter: Why don't you come home? I know
Washington must be pretty now, with the cherry trees
blossoming, but here in Atlanta the peach trees, too, are in
full flower. Your mother and I can't understand why you
still haven't made up your mind firmly about what you
want to study. Last year it was English and literature. This
year it's that silly stuff about Latin American history.
What practical use can that be?

Your mother is not feeling very well. She has phlebitis
and must stay in bed, and we are all quite worried about
her health. Like me, your mother was sorry you didn't
come to see us during your last summer vacation, and

now you tell us you can't come next Christmas. Why hate
the South so much? After all, in Washington there are
more Negroes than whites. You complain in your letters
that you have no friends there, and that you are not happy.
Then why do you persist in living in the city which you
yourself find monotonous and uninteresting? Come on
home, baby. You ought not let your life be ruined by
things that happened so many years ago and that you were
not to blame for at all. And if anyone is guilty in all that, it
is I, and God's my witness I'm not sorry for what I did."

Glenda ripped the letter across in a brusque gesture,
throwing the pieces into a wastebasket. Her father had no
right to bring up that subject!

She felt an unexpected longing for a bath. The same
thing happened several times a day, even in working
hours. It was the sudden feeling—absurd, she recognized,
but invincible—that she was dirty, that she smelled bad,
and that other people avoided her with repugnance. The
notion made friendly contacts difficult for her, turning her
into a withdrawn person, distrustful, unsociable.

She went into the bathroom and undressed. But before bathing she looked at herself in the dressing-table
mirror, running her hands over her breasts, her abdomen,
her pubis—not with voluptuousness or vanity, but with a
kind of clinical curiosity, looking for any hard spot that
might be the sign of a malignant tumor. She was forever
possessed by the notion that she was going to die of
cancer, possibly of the uterus. She tried, but in vain, to
bring herself to her senses. There were moments when she
could even laugh at her obsession. But it was useless; the
evil presentiment continued, darkening her mind, torment-
ing her life.

Suddenly she was struck by the suspicion that male
invisible eyes were spying on her. In an access of startled
modesty she wrapped herself in a towel. She let it fall only
when she stepped under the shower and opened the
faucet. She rubbed herself with soap, lathering her body
profusely. It was good to get clean. She did not love her
body. On the contrary, she had a certain loathing of it. It

was hard to be a woman. When her menstrual period came, she had the impression that her smell was contaminating the whole city. She became peevish, surly, at such times, and had the impulse to hide, to disappear from the face of the earth. Thinking of these things, Glenda rubbed herself so furiously that she actually scratched her arms, her breasts, her legs, with her own nails. I've got to do something, she thought, or I'll go crazy.

She dried herself, soothed by the tepid water. She went back into the bedroom, half smiling at her exaggerations. Sure, girl. It's all just fancies. It's a question of mastering your nerves. Take it easy!

She put on pajamas, returned to the living room, sat down at the writing desk, where she had the typescript of the thesis which she was going to present for her degree at the end of that academic year. She had thought that the Republic of El Sacramento, because it was a small, little-known country, would not offer many difficulties for an interpretative study. Sometimes she went so far as to believe she had done a good job. But the hours of doubt prevailed over those of optimism. She considered the thesis superficial, puerile. Perhaps it would have been better to specialize in, say, biology. Or sociology. Or nothing!

She picked up the envelope lying beside the typescript. It contained an invitation to the reception that the new ambassador from El Sacramento was giving for the diplomatic corps the following Friday. On the bottom there was a note from Pablo Ortega, written by hand. "Don't fail to come. I've read your thesis. We'll talk about it. I promise you won't be bored at the party."

Glenda lay down again on the sofa and thought about Pablo. She still did not know what to think of him, but she mistrusted what she felt—and that left her a little apprehensive. She had found the young man attractive in a way that she could not define clearly. The Sacramentan was perhaps the first man who had interested her—a little. She had liked his serious, manly face and his dry, almost monochord voice, free of that hypocritical theatricality so common in diplomatic circles. She also liked the fact that

Pablo Ortega, different from the majority of Latins she knew, did not have the look of a gigolo, and had not treated her as if he considered her easy prey. Too bad that his skin was so dark. But what did it matter to her whether he was dark or light? she thought rebelliously, turning over on the sofa and lying face down with a pillow pressed against her stomach.

She considered the invitation, mentally saw Pablo's handwriting, analyzed it. It was large, resolute, clear. It seemed to indicate generosity, frankness, and manliness. Yes, it was too bad that he had that Moorish tone to his skin.

She wondered what he had thought of her thesis. If he didn't like it, why didn't he say so right away? Does he think that he can lure me to the reception just with the guarantee that I won't be bored? Can he be so sure that his company is going to be so pleasant to me?

She mentally reviewed the dresses that she could wear to the reception. There were not many. Maybe the most appropriate one would be the black taffeta. But she was not yet sure that she was going to the party. She knew that sort of gathering. People were jammed into a room, elbowing each other, drinking and shouting, not really aware of what they were drinking or of what they were saying to each other. They merely stunned themselves. Actually nobody enjoyed himself. She wasn't going! Why should she? Just because of Ortega's postscript? They could discuss the thesis another time. She tried to blot Pablo's image out of her mind. She failed.

The young man must have a problem. It was plainly seen in his face. Problem, or problems. And the idea that he might *not* be happy made her feel, somehow, inclined to help him, to gain his trust, lead him to pour it all out to her. Perhaps Ortega might be the friend she needed. But did she really need a friend? And must that friend necessarily be of the opposite sex? She feared complications. She had regretted it every time she had consented to go out in the evening with some acquaintance. Eight out of ten tried to kiss her. Five out of ten tried to take her to bed by force.

She took an antacid tablet from her pajama pocket and put it in her mouth, letting it dissolve on her tongue. Pablo Ortega y . . . what? There was another name she could not remember. What blood ran in his veins? Indian and Spanish? His features were neither Indian nor Negro. The Moors had occupied the Iberian Peninsula for many centuries. Pablo must have Moorish blood in his veins. The Moors were Africans. But what did that Latin American embassy secretary's blood matter? All blood was dirty. All human beings were condemned to filth, both of body and of mind. All. Oh, God! She had another night to get through. The television programs were unbearable. Read a book? The books that were being published now dealt only with unpleasant themes: homosexuality, racial violence, resentment, despair. When they were not written by Negroes, they were, most of them, by Jews.

Glenda thought of phoning a friend. But what to say to her? She could get in her car and drive along the streets near the Potomac, aimlessly. Then she would come back, take a barbiturate and try to sleep. Why not take fifty seconal tablets at once?

Maybe suicide was the solution. But was she really sincere in thinking of suicide? No. She would kill herself only if she knew for sure that in her vital organs a cancer was growing, like a deadly flower. She pressed the pillow harder against her stomach.

Near ten o'clock that night the telephone rang in Clare Ogilvy's apartment.

"Hello? Who is it?" she asked, annoyed because she was enjoying her favorite television program.

"This is Monsieur Michel."

"What's the matter?"

"Miss Ogilvy," the butler said softly, "it is a confidential matter."

"Speak louder, man. What's it all about?"

"I am in a difficult situation, miss. It is concerning the reception next Friday. Excuse me, but I find it dangerous to talk about this in the chancellery." Clare heard the butler's social throat-clearing over the wire. "*Bien,* as you know, for ten years Beauchamps Frères have been our caterers. A respectable firm, first-class food, attentive employees, in short, an impeccable service—"

"I know, Michel, I know. What's your problem?"

"Something lamentable has occurred. General Ugarte this time has invaded my territory, taken over the catering, and given the contract to Parker & Baker, Caterers."

"Perhaps he has obtained more favorable terms," Clare ventured without conviction, gazing at the television screen—she had lowered the volume in order to answer the telephone.

"Not at all, Miss Ogilvy! Twenty percent higher. And I need not tell you who is going to pocket that nice percentage."

"Patience, Michel. The loser in that is the treasury of the Republic of El Sacramento. I am very sorry, but I can do nothing."

"*Mais,* mademoiselle, see my position. I had already promised Beauchamps Frères, as I have every year. *C'est calamiteux!*"

Clare was eager to get back to her program. She thought of the butler's face—the rosy orifice of his mouth, which the long nose all but hid, his blinking eyes, his half-obsequious, half-sour expression.

"Well, that's the way it is, Michel. What a misfortune! This time *you* will lose your usual ten percent, won't you?"

"Mademoiselle!"

Clare Ogilvy hung up.

Close to eight o'clock that same evening the automobile of the Embassy of El Sacramento had stopped before the portico of the embassy residence. Aldo Borelli had jumped out, opened the door of the vehicle, from which Rosalía Vivanco emerged with the collar of her coat turned high, covering half of her face, her head wrapped

in a kerchief tied under her chin. She pressed the button at
the door, which Michel opened to her, and went into the
mansion. The chauffeur returned to his place, and the lady
who had remained inside the car ordered, "Drive slowly
through Rock Creek Park." Aldo Borelli obeyed. He was
beginning to get alarmed. From what he had seen and
heard those last few weeks, he could have few doubts as to
the intentions of the fat old cow lolling on the back seat.
Her powerful, nauseating perfume assailed his nostrils like
a kind of libidinous invitation. *Mamma mia!* What he
wanted was to live peacefully with his wife and accumu-
late a little extra money so he could send for his younger
brother from Italy. If the general's wife were young and
pretty, there would be no problem except, perhaps, the
risk of getting caught redhanded by the general.

"A pretty night, Aldo."

"Very, signora."

The Italian looked at his passenger in the rearview
mirror. Physically she reminded him of certain Sicilian and
Calabrian women, corpulent and mustached. But the Sicil-
ians and the Calabrian women in general had a high sense
of honor and decency. They were faithful to their hus-
bands. In Sicily and Calabria honor was washed clean
with blood.

There was little traffic in the park. At a crossroads
Aldo hesitated. "Where are we going, signora?"

"Let's go see the cherry trees. Follow the banks of the
river and go by the Jefferson monument. As far as the
obelisk."

The obelisk! Ninfa Ugarte mentally caressed the
carnal image which the stone had evoked for her. What
she was doing was risky, and, because it was risky, exciting. A friend had told her once that the emotion of hunting
the game was even stronger than that of killing it.

"Are you married, Aldo?"

"Sí, signora."

"How old is your wife?"

"Twenty-eight."

"Is she pretty?"

"I think so, signora."

"Have you any children?"

"Two, signora. A boy and a girl."

Ninfa gazed in fascination at the sturdy young neck of the Italian.

Minutes later, when the Mercedes-Benz was passing the monument, Ninfa praised the beauty of Washington. Did Aldo know El Sacramento? . . . No? What a pity. He should. Cerro Hermoso was in a green valley. The climate was delightful. The city a jewel, with its ancient mansions from colonial times. The cathedral—*Dios mío!*—was lovely. Pure plateresque style. (If he asks me what plateresque is, I'm stumped.)

When they were once more drawing near the banks of the Potomac, the chauffeur asked, "And where to now, signora?"

"We have to kill time, Aldo. I promised to go for my friend around eleven-thirty. Let's ride over in Virginia."

Madonna! Aldo Borelli shouted to himself. If General Ugarte ever hears about this, I can lose my job and even get a thrashing.

The car crossed Memorial Bridge and then took the road to Alexandria. When the blue lights of the airport came in view, Ninfa ordered, "Stop the car yonder, near the river."

Damned old hag! Aldo turned the car off the paved roadway and approached the river's edge. From the center of the airport a vertical beam of violet light rose to the sky.

Ninfa Ugarte squirmed on her seat, and, groaning softly from the effort, opened the door and got out. Aldo Borelli was already a little excited, despite himself, by the anticipated prospect. It was all ridiculous, besides being dangerous. He imagined himself telling the story to his wife when he got home that night. "Just imagine, Antonietta, the general's wife made me stop the car in a deserted spot, near the river, and . . ." His thoughts were interrupted by the click of the door to his right. The warm, voluminous, perfumed presence of Ninfa Ugarte made itself felt beside him. "Here on the front seat," she said in excuse, "I can see the planes better." In fact, at short intervals planes were landing at the airport or taking off from it, flying low over the water. Aldo Borelli gripped the steering wheel hard, facial muscles stiff.

"A man like you, Aldo," whispered Ninfa, her fat hand resting on the chauffeur's knee, "ought not to be content with this occupation. You could be a movie or a television star."

A plane droned past toward the airport. Aldo Borelli gritted his teeth and remained silent, staring hard at the water, on which the lights from the river banks were tremblingly reflected. Ninfa Ugarte was panting, her heart beating faster and harder. And suddenly, with the precipitation and greediness of a fat little girl, she pulled the zipper of Aldo Borelli's trousers.

Bill Godkin reached his apartment on R Street just before eleven-thirty. Before going to bed, he decided to smoke one more pipe. He sat in the living room, looking at his possessions. A big-game hunter, he reflected, has the mounted heads of tigers, lions, panthers, boars, and so forth on his walls. A hunter of men, like himself, keeps the portraits of his "victims." His walls were full of photographs of famous personalities whom he had interviewed during his three decades of journalistic life. Autographed pictures of Gómez of Venezuela, Sandino, Cárdenas, Pérez Jiménez, Vargas, Ubico, Somozo, Santos Dumont, and Gabriela Mistral were among them. He got up to examine more closely, with a special curiosity, the enlargement he had had made of the photo which in 1925 he had taken of Juventino Carrera surrounded by his general staff, high in the Sierra de la Calavera. There stood the bearded guerrillas, with their broad-brimmed hats, their cartridge belts slung over their shoulders, knives and revolvers at their belts. He concentrated his attention on the tallest of the men. Even in that time-yellowed snapshot the observer could see that Gabriel Heliodoro had the most expressive face of the whole group.

Bill sat down again. In every corner of the apartment he had *recuerdos* from the countries of Latin America that he had visited. On the mantlepiece he had placed the *árbol-de-la-vida* group, carved and painted, which he had bought from a Mexican Indian artist. There it was in its innocent polychrome, with its little birds, flowers, children, and angels. The *torito* from Pucará standing beside the *árbol-de-la-vida* had been given him by Haya de la Torre on the day when he had interviewed the Aprista leader for the first time. The leather-covered *boleadoras* he had got from an Uruguayan politician. Specimens of black ceramic from Chile, maracas from Colombia, and Peruvian, Mexican, and Ecuadoran rugs adorned the living room and his bedroom—and every object had a history. Beside the armchair where he was now seated, next to the tobacco humidor on a round side table, shone the chased-silver hilt and sheath of the knife presented to him by Getulio Vargas, which he used as a letter opener.

His pipe finished, Godkin headed for the bedroom, pulled off his clothes, put on his pajamas, went into the bathroom, and began to brush his teeth—80 percent, he reflected, put their left hands to their waists while they are brushing their teeth. He tried every way he knew to avoid looking at the face which the mirror insisted on showing him. But there was a moment when he thought the man in the mirror wanted to speak to him; there was nothing to do but face up to him.

Well? the other seemed to ask. Nothing, he responded in thought—absolutely nothing. Life goes on the same and it's better not to discuss the matter.

With the toothpaste foam running down from a corner of his wide, ill-designed mouth, Godkin stood analyzing himself. If God had given him one of those faces that women like, such as Pablo Ortega's, for example—or like Orlando Gonzaga's—would his life have been very different from the way it had been? And if he were six-three with a face like a Mayan idol, like Gabriel Heliodoro? Rather, if all the passions, the impulses, and the daring of

the new ambassador of El Sacramento animated him,
would he, Godkin, be merely a solitary widower today,
chief of the Latin American Bureau of Amalpress?

He thought of his late wife. Poor Ruth! What could
she have seen in him to accept the timid, ill-timed proposal
of marriage he had made to her on the terrace of that
Caribbean hotel? Poor girl! She had the soul of a missionary. She would have looked good in a Salvation Army uniform. Bill smiled. He had often imagined Ruth dressed in
the uniform, singing and playing a tambourine on a West
Side street corner in New York. The thought moved him to
tenderness.

He again examined his own image with a critical eye.
Hair the color of rhubarb, now sparse. Skin of a pinkish
white, spattered with freckles. Light gray eyes, nearly
empty of expression, like the eyes of statues. And speaking
of statues, someone had once told him that, with his
broken nose, he looked a little like Michelangelo. He recalled his trip to Europe with Ruth—the trip with which
she said farewell to the world. In the church of Santa
Maria del Fiore, in Florence, he had experienced the
greatest artistic emotion of his life before the *Pietà* of
Michelangelo. Looking at it, he, who until then had had
little enthusiasm for sculpture, had felt something like a
blow on his chest in an impact that knocked his breath out.
Tears had come into his eyes. Ruth had pressed his arm,
tenderly, whispering in his ear, "Darling, how much the
figure holding the dead Christ looks like you!" Great consolation to have a broken nose like Michelangelo Buonar-
roti's!

Godkin lay down on the bed and began reading the
evening paper. Fidel Castro was still making news. The
Dominican dictator was snarling threats at the Cuban revolutionary government. The Secretary of State's condition
was hopeless—a new man had to be appointed. The President had informed the NATO Council, meeting in Washington, that its member nations must be prepared to live
in a state of tension and daily wrangles with the Soviet

Union. Red China had invaded Tibet. A lovely world! A brave world!

Godkin turned to the nonpolitical news. One item announced that there was now a very popular sport that students were engaging in from South Africa to California. The answer to a question of transcendental importance was being sought: How many persons can get into a phone booth? St. Mary's College in California claimed that it had won the world championship by putting twenty-two students inside such a booth. Bill shook his head in wonder, growling, "Didn't they have anything better to do?"

On another page he read that Mrs. Eleanor Roosevelt had bought a camel in Israel for $77 as a present for her granddaughter, but the Department if Agriculture had not permitted the entry of the animal into the United States because of the danger that it might be a bearer of hoof-and-mouth disease. Well, not all was lost, the journalist thought. The night before, sixty million eager Americans had watched on TV the Oscar awards telecast from a Hollywood movie theater. Sixty million! Bill thought, throwing the paper on the floor and putting out the light. Sixty million pairs of eyes fixed on a luminous quadrangle on which was unfolded a fantasy around another fantasy, a lie inspired by another lie. It was the supreme glorification, the greatest triumph of the world of make-believe. And backing the silly spectacle, as always, was a company that wanted to sell its product.

He closed his eyes. He thought of Ruth. Then—odd! —of an adolescent he had seen that afternoon lying on the grass under the flowering cherry trees—her well-modeled bust in a tight sweater of bright yellow which outlined her breasts in sharp relief. She looked like a fruit just fallen from its tree. No. She was a yellow flower, or better yet, the Goddess of the Forsythias. He had looked at her with eyes that were at once male and paternal. He did not know for certain whether he desired the young creature for a daughter or for a mistress. At all events, the Goddess of the Forsythias had sharpened for him the sense of time lost and irretrievable.

11

D R. JORGE MOLINA loved his solitude and the things in his apartment with a love that sometimes seemed to him not only of the spirit but also of the flesh—whenever he looked around the little room that served him as a study—the walls lined with plain shelves crowded with books; the floor of narrow, polished boards, bare of rugs; and the table he had bought at an auction in Alexandria, the old, spacious table on which stood the big lamp of colonial design, and on which were scattered dictionaries, old brochures, papers, and a whole collection of cheap wooden penholders, with Mallat pen nibs, just like the ones he used in school in his boyhood; whenever his fingertips touched the spines of the rare books he possessed, bound in leather, or when he opened them to smell their pages, yellowed odor of time, he came to experience something like a series of minute, repeated, dry orgasms.

For more than two hours he had been sitting at the table, trying to set in order his notes and plans for the biography of Don Pánfilo Arango y Aragón. As his back was hurting, he got up, and with both hands on his waist he started pacing up and down. He could not stay seated for long. He suffered—his doctor in Cerro Hermoso had told him—from a degenerative disc disease. After showing him the X ray, which revealed a lateral curvature of the spine, the doctor had added, smiling, "The spinal deviations, my dear fellow, are the price we pay for being bipeds." On humid days the pain Molina felt in his left shoulder and arm was dull, almost constant, but bearable. But if he made any abrupt movement of arms or head, the pain that flashed from his neck down to the tip of his fingers was so sharp and tearing that if it lasted more than half a minute it would be unendurable.

Rubbing his arm and trying to hold his body erect, the minister-counselor was now walking back and forth, from the wall on which hung a map of El Sacramento of the eighteenth century (authentic) to the opposite wall, where the portrait of Don Pánfilo hung, bearing an affectionate inscription. The only other photograph that Molina had in the house was his mother's, and he kept it in a silver frame on the bedside table in his bedroom.

When he worked at home in the evening, the minister-counselor wore the habit of a Franciscan friar instead of an ordinary bathrobe, and thrust his feet into sandals. This gave him an exquisite pleasure which he could not have explained. He could imagine the ridicule to which he would be exposed if anyone should see him dressed like that. They might think him a maniac, a lunatic, even a pervert. However, that danger was remote; he never invited anyone, no matter who, to his apartment. None of the persons with whom he had contact knew his address, not even his colleagues in the chancellery. He neither had nor wanted a telephone. He used a public phone when one was necessary.

That evening, after he had started work, he had held an imaginary silent dialogue with Don Pánfilo. Now, however, the voice of Leonardo Gris came into his head. "I repeat. How are you going to treat your subject? With the passion of a friend or the cool serenity of an historian?"

It was a pertinent question which he himself had often asked, and continued to ask himself. The present archbishop primate of El Sacramento was a controversial figure. His enemies accused him of following a twisting, Machiavellian political line, by virtue of which he was always in the good graces of the president of the republic, whoever this might happen to be. An orator famous for his eloquence, he knew how to be silent, when silence suited him in the political game.

"Look here, Leonardo," the minister-counselor thought, "one sentence of my dear friend Don Pánfilo can serve as a key to the secret of his politico-social conduct.

One day he told me, 'My dear Molina, sometimes to defend the Church of God we have to feign dealings with the devil and his representatives on earth." He heard the exile's laugh. "Your friend's political theology amuses me."

Jorge Molina tried to cast out of his mind the figure of his political enemy, as a monk in his cell exorcises an evil spirit. He halted, straightened up, moved his head from side to side, then sat down again at the table and fumbled with books and papers. He possessed everything that had been written—biographies, pamphlets, articles—on Don Pánfilo Arango y Aragón. He had before his eyes the famous autobiography of the archbishop primate, *Confiteor*, in flowing, correct Castilian. He had also obtained photostatic copies of nearly all the correspondence of his subject, from the letters he had written to his parents as a boy in a boarding school, to those which had come out of his privileged pen in the seminary days. (What jewels, these last, what precious gems of limpid brilliance!) Among them, the most important were those which the young seminary student had addressed to the then archbishop primate, Don Herminio Ormazábal, his friend and spiritual counselor. To collect all this material, the classification of which he was only just finishing, had taken Molina more than two years.

He picked up the sheet on which he had outlined the plan of his work—the order of the chapters, all of them with cross reference notes—see such-and-such a letter, or page so-and-so of this-or-that book—and made additional, new suggestions. After less than half an hour his eyelids began to droop with drowsiness.

He turned out the lamp, went into his bedroom, prepared for bed, and, as he always did, knelt down by the bed and repeated the *Sequentia: Veni, Sancte Spiritus, et emitte caelitus lucis tuae radium. . . . Veni, pater pauperum; veni, dator munerum! veni, lumen cordium.*

While he was murmuring the prayer, he felt the invisible presence of Gris in the room. In vain he attempted to summon Don Pánfilo to his aid. The exile whispered to him, "Don't you see that you're sending a message with no address on it?" *Lava quod est sordidum, riga quod est aridum, sana quod est saucium.*

He invoked a grateful recollection—Don Pánfilo, in his time as monsignor, splendid in his priestly vestments, preaching from the pulpit of the cathedral. His voice—in which metal, wood, and velvet alternated—filled the plateresque sanctuary of the temple, blending in such a way with the smoke of the incense that both seemed to participate in the same fragrance. *Flecte quod est rigidum* . . . "There are periodic stiffenings, which Mother Nature creates, Jorge, and which horrify you. Why, if they are natural? Why be ashamed of your body?" For an instant Molina seemed lost. He managed, however, to pick up the thread of his prayer. *Da tuis fidelibus, in te confidentibus, sacrum septenarium. Da virtutis meritum, da salutis exitum, da perenne gaudium. Amen.*

He lay down and closed his eyes. He thought how perfect everything would be if he could recover his faith in God.

When the foreign minister of El Sacramento, in 1933, gave Don Alfonso Bustamante the mission of redecorating to his taste the interior of the Washington embassy, until then poorly and atypically furnished, the old diplomat gave himself up to the task with such zeal and enthusiasm that he ended by supplementing from his own purse—the wealth of a rich widower with no heirs—the inadequate appropriation which his government had allotted for the purpose. Through the twenty-odd rooms, large and small, of the mansion on Massachusetts Avenue Don Alfonso paid homage to several Louis of France, not failing, however, to pay expressive tributes also to his admiration for the Italian Renaissance, and never forgetting his cultural and sentimental duties to his *Madre España*, land of his ancestors. A great admirer of Isabela la Católica, about whom he had written a monograph, privately printed, 1924, Don Alfonso had the delicate thought of having the presidential apartments—inaugurated years later by Gen-

eralissimo Juventino Carrera himself on the occasion of his
first and last visit to the United States, at the invitation of
Franklin D. Roosevelt—decorated in the purest Isabeline
style, which the diplomat-humanist customarily described
as a "combination of Mudéjar sensuality with Gothic mysticism and Renaissance refinement."

It was, therefore, on an ample Isabeline bed that Gabriel Heliodoro Alvarado and Rosalía Vivanco were now
lying, completely nude. They had made love in a manner
such as to honor the Mudéjar sensuality as well as the
Gothic mysticism and the Renaissance refinement. At
that moment, at least, they found themselves satisfied,
both of them, a tepid lassitude permeating their bodies.

Gabriel Heliodoro liked to make love with all the
lights on, but as Rosalía preferred semidarkness—for she
was still prudish about her own nakedness—there was
only one discreet blue light in a corner of the room.

The ambassador was lying on his back, his legs a little
apart one from the other. Rosalía was lying on her lover as
though riding his left thigh, her head resting on her man's
broad chest. Gabriel Heliodoro was caressing the girl's
hair with his left hand, while his right was lightly stroking
her back from the neck down to the end of her spine,
enjoying the pleasure, now almost innocent, derived from
the touch of her satiny skin and the firm, warm elasticity
of her flesh. For several minutes they had both been silent,
and from the rhythm of Rosalía's breathing, the warmth of
which he felt on his chest, Gabriel Heliodoro thought she
must be asleep. He made an attempt then to breathe carefully, without inflating his thorax too much, in order not to
wake her.

Suddenly she asked softly, "How is all this going to
end?"

For an instant he remained silent, as if he had not
heard the question. Then he said, "For you, everything
will end well. You are young. You are beautiful. The world
is yours. But I have the presentiment that *I* am going to
end in a violent way."

"Don't say that," she protested, kissing his chest repeatedly.

"The price of a violent life, my love, is a violent death."

"Not always."

Now she was passing her hand over her lover's shoulders, her eyes shut, as if she were sculpting him blindly. "You have the body of a man of forty."

Gabriel Heliodoro was not able, nor did he attempt, to conceal the joy he felt at these words. "I've always loved my body since I was a boy. I liked to look at my face in the mirror of the waters—in rivers, in brooks, in lakes."

"Weren't there any mirrors in your house?"

He did not answer. He remembered that his mother owned a cheap mirror, the kind with a gilt frame one can buy at fairs. It was in front of this mirror that she used to comb her hair and put on her makeup. Many times Gabriel Heliodoro had seen the men who slept with his mother straightening their ties and their military tunics and *képis* in front of the same cracked glass. That was why he hated the mirror so much. One day he had broken it with a stone.

Gabriel Heliodoro frowned. Had he really broken his mother's mirror, or had it all been a dream? Lately, when he thought about scenes from his past, he found it difficult to separate what had actually happened from the things that he had dreamed or simply imagined.

"Didn't you have a mirror in your house?" Rosalía repeated.

"I don't remember." And in the tone of one telling a dream he went on, "The most important thing in the world to me has always been my body. I've never been ashamed of it or of the things that it demanded of me. I used to think this way. If God gave me a body it was for me to use and use well. What good is it to save the body? To be eaten by time? Or by earthworms?"

He stopped to kiss Rosalía's hair.

"And do you know something? A person's intelligence

is not in his head, but in his body. The body knows what it
wants. A man must learn the language of his body."

She listened, smiling, her eyes still closed, surprised to
hear him say such beautiful, disturbing things.

Gabriel Heliodoro felt Rosalía's breasts on his chest,
reminding him of the ripe mangoes of his childhood, in the
forests of Soledad del Mar. He could feel them, heavy, and
yet, at the same time, tender, and this produced a strange
emotion in him. He took them delicately in his huge
hands, closed his eyes, and was in the mountains, fifteen
years old, caressing the breasts of Juana la Sirena, the first
female he had loved in his life. It was a green memory,
redolent of grass, warm earth, forest, and seawind.

"What time is it?" Rosalía asked.

"Don't think about the clock."

"Doña Ninfa promised to come before midnight."

"Let her wait."

Rosalía, however, was already standing beside the
bed, clad in her lover's bathrobe. "Be patient, darling, I
have to get ready to go." She bent over him, gave him a
quick kiss on the mouth, and barefoot, ran to the bathroom.

Gabriel Heliodo lay thinking with anticipatory bore-
dom of the loneliness of his night. He was going to be left
alone in that big house. To go to sleep early did not appeal
to him. What to do, then? The television programs had no
attraction because he could not understand English. He
might go out alone for a stroll around the neighborhood.
Or write a letter to Francisquita. Perhaps the best thing
would be to prepare the rough draft of his report to the
Generalissimo, describing his first encounter with the President. Then he could take up some book or other to read
and summon sleep. But the really nice thing would be to
go to sleep and wake up at dawn in Rosalía's arms.

Such a desire for her assailed him that, on hearing the
sound of the water from the next room, he had an idea
that was born of his body and that took possession of his
head. He got out of bed and ran to the bathroom. He saw

his mistress under the shower, a rubber bathing cap protecting her hair, water and soapsuds running down her naked body.

When she saw him, Rosalía made an instinctive gesture of modesty. He got in next to her and clasped her full against his own nude body.

"No!" she babbled.

Without saying a word he laid her down and possessed her, with the water from the shower falling hot and steaming on his back.

Pancho Vivanco had parked his car in a side street off Wisconsin Avenue, near the intersection of Massachusetts, and had been walking back and forth for nearly half an hour on the sidewalk facing the embassy, his eyes fixed on the mansion. He saw no light in any of the windows of the upper story, where the bedrooms were, but he was positive that at that hour Rosalía was in the bed and the arms of Gabriel Heliodoro. The thought produced a physical pain in his chest and in his head. He was breathing a little heavily. He slipped his right hand into the pocket of his topcoat and rolled between his fingers, obsessively, the cylinder made with a dollar bill.

What to do, God above! What to do? He stopped, half hidden behind a tree in the park, and stood there waiting for—not even he knew what. There were moments when he thought of walking into the embassy residence and putting a bullet in his own head, there in the entrance hall at the foot of the stairs. The notion gave him the morbid joy of imagining Rosalía's remorse and the scandal, which would jeopardize Gabriel Heliodoro's situation both in Washington and in El Sacramento. If he, Pancho, committed suicide, he would leave a letter asking that his body be buried in Cerro Hermoso. Rosalía would have to accompany the corpse back to their country. All dressed in black, the hypocrite! But no! She, poor girl, was not to blame. The culprit was himself. A short, fat, ugly, greasy-skinned man. Then why had Rosalía married him? Of course, her Aunt Micaela had forced her into it, to get rid

of her. And Rosalía had wanted to get away from the
virago.

Perhaps at that exact instant the two lovers were
naked and in each other's arms, disparaging him, Vivanco,
ridiculing him. She would tell the ambassador that she was
in the habit, on retiring, of bolting the bedroom door in
order not to have to yield to her husband. And the Indian
would utter a guffaw. It was possible and probable that
Rosalía disclosed to her lover other intimacies that
demeaned him, Vivanco, as a man. Bitch! Common scum!
Another shameless hussy was Ninfa Ugarte, who had gone
to pick up Rosalía at home at seven-thirty on the pretext
that they were going to the movies together, and yet she
had taken her directly to the ambassador. The procuress!

The image of Gabriel Heliodoro now occupied
Pancho Vivanco's whole mind, as he imagined himself putting five revolver bullets into that huge body. One in the
face. Another in his belly. Three in his genitals. But would
he really have the guts to do a thing like that? Hardly!
Suicide was the solution, he concluded, squeezing the
paper cylinder in his fingers. But the main thing was to get
Rosalía back. He felt sweeping over him an ardent, furious
desire for her body. It was strange. He did not understand
or want to understand; it was precisely because he knew
that the adulteress was going to come home sated, soiled
with the saliva, the sweat, and the semen of another man
that made him desire her more than ever.

And there behind the tree, looking at the front of the
mansion, where three windows were now illuminated, he
made plans for the night. He would go into Rosalía's room
before she had time to lock the door, and would force her
to have intercourse with him even if he had to violate her,
bludgeon her, choke her. And he would take her in the
way that would defile her worst!

He caught sight of the form of a man who was
rounding the embassy. The night watchman. He went off
whistling under his breath, along Massachusetts Avenue
toward Wisconsin, and reached the corner of Wisconsin almost out of breath. He headed for a nearby drugstore,

went in, sat down at the counter, ordered coffee, drank it, without sugar, absently, thinking of his plan for the night. He looked around. He liked the florescent light in the drugstores, their miscellany of smells, the gleaming, polychromatic atmosphere. Paying for his coffee, he went over to the newsstand, picked up a copy of *Time,* leafed through it with vague attention, restored it to its place, and then went to the counter where various office supplies were displayed. He picked up a box of Crayolas, opened it, and the smell of the wax sticks brought to his mind the image of his best childhood friend. His name was Sidney, he was American and the son of a high official of the United Plantations Company. Pancho thought him as handsome as a prince out of Andersen's tales; he envied him not only the blue of his eyes and his pink dry skin, but also his clothes bought in New York, his bicycle, his mechanical toys, and especially the scores of colored wax sticks (*Made in U.S.A.*) with which the lad drew his fanciful designs. Vivanco remembered perfectly—how could he forget—the name of the colored pencils—Colorola—written in black letters against a blue sky under which redskins on horseback were chasing a herd of buffalo. Ever since he came to the United States, Vivanco had been hunting Colorolas in drugstores and stationery shops, as one seeks his lost infancy. No. Rather, as if the simple name, Colorola, could have the magic virtue of bringing Sidney back to life. (His friend had died in action on Guadalcanal, as a captain in the U.S. Marines.) But no one in Washington seemed to be acquainted with that brand of crayons—and now, smelling the Crayolas, Vivanco mentally saw the golden-haired boy with whom he had secretly smoked his first cigarette behind the wall of the schoolyard; the boy who had taught him those exciting hand games forbidden by the grownups.

At that hour Dr. Leonardo Gris was receiving a special visitor in his apartment. The lights were out, and the room was as though dissolved in the shadows of a morning half-darkness, which recalled to the exile a moment of his adolescence when, after a sleepless night, hunched over books on the eve of examinations, he had gone out to wander through the streets of his suburb, waiting for sunrise. The late visitor was sitting in an armchair in the darkest corner of the room. For over half an hour they had been talking in low voices.

"I have told you, and I tell you again, it is dangerous for you to come here," Gris said softly.

"Why?"

"These last few weeks I have been followed by a man who is quite certainly in the pay of our embassy."

Miguel Barrios sketched an impatient gesture. "Well, anyhow, this will be our last encounter in Washington. I am leaving the city in two days. If anyone follows me, I shall know how to throw him off the track. I have had practice in such things."

Barrios was a man of forty-odd years, tall and angular, with a long neck and a prominent Adam's apple. His eyes, sunken in their sockets, held a gleam and a fixity so intense that they perturbed Dr. Gris for a reason that he had not yet succeeded in discovering. In his face, as in that of Jorge Molina, there was something ascetic. The man spoke with the preciseness of a schoolmaster. Indeed, he had been a teacher in a secondary school. Gris remembered having met him at least once, at a school celebration, in his days as minister of education.

"I have obtained the arms and munitions that we needed."

"Where?"

"In Florida. A friend of ours, a rich American who owns a yacht, offered to transport the material from Miami to Havana. He is in the habit of making pleasure voyages around the Caribbean. No one will suspect him. He generally goes to Puerto Esmeralda every year, to gamble in the casinos."

"A trustworthy man?"

"No one is entirely trustworthy, Dr. Gris. But in this

conspiracy in which we are engaged we are obliged by circumstances to use the technique of calculated risk. The American to whom I refer says he is heart and soul on our side. I prefer to believe that he is just attracted by the idea of adventure, of danger. In the war he was a lieutenant in the OSS."

How curious, thought Gris, The leader of the revolution which was intended to overthrow Carrera, that strange pale man dressed in black sitting in the corner, with his long skinny hands gripping the arms of the chair, was still an enigma to him.

"Where do you plan to make your first landing?" he asked. But he immediately added, "No. Don't tell me. Better that I should not know."

"I shall not leave any information written down, but it is necessary for you to have a general idea of what we are planning to do. Nearly all the sergeants and at least two-thirds of the officers of the garrisons of Puerto Esmeralda, San Fernando, Oro Verde, Los Plátanos, Páramo, and Soledad del Mar are with us. They are only waiting for the news of our first landing to rise in revolt. In Cuba we have several contingents of Sacramentan exiles, well armed and trained, ready for the invasion. If our initial plan fails, we shall go to the Sierra, and from there, with our guerrillas, we shall try to galvanize national and world opinion. The moment that the revolutionary troops tread home soil, agitation will start up in the university, in factories, in the streets, in the fields—acts of sabotage, passive resistence, agitations of every kind. But if the garrison at Puerto Esmeralda comes over immediately to our side, which is not just a possibility, but a probability, then our victory will be swift and explosive."

Leonardo Gris went to the window and looked out. He saw no suspicious form in the vicinity. He turned to his visitor and asked, "What can I do to further the movement?"

"Continue publishing your articles and giving your lectures, Doctor. Seek to enlighten official and public opinion in this country, both so essential to the success of our movement of liberation."

"The newspaper editors seem to be tired of my letters. I have had several rejected already."

"You still have the lecture platform left to you. Your university chair, up to a certain point. And your mere presence here, Dr. Gris."

The professor nodded. "Will you have some coffee?" he asked suddenly, as if to warm the chill of the silence that followed.

"No, thank you. Coffee gives me insomnia."

A strange thing, Gris reflected. This was the third meeting he had had with Barrios, and yet between them nothing had been established that resembled, even distantly, a feeling of comradeship or even cordiality. Whose fault? wondered the exile. Mine or his? Or of both? He looked at Miguel Barrios and had the clear impression that the latter was already seated on the throne, or, rather, in the chair of the president of the Republic of El Sacramento.

From afar could be heard the sound of a siren. A fire, perhaps, thought the professor. He remembered the *Noche Trágica*, in which prolonged howls like that one had pierced the dawn at intervals, and from the window of his room in the Embassy of Mexico he had seen the glare of the fires at several points in the beleaguered city.

The silence continued, and Gris sought to recall what he had been told about Miguel Barrios. He knew that the man had been a prisoner and had suffered abuse and mal-treatment at the hands of Carrera's police.

It was Barrios who broke the silence. "I know that you are on good terms with one of the secretaries of embassy—"

"That is true. Pablo Ortega. It was he who, on the night of Moreno's fall, took me at the risk of his own life to the embassy where I requested asylum. He is a person whom I trust implicitly."

"Son of a large landowner. Member of one of the

powerful families which govern and render our land and people unfortunate. Lackeys, all of them, of the Sugar Emporium and of UNIPLANCO."

"I assure you that Pablo is not happy with his position and that at heart he is with our cause."

"It is very easy to say these things when one lives in Washington, earns a good salary, and has an expensive automobile. Those sentiments and political opinions which you say Ortega nurtures at heart must come to the surface as soon as possible and be transformed into action. That is the only way I can believe that he is really with us."

"Well, only time can confirm or deny what I have said about Pablo Ortega."

"Let us talk no more of the young man. Do you know Roberto Valencia?"

"I have an idea I have heard the name."

"Valencia is a sincere revolutionary. He fought beside Fidel Castro in the Sierra Maestra. After the victory of the revolution in Cuba, he did not sleep on his laurels. He began to work with us. He is going to be my right arm."

Gris sat down again. Now he remembered Valencia. In his student days the youth carried on an intense work of revolutionary agitation and propaganda in the university. He had been arrested more than once.

"Valencia has a good head," Barrios said. "He knows what he wants, he knows guerrilla technique better than anyone. He is, in short, a man of thought and action, a thing rarely to be found among our people, Doctor."

Gris risked a question which he immediately regretted. "Have you any idea of when the armed movement will begin?"

The other hesitated slightly. "Perhaps within two or three months. It will have to break out before the November elections. Everything indicates that Carrera, to avoid them, is going to execute a coup d'état, close the Congress, arrest his opponents, and remain in power. At the moment he lacks only a pretext."

Miguel Barrios rose to his feet. "Well, I am going to leave. Now, perhaps, we shall see each other again only in

Cerro Hermoso." He said these last words in a serious tone
in which there was more solemnity than hope.

"Have you anything to say to me?"

"No. I only want to tell you, Dr. Gris, that if we decide to create a Sacramentan government-in-exile, you will
be chosen to head it."

"Count on me. And thank you for your confidence."

He helped Barrios into his overcoat.

"I don't know whether you recall, Professor, that my
wife and my children were murdered by Zabala's police."

"I am very sorry," the exile muttered awkwardly.

"So am I, Doctor, believe me. But the hour is not one
for condolences and sentimentalities, but rather one in
which to act and to hate."

Is it indispensable to *hate*? Gris was about to ask, but
restrained himself.

"One moment," he said. He went to the window again,
leaned out, and scanned the street to right and to left. It
was deserted. He turned back to his visitor.

"I think the best plan is for me to go out now toward
the river. Give me five minutes by your watch, and then
leave the building and go toward the city. If the man in
the light raincoat is anywhere around, he will certainly
follow me."

Barrios nodded. Gris drew on his topcoat. They went
downstairs. At the street door, the revolutionary leader
spoke.

"I believe that the next news you will have of me will
be through the newspapers."

They shook hands and separated.

II

The Party

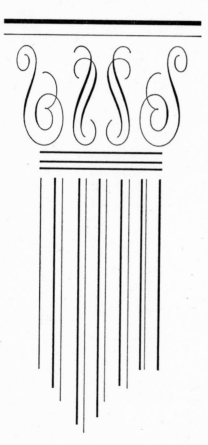

12

In Bill Godkin's opinion a man can be natural, spontaneous, and free only when, on getting home in the evening, he takes off—along with the mask that he has been obliged to wear in his social contacts—the clothing that he has worn all day long and slips into some old trousers and a pair of shoes that are on intimate terms with his feet. It was for this reason that the chief of the Latin American Bureau of the Amalgamated Press did not feel at ease when, that Friday evening, he entered the Embassy of the Republic of El Sacramento wearing his navy-blue serge, the best outfit in his diminished wardrobe, the wardrobe of a widower careless about his clothes. He was too conscious not only of the fact that he was wearing a rather rumpled suit, but also of the perhaps excessively gaudy color of his tie. (Ruth used to say that ties in tones of red go well with clothes of any color.) His shoes, which he had polished himself, pinched his feet a little. And as he had shaved hastily only half an hour before, his sensitive skin was broken out in dots of blood that had coagulated and which he now felt in stinging bumps when he ran his hand over his cheeks. He hated large social gatherings as much as he loved to talk with two or three friends in quiet, discreetly illuminated nooks. He appeared at diplomatic receptions only through his sense of professional duty.

He stood for some time in the entrance hallway of the embassy with his hat in his hand and his dead pipe in his pocket, hoping against hope that nobody would demand his card of invitation, for he had left it either at home or at the office.

Michel approached him, bowed slightly, and asked his name in order to be able to announce it to the ambassador, who was at the door of the reception salon at the head of the receiving line. The butler had not yet got his name straight (Bodkin? Godpin?) when Gabriel Heliodoro caught sight of the journalist and, coming over to him with open arms, exclaimed, "*Hombre!* How long it's been!" He embraced him with such enthusiasm that, somewhat abashed, Godkin almost felt he was a V.I.P. He discovered that Gabriel Heliodoro's presence was still quite pleasant in spite of the unsavory stories that he knew about him.

The ambassador took Bill's hat from the newspaperman's hands and tossed it to the butler like a forward pass in football. Michel caught the black, shapeless "thing" without losing his continental aplomb.

"Come in, Godkin," Gabriel Heliodoro said, pulling the other by the arm. "This is your house. But don't go away without first talking to me. We have a lot to talk about."

He introduced Bill to the next in line.

"Señora de Vivanco, who is doing the honors of the house today."

Godkin took the brunette's hand, thinking her very pretty, and thought also, touched, Another message from God? No. This one must be from the devil. The Ambassador has good taste. But Rosalía was introducing him already to the man standing beside her.

"Do you know the minister-counselor?"

"Of course," Bill replied. "How are you, Dr. Molina?"

From the formal, dry manner of the other's greeting Godkin inferred that his stock with the Sacramental diplomat was low. It must be on account of some news stories which the Amalpress correspondent in Cerro Hermoso was currently filing with his news agency, unfavorable in general toward the administration of Juventino Carrera.

The next figure in the line was General Ugarte, resplendent in a gaudy uniform—turquoise-blue tunic with gold buttons and black trousers with a crimson stripe down each side. He displayed several decorations on his chest, including the Order of the Golden Puma.

"How are you, General?" Godkin asked.

The other grasped his hand, his face blank. Suddenly, his face lighted up, his lips drew back, two gold teeth glinted, and the little eyes smiled.

"Ah! Our *Gringo Rubio!* Well, how goes it?" and he embraced the journalist. Turning to the lady at his side, he asked, "Ninfa, don't you remember this gentleman who dined at our home in Cerro Hermoso? What year was that, mister?"

Surrendering her fat hand, soft as a dove, to Bill Godkin the general's wife exclaimed, "Of course I remember!" And she lowered her voice confidentially, "I know you appreciate our national dishes. Well, I have a sensational piece of news for you. Don Gabriel Heliodoro had a cook from Soledad del Mar brought here by plane especially to make the famous *empanadas sacramenteñas* for this reception. Don't fail to try them." She bunched her fingers against her lips and then opened them as if blowing a kiss. "They are divine! Just go on in and make yourself at home." And she practically shoved Bill toward the door.

By that time there were more than two hundred guests in the reception salon, a room of majestic dimensions and profusely lighted. Whenever he entered that part of the embassy, Bill Godkin felt a little dazed at the extravagant wealth of its decor. From the high wooden ceiling, ornamented with oil paintings inspired by eighteenth-century artists, hung an imposing chandelier, like a rigid, iridescent crystal flower. In designs that dazzled the eye, the colors of the Sacramentan flag, yellow-gold and red, predominated in the silk brocade that covered the walls as well as in the upholstery of the chairs, sofas, and couches. The chandelier was reflected in two great Venetian mirrors in golden frames, set into the center of the long walls, face to face, above consoles of roseate marble. It was said that Don Alfonso Bustamante had been in the habit of carrying on dialogues with his own image in front of one of these mirrors, late at night, after the last guests at his parties left the mansion.

In an automatic gesture Godkin pulled his empty pipe out of his pocket, stuck the stem between his teeth, and started ambling slowly among the warm, perfumed multitude. He had the impression that he was wandering without map or compass among the trees in a tropical forest, not necessarily virgin.

The party, he estimated, was reaching that point at which the surface ice was beginning to crack, the first glasses were emptied, filling stomachs and stimulating heads, and the voices, at first restrained and formal, were rising, taking on a more metallic timbre, and the pallid, conventional smiles of the first minutes were becoming bold enough to turn into laughter, which would soon be loud.

A waiter passed bearing a tray full of glasses of a yellowish liquid. To be doing something, Bill took one. He drank a sip; it was whiskey of the finest quality. He began to catch sight of acquaintances. The first was the ambassador of Peru, who smiled and waved at him in friendly fashion. A high official of the Department of State greeted him with a nod. He saw the chargé d'affaires of the Embassy of Brazil chatting with one of the "sacred cows" of Washington.

He passed by a group in which French was being spoken, and immediately another whose conversation seemed to him Scandinavian. (A woman friend had remarked one day, "If Death speaks any language, I'll bet it's Swedish.") He stopped momentarily to listen to what four ladies of Latin American appearance were saying. In excited Spanish they were discussing the merits of a sale of winter dresses in one of the great local department stores. In most of these groups, Godkin noted, Castilian predominated. He considered himself a specialist in the Spanish spoken in Latin America. The Uruguayans and the Argentinians temper the language of Cervantes with the garlic and the oregano of Italy. One of the secretaries of the Argentine Embassy had got angry on hearing him humor-ously describe the typical Argentinian as "an Italian who speaks Spanish but is convinced that he is English." The Castilian spoken in Mexico has a half-affectionate, half-playful intonation that leads us to think all Mexicans are cousins of Cantinflas. The Cubans speak a puffy sort of Spanish with a lot of wind and flaccid cheeks. As for the Venezuelans and the majority of the Caribbeans, when they talk they give the impression of magnetic tapes played backward at top speed. Bill liked especially the clear Spanish of Colombia and Chile.

"Bill, old man!"

The newspaperman saw Clare Ogilvy's figure emerging from the crowd, swathed in the chiffon of a sky-blue dress.

"Clare, how nice to find a familiar face when I'm lost in a foreign land!"

They shook hands. Then she led her friend to a corner where they could talk a little, and listen to each other without having to shout. La Ogilvita made a gesture with her head that took in the whole salon.

"What do you think?"

"Quite a party."

The secretary sniffed loudly, twisting her nose and mouth to one side. "I wanted to arrange a smaller reception, limited to the Latin American group, a few Department of State officers, society editors, and people of the press. It would be cheaper and really more entertaining. But no! Don Gabriel Heliodoro insisted on having a reception in the grand style. You know we have more than eighty diplomatic missions in Washington. We invited them all!" She laughed, clutching Bill's arm. "I wish you could have seen the startled expression, mixed with glee and delight, on Don Gabriel Heliodoro's face when the ambassadors of Ghana and Iraq arrived in their native costumes. He nearly clapped his hands when he saw the wife of the ambassador from India in a beautiful fuchsia sari. Our ambassador is having as good a time as a boy in a circus."

"Did you invite the Soviet ambassador, too?"

"Of course. On the express command of Don Gabriel Heliodoro. The Russian has already arrived. It was a memorable encounter. The two giants engaged in a clasping and shaking of hands that seemed endless, smiling at each other. The Russian, as you know, speaks fluent English, but our Don Gabriel Heliodoro *no habla* anything but Spanish. And speaking of that, I've been right beside him, interpreting, ever since the first guests began arriving. I've left Pablo in my place, to get a chance to catch my breath." She stood on tiptoe to look over the heads between her and the door. "I must get back to my post. See you, Bill. Have a good time!"

Clare Ogilvy departed, as though borne away on a blue cloud, in the direction of the receiving line. Bill Godkin's eyes followed her with genuine liking.

Pablo Ortega was in the middle of the salon looking from one side to the other, seeking Glenda Doremus—but without much hope of finding her—when he felt in his back the pressure of a finger and heard a friendly voice:

" 'Hands up!' shouted Buffalo Bill."

"Gonzaga!" he exclaimed, turning around and clasping his Brazilian friend to his bosom.

"Restrain your Latin exuberance," the latter cautioned him. "I see Anglo-Saxon and Scandinavian eyes on us with an expression of disapproval."

"I'm expecting my guest of honor."

"The little Japanese?"

"No. An American. I've seen her only once, but I telephoned her this morning, and she promised to come."

"Interesting?"

"I'm still not quite sure about that. But I think so."

Gonzaga eyed the ceiling, remarking, "Titito was right. In the decor of this salon are mingled at least three Louis of France, the XIV, the XV, and the XVI. In this ambiance I shouldn't be surprised to find Don Gabriel Heliodoro dressed as Louis XV sitting on a throne." He lowered his voice to add, "Just now I had the pleasure of clasping the soft hand of Madame Pompadour."

Pablo paid no attention to his friend's last words, because he had glimpsed someone and was on the verge of panic.

"Look who's coming yonder," he said to Gonzaga, already hunting a way to avoid the encounter. "The thin, pale woman in black."

"Who is she? Death?"

"You mean you don't know her? That's Augusta Schneider, man! The queerest stories are told about that Viennese. They say she was held prisoner in a Nazi concentration camp for a year and lost her reason. A mild type of madness, you understand. Liberated by the American forces, she came to this country. She had an uncle here, who died, leaving her a small fortune. She attends every party in all the embassies. Nobody sends her invitations, but she always turns up. She has a mania for talking Spanish and a certain weakness for Latin Americans of our type, Gonzaga. She's a pain in the neck—everybody runs from her. Let's pretend we don't see her and head straight for the other door."

Too late. Augusta Schneider was there in front of them, smiling her pallid smile. She looked like a watercolor portrait—straw-colored hair, faded gray eyes, very white skin, vague features—a face that might fade away forever if it were not restored in time. Augusta was smiling at Pablo, who in his turn was smiling at Augusta. As for Gonzaga, he smiled at both. Ortega knew that the same old dialogue was going to be repeated.

"I know you," the Austrian lady murmured, pointing her long, fleshless forefinger at him and half closing her eyes in a coquettish expression.

"Of course you do, señorita."

"You are a Chilean, aren't you?"

"No, señorita, I—"

"Don't tell me, let me guess. Ecuadoran!"

"No," Pablo replied, serious in spite of the faces Gonzaga was making at him behind the Viennese woman's back.

"Mexican?"

"No."

"But you are a diplomat."

"Yes."

"Peruvian?"

"No."

"Then you must be—"

"A Sacramentan."

"That's it! I knew I knew you. My name is Augusta. And yours?"

"Ortega. Pablo Ortega."

"A great pleasure," said the young woman, extending her fragile hand, which the diplomat held in his for a couple of seconds.

Suddenly Augusta Schneider's face brightened. She had seen the wife of the ambassador of China, one of the most influential feminine figures in the diplomatic world of Washington. She forgot Pablo and headed for the Chinese lady, exclaiming, "Oh, Mrs. Koo!"

"Saved by the gong!" Ortega sighed.

"Now it's my turn," Gonzaga said, resigned. "There comes *my* sweetheart. God is punishing me."

Mrs. Patricia K. Woodward, now in her seventies, was a lady widely known in the social circles of the capital. She was proud of being a friend and boon companion of the President's wife. Maternally tender toward Latin Americans in general, she was studying Spanish along with a group of ladies—most of them wives of American senators and representatives—and, as Gonzaga usually put it, after three years' study she had learned barely a half-dozen phrases, such as *Buenos días, amigos! Hasta la vista; Qué rico!* and *Muchas gracias.*

She caught Pablo Ortega's chin and shook it gently. "I like you very much, Pablito, but I confess that Gonzaga is my favorite Latin American. I want to introduce him to a charming girl. We must get this incorrigible bachelor married. Come along, Orlando!"

The two went off toward the state dining room, where the table was laid with refreshments. Pablo's eyes followed them. Tall, lean, the pendulous skin of her face flaccid and drooping despite her many face-lifting operations, her hair dyed strawberry blond, Mrs. Woodward was famous for, among other things, her necklaces, bracelets, and pendants, generally of an exotic type—relics, amulets, and fetishes from Africa, Polynesia, and Malaya. She used lavish makeup and dressed garishly. Pablo decided that she seemed to be imitating in real life those character actresses who imitate onstage the overdressed women of real life.

When Ortega turned around to make his way to the entrance hall, he found himself facing Miss Kimiko Hirota.

"Ah!" he exclaimed, clasping the hand she was holding out. "When did you arrive?"

"A few minutes ago."

The girl's head, with black, gleaming hair, barely reached her friend's shoulder. Her round face, with the prettiness of a porcelain doll, always awakened in Pablo the tenderness of an older brother despite the innocent insistence with which those oblique eyes stirred the male in him.

Ortega stopped the waiter who was passing with a tray loaded with glasses.

"What are you drinking?"

"Ginger ale."

He managed to find one on the tray. "We must take tea together some day," he said, absent-mindedly, watching the doorway.

He felt well. His head was not aching, and the possibility of seeing the American girl, whose image had not left his mind the whole day long, produced in him an exaltation which he called a white drunkenness, for he had not yet taken a drink.

"You owe me a *haikai*," said Miss Hirota.

"True. I have it with me." He handed a card to his friend.

WINTER

On the white snow
The rigid blue blot
Of the dead bird.

Kimiko read and re-read the *haikai* a long time. Then, head still down, she stammered, "It is so sad!"

"Agreed. But it happened. I saw the scene from one of the chancellery windows last winter."

"Why, this is spring!" the Japanese girl exclaimed.

Pablo hardly heard what she was saying, for his eyes and attention were on the salon door.

"Are you expecting someone?" Kimiko asked.

"A friend, I mean, a girl. As she knows no one here, I must be with her as soon as she comes."

He bent over, took both Miss Hirota's arms in his hands with the care of one who picks up a fragile, rare statuette. "Will you excuse me for a moment? Make yourself at home, I shall be back right away."

Kimiko nodded repeatedly, like an obedient child. And when Pablo Ortega moved away, she stayed where she was. The card, like a dead bird, seemed to be heavy and inert in her hand.

13

FROM THE MOMENT the first guests began arriving, Gabriel Heliodoro Alvarado, as Clare Ogilvy had begged and as protocol required, had made himself stay in the reception line, but only with the impatience of a fiery horse at the starting gate, eager to dash off along the track. At frequent intervals he would look into the salon. At first it had all been amusing; there was the anticipation of surprise, a kind of guessing game—who'll come next?—and it was always nice to meet new faces, specimens in that great showcase of races and countries that was the diplomatic world of Washington.

As the salon filled, however, and the sound of voices and laughter rose, Gabriel Heliodoro no longer paid any attention to the introductions. He felt exactly like a rest-

less man who has bought a ticket for a show and wants to
see and enjoy it from the start. It would be the limit if he
couldn't share in his own party. And finally the time came
when, unable to resist any longer, he requested Molina to
take his place and he broke away.

The salon, now completely filled, offered a lively,
kaleidoscopic play to the richness and variety of which the
women's colorful dresses, the paintings on the ceiling, the
brocades on the walls, and the mirrors, which multiplied
the lights of the great chandelier and the candelabrum all
contributed. This produced in the ambassador of El Sacramento a joy that was not only of the spirit but also, and
principally, of the body. He inhaled pleasurably the good
smell of perfumed people, tempered by the alcoholic odor
of the drinks, by the smoke of cigarettes and cigars, and—
yes! yes! yes!—how good it was to catch the scent of the
indescribable but exciting odor of a room in which clean,
upper-class women are gathered! A thrill ran over his
whole body from his scalp to the soles of his feet. *Cojones!*
It was a whale of a party!

Several persons approached him, and those who knew
Spanish praised the house and the party. Gabriel Heliodoro thanked them. If the speaker was a woman, and
pretty, he would take her hand and kiss it. If it was a man,
he would give him a friendly pat on the shoulder and continue his wandering through the crowd. "Aren't you drinking anything?" he asked a tall gentleman, blond and bored-
looking. The other, with a polished shrug of the shoulders,
answered, "Sorry, sir, I don't speak Spanish."

"O.K., O.K." the ambassador exclaimed. He called to a
passing waiter. "Here, *mozo!* Bring something for our
friend here." The waiter knew no Spanish either, but that
did not prevent his interpreting correctly the host's request.

A high official of the Embassy of the Dominican Republic, who had already swallowed his third cocktail and
whose eyes were shining and whose tongue was loose,
caught Gabriel Heliodoro by the arm, took him over near
one of the mirrors, and said to him in a rather slurred

voice, "My dear Ambassador, why don't we join forces, my country and yours, to invade Cuba, eh? What do you think of the idea?"

"*Hombre!*" the Sacramentan smiled, taking it all as a joke. "It's an idea. But who'll finance the operation? The gringos?"

"Why not? Why not? It's to their interest. But they don't understand!" And the Dominican shook his head as he dropped his arms in a gesture of discouragement. "They are obtuse. El Benefactor has ordered planes, tanks, machine guns, ammunition from firms in this country, and what does the Pentagon do? It merely advises the President to decree an embargo on war materiel for the Caribbean zone." He gripped the Sacramentan ambassador's arm. "But I'm going to tell you one thing, my friend. As for the air force, we are better prepared than Cuba. We have eighty fighter planes, fifty-odd of them jet planes. The Cubans haven't more than sixty. It's just as I tell you. We have to invade Fidel Castro's island before it's too late. The Beard is a Communist. Believe me, he's a Communist. He may deny it in public, but he's dominated by Che Guevara and his gang. This is the time!" the Dominican wound up with a prophetic air. He suddenly abandoned his interlocutor to set out on the trail of a passing waiter with a tray full of glasses.

Gabriel Heliodoro stood there looking at himself in the mirror, straightening his tie. If Trujillo thought that his *compadre* Carrera would enter into an adventure of that sort, he was crazy.

He turned around again and went to take up a position in the center of the salon directly beneath the great chandelier. What country was that elegant black from, dressed in Western fashion but with a little cap like that of an organ-grinder's monkey on his head? From Guinea? Or Ghana? No. The ambassador of Ghana was the one in the long white nightshirt.

With a critical eye he examined the tiny Chinese woman who was talking with the wife of the ambassador of Pakistan. He thought her slit skirt, showing her leg, was exciting. Ah, but they were thin, badly shaped legs. Nor did he care for her face, with its yellowish pallor and beady little eyes.

At this point a black-bearded gentleman (This one is a Hindu, I'll bet) with long feminine hair covered by a turban, but dressed in occidental style, approached him, grasped his hand, and said something in English—or in French. Gabriel Heliodoro smiled and exclaimed automatically, *"Merci beaucoup,* mister, *merci."* He gave a little pat on the Sikh's shoulder, and the Indian moved off toward the entrance door.

The ambassador recalled a sergeant of the 5th Infantry, large, dark, and bearded, whom he had known and hated when he was a boy. A voice sounded in his mind, muted, a voice that seemed to come from the ends of time, across seas and mountains:

"Gabiliodoro! Gabiliodoro! Come right on home!"

Gabriel Heliodoro looked at his reflection in one of the mirrors. I wish she could see me now, he thought. But if she did, she would not understand, nor even believe her eyes. She was an ignorant woman. She had never learned to read. Her body was her only talent, her capital, her work tool. Through her bed had passed the whole infantry regiment of Soledad del Mar. On Saturdays (Was it true or had he dreamed it?) she gave special discounts for enlisted men. *Gabiliodoro! Gabiliodoro!*

In the mirror the ambassador saw Ernesto Villalba enter the salon, arm-in-arm with a blonde woman of majestic bearing, a good deal taller than her escort. He turned swiftly and went to meet the recent arrivals. For a moment he lost them in the crowd, but his hunter's instinct finally led him straight to the beautiful stranger.

"Don Gabriel Heliodoro," said Titito obsequiously, "I wish to have the pleasure and the honor of presenting my friend Frances Andersen Warren. Mrs. Warren, this is the ambassador of El Sacramento, our host."

Gabriel Heliodoro took the hand which the woman offered him and deposited on it a sonorous kiss, which

Titito thought barbaric in its avidity. The lady turned to the secretary and scolded him in Spanish.

"You forget that I am no longer Mrs. Warren. My divorce became legally effective last week."

Titito bowed and begged her forgiveness. Gabriel Heliodoro, dazzled, looked at the guest and wondered, Why is it that these *maricones* always get the pretty women? The one before him now had a ripe wheat field on her head, a sea in her eyes, and snow on her skin, yes, but snow touched by the rosy glow of the first morning sun! And those breasts—*Virgen de la Soledad, madrina mía!* And her features—what a picture! Her mouth was wide (he had a weakness for women with large mouths), her nose straight and thin; and the line of her neck and jaw could have been drawn only by an artist like God our Lord. And while Villalba was giving him a succinct biography of Miss Andersen—she had been born in the Middle West, had Danish grandparents, her ex-husband had been naval attaché of the United States in several South American capitals—Gabriel Heliodoro gave himself up to the exciting task of undressing her. Her hips, different from Rosalía's, were boyish in their straight line and promised long, rounded thighs. And only to think of the word "divorced" fired the ambassador's imagination and vitals. He took Miss Andersen's hand again, this time between both of his, saying eagerly, "My dear lady, this house is yours, and I am your servant." He released the long, warm hand when he saw out of the corner of his eye the blood-red of Rosalía's dress approaching.

"Ah, Miss Andersen, I should like to present to you Señora de Vivanco, representative of Sacramentan beauty in Washington. Rosalía, my dear, this is Miss Frances Andersen. I am going to have Titito promoted to first secretary for having brought such loveliness to our party."

In a fraction of a second the two women exchanged appraising glances. The American smiled and bowed, with her hands at her sides, however. Rosalía, who had already started to lift her right arm with the intention of shaking hands, contained herself. On being introduced to a person, no matter what the sex, she never knew whether she ought to offer her hand or confine herself to a mere inclination of the head.

"A lovely dress you have," Frances smiled.

"Not as lovely as yours, señora," Rosalía replied. "It is the color of ice, isn't it?"

"Exactly."

The Sacramentan woman examined the *gringa* from head to foot, critical and on the hostile side, while Titito and Gabriel Heliodoro, both with lighters at the ready, were disputing the privilege of lighting the cigarette which Miss Andersen had put to her lips.

At a short distance Pablo Ortega and Bill Godkin were watching the scene. They saw Gabriel Heliodoro, pushing Titito aside, light the blonde lady's cigarette and then say something to the secretary, who went off immediately toward the dining room in his sinuous mincing walk through the throng of guests.

Ortega, who knew Frances Andersen from other parties and places, gave the journalist a few bits of information about the beauty.

Orlando Gonzaga, who had managed to free himself from Mrs. Woodward, joined the two friends and, seeing where they were looking, remarked, "Either I'm badly mistaken or Señora de Vivanco has a rival in prospect. She'd better take care—"

"Don't worry about her," Pablo responded. "Rosalía must have sensed the peril already. Look how she is studying the other."

"And between those two thoroughbred fillies stands our Gabriel Heliodoro like a stallion at stud on the eve of retirement. Frankly, if I had to choose between those two, I'd take the brunette. She has more warmth, a background of *sangre y arena*, guitars, flowering almonds, something of Arabia, all mixed with the sun and the wind of the Caribbean, while the other reminds me of a goddess out of the mists of the Scandinavian fiords. The Swedes and the Norwegians, I know from my own experience, are healthy and ardent, but who can live all his life on a diet of fish?"

Godkin only smiled. Pablo took an arm of each man and said, "Miss Andersen gives me the impression of a diamond—something precious, scintillating, rare, expensive, but hard and rather cold."

"Look what magnificent breasts those two females possess!" Gonzaga observed. "They look like battleships armed with cannon, facing one another ready for battle. And see how they are attracting men's attention. Bill, take note of the dopey faces on that colleague of yours from the Associated Press and the fellow at his side. Both are in ecstasy! Bill, old boy, your compatriots are still in the oral phase. They drool at the sight of women's breasts. Psychologically, they are suckling infants. Just look at the success of the TV and movie stars in this country when they have big bosoms. In Latin America we get over that at the right time. As for me, I was fed at the breast until I was two years old—and at the breasts of a black woman."

At that instant Don Gabriel Heliodoro, holding the blonde's arm with one hand and the brunette's with the other, led them off toward one of the salon doors. Clare Ogilvy appeared on the trail of her chief and touched him on the shoulder. The ambassador turned around and the secretary said something in his ear. He made a grimace of annoyance and retraced his steps, but without releasing his beautiful prizes.

There was a sudden commotion in one part of the room. It was as if an unexpected wind had ruffled the surface of the waters. Miss Potomac was making her triumphal entry. Surrounded by admirers, she came forward in a slow, majestic march, interrupted here and there. She was like a great caravel brave with banners, all sails bellying full, sailing over a sargasso sea. Squeezed into a black silk dress embellished with long glass beads, she was holding in her fingers, aglitter with rings, a long holder with a smoking cigarette in it. As she came, her hoarse, semimasculine voice was uttering her habitual

epigrams, which provoked subservient laughter in those
who were around her. She was famous for her barbed remarks. In the exact instant when the host approached to
greet her, Miss Potomac was slandering a columnist competitor of hers who was in the habit of giving great parties,
which she could not afford, for blue bloods and millionaires, and for that reason was always in a chronic state of
financial insolvency.

The three friends gave the "sacred cow" only a few
seconds' attention. Godkin turned his back on her and
spoke to Gonzaga.

"Well, how did you manage to escape Mrs. Woodward's claws?"

"My savior was the ambassador of South Korea, who
started a conversation with her on outer space. I made the
most of the opportunity to pull out of orbit."

"Mrs. Woodward," Pablo said with a smile, "is one of
the monuments of Washington."

"Do you know what I've discovered?" asked Gonzaga.
"That lady is highly representative of several million
women of this country who pattern their behavior on a set
of ready-made notions that in reality are nothing but
myths."

Bill Godkin asked Gonzaga to explain his idea further,
but he could already foresee that his Brazilian friend, as
usual, was going to bear heavily on caricature.

"Well, some of these myths can be synthesized in such
phrases as, The American way of life is the best in the
world. . . . What's good for General Motors is good for the
United States. . . . Negroes are a hopelessly inferior race.
. . . Nearly all Democrats are crypto-Communists. . . . The
Chinese, especially the Reds, are bandits and Mao-Tse-
tung is a new incarnation of Dr. Fu Manchu."

Godkin smiled. "I think you are doing a great injustice
to American women by taking Mrs. Woodward as representative of them."

Gonzaga cordially seized the journalist's lapel.
"Maybe there is a little exaggeration in what I just said, but
there's a lot of truth, too. This country feeds on gilded

myths, sugar-coated and imposed on the public finally by your mass media. Your magazines, newspapers, movies, television, theater, all of which constitute the most prodigious, rich, alluring and efficient net of propaganda ever invented by man, are devoted to the diffusion of legends and myths. They feed the public with fairy tales or horror adventure. They oscillate between Poe and Pollyana, with way stations for Dick Tracy and Superman."

"Anybody listening to you talk, Gonzaga," Godkin said, "would not understand how it is that, with so many defects, illusions, and dumb innocence the Americans could have built one of the richest and most comfortable countries on this planet."

Gonzaga let out a laugh. "Don't get mad, Bill, and don't take me too seriously. I've had three whiskies and I haven't eaten anything yet." He turned to Ortega and said, "Give Bill the recipe for manufacturing an American."

Pablo, who was on tiptoe looking toward the main door of the salon in the hope of discovering Glenda Doremus, answered, "It's not worth bothering about."

"Come on, man! Bill knows you and I criticize the gringos only out of mischief, never with malice."

Ortega turned to the newspaperman. "To make an American, pour into a pot a portion of *homo faber*, and another, a little smaller, of *homo ludens*, then add a pinch of self-righteousness and set the mixture to simmer."

Godkin was about to formulate his protest, because, to begin with, he thought he himself had a touch of *homo ludens* but almost nothing of *homo faber*, when he saw Clare Ogilvy coming.

She tugged at Pablo's arm and whispered to him. "I have a confession to make."

"Make it."

"I betrayed you today."

"With whom?"

"With Don Gabriel Heliodoro. As soon as I got here, he embraced me and kissed me—imagine! He is a sorcerer. You can say what you will about him, *today* I won't believe it. I adore that man. Forgive me, Pablo," she added in the tone of one writing the end of a suicide note, "yours forever, Ogilvita."

"When do we eat?" the Brazilian wanted to know.

"Don Gabriel at this very minute is convoying a blonde and a brunette toward the dining room," the secretary informed him. "We'll first have the ceremony of introducing to Washington society the famous *empanadas sacramenteñas*. Come on, before the barbarians attack the table and strip it bare."

On the way she told Pablo how Don Gabriel had behaved in his encounter with Miss Potomac. He had thanked her for what she had said about him in her column. He had kissed her hand, praised her dress, and made it plain that he thought her youthful. A veritable seducer. "Of course in the translation of his compliments I took care to delete some exaggerations and unsuitable details. But of one thing I am certain—our ambassador is a success."

Contrasting with the splendor of the salon, the dining room adjoining it, in low Renaissance style, had a restful sobriety. The floor was of brick—now without rugs—and on the walls were Belgian tapestries inspired by Raphael's designs. The furniture spoke of a time when nostalgia for imperial Rome and classic Greece had not yet become acute among the artists of Italy and their patrons. Don Alfonso Bustamante, nevertheless, had thought it a good idea to break the severity of the decor by having the high-backed chairs upholstered with an imitation of fifteenth century Venetian velvet, with stylized artichokes in the middle of garlands embroidered in gold thread on a wine-colored background. The carved walnut table was of simple design, almost monastic, and around it the old diplomat, at dinners that marked an epoch in Washington, used to seat more than twenty guests.

This long table had been transformed by Parker & Baker, Caterers, into a *buffet froid*. (*"Dégoûtant!"* Michel Michel had muttered, wrinkling his nose when he saw the food.) Among floral arrangements, which the butler

thought detestable (*"Le goût américain, vous savez . . ."*),
were aligned platters with apparently whole turkeys, but
which in reality had been sliced ready to serve; slices of
leg of mutton and pork; baked, sugar-glazed hams riddled
with cloves and surrounded by pineapple slices; a rich
variety of salads that looked more like products of a dark-
room than of the kitchen; slices of beef tongue in spicy
sauce; and great dishes of hot rice, which Miss Ogilvy had
ordered at the last minute, thinking of the Latin American
and Oriental guests. There were also fish, enormous whole
fish, covered with a white layer of gelatine upon which
was designed (*"Quelle vulgarité!"*) the flag of El Sacramento.

Without releasing his ladies' arms, Gabriel Heliodoro
took them over to the buffet and thus gave the signal
awaited by the guests who were crowding around the
table. Under the critical eye of the butler, waiters were
bustling all about, and some of them were already beginning to serve the first guests who presented their plates.
Suddenly something occurred that created a great sensation in the Renaissance dining room. Three waiters entered
bearing long platters full of hot, golden pastries dusted
with confectioner's sugar.

"*Las empanadas!*" Ninfa Ugarte exclaimed in ecstasy.
A flock of her female compatriots ran to meet the waiters,
uttering little cries of patriotic gluttony. Doña Ninfa, who
had already stuffed a pastry into her mouth and thus had
her mustache and chin spattered with sugar, raised her
arms and cried out, "Wait, *chicas!* Be civilized! Where is
your Sacramentan hospitality? Let the visitors first taste
the pastries." Her words were lost ineffectually in the
midst of the frenzied hubbub of voices, and her person was
physically involved in the melée around the waiters. Beside the door the ambassador of Ghana, a tall black of
imposing aspect, clad in a white tunic, was smiling at the
scene, showing his beautiful white, regular teeth. And
Orlando Gonzaga, who had come up arm-in-arm with
Godkin, ravenous for food, whispered into his ear, "I wonder whether they provided a roast of human flesh for those

representatives of the new African republics?" Godkin growled, "I'll bet those blacks are more civilized and cultured than you, or me, or the majority of the people here tonight. Many of them have been to Oxford or Cambridge."

At one end of the table Michel was eying the "bacchanal" with an expression of repugnance which accentuated the furrows that habitually enclosed his mouth in a parenthesis of disgust. Gabriel Heliodoro signaled to him.

"Michel, have a tray of pastries brought to us."

The butler gave the order for the pastries and the ambassador of El Sacramento invited Frances Andersen and Rosalía Vivanco to help themselves. The Sacramentan woman picked up an *empanada* and put it to her mouth almost with the air of one carrying out a sacred ritual. The American followed her example, but with a ceremonious, fastidious indifference, she merely nibbled at the pastry. The brunette bit into hers with gusto, just managing to keep the fine stuffing from escaping out of the corners of her mouth. Gabriel Heliodoro, never taking his eyes off Miss Andersen's face, was watching when her small teeth seemed to gain animation, and finally she put half of an *empanada* into her mouth, a gesture that inflamed the erotic imagination of the ambassador.

"How do you like it?" he asked, gleefully. "How about it?"

"Delicious!" the American replied, helping herself to another pastry.

The ambassador was exultant. "Have you ever in your life eaten more delicate pastry? But the secret, my dear lady, is in the stuffing."

"Chicken?" Frances asked.

"Chicken mixed with beef, mutton, pork, and shrimp, all seasoned with herbs that are found only in our country. The recipe for these pastries comes from colonial times. Oh, Michel, bring us some champagne!" A little later, glasses in hand, the three were exchanging toasts.

The dining room was now completely jammed with

people, and around the table the din was infernal. Two of the fish had already been cut. A nostalgic Sacramentan had taken care to remove his portion without breaking up his country's flag, which he ate, reverently grease-smeared.

Ninfa Ugarte and her husband were next at the table, helping themselves enthusiastically.

"The pork is wonderful," she advised him.

"But . . . how about my cholesterol?" he hesitated.

"*Mierda* on your cholesterol!"

In the middle of the lively agglomeration, Gabriel Heliodoro lost sight of both Frances and Rosalía. He was about to help himself to a chicken leg, nicely browned, as he liked it, when he saw on the other side of the table, smiling at him, an American general in uniform.

With the speed of light the ambassador's mind transported him to Soledad del Mar. A summer evening in 1915. He was twelve, and was spying on the bivouac of the United States Marines. A sergeant was waving a chicken leg in the air. The barefoot, ragged, ravenous boys of the town raised their arms and yelled, "Throw it! Throw it!" The American threw the piece of chicken toward them. Gabriel Heliodoro, the tallest of the lot, caught it before it fell on the ground, held it to his chest, and tried to escape. One of his mates seized him around the knees and he fell, crushing his nose against the ground, but he did not let go of the chicken leg. The others threw themselves on him, yelling, and tore his shirt, scratched his back, bit his arms, hammered his head, and left him only when other Marines came up and started throwing among them some nickel coins which had the image of a buffalo in relief on one side. Gabriel Heliodoro dashed to the church and ran inside, panting from the fight and the running. He began voraciously gobbling the chicken leg, which tasted of gringo flavor, sweat from his own body, dust, and blood— the blood that was running warm from his nose. While he ate he stared at the image of the Virgin, his patroness. He was a little ashamed for having accepted the left-over food of that foreign unit that had landed in Soledad del Mar especially to kill Juan Balsa and his guerrillas.

For a magical instant Gabriel Heliodoro succeeded in recapturing the images and sensations of that remote episode of his life.

He smiled now, looking at his plate. On an impulse he speared the leg he had chosen for himself, using a fork, and practically threw it onto the plate held by the general, who at first seemed a little startled, even offended, but immediately, discovering cordiality in his host's gesture, nodded his thanks.

14

P ABLO HAD ALREADY given up hope of seeing Glenda Doremus when the girl appeared in the salon doorway. At first he did not recognize her. Curious how our fancy deforms memory's images; Glenda now seemed to him prettier and less dramatic than the first time he had seen her. He went to her, took her hand warmly, and thanked her for coming.

"Be patient with me," the American girl pleaded in her crepuscular voice, which Pablo liked so much. "This is the first diplomatic reception I've been to."

"In all your life?" he said, surprised.

"In my whole life."

"Fine! Let's take a turn around the room. There are some interesting fauna here. That tall man is the ambassador of Ethiopia." Glenda did not seem very interested in the African diplomat. "The fat, dark gentleman with the face of an attractive Buddha on a slenderizing diet is the ambassador of Thailand. And there is the wife of the ambassador of France, one of the most elegant ladies in Washington."

He took Glenda's arm and sensed—or could it be an illusion?—that she shrank from contact with his hand as if she found it unpleasant. He did not, however, relax the pressure of his fingers.

"Ah! Here is my friend Orlando Gonzaga, first secretary of the Embassy of Brazil. Be careful, he's a dangerous man."

The Brazilian took the hand extended to him by the American. Pablo strolled on with his guest, leaving his friend behind.

"Bill!" he exclaimed. "Come and meet a fellow countrywoman of yours."

After leaving the journalist, they came to a man who was gliding among the guests with the graceful, airy movements of a dancer. "This, Miss Doremus, is my colleague Ernesto Villalba."

Titito looked at Glenda Doremus from head to foot, and immediately classified her: clerk in the Pan American Union. Parties are not her forte. She makes herself up badly. Hasn't good health. The dress is horrible. But Pablo is falling for her.

"You must excuse me," he said. "I have a sad mission to carry out. Our ambassador ordered me to show the house to five ladies of Washington society, all of them VIP's and interested in Latin America. Good-by! A pleasure to meet you, miss."

When Pablo presented a swarthy gentleman with black mustache to his companion, he kissed her hand. "A sus pies, señorita."

A little later, well away from the gallant, she asked, "Why 'at my feet'?"

"It's an old formula of Spanish courtesy. Don't you like it?"

"I hate all formulas," she said acidly. "Especially those of courtesy."

Pablo smiled. He felt happy. With Glenda's presence the party was taking on a new and exciting meaning for him. Now he was certain that he liked Glenda Doremus physically, but his intuition told him, nearly bellowed at him, that he was going to have problems with her, differences of opinion, personal clashes, conflicts of every kind. But why did he feel these presentiments when they had talked so little with each other, and when the academic thesis of this girl from Georgia was as impersonal as a newspaper item?

"Pablo! Aren't you introducing me to the beauty?"

Gabriel Heliodoro had appeared in front of them, having just emptied his third glass of champagne. The introductions were made. The ambassador spilled out his charm upon the American girl, who reacted with an almost hostile coldness.

"Make yourself at home, señorita, this house is yours. Pablo, look after her. Make her eat some *empanadas sacramenteñas*. We'll see each other later, miss."

"Does he have Indian blood?" Glenda asked, her eyes following the ambassador, who was moving away toward a beautiful woman dressed in scarlet.

"He must have," Pablo responded. And, knowing that he was going to start an argument, he added, "Is that of any importance?"

"That what?"

"The type of blood a person has in his veins."

"You think not?"

He expressed his indifference to it with a grimace. Glenda then made the second attempt to free her arm from his grasp. But Pablo did not release it.

It was at that moment that he caught sight of the ambassador of Haiti, and decided to make an experiment. "I want you to meet a friend of mine," he said, leading the girl toward the Haitian diplomat, who was in the center of the room, an empty glass in his hand. Perceiving that she was going to be introduced to a Negro, Glenda tried to turn aside. "No!" she exclaimed. Pablo, however, gripped her arm harder and continued pulling her along with him. Why this ferocity, he asked himself, this desire to dominate and hurt her?

"Please," she begged, trying to disengage herself. "I don't want to. I won't. You have no right to make me."

Pablo, nevertheless, still smiling, forced her to approach the representative of Haiti.

"Mr. Ambassador, this is my friend Miss Glenda Doremus."

The diplomat smiled, bowed, and extended his hand. The American hesitated an instant, gave the Haitian the tips of her fingers, and withdrew them hastily. Pablo noticed that she had turned pale.

"With your permission, Mr. Ambassador," Ortega excused them. And he marched on with his prisoner. Glenda was his prisoner. Now I know, he thought, now I'm positive. She's a racist. She shook hands with a Negro; her stomach must be in convulsions. He noticed drops of perspiration on her forehead, and she made a third attempt to escape.

"You are bruising my arm," she complained, giving him an angry look.

"All right. I'm going to let you go." He was still smiling. "But don't run away. We have to talk."

They walked on several steps in silence. Abruptly she stopped. "Why did you do that? I said I didn't want to be introduced to that Negro."

"More than a Negro, he is a human being."

"I didn't come here to take lessons in ethics and morality."

"Don't be silly!" Pablo burst out, surprising himself at his own behavior. Never in all his life had he behaved like this with a woman. "I appeal to your sporting blood," he said, offering her a cigarette. She refused with a shake of her head. He lit his and began to speak. "This embassy is legally territory of the Republic of El Sacramento, therefore I am in my own land."

"The more reason to act like a gentleman," she retorted, looking around her. The mass of people, the temperature of the room, the din of voices, the smells of food wafted from the other room all contributed to leaving her in a dazed state. Her stomach began to feel queasy. "I'm leaving," she muttered.

He took her arm again, but tenderly this time. "Don't go, please. I need to talk with you. We haven't discussed your thesis yet."

"I didn't come here for that."

"Why did you come, then?"

She looked surprised. "What an idiotic question! I came because I was invited. I came because you insisted and I promised I'd come. Are you drunk?"

"I haven't drunk anything yet. Not even water."

"Have you taken some drug?"

"It isn't my custom to take drugs. What do you think I am?"

They were silent for some seconds, eying one another, both scowling. "Do you plan to discuss my thesis in the midst of this inferno?"

"No. I detest these social gatherings as much as you do. I am going to break a rule of the embassy now, the one that prohibits its secretaries' giving their exclusive attention to a single guest. Let's go find something to eat and drink and then we'll take refuge in a quiet corner. O.K.?"

She shrugged, as though in resignation. They went on to the next room. Pablo filled two plates and put them on a tray together with a bottle of champagne and two glasses. "Let's find out whether the library is deserted."

They went out into a hall under the great stairway of the central lobby, and entered the library. In one corner two men were talking. Pablo recognized them—Dr. Jorge Molina and a professor from George Washington University. The former was saying in his didactic voice, ". . . so that destiny is the direction of the existence toward the essence. I would say even that . . ."

He lowered his voice on seeing the newcomers. Bending toward his companion, Pablo whispered, "That oil portrait above the mantel is President Juventino Carrera."

Glenda found no interest in the painting, in which the Generalissimo was imitating the classic pose of Simón Bolívar.

They left the library, and after passing through halls and rooms of varied sizes, which to Glenda seemed imitations in miniature of the Hall of Mirrors in the Palace of Versailles, they came to a small room at the back of the left wing of the mansion.

"This is my favorite nook in the embassy," Pablo said. "According to the experts the furniture is pure Spanish

Renaissance. Do you see that desk yonder in the corner? It is a genuine *vargueño*."

Miss Doremus had never heard of a *vargueño*, nor was she interested in learning the history of the piece.

Pablo set the tray on a low table in front of the sofa on which Glenda sat. For an instant he was occupied with opening the bottle of champagne. Finally the cork leaped out with a bang, flew toward the ceiling, and fell on the fluffy carpet while the foam gushed out of the neck of the bottle. Pablo filled both glasses.

"Let's drink and make up," he proposed, sitting down in an armchair facing the girl, who had merely picked up her glass while Pablo was taking his first sip.

"Aren't you drinking?"

"It may make me sick at my stomach."

"Not at all. Drink. Stomach ailments are generally the products of our imaginations. Don't tell me you are not going to eat, either."

She glanced at the plates on which, with slices of turkey and a salad with a dressing of dubious-looking color and aspect, she saw two pastries shining with grease. Pablo quickly emptied his glass.

"Why did you force me to shake hands with that Negro? There was no need to. He was not in our path. You deliberately headed me to him. Did you want to test me?"

"Exactly."

"Very well, so now you know I detest Negroes. The question is closed. I respect your tastes and convictions and you ought, in exchange, to respect mine. But anyhow, I think you were rude."

Pablo refilled his glass. "You're furious with me, aren't you?"

"Speaking frankly, I am."

"Will you accept my humble apology?"

"I told you, I detest formulas. And please don't ever again use that detestable word."

"Which?"

" 'Humble.' "

"All right. Let's eat."

He handed one of the plates to Glenda, who played with her salad with the fork, without appetite. Pablo got up and went to the door by which they had entered, and locked it.

"Why did you do that?" she asked, rising in alarm.

"I don't want us to be disturbed."

"Open that door!" she ordered, harshly.

He came back to her as if he had not heard the command. "Sit down, Glenda. Be calm. I'm not going to try to rape you."

She grew pale, and for a moment an expression of hate twisted her face, giving an evil glint to her eyes. "Never pronounce that word again in my presence," she said thickly. She sat down, opened her purse with trembling hands, and took out a cigarette case. Pablo offered her the flame of his lighter. The cigarette shook in the girl's hands. Finally, after nervously expelling a puff of smoke, she looked at the diplomat.

"Mr. Ortega—"

"Please call me Pablo."

"Very well. Pablo, you are a strange man. The first time I saw you, at the embassy, I had a different impression. You looked like a well-balanced, intelligent—how shall I say it?—suave person. A man I could trust, in short. Now I see you are like all the others."

He faced her in silence for an instant. "Glenda, to be quite frank with you, from the moment you entered this house I have been playing a part. Pablo Ortega in the role of the strong, dominant male. I'm not at all like that, believe me."

"Then why are you pretending to be what you're not?"

"I don't know. Maybe because you awaken dormant instincts in me"—he smiled—"or else because at heart— well, I don't know, perhaps I'd like to be the type I'm impersonating. But it's of no consequence. Let's be friends, that's what matters."

"Frankly, I don't know what to think. I'm sorry I came. And if I came it was because of you." She paused, and then asked, "Why don't you go attend to the other guests? Why this special interest in me?"

"You think it unpleasant that a man should be interested in you?"

"Yes, because whenever it happens, it all turns out badly."

"You are very pessimistic, Glenda. But come on, eat and drink something."

She cast an indecisive glance at the plate she had rejected, replacing it on the table.

15

MINUTES LATER, calmer, she had managed to eat, besides two small pieces of turkey, half a pastry, the stuffing of which she thought too highly seasoned and sickening. At Pablo's urging she had drunk a few swallows of champagne, but cautiously, almost in fear, thinking of how she would feel the next day.

Ortega, meanwhile, had emptied his third glass, and, standing in front of her, was ready to tell her frankly what he thought of her thesis on El Sacramento.

"I want a sincere criticism," she insisted, folding her arms and pressing them against her stomach, merely as a precaution, because she was not yet feeling any pain or nausea.

"Very well," said Pablo, still not quite sure why he found such pleasure in being so aggressive toward the girl. "Your thesis shows not the slightest sense of historical perspective, and is full of untruths."

She frowned, feeling his words not only with her mind but with her whole body.

"Untruths? How? Why?"

"To begin with, you have used unreliable sources of information."

"But the data I used were furnished, for the most part, by your own embassy!"

"That's exactly why I call them distorted, false."

"You're drunk."

"Maybe so, but that doesn't make what I've just said any less true."

Glenda stared fixedly at the design of the rug at her feet.

"Of course, in your thesis there are some indisputable facts," Pablo continued. "El Sacramento is really an island, it stands in the Caribbean Sea, it was discovered in 1525 by one of the captains of the Spanish conquistador Francisco Fernando de Córdoba, one Leandro García Escala, who founded Puerto Esmeralda on the northwest coast of the island and later Cerro Hermoso on the central plateau. But the story of the tawny puma that mounted guard at the mouth of a silver mine and devoured only Spaniards, while it spared the natives, licking their hands, is no more true than the tale of the she-wolf that suckled Romulus and Remus."

"I read, in a book that Dr. Molina lent me, that the existence of that puma was verified in old documents from colonial times, so that today the animal appears on the arms of El Sacramento."

"A myth, believe me."

Glenda leaned forward, pressing her hands to her cheeks and leaning her elbows on her knees, and raised her eyes to the diplomat. "Can't anything be salvaged from what I've written?"

"You can be."

"Don't pay me compliments! I abominate such things. I am speaking seriously. I have to hand in my thesis next month."

Pablo shrugged. The wine was making him talkative, happy, ethereal. For some strange reason he was finding Glenda Doremus's company pleasant.

16

GABRIEL HELIODORO had succeeded in getting Rosalía to one of the small rooms at the back of the east wing of the mansion, and, once inside, he turned on the light, locked the door, clasped his mistress to his heart, and applied his mouth to her lips like a leech, so violently that the girl uttered a moan of discomfort.

"*Ay!*" she complained, when she finally succeeded in freeing her head and throwing it back. "You take my breath away."

She buried her face in his chest, and stood panting, listening to a heartbeat, she could not be sure whose—hers, his, or both as one. Gabriel Heliodoro's embrace did not slacken. He kissed her hair, ran his hands down her back, her breasts, her hips, and she felt a turgescence throbbing against her abdomen. To her mind came the image of an old family doctor, a yellow little man, bald and skinny, enveloped in a sort of white smock. And he told her, stethoscope in hand, "You are a vagotonic, fated to feel all of life's emotions, both good and bad, in a more intense way than other people. But don't worry. It isn't really a disease." If a verse, a melody, a scene in a novel or a film or a drama moved her, she felt the emotion in the form of a thrill that ran from her head to her feet. On some days she had the sensation that parts of her body were as though anesthetized. Now she was sure that, after all the strong sensations she had experienced that evening, she would feel as if she had been beaten—beaten not only on her flesh but in her mind.

"I want you to spend the night with me," Gabriel Heliodoro murmured in her ear, biting the lobe.

"But how can I? What am I to say to Pancho?"

"Whatever you wish."

"Impossible! The night before last he forced his way into my room and refused to leave. He *made* me go to bed with him."

"Did you . . . sleep together?"

She hesitated for an instant. "He threatened to beat me. I couldn't help it."

"The dog!"

"You forget that he is my husband."

"Yes, but I, *I* am your *man*."

Rosalía kept her head nestled on her lover's chest. "I can't bear this situation any longer," she murmured. "My life is a hell. When we are at home, sitting in the living room, facing each other, which rarely happens, he just sits there in silence, looking at me with those doglike eyes, sad, full of hurt. He sighs, shoots his little paper birds, looks at me again, and seems to want to say something but hasn't the nerve. When bedtime comes, he begs me not to lock the door of the bedroom." She stopped for a moment, and her fingers absently straightened the handkerchief in Gabriel Heliodoro's breast pocket. "Once in a while a fit of fury comes over him and he threatens to kill me, kill himself, make a scandal, throw himself out of the apartment window, drown himself in the river. Today, when we were getting ready to come here, he suddenly burst out crying. I didn't have the nerve to ask him why he was crying. Then he started doodling absent-mindedly with his colored pencils, as if I didn't exist. At night he takes drugs to sleep, and in the morning he gulps tablets of another kind to stay awake. Where is all this going to end? Where?"

As his only answer Gabriel Heliodoro again kissed his mistress' lips, this time with more tenderness than sensuality.

"Will you stay or not?"

"How can I?"

"I'll have Ugarte invent a special, urgent job in the chancellery to keep Vivanco busy until daybreak. We'll say that you went to Ninfa's with her."

"It's madness!"

He released her from his embrace. She straightened

up. They stood face to face in silence. Rosalía then let escape the words that had seemed to stick in her throat:

"Do you think I didn't see your eyes on the American woman?"

"God gave me eyes to see."

"You are enchanted with her—confess it."

"No normal man can remain indifferent to the beauty of a woman."

"You want to sleep with the *gringa*, don't you?"

Gabriel Heliodoro smiled.

"And you . . . do you want to hear a truthful answer, or a lie?"

"The truth."

"Then you must know that I want and am going to sleep with her. But that doesn't mean I'll stop desiring you like a madman, Rosalía, because *you* are my real wife!"

Francisquita's image flashed into his mind—at nine in the morning, taking her tea and toast in bed, a lace cap on her head, a bed jacket over her shoulders.

Rosalía turned her back on her lover, went over to the mirror and stood before it fixing her hair, powdering her face, and touching up her lips. Gabriel Heliodoro watched her, desire pulsating through his body. Rosalía was his woman, but he also desired the other, the blonde with the air of a goddess. Not that he thought her more desirable than the brunette—never! But there was in Frances Andersen an air of pride which he wanted to break, a certain cleanliness that he wanted to soil. He sensed in that white and radiant woman, in spite of her probably numerous sexual adventures, a certain virginity which he wished to tear away.

Rosalía, who could see the ambassador's image reflected in the mirror, told him, "Wipe your lips with your handkerchief, they are stained with lipstick. Dust off your lapels where my head rested."

Gabriel Heliodoro smiled. "These stains are decorations. Other men will envy me when they see them."

Rosalía turned around, went up to him, and with her

handkerchief wiped his lips and then flicked her fingers over his lapels.

"Now let's go back to the salon."

"Yes, my love."

At the door, as he was turning the key, he asked, "Will you stay or not?"

"Why don't you invite the American?"

"Your jealousy excites me all the more. Stay. I promise it will be the best night of your life."

"I don't know, I don't know. For the love of God, let me think!"

She opened her purse, took out of it a little vial of belergal, opened it, and shook out two of the tablets into the palm of her hand, put them in her mouth, and swallowed them.

"Who goes first?" she asked.

"We'll go together, my love."

Gabriel Heliodoro opened the door, took his mistress' arm and led her toward the reception salon. On the way Rosalía decided to go to the ladies' room. She needed a few minutes of quiet to collect her wits. The ambassador entered the salon alone.

The first person he encountered was Bill Godkin, a solitary figure propped against the door frame, placidly smoking his pipe and watching the increasing animation of the guests.

"Ho, *Gringo Rubio!*" the ambassador exclaimed, slipping his arm around the journalist's shoulders. "*Hombre,* why haven't you come to see me yet? I've been in Washington more than a week. Were you waiting for an invitation? Why, you are one of the family. Do you think I have forgotten that memorable encounter of ours in the Sierra de la Calavera, in 1925? Oh, Dr. Molina!" he called, seeing the minister-counselor and beckoning him over.

"This rascal," the ambassador said with a friendly look at Godkin, "has been writing stuff against our administration. Look, Bill, the Generalissimo is offended with

Amalpress. After all, you fellows have been very unjust and ungrateful toward him."

Bill Godkin, who was already expecting the reproach, merely smiled.

"You must visit El Sacramento," the ambassador continued. "Go take a look at the public works that El Libertador has been carrying out. Consider yourself officially invited. Dr. Molina, we'll make the invitation formal later on. But go, Bill. When you will and how you will. All expenses on us. You'll have the opportunity to see the new houses that the government is building for workmen, the roads that have been opened these last three years. You will find Congress functioning normally, the press free, and the people happy. How is it you fellows can call my *compadre* a dictator, eh? How?"

Catching sight of Titito Villalba, who was coming out of the dining room arm-in-arm with Frances Andersen, Gabriel Heliodoro immediately forgot the newspaperman and hurried toward the couple, wondering, rather annoyed, Can it be possible she likes only pansies?

Dr. Molina exchanged a couple of words with Godkin but was snatched away by a tall gentleman, dressed all in black, with a waistcoat up to his neck and a clerical collar. After the two men went off, Godkin identified the priest. Of course! That worldly padre was an ubiquitous figure at parties in the Latin American embassies. Author of a laudatory biography of El Benefactor (*Trujillo: A Portrait*), he was famous for his weakness for dictators and decorations. He had already been decorated by Pérez Jimenez, Rojas Pinilla, Anastasio Somoza, and Rafael Leonidas Trujillo. According to all the signs, his last article on Juventino Carrera would get him at least the Order of the Silver Puma.

Once more alone, Godkin asked his favorite phantom, What's the explanation, Ruth? What's the answer? His wife's image came to his mind as he had seen her in the last days of her life, emaciated and livid, on her bed, gradually approaching the end. Before her death, Ruth had begged him to continue his "search." One day, perhaps, it might be given him to understand the language of God, to arrange in a revealing message those lovely "words" which the Creator had scattered in the universe and in nature, words represented by the colors of the sky, the grandeur of the stars, the corollas of flowers, the laughter of little children, the purity of lakes, the plumage of birds, the power and mystery of the sea, and, above all, the capacity bestowed by the Creator on man to love and to produce beauty. And in the moment when Ruth, in her faint voice, was saying these things to him, through his mind had meanly passed the idea of asking her what part in the divine syntax the "words" like cancer, leprosy, war, and man's capacity for hating and destroying his fellow man might play.

Now Bill Godkin had hundreds of single words right there in the salon of the embassy, and was vainly trying to set them in order in such a way that they would make sense in a message or at least in a phrase, however crazy it might be.

The worldly cleric held forth for several minutes to Jorge Molina on the personality of Juventino Carrera, whom he had had the privilege of meeting personally on the occasion of his visit to El Sacramento less than a year before. Molina was not paying much attention to him. He limited himself to affirmative nods of the head, in increasing impatience. He felt relieved when the clergyman left him to meet the ambassador of Colombia.

He then returned to his solitude, to his exquisitely pleasant seclusion in the midst of those hundreds of people. He felt a certain voluptuousness in wandering among the guests without loving anyone, without being interested in anyone, without belonging to anyone, doing nothing but listen to scraps of dialogue here and there in many languages. What futility! What insincerity! Hypocritical was his opinion of the open-faced smile of the ambassador of the Soviet Union, who shortly before had announced to the ambassador of France in his fluent English and with his Rotarian smile that Russia intended to place two or

more astronauts on the moon before 1970. Nor had he the
slightest regard for the perilous innocence of the functionaries of the Department of State, the men of the Latin
American Bureau, the famous "specialists" so preoccupied
with statistics, those big men of athletic bearing and inex-
pressive faces who thought they could relegate the task of
ratiocinating to electronic computers.

His compatriots also displeased and sometimes em-
barrassed him. A few minutes earlier he had overheard in
one of the smaller rooms a comic dialogue between two
young Sacramentan women. They were standing in front
of a painting by Van Gogh.

"Who painted that?" one of them asked.

The other went over to the painting, looked at the
signature, and said, "Ban Go."

"Bangó?"

"That painter that cut his own ear off. Didn't you see
the movie about him?"

Molina's back ached. He felt a desire to lie down on
the hard planks of the floor, to make the pain go away. He
glanced at his wristwatch. Nearly eight-thirty. Looking
around the room he saw no sign of diminishing enthusiasm
in the people who were eating, drinking, laughing, and
talking.

He thought about Gabriel Heliodoro, whom he had
seen slip out of the salon not long before, leading his
mistress by the arm. It made him indignant to see a man of
that moral and intellectual fiber as ambassador of his
country to the United States. He was a scoundrel and a
barbarian. All he had was good looks and boldness. What
could President Carrera have been thinking of when he
decided to appoint his *compadre* to such a post? Don Alfonso Bustamante must be turning over in his grave.

He saw the ambassador of Ghana two steps from him.
The splendid Negro was smiling at him. Molina only inclined his head and went on his way. He had no racial
prejudices like the Americans, but he was not dying of love
for the Negro. It annoyed him to see the representatives of
the new African republics there. Republics? They were no

more than agglomerations of semibarbaric, if not completely savage, tribes. Many people nowadays were proudly repeating the expression "end of colonialism." Ah! The world would yet look back with nostalgia on the time when the sun never set upon the British Empire! And the persons indirectly responsible for that ridiculous proliferation of African states were the intellectuals of the stamp of Leonardo Gris, the famous liberals who were constantly talking and writing about liberty and self-determination, as if there could be freedom where no sense of responsibility existed, not even common sense, and as if it were possible for those pseudo-nations formed—or deformed—by tribes who devoured each other, not only in the figurative but sometimes the literal sense of the term, to exercise self-determination.

As he abruptly turned aside to see where a stentorian laugh was coming from, Molina felt a ripping pain, a streak of fire that ran from the nape of his neck to the fingertips of his left hand. He stood for some seconds with lips tightly compressed, groaning very softly. Then, relieved, he decided that the only thing to do was to sit down in a chair with a straight, hard back. He headed for the library, hoping to God (*God?*) that it was deserted. He would take up some book or other and stay there reading until the end of this unbearable party.

For some instants the consul's eye followed the minister-counselor. He did not like Dr. Molina, but he respected him. Himself, Vivanco, nobody liked, he reflected, sighing. Nobody respected him. Not even himself. He was horned. A meek cuckold. A coward. Everybody knew that his wife was sleeping with the ambassador. He sensed it in the way they looked at him. Some showed pity in their eyes. Others, irony. Many, contempt.

He turned around and saw his own image in the Venetian mirror and mentally addressed yet another series of insults to himself. He felt, inside, three different persons: the insulter, full of a delirious rage; the insulted, a poor sad and depressed man; and a third ego who cen-

sured the insulter and pitied the humiliated one. But he
did not love him.

He brusquely turned his back on the mirror. What
gave a certain expression of weakness to his face, he concluded, was the virtual absence of chin. He wiped his
glasses with his handkerchief in meticulous deliberation,
and then, replacing them on his nose, adjusting the ear-
pieces over his ears, he set out across the salon aimlessly.
Where could Rosalía be? Where was the ambassador? He
tried not to lose sight of them and at the same time wanted
no one to notice that he was keeping watch over them.
When he suspected that someone had discovered his anxiety to locate the lovers, he donned his mask; he stuck his
hand in his pocket, caressed the paper cylinder, and began
to whistle under his breath.

The interest displayed by Gabriel Heliodoro that evening for the lovely unknown lady presented to him by
Titito had caused in Vivanco a certain irritation which he
himself could not explain clearly. Would it not be a solution if the ambassador fell madly in love with the American and forgot Rosalía? There would then be some hope
that he, Vivanco, might recover his wife. He would request a transfer to some other embassy or consulate and
could then commence a new life with her. The strange
thing about it, however, was that he had felt almost insulted himself, personally, on perceiving that Gabriel
Heliodoro was devouring the blonde with his eyes and
besieging her with special attentions.

Later he saw Rosalía return to the salon. He noted
something peculiar about her eyes. Yes, his wife had been
weeping. He knew that expression. What could have happened in the long minutes when she and her lover had
remained absent from the salon? Had they gone up to the
bedroom? And there she was now, looking from side to
side, certainly hunting for her man. Whore! Tramp! The
terms exploded in his mind, but without force, without
echo.

He remembered what had occurred two nights before.
He had almost had to beat Rosalía to make her go to bed

with him. She had yielded with tears in her eyes, but that, far from inhibiting him, had whetted his desire. "Please, Pancho, turn out the light." "No, darling, I want to see your face." "For the love of God, make it quick, I'm just dead tired." He had had his moment of courage then. "You slept with the ambassador today, didn't you?" "Pancho, leave me alone!" "Did you or didn't you?" She had shut her eyes, disheartened. "If you know, why do you ask?" And then he had begun undressing her with a voluptuous deliberation. Rosalía remained motionless, eyes closed. And he licked her body all over, avid, eager, panting. Her indifference exasperated him. He was like a madman. "You like him because he's a giant, don't you?" She was still silent. And he gave quick bites on her neck, breasts, thighs, pubis, knees, legs. And he smelled her, seeking on her body the smell of Gabriel Heliodoro. "He makes you enjoy it, doesn't he?" Tears kept stealing down her cheeks as she bit her lips in order not to burst into wailing. At last, tremulous, he covered her with his white, flaccid nudity, penetrated her furiously, and at the moment of the orgasm, sensing the presence of the other man in his bed, he had so keen a pleasure that he began groaning as if he were wounded. Rosalía shoved him off, jumped out of bed, ran to the bathroom, and locked the door. He had remained, lying face down, embracing the pillow, and suddenly had broken into tears, like a child.

17

PABLO WENT to the door of the library and opened it. He had a feeling of being up in the air, in a state of levitation, with his body remaining in a vertical position. His head was beginning to ache dully.

In the hall he took Glenda's arm and led her toward the great salon, at the door of which the girl halted, like a child hesitating at the edge of a tangled, dark forest she must traverse. Orlando Gonzaga came to meet them. Pablo, who knew his friend well, saw that he was drunk.

"You want to hear a good joke? Just now I was arguing racial problems with a Texan and I told him my version of the Last Judgment. Listen. The celestial trumpets sound, an apocalyptic voice reverberates throughout the universe, announcing that the trial is going to begin. Humanity is trembling. The Texans automatically reach for their revolvers, but they immediately realize that the gesture is futile, because God must be faster on the draw. The whole world's population concentrates its attention on heaven, where, immense and luminous, the throne of the All-Powerful appears. Sounds of trumpets, harps, lyres, celestial songs of angels, etc., etc., are heard. The Archangel Gabriel, master of ceremonies, announces that the Creator has just seated Himself on the throne. The Texans lift their eyes to heaven and with fear-stricken eyes see that God our Lord is a Negro! Well, my Texan didn't like it. What do you think, Pablo?"

"We'll talk later, Gonzaga. Miss Doremus is a little indisposed."

Ortega did not need to look at Glenda's face to sense that the Brazilian's story had shocked her.

"Let's go, Pablo."

They left Gonzaga behind and began boring through the crowd, bound for the entrance. Glenda's feeling of nausea was increasing. Surely it was because of the heat of bodies in such proximity, the smell of the Sacramentan pastries floating in the air, mingled with the fetid sweat of the Negroes who were present. She collided with a fat woman who was wearing an already withered orchid on her bosom. The woman smiled—"Sorry, dear!"—and Glenda imagined herself eating the orchid, which heightened her queasiness. Suddenly she came across the black and shining face of an African ambassador. Immediately she glimpsed a swarthy woman with her lips gleaming with grease, her mustache speckled with sugar. Many people's breaths were redolent of that horrible seasoning.

Glenda walked on in a daze, led by Pablo, pressing her purse against her stomach, breaking out in cold sweat, feeling a weakness in her legs.

"Quick, I feel sick!"

They succeeded in reaching the entrance hall and at last getting out to the portico. The coolness of the night relieved her a little. She leaned against one of the columns.

"Glenda, can I go get some medicine for you?"

"No. Please ask them to bring my car right away." She told him the number, make, and color of her car—information which Pablo passed on to the embassy doorman.

"I'll come with you," the diplomat said, when Glenda's car stopped in front of them.

"No, Pablo, for God's sake let me alone!" She ran to the car, got in, and sat down.

"Glenda, you're sick. You can't go home alone."

She was livid. Her lips were quivering. She sat for a moment with her hands over her eyes, her stomach in upheaval. "Be patient, Pablo, try to understand."

"It's all right, I understand. When do we see each other again?"

She shook her head negatively as she started the motor. "I don't know. I don't know."

The automobile pulled away with a jerk. Pablo's eyes followed it until it disappeared from sight. Then he lit a cigarette, and, annoyed with himself, his head throbbing with pain, returned to the party.

III

The Merry-Go-Round

18

THE AMBASSADOR of El Sacramento was formally installed as a member of the Council of the Organization of American States in the third week of April. On entering the building of the Pan American Union, he was instantly attracted by strident voices that awakened the boy dormant in him. He detached himself from the advisers accompanying him and hurried to the Tropical Patio, where two macaws in colors so glistening that they seemed to smell of wet paint—scarlet, green, blue, yellow —were excitedly lurching and shrieking on their perches. Gabriel Heliodoro approached one of them and tried to catch its beak, which excited the colorful creature still more, and then he began saying things to the bird in a language which Titito Villalba had never heard in his life. In vain the secretary sought to show the other curiosities of the patio to his chief. Paying no attention to him, the ambassador approached the other macaw and repeated the game.

At that instant a group of tourists appeared in one of the entrances to the patio, and the guide called the visitors' attention to the tropical trees, represented there by a rubber tree, a banana plant, a coffee tree, and a yerba-maté. The central fountain, as the guide explained, was of rosy mable and "you will observe that the figures sculpted on the fountain are of Maya, Aztec, and Zapotec influences, and the designs of the mosaic in the pavement . . ." Useless! The stentorian voice of Gabriel Heliodoro and the squawks of the macaws created such pandemonium that the guide had to fall silent in annoyance and wait.

Comprehending the situation, Titito suggested to the ambassador that they should go up to the upper floor, since the time for the ceremony was drawing near. Still fascinated by the birds, Gabriel Heliodoro asked, "Are they compatriots of ours, Villalba?" In his boyhood he used to go into the jungle around Soledad del Mar to catch live macaws exactly like these. He would sell them to American tourists for two dollars each. Titito answered that he regretted to inform him that the two specimens present were natives of Guatemala. "Well, make a note, Villalba. We shall have two Sacramentan macaws found to give as a present to the Pan American Union, in the name of our government. A male and a female, because—I don't know whether you know this—the macaw is monogamous." Titito shook his head, thinking, Well, I can't say much for his taste.

Minutes later, followed by Dr. Jorge Molina—who had drawn apart in embarrassment at seeing the scene in the Tropical Patio—by Pablo Ortega and by Ernesto Villalba, Gabriel Heliodoro Alvarado slowly climbed the marble staircase leading to the second floor. It was another great moment in his life. In the Hall of Heroes and Banners, he found the other ambassadors waiting for him. He went forward to distribute handshakes and embraces— "My dear Ambassador!" "*Qué tal, amigo?*"—and then they all headed for the Council Hall.

In the chancellery Gabriel Heliodoro was working, sitting at his *bureau ministre* under the painted eyes—but what realism, what life those eyes had!—of Don Alfonso Bustamante, who watched him from the opposite wall with a severe expression. The portrait, from the waist up, had been painted academically by an American artist, and depicted the illustrious diplomat dressed in black. The button of the Légion d'Honneur was like a glorious drop of crimson in the lapel of his cutaway coat. The fleshy, ruddy face of Don Alfonso, crowned with long, white, satiny hair, stood out against a fire-red background. As the artistic Titito had already remarked, the color scheme of the picture went very well with the decor of the office: the walls paneled in walnut, the velvety cherry carpet, and the heavy mahogany furniture of a deep chestnut brown.

Whenever he lifted his eyes from the papers he was working on, Gabriel Heliodoro encountered the presence of Don Alfonso, who seemed to observe him with a critical expression. And when the new ambassador of El Sacramento rose and began pacing up and down—for he had discovered that he thought better on foot, walking, than either sitting or lying down—he had the impression that the old diplomat followed him with his eyes. There was no escaping them. Gabriel Heliodoro told Miss Ogilvy one day, "Have you noticed, Clare, that the devil of a painter made that portrait in such a way that, no matter where a person stands in this room, Don Alfonso's eyes are always on him?"

"If you'll forgive the joke, Don Alfonso is the symbol of the national conscience."

The ambassador laughed heartily and replied that his country deserved a younger and gayer conscience than that. He was now examining the documents relative to the proposed construction of the great asphalt highway that was to cross the Cordillera de los Indios, climbing and descending mountain slopes, entering numerous tunnels, and at last realizing an old dream of the Sacramentans— the swiftest link between the important centers of the north and the backward southern provinces of Oro Verde and San Fernando.

Dr. Molina appeared frequently in the office, bringing papers, diagrams, explanatory notes—*Santo Dios!* what a tiresome stuffed shirt!—and always with that grave and cautious air, as one who feels the weight and responsibility of much learning. When he referred to him in conversation with the secretaries, Gabriel Heliodoro called him "Mr. Encyclopedia Britannica."

Sometimes the ambassador would glare fixedly at the photocopies of the projects, at the maps and estimates of the American company that was going to undertake the gigantic work—he was reading the technical opinions which Sacramentan engineers, representatives of the government, had given on the matter—and he would yawn, scratch his head, feel the weight of drowsiness on his eyelids, shout for Miss Ogilvy—he had not yet got accustomed to pressing the button for her—call for a coffee, light a cigar, start pacing to and fro, casting slanting and half-hostile looks at the portrait of Don Alfonso, sit down again, and try to understand what was designed or written on that mass of papers. In a few weeks he would have to face the Undersecretary of State for Latin American Affairs in the Department of State. He needed to have his "lesson" learned and on the tip of his tongue in order to impress the gringo favorably. Of course, the important thing was to get the loan. The fight would be tough, but what the devil!—he liked to fight.

On some afternoons, overtaken by an acute sense of unease, almost of asphyxia, because he felt like a prisoner in such an overheated atmosphere, he would shout at Miss Ogilvy as he passed, "I can't stand this mausoleum any longer, I'm going to get some air"; and he would sally out of the chancellery without a hat to stroll in the park, talking to himself, thinking aloud about his problems and plans. He loved the Sierra, the open air, the limitless spaces, and never in all his life had he felt freer from oppression and happier than when he had been in the mountains with the guerrillas of Juventino Carrera. It was good to sleep under the stars, even when he woke up with frost on his face and eyelids, and his cheeks, from sheer cold, actually felt as if they were burned.

When the air at the end of April had lost the last trace of winter and the days grew warmer, the central-heating radiators were cut off in both the residence and the chancellery. And one morning, on reaching his office, Gabriel Heliodoro told his secretary, "Open the windows, Clare, and invite the spring to come in."

Now, when he interrupted his work, he would go to the window and stand watching the birds in the trees, and with the odd impression of being "in a foreign picture postcard" he would contemplate the chimneys rising solemnly above the roofs of the Embassy of Great Britain. He would fill his lungs voluptuously with the perfumed, cool air. Once, as he caught the green scent of grass, an image limned itself in his mind—Juana la Sirena! Alive, as alive as if he had her there before his eyes, in the flesh.

He was fifteen, and for two lunas a week he herded goats in the mountains near Soledad del Mar. When the desire for a woman came on him, he would satisfy it on the bodies of the patient nannies. He knew it was a sin, but the desire of the flesh was stronger than the fear of hell or of the reprimands of his confessor. One day he was caressing the back of his favorite goat, preparing her for the act with magic words of his own invention, when he heard a voice. "Gabriel Heliodoro, why do you do that with animals?" Startled, he turned toward the voice and saw Juana. She was one of the prettiest brunettes in the town. One day Amalio, the fisherman, had gone out to sea alone in his boat and at nightfall had returned bringing the woman with him. When they asked him who she was, Amalio answered with a smile, "A siren I picked up in my net, out at sea."

Gabriel Heliodoro looked at her now, ashamed, with the proof of masculinity swollen and ready for action, throbbing with desire. When he realized the situation he shrank away, turned his back to Juana, and, manipulating his straw hat in the quick movement of one who is catching a bird, hid the thing.

Juana drew near with a kindly smile, stroked his head, and asked, "Don't you know what God made women for?" He stared at the ground, panting. That caress of her hand thrilled his whole being. He felt the warmth of Juana la Sirena's body, which smelled of sea, salt, and sun. She took his hand and led him to a wood. Without saying a word, she lay down on the grass, lifted her dress, baring her legs, her thighs, her belly. The old crones of Soledad del Mar lied. Juana's body was not scaly like a fish. It was smooth, clean, and sapota-colored. And for the first time in his life the boy saw the nakedness of a woman. Juana raised her arms. "Come?" With wet eyes, tremulous with desire, with fear, with a nameless shame, he lay down on top of her. He had a spasm almost as of death, his groans of joy turned into sobs of pleasure and gratitude. Amalio's woman got up, let down her dress, and again stroked his hair. "You see how easy and how nice it is?" He nodded, unable to look directly at Juana. And when he summoned up courage to face her, it was as if he saw her for the first time. She was the most beautiful creature in the whole island, in the whole world. Her voice had something of the sound of a conch shell. "Don't be afraid, I won't tell. I hope you won't, either. It's a secret of ours, just ours, all right?" He said "Yes!" with his whole body. He understood, he understood, ah, how well he understood! And when he recovered the use of his tongue, he swore by the Virgin that he would never tell anybody, not even his father confessor. And then Juana told him something that swelled his breast with a pride so great that it could hardly be contained in the broad horizons of the *cordillera* and the sea. "You are a man." She took a few steps, stopped, turned around, and added, "You can expect me every Friday at this hour. I'll be back." He nodded, dazzled. The goats grazed quietly; the wind stirred Juana's hair and clothes. And she went off down the slope toward the town.

That was the happiest day in his life. But there were other happy days. Every Friday at the same time Juana came back, and they made love under the trees on the grama grass. One day he realized that he was deeply in love, and began to feel jealous of the fisherman who slept every night in the same bed with Juana. He would prowl around their house in the early morning hours with a pain in his chest, wishing for Amalio's death. He went to sleep and he woke up thinking of his love. Now the mountains without Juana's presence seemed like deserts. He loathed the goats. But Juana always came on the day and hour appointed.

Oh, that terrible Thursday in December! The town

awoke to excitement. Amalio, returning early from the sea and catching his wife in bed with a sergeant of the infantry regiment, had murdered them both with his fish knife. Gabriel Heliodoro, despairing, lacked the courage to view the body of his beloved. He went to the church to weep, kneeling at the foot of the image of the Virgin, his patroness. From afar he followed Juana's funeral procession. Perched on the cemetery wall, he watched them lower her coffin into the depths of the grave and then cover it with earth. Next day he went up into the mountains with his goats. It was Friday. At the hour when Juana used to come, he imagined that she had really come, and the two of them, hand in hand, went into the woods. She lay down in the usual spot and he covered her with his body. The smell of grass was the smell of Juana. The earth was Juana. And then he loved the earth, that first day of his widowerhood. And he left the grass damp with his semen and his tears.

19

GABRIEL HELIODORO detested bureaucracy and believed that there was an excess of *papeleo* in his embassy. He told Titito one day, "Don't you think men would be happier if they wrote less, used less paper? What did God give us the faculty of speech for?"

Villalba replied, "In my opinion, men are divided roughly into two groups, the oral and the graphic. Oscar Wilde, for example, was an oral." To me he was something else, thought Gabriel Heliodoro. "André Gide was a graphic," Titito went on, "that is, he expressed himself better in writing than in speaking. And you, Your Excellency, are an oral." And to himself he ended the sentence, ". . . and an uncouth fellow." Gabriel Heliodoro looked at the secretary for some seconds, feeling like telling him where he could go. However, he swallowed the bad word. He picked up the papers that the other had brought to him, and resignedly started signing them.

Clare Ogilvy did what she could to reduce the mountain of paper in the chancellery, but her efforts in the majority of cases were nullified by the stupidity of Ugarte and his protégés, by the pedantry of Dr. Molina, and by the carnal love which Vivanco devoted to papers and to the bureaucratic ritual. Three times a week, in the morning, La Ogilvita gave English lessons to Gabriel Heliodoro. She found her pupil intelligent, possessed of a good memory, capable of storing up with relative rapidity the English words he was learning. His problem was pronunciation. Whenever he attempted to say something in the language of his beloved Lincoln, his tongue seemed to take on the weight of tin. His teacher found his pronunciation defects hard to eradicate.

"Say *very well.*"

"*Bayri gwel.*"

He would say the *v* like a *b* and pronounce the *w* as if it were *gw.* If an unforeseen consonant turned up at the end of a word, the pupil devoured it pitilessly. Instead of *that* he would say *theh.* For him United States was simply *Yoo-nigh Estéh.* La Ogilvita made considerable effort not to laugh at these things. But Gabriel Heliodoro himself laughed frankly at his inability to learn "that language of barbarians." And clapping the book shut, and uttering a jovial guffaw, he would stop the lesson.

Gabriel Heliodoro had a kind of allergy to the presence of Pancho Vivanco, not only because "that lump of suet" was Rosalía's husband but also—and perhaps mainly—because the consul was tediously meticulous and fond of minute detail in the affairs of the service. If only the man would do and say all those things with a certain circumspection and naturalness, one could still bear him. But the mollusk was obsequious, servile. "Excuse me, if Your Excellency permits me," etc. While he was signing papers, Gabriel Heliodoro hated having him standing by the desk, constantly rolling his famous dollar bill in his fingers. It was as if Vivanco's eyes were smearing him with a cold, viscous slobber that smelled bad.

Sometimes, the matter completed, the consul would gather up the signed papers and stand there as if he wished to say something to his chief. "That is all, Vivanco. You may go." Rosalía's husband would hesitate a second or so longer, as if he had not understood the ambassador's words. At last he would turn around and go away. Gabriel Heliodoro followed him with eyes full of dislike, wanting to get up and apply a hard kick on his consul's fleshy hips.

As regards Dr. Jorge Molina, though, his feelings were different. Gabriel Heliodoro admired, reluctantly, the minister-counselor, but did not like him. To have to be nearly always under his subordinate's thumb in chancellery matters was not a situation to make him happy. As much as he could, he avoided consulting him directly. He was waiting, with a schoolboy's gleeful excitement, for the day when he could catch Dr. Molina in an error. The devil of a man, though, never made a mistake. He knew everything. He did everything well. All right, what else could you expect? He had studied for ten years in a Catholic seminary. Furthermore, Gabriel Heliodoro reflected in his better moments, it was really a bit of luck to have a man of the caliber of his minister-counselor to whom he could entrust the chore, usually boring and at times delicate, of representing the Republic of El Sacramento on the many committees of the OAS.

His antipathy for Jorge Molina grew on the day that Titito, in a conspirator's whisper, informed the ambassador that the man was chaste. Gabriel Heliodoro slapped the desk and exclaimed, "Now I know why that frustrated priest never laughs!"

Titito . . . the ambassador had ambivalent sentiments with regard to his second secretary. He considered that his effeminate gestures, his dancer's mincing walk, his contralto voice, and his pastel-colored clothes not only demoralized the embassy but were a blot on the escutcheon of the republic. Still, in all probability there wasn't a single one of the eighty-odd diplomatic missions in Washington that didn't have among its personnel at least one homosexual, overt or covert. But he preferred aides in his chancellery who were indisputably male.

Nevertheless, he had to admit that Ernesto Villalba, besides being intelligent, was witty and frequently enlivened the chancellery routine with his jokes, gossip, and opinions. Gabriel Heliodoro had nearly died laughing when one day, with the most serious expression in the world, Titito had professed to be convinced that La Ogilvita in reality was a man who had turned into a woman, thanks to a surgical operation.

There was another powerful reason for the ambassador's tolerating the secretary. Titito was an intimate friend of Frances Andersen.

"How is our goddess?" he asked one day, shortly after Ernesto Villalba got back from a quick trip to New York. "I haven't seen her since the reception."

"Miss Andersen?" the secretary said languidly. "I came across her in Manhattan, in the lobby of the Metropolitan Opera, during the intermission of the performance of the Bolshoi ballet. She was wearing a tiara on her head, a dress—"

"Wait! I don't give a damn how Miss Andersen was dressed. What I want to know is when I can undress her. Is she coming back to Washington?"

"In a week or two, is what she told me."

"Listen, Titito, you can't be ignorant of my interest in that creature."

"Ambassador, I can be anything but obtuse."

"All right. When Miss Andersen arrives, I want you to fix up a meeting with her for me, but in the greatest secrecy. The rest I'll take care of."

Villalba bowed his head slightly and laid his hand over his heart. "If Your Excellency will permit it, I suggest that you send her some flowers as soon as she arrives."

"I'll send tons of them. And how about my sending her a jewel as a present, eh?"

Titito hesitated. "We have to go slowly. She may be offended . . ."

Gabriel Heliodoro suddenly became aware of the ridiculousness of the situation. He—of all people!—was taking lessons from a pervert on how to win a woman. He had a fit of laughter, after which he took a cigar out of his pocket, bit off the tip, stuck it between his teeth, lighted it, and paced back and forth, smoking, under the implacable gaze of Don Alfonso Bustamante.

"I'm going to ask you a very important question, Titito. Has Miss Andersen any . . . any affair on now?"

The secretary shrugged his fragile shoulders. "I only know she has a lot of suitors. There's a Philadelphia playboy, a rich young fellow, who is running after her. The innocent child is twenty-odd years old, and he's pretty!"

Gabriel Heliodoro made a contemptuous gesture. "How old is our friend?"

"She must have already said good-by to thirty."

"That's what I figured. A fine age! But I don't think an intelligent, mature woman wants to to to bed with a twenty-year-old kid."

Well, I would, with much pleasure, Villalba thought.

About that time Gabriel Heliodoro received a confidential letter from President Carrera, its envelope sealed with wax.

"My dear *compadre:* The situation here is not good. As you know, the Constitution requires that we hold presidential elections in November of this year. I thought I was ready to hand over the government to my legal successor and retire once and for all to my plantation at Los Plátanos, since I am a little sick and very tired. Unfortunately my mission is not yet completed. I want to leave the great works of the Trans-Sacramento highway at least started, and many other undertakings that I've begun, finished. Besides, I do not think that our country is prepared to endure the commotion of a presidential campaign. They say that the devil knows a great deal more because he is old than because he is the devil. Well, this *compadre* of yours, an old fox, has caught the smell of something in the air. I can sense a certain restlessness not only in the university, among professors and students, but also in the streets, and even in the highest circles of our society.

"The day before yesterday I called the Cabinet together to find out just what they had done about the suggestion I made some time ago to send to the Congress an amendment to the constitution that would permit my second re-election. They had sworn to me that the amendment would be approved by early March, at least. Now it is nearly May, and no action to date. The minister of the interior told me that, in his opinion, the discussion of such an amendment would be a dangerous thing, for it would provoke animus and offer the leftists a pretext to begin agitation. I lost my head and yelled a couple of nasty things at Allende, who turned red and lowered his head, but said not a word. When I asked him, out of pure irony, whether the *señores ministros* had already chosen a candidate to succeed me, he answered yes. Imagine who it is! Dr. Ramón Tejera, president of the Surpeme Court! Allende then embarked on a long rigmarole about Tejera's being a cultured citizen of integrity, a respectable figure as a judge, a nonpartisan man, capable of winning the support of the majority of the electorate. I lost patience again and roared, 'In my opinion Dr. Tejera is a candidate for an old people's home. He's nearly eighty. You are all crazy!' No one answered back. What they want is a puppet president who those landowners, bankers, and industrial captains can manage at their good pleasure. They know they can't do that with me. Now I see you were right when you told me I was surrounded by disloyal folk. It's the limit! They had already made out a ticket of candidates without consulting me, and were soft-soaping me with the promise of obtaining approval of the amendment.

"What measures am I to take, then, to keep this country from falling into the hands of the Communists or of the Sacramentan plutocracy, which at bottom has never accepted me, never resigned itself to being governed by a man of humble origins like me? The solution, as I see it, is a new coup d'état. I conferred secretly yesterday with the minister of war, who thinks as I do and guarantees me the total and unconditional support of the army. We have to act before November, but we need, as you well know, a good pretext for closing Congress and decreeing martial law. After all, we have to take into consideration world opinion, especially that of the United States and that of the Organization of American States. Yesterday I lunched here in the palace with the American ambassador and the archbishop, and you may imagine why I invited those two. I sounded out the gringo, who has the look and the laugh of a dunce, but he is a wily one, and I came to the conclusion that he, too, wants to see the last of me. Without beating about the bush I asked Don Pánfilo what his opinion of the amendment was. The man made a very pretty speech with that skill and that elegance you are acquainted with, but he evaded the point. It is natural that the archbishop wants to see as chief of state a sanctimonious wafer-guzzler like Dr. Tejera, who goes to Mass every Sunday.

"This being so, *compadre*, the thing to do is wait for the agitators to stick their heads out, and then act. If they don't before November, we'll have to invent a new subversive plot and once more use the bogeyman of communism to frighten both the Department of State and that class which your friend Gris, that exiled scum, calls 'the rural oligarchy.'

"The devil of it is that any politico-social upheaval just now can prejudice that business of the loan. I need not repeat that the dream of my life is to leave the Trans-Sacramento road at least begun, and that I should be the happiest man in the world if that highway should bear my name.

"Send me at your earliest convenience your opinion on all these problems. Sometimes I regret having sent you to our Washington embassy. You are one of the few men of whose loyalty and friendship I have no doubt, and never have had. But stay there for the time being and try to dig up that loan, which is vital for our land. As for the rest, let's let things take their course. I have faith in my lucky star. Before November we'll find a good pretext for the coup.

"I authorize you to show this letter to Ugarte and no one else. After you do so, it would be best to burn these pages. I have always had a horror of things written down. With an affectionate embrace from your old friend and *compadre*

Juventino."

The letter left Gabriel Heliodoro in a ferment. For a long time he had suspected the existence of that "white revolution" led by Ignacio Allende, minister of the interior, with the aim of avoiding Carrera's re-election and of imposing a candidate of the so-called Sacramentan elite. And the Department of State and the archbishop were in on the game. Now he understood—how stupid he had been!—the reason for the foreign minister's having been in such a hurry to send him off to Washington, and the reason why Congress had approved so swiftly and unanimously his nomination to the post of ambassador. It was obvious that Gabriel Heliodoro was a stone in Allende's shoe, a hindrance to his group. And he, idiot that he was, had fallen into the trap. Why? Why? Of course, he had been dazzled by the title of ambassador, by the opportunity to shake the President's hand, to spend at least a year in the beautiful embassy residence—yes, and to perform a service to his country by negotiating the great loan. Moreover, he found pleasure in the prospect of living near the Lincoln Memorial, of tasting the flavor of Washington's social gatherings, and of enjoying a few months' freedom with Rosalía. And—what the devil!—a man must be frank with himself and recognize certain things: he wanted to rest a little, get away from Francisquita's chronic ailments, Francisquita's voice, from that cream-whitened face which he was forced to see in bed every night, from that woman who had never felt the least sexual pleasure and who had always been ashamed of her own body—and of the bodies of others. And, when all's said and done, hadn't he made a bet with himself and the world that some day he would occupy a very, very important job?

He summoned Ugarte, and when the general entered the office, Gabriel Heliodoro locked the door and handed him the letter from Juventino Carrera. He grew impatient with the slowness of the other's reading. In vain did he seek any reaction in that broad, bronzed face. Nothing. It was the face of an illiterate sphinx. The eyes? The eyes of a snake on the lookout for a chicken. After several minutes, which to Gabriel Heliodoro seemed interminable, the military attaché folded the letter from his president and returned it in silence.

"Well? What have you got to say?"

"I say the situation doesn't look at all good."

"Yes, but we'll get out of this jam the way we've got out of others that were even more serious. We can't hand over the government to Allende's gang, much less to the leftist rabble."

"You really think that old shit-pants Allende picked has a chance to win the election? And if he does, you think he can govern without Carrera's support, when Carrera has the army on his side?"

"Of course not. That makes me feel a little easier, but only a little. The real solution would be a coup d'état. I give you my word, I feel like taking the plane tomorrow to Cerro Hermoso to go shake up the Cabinet and the Congress, and bring them to their senses. But you know—I can't just drop these negotiations for the loan. I've got an appointment set at the Department of State, although I suspect those gringos are going to screw us up royally."

Ugarte broke into a mute laugh which was most perceptible in the shaking of his shoulders.

"Maybe we can help the president better here, indeed." He took a piece of paper from his pocket, and handed it to his friend. "I got this communiqué today. 'Most confidential,' as you see."

The paper bore the stamp of the Ministry of War. Gabriel Heliodoro read, "We have reasons to believe that

Dr. Leonardo Gris is the center in Washington of a conspiracy which has as its objective the invasion of our island and the revolt of federal troops as well as peasants throughout the national territory. It is urgent and indispensable to discover not only the plans of the subversive movement but also the names of the persons on whom the revolutionaries are counting here in El Sacramento for acts of sabotage and terrorism and for taking up arms at the first signal. The best way to get what we want is to enter the Gris apartment and search all his papers. We recommend the maximum precautions in the operation in order to avoid complications with the American authorities."

Gabriel Heliodoro returned the paper to Ugarte quickly, as if it were burning his fingers. The ambassador could not imagine what his military attaché was scheming.

"Pretend you didn't show me that document, understand? You are responsible to the Ministry of War, not to me. Do what you think fit, but I have just one request—don't tell me anything. Absolutely not a thing, whatever happens."

"Do you mean then that I have *carte blanche* to act?"

"If you have, it's not over my signature. I wash my hands of it. I wash them with plenty of soap and water. I don't want them soiled with blood. I know what you're thinking. I don't endorse violence."

The military attaché smiled. "Who's talking about violence?"

"Keep in mind that the American police are very efficient."

"But not infallible."

Before leaving the office, Hugo Ugarte said, "One thing I want you to know, Gabriel Heliodoro. If the situation does get worse, I'm off to Switzerland, where nobody can extradite me. I'm too old to stand imprisonment. And you know that if the opposition wins, there'll be a reward on my head. They'll stand me up against the wall and pin decorations on my chest with bullets."

And with this statement the ex-chief of police withdrew. Gabriel Heliodoro waited a moment, barely managing to hold in his wrath. He looked at Don Alfonso's portrait and, as if the old ambassador could hear him, exploded, "The coward! The ingrate! The egoist! The cuckold! He'll run off to Switzerland with that cow of a wife, who's deceiving him with my chauffeur, in *my* Mercedes!"

He felt a great need to unburden his heart, by talking to someone who was a real person. Who could it be? Molina was a block of ice and a pedant. Miss Ogilvy, a foreigner. Titito, a frivolous butterfly. Vivanco? It was revolting even to think of that slug. The man was Pablo. But Pablo doesn't like me, Gabriel thought. No matter what I do to please that boy, he remains distant and indifferent. Besides, Pablo was a friend of Gris. It had been thanks to the intervention of Don Dionisio Ortega y Murat's son that Gris had escaped being captured and killed on the Tragic Night.

Ah! The thing to do was to telephone Rosalía and fix up a date with her for somewhere. Yes, he could pick her up in the car, they would ride in the park. He picked up the phone. Immediately he heard La Ogilvita's voice.

"Yes, Mr. Ambassador?"

"Connect me with *that* number."

20

PABLO ORTEGA again visited Dr. Leonardo Gris in his apartment on Q Street. There was not a place in all Washington where he felt more at home than in the room which his friend had gradually furnished in accord with his taste for American colonial and early English. The things found there Gris had bought during his years of exile, in "thieves' markets," in remote suburbs of the capital, or at auctions in Georgetown. He selected rugs, furniture, lamps, pictures, all with the affectionate care of one who is choosing his friends. That was certainly how he had succeeded in giving the room such a welcoming air, as if each object in it bore some mysterious cargo of time, dream, and rich experience of life. On the walls, wherever the book-filled shelves left an open space, reproductions of Goya engravings, especially the *Caprichos* and the *Disasters of War*, could be seen against the faded rose of the wallpaper. And in one corner of the room, shut into its black case, the cello was almost like a human presence.

On that late afternoon in early May, Gris received his friend with a special coffee, which they drank quietly, talking idly about music and literature. After a silence which Pablo felt like a kind of graphic symbol intended to separate two paragraphs, the exiled man spoke.

"I dreamed of Moreno again last night. I don't recall the details of the dream, but the gist of it was something like this. I was a boy, I had to get out of bed to go to school, but I had a hard time doing it. My eyes were heavy and I wanted to sleep longer. I heard a voice then, calling me, 'Leo! Leo! Get up, lazybones!' I opened my eyes with great difficulty and saw beside the bed a form that was both my father's and Dr. Moreno's, in a fusion."

"It is curious how some people, or maybe all, have an anthropomorphic conscience. Yours takes the form of Dr. Moreno."

"I think I can explain the dream. I have spent these last several days working on my essay on Góngora, listening to baroque music, and attending to my course at the university. It has been, in short, a tranquil, happy week. Dr. Moreno appeared in my dream to make me 'get up from bed and fulfill my duty.' It's just that I had completely lost contact with the revolu—" He stopped abruptly, smiled and added, "All right. I know you prefer to hear nothing on that subject." He paused anew,. and then, "Who is your conscience, Pablo? Your father?"

The other shook his head. "No. Maestro Natalicio."

"The folk artist of Soledad del Mar?"

"Exactly. Do you know him?"

"I know his works, but I have never seen the man."

"To me Maestro Natalicio symbolizes the dignity and patience and endurance of the common people, of our people, Dr. Gris. I don't know whether it's my imagination, but I believe I sensed it the moment I met him, when I was still a boy. I used to hear that he could be a rich man if he would accept the offers he received to industrialize his figurines. But he refused. He was even a little ashamed to traffic in his sculptures. He preferred to sell the fruits of his orchard. He has remained what he has always been, a man of the land, sunburned, barefoot, with his white cotton clothes and his straw hat."

"I consider his figures admirable," Gris said. "I remember some painted horses with eagle wings and unicorn horns, some pumas with human faces, figures that were a mixture of vegetable and animal, and—oh yes, some delightful angels."

"Maestro Natalicio is illiterate. He barely learned to write his own name, which he carves on his works. He never had a teacher of sculpture. His skin has a touch of the color of the clay with which he works. I have always thought his hands impressive—hands with an expressiveness of their own, hands with integrity—I would say, the hands of a saint. St. Francis of Assisi might have had hands like those."

"Is he still living?"

"I think so. He must be close to seventy. I haven't seen him for more than six years now." Pablo smiled at his memories. "When I was a kid I liked to visit the Maestro's house. It was a poor hut, roofed with straw, the floor of hard earth, almost at the edge of the sea. Natalicio had five or six children. They all played with clay. They would make little figures, some well, others poorly. One thing that delighted me about that house was the clean 'fat' smell of clay pervading the air. I would sit for hours watching Don Natalicio modeling or painting his figurines. Sometimes he would let me play with his colors. But most of the time I watched in fascination as those nimble fingers gave shape to the clay. I thought that God must surely have made the world and the first man that way. And, speaking of God, one day I looked at some examples of the strange fauna created by the artist, and I asked him, 'Do those animals really exist, Maestro?' He winked, smiled all over his face, and answered, 'A man can make creatures that exist, but he can invent, too, with due respect, those that don't, the ones that God our Lord forgot to make, surely for lack of time, because six days is very little to finish up a world.' "

Gris smiled. "If my memory doesn't fail me, Chamorro's police kept pestering Natalicio a good deal."

"They did indeed. Now and then the artist would leave the field of imagination to make what nowadays is called *art engagé*. When Juan Balsa was in the Sierra with his guerrillas, Don Natalicio would make portraits of the hero in painted clay, and the figures would be passed from hand to hand, set up in niches, all but adored like images of saints. He also sculpted groups that sometimes seemed like pamphlets of political and social criticism. A soldier of the police beating a peasant. A gringo from UNIPLANCO riding a peon, whip in hand, a cigar stuck between his lips. The district judge receiving money from a big shot for a favorable decision. There was, I heard, a district police chief in Soledad del Mar who used to maltreat his prisoners. Maestro Natalicio made a caricature of the man in clay, showing him with whip in hand flogging a man of the people, whose slashed torso was bleeding. The likeness of the police chief was so good that the statuette was passed around in the city like an underground cartoon. But there is always a stool pigeon to squeal on a man. Maestro Natalicio's house was invaded by the police, who broke up all his figurines and tools and beat the artist, his wife, and his children. Had it not been for Padre Catalino's intervention, Natalicio would have rotted in jail. But he set up his workshop again and went on working. And as the police never took their eyes off him, he took to sculpting angels, using his youngest children as models."

Pablo got up, leaned out of the window, and looked to right and to left to see whether he could spot the man in the gray raincoat whom he had glimpsed on arriving. But Gris, with a question, made him turn around.

"And what does Natalicio represent to you, today?"

Pablo faced his friend. "Many things. To begin with, he has several qualities which I cordially and *almost* humbly envy him—artistic integrity, human genuineness, intimacy with nature . . . as if the clay he works with transmitted to him through his fingers secret messages from the earth. Yes, and also immunity to sophistication."

"Only that?"

"Oh no. As I said, he is my living conscience. Whenever I get my monthly check in the chancellery, I think of the miserable people of El Sacramento that Natalicio, in a certain way, represents for me. I don't recall having dreamed of him, but his face comes to my mind with a frequency that is at times obsessive. Of course, I can go for days without thinking about him, but whenever I begin to enjoy myself at a party, to like the company—in short, to feel happy—then the image of Maestro Natalicio pops up in my mind and I am immediately pricked with remorse, with the feeling that the price of my pleasure and my comfort is the disease, the hunger, and the wretchedness of my people. Generally at these times I see him squatting on the ground in front of his hut, the sun striking full in his face, the wind from the sea stirring his mustache and his grizzled, sparse little beard. He looks at me and says nothing. He asks for nothing. On some occasions only his hands speak to me."

Pablo walked a few steps around the room and stopped before one of the Goya engravings, in silence. Gris was slowly shaking his head in comprehension.

"I wonder whether Gabriel Heliodoro has a conscience, too," he remarked.

Pablo turned to his friend. "That is what I have often asked myself. Perhaps the ambassador's conscience is his mother. You know she was a prostitute. Those who knew her personally say that she had been really quite pretty, but being wasted away by venereal diseases and ill treatment, at forty she looked like an old woman of over sixty.

When Juventino Carrera returned victorious from the Sierra and gave a very good job to Gabriel Heliodoro, many people expected him to go back to Soledad del Mar to help out his mother, to take her away from her wretched life in the lowest class of prostitution. But he didn't. When he visited his home town two years later, the poor woman had died and nobody, not even the vicar, knew for certain where her body had been buried."

Gris was pensive for an instant, and then inquired, "How are your relations with that man?"

"Gabriel Heliodoro? Well, it would be easier for me if I could succeed in hating him, despising him, or, better yet, take no cognizance of his existence. But the fellow is ingratiating, all-enveloping, and every time I feel inclined to like him, I can't avoid the thought that in doing so I am once more betraying Maestro Natalicio and his people."

"I believe the amorality of that man has a strong element of fascination for you."

"Do you really think so?"

"All intellectuals are much alike in that, Pablo. We secretly envy the men who use their bodies without scruple, denying themselves nothing."

Ortega sat down again. "But believe me, in spite of all his blusterings and his noisy external gaiety, Gabriel Heliodoro has his hours of depression. I have already caught him in those somber moments when his Indian side prevails over the other or others, and he remains withdrawn, motionless in a corner, his face gloomy. Whenever he falls into one of those depressions, he ends up by paying a visit to the Lincoln Memorial."

"Has he committed many diplomatic blunders?"

"No. On the contrary. He is a success. I was present at the discussion which, with Dr. Molina's and my assistance and advice, he held with the Undersecretary of State, who speaks and understands Spanish well. Gabriel Heliodoro surprised us by his familiarity not only with the financial but also the technical side of the plans for the great highway which our newspapers call Trans-Sacramentan. The undersecretary seemed to me favorably impressed. Don

Gabriel took care to skilfully insert a few anecdotes into the presentation and made the American laugh delightedly. In spite of everything, nothing has been decided definitely about the loan. It seems that the United States government prefers to postpone a final decision on the matter until after our November elections."

"And how does the ambassador treat you? He spills tons of charm on your head, I suppose."

"I'll tell you a story. Yesterday he called me to his office and invited me to take a ride with him in Rock Creek Park. I thought he looked very depressed. I considered the invitation peculiar, but I accepted. We got out of the car at one spot in the park and set off walking along the ravine. First, Gabriel Heliodoro talked about birds, trees, and flowers. He told me how fond he is of a Japanese red maple in the embassy garden. He said an interesting thing. 'Do you know what I feel in the presence of that tree, Pablo! I feel that I have no intimacy with it. I can't speak to it with the familiar *tú* as I do to the cedars, the cacti, the plantains, and the palms of Soledad del Mar. And this country is much like that bronze tree. Pretty, very tidy, nice . . . but I know I'll never be able to be its bosom friend.' He was silent for several minutes, watching a flock of white ducks marching in Indian file ahead of us. I looked at the man's face and saw on it so great an expression of sadness and loneliness that I was sorry for him and at the same time irritated with myself for pitying a scoundrel, the table companion of a dictator, a dealer in shady transactions, a usurer, an exploiter of the misery of our people. To be sure, Gabriel Heliodoro has a lot of the ham actor in him, but I don't know . . . in that moment I felt that he was not acting. His sadness was genuine. Suddenly he asked me, 'Why don't you like me, Pablo?'"

Gris burst out laughing. "Ah, how well I know that type of man! Despite all his formidable masculinity, his outsized male pride, he has a markedly feminine component. Obviously the sorcerer, the consummate seducer, cannot admit that anyone can resist his charms."

"I mumbled half a dozen words that meant nothing.

He grabbed my arm cordially and embarked on a lively autobiographic narrative. He talked about all the ill treatment, imprisonments, beatings, and violence of which he had been the victim in infancy, in adolescence, and in his youth, in the days of Chamorro's dictatorship. At last he said, 'You must not judge me hastily. A lot of lies are told about me. Maybe one day you can understand.' "

Gris moved in his chair and crossed his legs. "Do you think you can?"

"Perhaps. That man must not be as simple as he looks. And after all, what do we know of one another? And of ourselves?"

The exile shook his head. "No. Let's leave the Final Judgment to God, if God exists. I am not interested in philosophical considerations about the character and the soul of your ambassador, Pablo. It is not a question of judging him *sub specie aeternitatis*, but in the light of historical time, which is expressed in millions of lives and human destinies. I am not interested in the theological sins of Gabriel Heliodoro, but in his social ones. He symbolizes a situation which, in my view, is criminal, cruel, and unjust, and which, therefore, must be eliminated if we wish to lift our masses out of the almost animal level on which they are suffering and up to a human one."

"Agreed, Professor, agreed. Nevertheless, that does not prevent me from observing Gabriel Heliodoro from the angle of the artist, with the impartiality which, for example, the novelist should have if he wishes to understand other people and, through them, himself."

Gris again dissented with a vigorous wag of his head. "Allow me to tell you that, in this hour and in this special case, impartiality is not merely absurd, it is criminal. You know how much I detest categorical statements. But the only hope for our land is in the downfall of Carrera and the oligarchy which supports him. Need I repeat that I hate violence? I have been thinking about that a great deal these last few days. A very great deal. I have concluded that there is a type of violence that I accept, sadly, I confess, but I accept. It is the violence that is employed to respond to violence. I shall not change a comma in what I have said with respect to my incapacity as a revolutionary. But I have taken a stand."

"With a grain of salt?"

"Perhaps with a drop of blood."

Ortega was now becoming aware of great discomfort. His head was beginning to throb with pain. He took an aspirin tablet out of his pocket, stuck it in his mouth, chewed and swallowed it, immediately drinking the cold coffee remaining in his cup.

"Dr. Gris, I'm afraid that henceforth your image may start working in my head along with that of Maestro Natalicio, as the incarnation of a feeling of guilt."

"Forgive me, Pablo, forgive me!" Gris said, laying his hand on his friend's shoulder. "I don't want you to think that I am trying to censure you. I am a clumsy bungler! We have discussed the thing so many times. I understand your position. I know that you are one of us but can do nothing for the present because of the state of your father's health."

"I have no assurance of that. Perhaps I am blackmailing myself, using that situation as an excuse for not making the great gesture, throwing up my job, and going off to join the revolutionaries, wherever they may be at the moment. It is very comfortable and pleasant to live in Washington, earn a thousand dollars a month, have a Thunderbird, be able now and then to visit the National Gallery of Art, spend the weekends in New York seeing good plays."

Gris rose, turned his back to his friend, and went over to his cello, took it from its case, sat down with it between his knees, tuned it for a few moments, and then said gently, "Now, to wipe away the bad impression I can offer only this."

He began to play, mutedly, something in which Pablo recognized the voice of Bach.

"Do you recognize it?" the exile asked. "It is the second movement of the *Easter Oratory*. Written for oboe and orchestra. The transcription is mine. Even badly played, this melody has a greater sedative effect than aspirin. Perhaps a bit melancholy. Don't think of the matter any more. Or hate me."

Pablo, now lying on the sofa, was listening with eyes closed. The almost human sounds from the cello sank into his brain, soothing the throb of his heart with the silk-cotton floss of the melody.

"You see?" Gris said, as he finished the piece. "Who is going to believe in a revolutionary like me?"

Then, when he was replacing the instrument in its case, he asked, "Do you like Chinese food? What about dining with me at the Oriental? It's nearby. We could walk that far."

Pablo declined, explaining that he had an appointment with Orlando Gonzaga. He gripped his friend's hand and left.

He got into his car, but before starting the motor he sat gazing hard at the building in which Glenda Doremus had her apartment. In spite of all his numerous attempts, he had not succeeded in seeing her again since the embassy reception. He had telephoned her the day after the party, to beg her pardon if his behavior had offended her. She had replied that no explanation or excuse was necessary, since they were not going to keep on seeing each other. He insisted, "But I want to be your friend." And she asked dryly, "Why?" He replied lightly, "What a question! Because I like you." One of those terrible telephone silences fell then. Afterward, the voice of the girl, less hard, came to his ears. "It's best for us not to meet again." And the connection was abruptly cut off.

He had called Glenda several times at the office where she worked. A woman's voice with a Spanish accent had replied that Miss Doremus was not in. Evidently Glenda had asked an office mate to tell that lie. More than once Pablo had thought of going to wait for her at the door of the Pan American Union at the time for her to leave work, but he had had to drop the notion because it was precisely between five and six o'clock that the ambassador was in the habit of summoning him to his office for some consultation or other, to give him the task of composing a letter, or only to talk.

Pablo sat asking himself how he would be received if he should go right now and knock at Glenda's door. He imagined a scene so disagreeable that he could feel his ears burning with embarrassment. He started the car and headed it toward the center of town. The pain continued to hammer at his temples.

21

IN APRIL AND MAY of that year no other diplomat in Washington had his name mentioned more often in the society columns than Gabriel Heliodoro Alvarado. There were items about the intimate dinners which he frequently offered in his residence to personalities like the Undersecretary of State for Interamerican Affairs and the directors of the International Monetary Fund, besides other exalted personages.

One of the best-known columnists of the capital stated in an extravagantly colored story that Don Gabriel Heliodoro, like a kind of oriental potentate, had sent home for a collection of precious and semiprecious stones, which he had distributed among the society editors and reporters —Miss Potomac had got an enormous aquamarine—and among some of the most famous hostesses of Washington, who repaid him for the presents with dinners and receptions. Thus the fame of his generosity as host, the excellence of his cuisine and his wine cellar, and his witty sayings—"An earthy humor," as another reporter put it, "very close to the land and to life"—was spread abroad.

One day, as he went into Miss Ogilvy's office on tiptoe, Titito Villalba asked in a lisping whisper, "How goes our Caliph of Baghdad?" But in the second secretary's irony it was easy to note a tone of admiration and affection for his chief.

The fact was that, with the exception of that erudite clam, Dr. Jorge Molina, the whole personnel of the embassy was enchanted with Gabriel Heliodoro. He was affable, outgoing, generous; he would breeze into the chancellery every morning, distributing sonorous, expansive good mornings, his teeth gleaming in smiles. Once he went so far as to stop an instant beside Merceditas' desk to run his hand over her hair. "Well, my girl, how goes it?" The poor girl wriggled all over, so moved that tears came into her eyes.

As regards La Ogilvita, she was as though mesmerized by the man. As for Ugarte, it was plain to be seen that the old bandit loved his former companion-at-arms.

Vivanco himself, who had every reason to hate the man who was sleeping with his wife, could not manage to hide from himself or from others the fascination which the ambassador exercised on him.

In mid-May, as the social season was almost coming to a close, Gabriel Heliodoro sent by air to El Sacramento for two folk groups, Los Indios Bailarines from Páramo and Los Campesinos Cantores from Oro Verde.

Both groups spent only a week in Washington, but, in Clare Ogilvy's phrase, they were "seven days that shook the world." There were thirty persons, all told: eighteen men and twelve women. By order of the ambassador, La Ogilvita took charge of both groups, taking on the functions of impresario, interpreter, governess, and tourist guide. Not one of her thirty wards spoke English. The first problem was housing. Two or three minor hotels refused to admit the hairy Indians from Páramo, with skin the color of a dried gourd. La Ogilvita then made a patriotic appeal to the members of the local Sacramentan colony, asking that each family receive at least three dancers into its home—an appeal that got results. She herself took two girls to her apartment, and Merceditas did the same. Titito chose the youngest and handsomest of the male dancers as his guest. Pablo undertook to give bed and food to two singers. A small group was installed in the embassy itself, to the honor of Monsieur Michel. A few hours after their arrival, the thirty artists were duly billeted, and La Ogilvita could breathe again. Her problems, however, had barely begun. Titito fell madly in love with his guest, whom he called "my Apollo of bronze." One night he made an indecent proposition to him; the youth, indignant, punched him in the face, threw him out of the apartment, and locked the door. Villalba, his eye encircled by a halo of purplish black, had to go to a hotel to sleep. Merceditas wailed complainingly that her guests were making a pigsty out of her apartment. The girls, both those in the group of singers and those in the corps de ballet, wanted to go shopping. Clare Ogilvy took them to the basement of one of the great department stores where a sale was advertised. Faced with the articles scattered over the tables or aligned on the shelves, such a fury of acquisition took possession of the Sacramentan girls that they started screaming and grappling with each other—"That's mine!" "I saw it first!" "Stupid!" "Idiot!" "Turn it loose!"—in the struggle over dresses, necklaces, hats, stockings, shoes, handkerchiefs. . . . In the middle of the lot, as imposing as a sergeant, La Ogilvita was attempting to restore order, bellowing, "*Muchachas! Muchachas!*"

Two guitar and harp players, middle-aged men, got drunk one day, started a fight in a bar, and wound up in a police station, where Pablo Ortega with great difficulty finally managed to free them. Three of four members of the group of singers, boys with a lot of brilliantine on their hair and exhibiting a rich collection of mustaches, sallied forth one night in search of females, for they wanted at all costs to sleep with "blonde *gringas*." When they did not find these as easily as they had expected, they started libelling the city that was so backward it didn't even have a whorehouse. That was civilization? That was progress?

The most pathetic note of the famous week was the attack of melancholy which overwhelmed the majority of the Indian dancers from Páramo, who, homesick for their natal land, stayed indoors, frightened at the foreign city with its barbarous language and strange customs. They would not eat, they would not speak, they refused to go out for rehearsals, and not infrequently they would burst into tears.

"If this lasts more than a week, I'll commit suicide!" Miss Ogilvy exclaimed one day. The ambassador offered the two groups a luncheon in the garden of the embassy. Michel eyed the savages with the greatest disdain, his rosebud mouth wrinkled in an expression of civilized repugnance as he watched them eating like animals.

Finally the two groups, in their typical costumes of dazzling colors, performed in the Salón de Fiestas of the Pan American Union before a large audience, which applauded them enthusiastically.

Gabriel Heliodoro felt like a circus impresario on an evening of a gala performance and good box-office receipts. He wanted to get up on the stage and announce and explain each number himself before its execution. He vibrated with the dances and the songs of his fatherland. And when the singers, accompanied by plangent harps and guitars, interpreted a popular ballad of Soledad del Mar that his mother used to sing, his eyes clouded over and the big man squirmed in effort not to weep.

On May 27 Gabriel Heliodoro represented his country at the funeral of the famous Secretary of State in Arlington Cemetery. The ceremony was touching in its simplicity. The tireless diplomat, who had flown distances equivalent to a round trip to the moon in the service of his people and of peace, was resting now, mute and motionless, in the cemetery of the heroes.

Returning to Washington alone in his car, Gabriel Heliodoro felt downcast. He thought of his own death, and once more to his mind came both the presentiment that his end would not be long in coming, and also the certainty that he would not have a hero's burial. Perhaps they would throw his blood-drained, bullet-riddled corpse into a common grave. Or leave it unburied to be devoured by black birds of the sky.

"Where to, Mr. Ambassador?" Aldo Borelli asked.

"Straight to the embassy."

That evening he dined alone. He exchanged a few words with Michel, whom he had summoned. The room was in shadow. There were two candles, spitted on long silver candlesticks, lighted on the table.

"Blow out these candles and turn on all the lights!" Gabriel Heliodoro exclaimed to the butler, who hastened to obey. "This is no wake!"

Dinner over, he wandered about aimlessly from room to room, comparing his solitude with Don Alfonso Bustamante's. He gazed nostalgically at the portrait of his daughters and grandchildren. He even began a letter to his Francisquita, but got no further than the second line. He turned on the television set; a western was halfway over. Gabriel Heliodoro waited to see the final duel. He switched off the set when a fellow with beautiful teeth appeared singing the praises of a well-known brand of toothpaste.

He sat down in an armchair, and, leafing through magazines, awaited Rosalía's arrival. And when, around eight o'clock, she telephoned to let him know that she could not come because a crisis had arisen, he was on the verge of saying a few cross words to her.

What to do that evening? He could call Ugarte and two other companions for a poker game. But the prospect of looking at the military attaché's face for hours and listening to his incessant sniffle and sucking of his teeth was not at all attractive. The ex-chief of police was a lousy card partner; he always wanted to win, and turned unpleasant when luck was not with him.

Before nine o'clock Titito telephoned to inform him that Frances Andersen had arrived in Washington that afternoon and had asked for news of her "dear ambassador."

Gabriel Heliodoro felt quite gratified.

"Did she, really?" he exclaimed, beaming. "And when do you think I can see that marvel of nature?"

"Tonight, if Your Excellency wishes. Frances might accept an invitation to go to a night club. If I may be permitted, I suggest the Blue Room at the Shoreham. Have you a pencil, Ambassador? I'll give you the phone number of the goddess of the fiords."

"Goddess of what?"

"Of the Scandinavian fiords."

"Oh. All right. Let's have it."

22

PABLO ORTEGA and Kimiko Hirota not only exchanged *haikais* by mail with some regularity, but also met at least once a month in a tea house on F Street. Their dialogue was carried on in low tones, which in his voice took on a warm dryness of autumn leaves, and in hers the quality of a music box playing melodies in staccato with only three or four notes. Generally they avoided personal matters and political themes. They behaved as if outside of time, within the magic space of a nameless, mapless country.

One day Orlando Gonzaga asked Pablo Ortega what pleasure he could find in drinking jasmine tea in the company of that "sketch of a woman." Ortega replied that his meetings with Miss Hirota were the equivalent of a flight into a kind of fourth dimension in which he rested from the chancellery routine, from the sameness of Washington life . . . and from himself. He added, "When I am with her I have the feeling that I have been transformed into something—fish, bird, tree, insect—in those hazy pictures of the Japanese *kakemonos*." His friend, tongue-in-cheek, retorted, "In my opinion, at the age of thirty you are satisfying the desire that you suppressed as a boy—you like to play with dolls."

That Saturday evening Pablo and Kimiko went to dine at the Genghis Khan, where they ate *sukiyaki,* drank *sake,* and conversed about the art of the *haikai.* She was wearing a silk dress of ultramarine blue, of great simplicity, which went very well with the old ivory tone of her skin.

"In the art of the *haikai,*" the girl said, "there is a series of tiny mysteries—allusions, quotations, images with double meaning, key words . . ."

She was talking in a manner which reminded Pablo of the exquisite flight of a butterfly.

"For example," Miss Hirota continued, "the poet, with a single word, can give the reader an idea of the season of the year or the hour of the day to which the poem refers."

"I know that flower is always a cherry blossom and therefore corresponds to spring."

"Yes. Cricket suggests night. The cuckoo announces nightfall. If the poet speaks of bell, the reader knows that it is the hour of dusk, because the bells of the temples of Japan always ring at that hour. And so on . . ."

"To me, the clangor of bells evokes morning things— golden light, Glorias, church feast days, hallelujahs."

Kimiko smiled, her cheekbones stood out, and for an instant her black pupils were almost hidden behind two oblique lines. "The Japanese bells," she crooned, "are very discreet. They have a crepuscular sound, with little resonance." She paused a moment, and then added, "Physical, that is."

For a while they quietly enjoyed the *sukiyaki,* which the waiter had prepared at their table. Miss Hirota took the bowl of *sake* in her delicate hands, lifted it to her lips, and sipped at it, without taking her eyes from her friend's face. Then she began talking about Zen Buddhism. She repeated the familiar story. One day a disciple of Gauthama Buddha approached him, handed him a golden

flower, and asked him to preach a sermon about his doctrine.

"Buddha took the flower," Kimiko went on, "held it
out from his eyes, and contemplated it a long while, in
silence. Do you know what he meant to suggest by that?
That truth is not in the description but in the contemplation of things."

"Perhaps some day I'll become a Buddhist monk,"
Pablo joked, "sit contemplating a flower—you, for example
—and suddenly, in a flash, attain the intuition of truth."

"But discipline is necessary to achieve that flash of
intuition. And patience. And humility. Some monks have
had the revelation only after ten years of contemplative
life."

Kimiko said that she was going to tell him a confidential story about a North American family of her acquaintance. She asked her companion not to question her about
names, because she would not reveal them. Pablo got the
impression that she was going to confide a dark secret, a
case of murder or incest.

"Imagine," she said gently, "this family has a garden
at their home. Every Saturday, the head of the family
mows the grass. At the appropriate time he prunes the
trees, from time to time he sprays insecticides on the
plants to kill parasites. The garden is lovely. The members
of the family photograph it in color, and in the summer
they eat and drink in the shade of its trees. And yet they
never commune with the garden, they have no intimacy
with it, they do not meditate on its flowers, its grass, its
earth. They only think of buying more things to adorn it
and make it more comfortable—benches, tables, an in-
flated swimming pool, plaster statuettes. And the garden
remains uncomprehended, a stranger. Isn't it horrible?"

Pablo gave a hearty laugh, which shocked the Japanese girl a little. Then, lowering his voice to the official
muteness of their conversation, he said, "I understand
what you mean. But the American man generally has the
engineer's view of the world. And it is that view that pre-

dominates in the occident. We want to conquer nature, tame it, in short, use it for our benefit."

"A purely material benefit," she protested. "And as a result the occidentals alienate themselves not only from nature but from each other, and each one from himself."

"Yes, our greatest problem has been to bridge the psychological distance which separates the subject from the object. Do you think the oriental philosophers have achieved it?"

"Without the slightest doubt."

"Admitting that the Japanese are in the majority Buddhists and therefore contemplatives, how do you explain the accelerated, almost obsessive industrialization of your country since the war?"

"That industrial mentality is to our real way of being as the artificially cultivated pearl is to the real one. We still have time and taste for contemplating nature and receiving her messages." She smiled again. "Yes, and for painting and writing poetry. Do you know that nearly a million Japanese cultivate the art of the *haikai?*"

Pablo refilled both bowls with *sake*.

"The Americans," Kimiko whispered, looking cautiously all around, "have no time or even the capacity for really enjoying the things they make. Worse yet. They think that *doing* is more important than *being, action* is better than *contemplation*."

A short pause followed, and then Pablo picked up the thread of thought. "One day I touched on that subject in a conversation with my friend Bill Godkin. . . . Do you remember him? The blond, freckled newspaperman who smokes a pipe? . . . He listened to me with his usual patience, and then said, 'What would become of us if it were not for the inventors, the engineers, the promoters and especially the scientists? If Western man, faced with the hardships, the discomforts, and scourges of nature, had remained in a state of Buddhistic contemplation, gazing at the absolute or at his own navel, what sort of situation would we be in today? To start with, humanity would be periodically decimated by plagues. Think of the progress just in physics and biochemistry.' And my friend enumerated a series of occidental discoveries and inventions which have contributed not only to improving but prolonging man's life on earth." Pablo laughed. "At that moment another friend of mine, Gonzaga, put in, 'Oh, Bill, what you Americans lack is the capacity for magic. This country is prosaically practical.' Godkin puffed at his pipe, looked at the Brazilian and answered, 'You Latins make magic with words. We do it with deeds and things. Do you want any magic greater than the one we're doing now, turning sea water into potable water?' "

Kimiko related several cases of friends of hers who had received messages from the absolute. Pablo listened to her in a rather skeptical silence, and then replied:

"Think of this monstrous contradiction. The Japanese general staff, which planned and executed the treacherous attack on Pearl Harbor, was wholly composed of Zen Buddhists. And the atomic bomb was invented, manufactured, and launched upon an open city by a nation confessedly Christian. Where is the nexus in all that?"

Ortega immediately regretted having said these last words, because a great sadness shadowed the face of the secretary of the Embassy of Japan.

They came out of the Genghis Khan and went to a movie theater. Pablo was fidgety. He squirmed in his seat and could not get interested in the picture. Kimiko's warm, perfumed presence beside him in the darkness of the theater began to disturb him. More than once he thought of taking her hand, but held himself back. The gesture would be like throwing a drop of grease on the painting of the delicate Japanese *kakemono*. He thought of Glenda Doremus and felt a physical nostalgia for her. The note he had written to her that morning returned to mind: "Don't be stubborn. Obey the spirit of the law of your country and grant this defendant the benefit of the doubt. I insist on seeing you. Telephone my apartment or the embassy."

23

ON THE FOLLOWING Monday morning, close to nine o'clock, Pablo parked his car as usual behind the embassy residence and walked across the park toward the chancellery. Under a sky of limpid blue, a warm and golden sun, already timidly promising summer, was shimmering rainbows on the wings of dragonflies and in the water from the sprinklers pinwheeling over the grass.

The first secretary was walking with hands in his pockets, head down, thinking of Glenda and wishing to find a message from her on his desk. Just as he raised his eyes, he saw a swift object—bird? dart?—sail out of Pancho Vivanco's office window, cut the air in a serene flight, and disappear, diving into the foliage of a tree. Pablo smiled. The consul was beginning his day by sailing out birds of paper. He went into the chancellery, greeted the taciturn man at the information desk, said a few kindly words to Merceditas—the pity that the ugly little creature sometimes awakened in him—murmured a neutral good morning to one of Ugarte's lieutenants—the one who was forever begging him for girls' telephone numbers—waved to La Ogilvita, whom he glimpsed down the hall, went into his office, closed the door, sat down at the desk, took a fountain pen and a blank sheet of paper, and wrote a note to Miss Hirota, thanking her for the pleasure that her company had given him on Saturday evening and composing a haikai for her:

> CONSULAR SERVICE
> With *cartes blanches*
> The Consul dispatches
> Doves of paper.

Still at his office window, Pancho Vivanco was staring in the direction of the ash tree where his paper bird had alighted, but after a while the image that filled his mind was that of his wife. Why was Rosalía so sad and depressed lately? What caused those sudden fits of weeping, those puffy eyes, those attacks of insomnia? She refused to talk to him, she repulsed the attempts that he made to comfort her. And now, there at the window, the suspicion that for days had been darkening his mind and that he tried in vain to thrust away was taking shape. *Rosalía was pregnant.* That was the terrible truth. And why not? It could only be that, he thought, rolling and unrolling the dollar bill in his fingers, trying to make of it a tighter and tighter, thinner cylinder. If Rosalía is pregnant, the child is not mine. I am absolutely sure of that. I've always taken precautions, at her request. But it matters little to that egoist to beget a child on his mistress, never thinking of the consequences.

The breeze stirred the branches of the ash, and the paper bird fell to the ground. And gazing fixedly at the white spot on the grass—the seagulls of his honeymoon dipped and circled in his aching memory—Pancho Vivanco stood pondering his and Rosalía's misfortune. What to do? If Rosalía chose abortion, who could she go to? The consul's lips trembled, a cold sweat dampened his forehead and his hands. Stupid? Now it was all clear. Rosalía *was* pregnant, but was ashamed to disclose her secret. She, who didn't want children! They had discussed the problem on their honeymoon. "Later, Pancho, after we have made the most of our youth. Not now. I don't like even to imagine what my life in Paris would be, looking after a baby. No."

Vivanco lifted his head and fixed his gaze on the ambassador's residence. The beast! The loathsome sperm of the Indian had sullied Rosalía's uterus and was now growing inside it like a malignant tumor. What to do, God above? What to do? The poor girl might, in desperation, have recourse to some quack. Ninfa, that indecent procuress, must know the addresses of some "angel-makers"; she would take her friend to one of those places. Rosalía would then run a deadly risk. He had to make her confess everything, so that he, her husband, could take the necessary measures that the situation required.

He took off his glasses, breathed on the lenses, and wiped them with his handkerchief. And while he was thus occupied he imagined a horrible scene: Rosalía bleeding to death on the table in a sordid consulting room. "Hello. Who's speaking? Mr. Vivanco? Come to the morgue right away. Your wife has just been found dead in a taxi. Hemorrhage." Who would be telephoning him? The police, naturally. There would be a scandal. Stories in the newspapers. But worst of all would be Rosalía's death. Livid, rigid, frozen in a drawer at the morgue.

Vivanco looked up at a plane passing low, making ready to land at the airport. He consulted his watch. It was time to start the day's work. He sat down at the desk, took some colored pencils out of the drawer, and started his habitual doodling with them on his memorandum pad. After several minutes, almost calm again, he began visaing passports and signing invoices with his customary loving interest.

Dr. Jorge Molina was also at his desk, studying the documents regarding the question to be debated that afternoon at the meeting of the OAS Council. It concerned sending an investigating committee to Nicaragua to verify the validity of that country's complaint that its territory had been invaded by a group of rebels coming in planes from Costa Rica.

He could not succeed, however, in concentrating on the typed text before his eyes. His attention wandered frequently to the memoranda which he had left on the writing able in his apartment and which reflected the doubts that were beginning to bother him about certain aspects of the life and the character of the man on whose biography he was working.

He rose, and immediately felt in his collarbone a sudden pain which flashed down from his shoulder to his left

wrist. He began to pace up and down. The specter of Gris
—his usual visitor at that hour—was there in his corner, in
his usual armchair, wearing that eternal gray tweed sport
jacket of his, lead-gray slacks, a soft-collared, rather wrinkled shirt and a dark tie, in a university professor's general
untidiness, which at bottom, paradoxically, has a certain
elegance about it. Molina knew what the phantom was
going to ask him.

"So you think you can honestly write a laudatory
biography of the archbishop primate of El Sacramento,
after all you know about him?"

"And why not? He is a fascinating personality."

"I don't deny that. But the man seems to me rather a
disciple of Machiavelli than of Christ."

"Question of point of view."

"I feel, too, that you are beginning to be preoccupied
by an unexpected personage who has emerged before you,
threatening to break up your initial plans."

"I know, you are going to talk about Padre Catalino.
It's true. I never imagined that the obscure provincial
vicar could be more than a vague shadow on the backdrop
of my history. And yet . . ."

Gris smiled. Motina continued pacing, both hands on
his hips, holding his body erect and wagging his head from
side to side.

"And yet the life of that village priest runs parallel in
time with Don Pánfilo's," Gris said, "and it constitutes a
parameter dangerous to the moral judgment of your hero.
By coincidence, both were born in the same year, 1890.
Pánfilo, in a sumptuous mansion of Páramo, son of a rich
family with traditions and vain airs of nobility, a family
whose fortune was made principally in the exploitation of
silver mines at the end of the eighteenth century. Am I
right? Good. Catalino, the son of peasants, was born, like
Jesus, in a stable."

"With all that vaunted logic of yours, which leads you
so far away from God, you are nothing but an incurable
romantic, Gris. Catalino was born, it is true, in a poor
cabin with walls of adobe and roof of thatch, and his par-

ents were peasants, but I don't think it right to throw in a man's face, like an insult, the fact that he was born well or ill. Ignacio de Loyola was noble and rich by birth, but that did not stop him from becoming what he was. Gabriel Heliodoro also was born in a stable, to use your expression, and you and I know that it made no saint out of him. On the contrary!"

Gris's laughter resounded in Molina's memory.

"While Don Pánfilo Arango y Aragón, table companion and bosom friend of the dictator, cultivates the friendship of politicians and millionaires, without ever arguing with them about their morals and habits—while, I say, the subject of your book frequents the upper worldly circles and in short lives the life of a prince, Padre Catalino Sender carries on his sacerdotal labors in the obscurity of a poor parish, and shares his daily bread, his bitter tortilla, in Christian fashion with the peasants, for whom he often intercedes with the powerful landowners."

Who was speaking now? He, Molina, or that diabolical exile? Or was it perchance a third person, a fusion of the two, in a monstrous symbiosis? Because the minister-counselor mentally heard an impersonal voice, colorless and toneless, which reached him now in the form of words, now in that of ideas or image syntheses.

"When Juan Balsa led the peasants in revolt against the dictatorship of Antonio María Chamorro and took refuge with his guerrillas in the Sierra, the young Padre Catalino, then recently ordained, often left his hut in Soledad del Mar and climbed the Sierra de la Calavera, at the risk of his own life, to hear the confession of the rebels and administer communion or extreme unction to them as the case required. During all this, in the Cerro Hermoso cathedral, Don Pánfilo was preaching furious sermons in which he referred to Juan Balsa as 'that atheistic, bloody bandit' and called down the wrath of God upon his head. Don Pánfilo was not only the apple of the old archbishop's eye—Don Herminio Ormazábal made him his private secretary—but also the *enfant gâté* of the society of the capital, which filled the cathedral on Sundays to hear the

beautiful sermons preached by the young priest, as elo-
quent as Cicero and as handsome as a pagan god of ancient Greece. And Don Pánfilo knew—ah, how well he
knew!—that he inspired real, unspiritual passion in the
women of the great world, whose tables—and beds, possibly—he frequented, and whose old wine he drank. In
those times going to Mass in Cerro Hermoso on the Sundays when Don Pánfilo was preaching was as entertaining
as going to a good play, because your hero, Molina, is first
and foremost an actor who can modulate his voice, make
dramatic pauses and underline phrases with opportune
gestures previously rehearsed. And have you noticed the
admiration he has for himself and for everything belonging to his person—his bearing, his features, his intelligence, his culture, his style, his voice, his hands—ah yes,
those patrician hands! A winner, in short, Molina! But
think of Padre Catalino dragging the hem of his brown
robe year after year through the dust or the mud of
Soledad del Mar, consoling the sick and afflicted, weeping
and praying when he cannot save a life or give food to a
starving man."

Jorge Molina approached the window and looked out,
unseeing, attentive only to his inner world. The "voice"
continued, implacable, a voice which he was now beginning to recognize as his own, very much his own.

"One day the government soldiers tried to force Padre
Catalino to guide them to Juan Balsa's hideout, because in
Soledad del Mar only he knew where the rebel leader was.
The vicar refused. They threatened to shoot him, torture
him, but the priest remained steadfast. It was then that
Chamorro's minister of war got Don Herminio to summon
the rebellious priest to the Archepiscopal Palace for a
formal reprimand. The archbishop asked the vicar
whether he understood that he was compromising the
Church with his conduct. Padre Catalino shook his head.
No, he did not understand it so. Don Herminio further
asked whether he was going to change his attitude thence-
forth. Padre Catalino replied that he would continue to
fulfill his priestly duty, that is, giving spiritual comfort to

those who sought it, but that he would not forget his duty as a man, which was that of helping those who were hungry for justice . . . and for the bread that nourishes the body, he added in his placid voice. And then the old archbishop, irate, punished the priest by exiling him to a parish even poorer than that of Soledad del Mar, at the far limits of the Province of San Fernando."

Now Molina was massaging his left arm with his right hand, moving his head to right and to left. It had done little good to have slept the previous night lying on the hard floor with no pillow.

"Come, Minister, come. Face the problem with courage. No one is listening to us, or watching us. Who was the confessor of Doña Rafaela, Chamorro's wife, in the last years of her life? Everyone knew that it was the then Monsignor Don Pánfilo. He was informed of all the moral iniquities of the matron, knew that she was manipulating her poor husband as a ventriloquist manages his puppet. He knew she was an adulteress and a cruel, selfish woman. And yet he continued to cultivate her friendship, to frequent her house. And when that dissolute woman had her mystic crisis—and you will naturally seek to convince your readers that Don Pánfilo was the one responsible for that 'change'—when Doña Rafaela retired to a convent, where she died shortly thereafter in an aura of sanctity, Don Pánfilo Arango y Aragón, over her coffin in the cathedral, preached a funeral oration that all but represented a prelude to the dead woman's beatification."

Molina turned back to his desk, picked up his pencil, and wrote on a sheet of paper: "Must not forget that, at the end of 1924, Don Pánfilo magnanimously asked the old archbishop to permit Padre Catalino's return to his parish of Soledad del Mar, and had his request granted."

Now the minister-counselor sensed that Don Pánfilo himself was also in the room, seated in a corner, splendid in his episcopal robes, his noble hands resting on the arms of his chair, a smile at once ironic and benevolent on his face, now wrinkled but still handsome.

"It is 1925. Juventino Carrera stirs up a battalion of

the 5th Infantry at Soledad del Mar to revolt and takes his soldiers to the mountains. Other garrisons revolt. Padre Catalino is captured by government troops and accused of aiding the rebels by carrying munitions of war and food to them, and of sheltering rebel fugitives in his own home."

Molina again writes: "Regarding the aid that Padre Catalino gave the revolutionaries of Carrera, no one better than Gabriel Heliodoro can testify to that, and furnish details. G. H. himself spent two or three days hidden in the church of Nuestra Señora de la Soledad, awaiting the opportunity to go up to the Sierra de la Calavera, where he joined the rebels. It seems beyond doubt that Padre Catalino personally served him as guide."

Jorge Molina walked to and fro between his two phantoms. Don Pánfilo was silent, but Gris was speaking.

"And what did your friend Pánfilo do when he saw that Chamorro's army was weakening, and agitation was beginning in the university and in the streets of Cerro Hermoso and of other cities and towns? He sought out Don Herminio and asked his authorization to go in secret up into the Sierra de la Calavera with the purpose of parleying with Juventino Carrera. The old archbishop was perplexed by the idea. 'Have you lost your senses?' he asked. 'No, Eminence, the monsignor replied. I am sure of Carrera's victory, Chamorro is at the end of his rope, and the Church must be on the side of the victors.' What did Don Herminio answer? Come now, Molina, you know that, you have the testimony of Don Pánfilo himself, your dear friend, who is so proud of that brilliant, astute political feat."

Now it is Don Pánfilo who speaks, and his voice fills the vault of the cathedral which Molina holds in his memory.

"Don Herminio told me, 'Go. But without my authorization. Go on your own initiative and at your own risk. If Juventino Carrera is defeated, as I expect and desire, and that attempt of yours at mediation, Pánfilo, comes to be discovered, I shall publicly declare that I knew nothing whatever about it. And I will deliver your head to the government—with heartfelt pain, but I will do it.' I smiled and replied, 'I accept the conditions, Eminence.' I left Cerro Hermoso at nightfall that same day, and next morning I reached Soledad del Mar, clad in the cassock of a simple campaign priest. Padre Catalino took me to the chief of the rebels, who received me with surprise and distrust. He asked, 'Wasn't it Your Reverence who a few months ago preached a sermon against me in the cathedral in Cerro Hermoso?' I smiled and nodded, 'I am not here to justify or excuse myself, but to reach an agreement which I deem to be to the interest of the revolutionaries as well as of my Church.' He decided to listen to me. My proposal was simple. I undertook to work upon certain key garrisons immediately, such as those of Páramo and Puerto Esmeralda, to get them to revolt within a few weeks, ending the campaign sooner and avoiding the useless loss of more human lives. I would also order the cessation of all preaching against the revolutionaries in all the churches. Carrera heard me out. He wanted to know what I was asking in exchange. I gave my conditions. I wanted him to promise me on his solemn word, given before the members of his general staff, the following—*a*, to respect the Church, its priests, its properties, its rights acquired to date—*b*, not to permit acts of violence, vengeance and sacking anywhere in the country—*c*, to enter Cerro Hermoso at the head of his troops in an orderly formation, and receive the symbolic key of the city from the hands of the archbishop primate, whose ring he was to kiss in public. Carrera drew aside and conferred with his men. He came back shortly thereafter and said that he accepted the proposal, but that it would be an agreement between gentlemen—he would not sign any written document. We sealed the pact with a handshake, and I went down to Soledad del Mar. I carried out what I had promised. In two weeks the federal garrisons of Puerto Esmeralda and Páramo—the commander of the latter was a second cousin of mine—revolted, and Chamorro fell."

Gris intervened, "But Carrera did not fulfill one of the terms of the pact. He did permit violence, looting, and revenge at least in the first days of victory. And the famous popular tribunals then set up were nothing but a mockery."

Don Pánfilo made a fluttering gesture. "No one, nothing is perfect in this world. But the fact is that the other clauses of the oral contract were carried out to the letter. Ah! I forgot one very important stipulation of the agreement. Carrera also promised that, once the period of consolidation of victory was over, he would convoke a constitutional assembly, adopt a constitution, and hold elections. He did not fail to keep his word."

Molina stared fixedly at one corner of the room, thinking again of the notes he had written the evening before. He remembered a paragraph: "It occurs to me now that Don Pánfilo represents the high bourgeoisie of the Church and Padre Catalino the proletariat."

Gris reappeared in his mind. "Ah! I am happy to see that my friend is using the Marxist nomenclature. Well, I would say more simply that Padre Catalino represents the real Church of Christ, that of the Good Samaritan, the Church of the saints and the martyrs."

"Think well, Gris. Without men like Don Pánfilo the Church would not be able to subsist on the plane of history. It needs heads as much as it needs hearts. It is thanks to the combined action of those two *forces* represented by Don Pánfilo and Padre Catalino that the Church maintains its admirable equilibrium between the spiritual and the temporal."

There was a silence. Molina was once more rubbing his aching arm, looking around the room, recognizing that he ought to get back to the study of the Nicaraguan document, but feeling that he could not read it now with the necessary attention.

"But don't run away from the rest of the problem. Let's leave the year 1925. I know that you are dismayed by the idea of bringing history up to date. Carrera was elected, re-elected. He robbed, killed, tortured. He got rich, and today he practices dictatorship disguised behind a democratic wallpaper façade, supported by a submissive Congress, wholly his, a Congress without a backbone, without ideas, without principles. During all those years there was peace between the Church and the state in El Sacramento. And Don Pánfilo continued to be a favorite guest in the Palace of Government, possibly pacifying his conscience with the parody of a Biblical phrase, 'To Carrera what is Carrera's, and to God what is God's.' "

"You oversimplify, Gris, because you hate Don Pánfilo. Men are not spheres or cubes, but much more complex polyhedrons than people imagine. I don't want to draw a caricature of my subject, but a portrait. Don Pánfilo also has great qualities of soul, of heart."

"Very well. When Carrera's police invented a Communist conspiracy as a pretext for a coup d'état, the famous Movement of National Salvation, do you think, then, that Don Pánfilo, an intelligent, shrewd man, didn't know that it was all a lie? And if he did, why did he keep still? Why did he connive in that crime of *lèse*-democracy? Another thing! Why didn't he raise his voice to have them stop the tortures to which political prisoners were subjected in the prisons of Cerro Hermoso?"

"One moment! More than once Don Pánfilo appealed to Carrera about that. I have proof of it. Gabriel Heliodoro is a witness."

"I know. Urged by the archbishop, Cerrera held an *inquiry* in which it was proved that everything evil said about his chief of police and his political prisons was sheer lies spread by the enemy.

"Don Pánfilo," the exile went on, "hand-in-glove with the United States ambassador, contributed to the downfall of Moreno and the return of Carrera to power."

"You must not forget the innumerable attempts the archbishop made to become Moreno's friend, to frequent the palace, to keep him on the path of moderation. Moreno repulsed him, always. God will judge Don Pánfilo Arango y Aragón. God, not you or I, will say the last word about that prince of the Church."

"You don't believe in God, Molina."

"Then, as that personage of Dostoievski's said, if God does not exist, all is permissible."

"Don't forget to include the sermon that Don Pánfilo preached in the cathedral a few days after the Tragic Night, in which he condemned Dr. Moreno's soul to hell, irremediably, because of suicide. And I doubt that he was really convinced that Moreno had committed suicide."

"You cannot make Don Pánfilo out to me to be amoral and a cynic."

"Dante must have had good reason to send some bishops to hell, in his *Commedia*."

"I shall be able to prove in my biography that Don Pánfilo ran the risk of losing his own soul in eternity to save his Church in historical time. In a way that makes him a martyr, too."

"Very ingenious! But don't forget to show Padre Catalino as an agent of Moscow, an emissary from Satan."

The minister-counselor sat down at his desk and covered his face with his hands. The voice continued:

"Jorge Molina, I challenge you to write a sincere biography of Don Pánfilo Arango y Aragón. The real hero of your story is Padre Catalino Sender. He knows less theology than the archbishop, but he has lived in accord with the spirit of the Sermon on the Mount. Don Pánfilo is holder of several decorations, which he displays in public. The parish priest of Soledad del Mar has as his only decoration a gastric ulcer. He symbolizes the real Church of Christ, the Church of love and compassion, the eternal and invincible Church, Jorge Molina!"

The ex-seminarian picked up a pencil and began drumming on the table with it. The truth was that, if he wished to reveal in his biography all that he knew of the life and character of the archbishop by deduction, induction, or direct and documented knowledge, he would end by not only losing the friendship of the subject of the biography but also prejudicing the Church which he loved so much, the Church into which he profoundly yearned to reinstate himself through the rediscovery of God.

Gris, like an angel of darkness, whispered into his ear, "Have the courage to plumb the depths of your motives! You don't want to displease your friend the archbishop in any way because you have the hope that some day he may breathe into President Carrera's ear the suggestion to make you ambassador of El Sacramento to the Vatican. The dream of your life!"

Jorge Molina seized the pencil in both hands and broke it in half.

24

CLARE OGILVY looked at her wristwatch and thought, The ambassador is late today. I wonder what's happened. She looked over the day's agenda. At eleven sharp Don Gabriel Heliodoro would receive the ambassador of Nicaragua in his office. At twelve-thirty he was to be in the Occidental Restaurant to lunch with one of the directors of the Eximbank. He would have to go to a reception in the Embassy of Ecuador at six.

And in the evening? La Ogilvita smiled mischievously. In the evening, naturally, her chief would take Miss Frances Andersen to some night club. Afterward, only God knew what would happen. Poor Rosalía! The secretary spent a few minutes revising the text of a speech which Pablo Ortega had written in English for Don Gabriel Heliodoro to deliver on the following Thursday at a luncheon in the National Press Club, where he was to be the guest of honor. To her now fell the task, not at all easy, of making a phonetic version of the speech, in such a way that the ambassador could read it in English. Good heavens! She looked at her watch again.

Some miles away from the chancellery, in the vestibule of a motel along the Lee Highway in Virginia, Aldo

Borelli was staring at the big electric clock mounted on the wall in front of him. He had to be back at the embassy by noon, at the latest, to take the ambassador to the Occidental.

Ninfa Ugarte, who had requested a room in which to rest for a while (*jos tu res wis mai ósban*), signed the registry card with the names Señor y Señora González and paid the twelve dollars for the day. It was the third or fourth time they had taken a room in that motel. Aldo Borelli felt ill at ease, not knowing where to put his hands or where to look. He noticed that the man at the desk stared at him in a funny way. Obviously the young fellow understood the whole thing. He knew that they were not husband and wife. Gabriel Heliodoro's chauffeur turned red. The situation was unpleasant and embarrassing for him. Worse than that, the more he thought about the affair, the more apprehensive he became. Suppose his wife should find out everything? She was already getting suspicious of the stories he told her to explain where the extra money came from that he was bringing home. "It's nothing, dear, the new ambassador very generously gives me fat tips. These ties? It was Don Gabriel Heliodoro that gave them to me, too. They're used, see? The shoes, too. Lucky we wear the same size. The shirts are a little large for me, but that's not surprising, the man has a neck like a bull." Ah, but if General Ugarte found out—*mamma mia!* —he was capable of putting a bullet in him.

Anyway, it was a relief to know that the ambassador was on his side, knew everything, and did not censure him. On the contrary, he protected him, allowed him to go out twice a week at that hour without uniform. That was the way Don Gabriel Heliodoro repaid the go-between's services.

"Number twenty-five, madame," said the receptionist, smiling, handing a key to his customer. "It's down the hall on your right, please."

She headed for the room and Aldo followed. A gigolo, nothing but a gigolo. He was getting money and presents for sleeping with that woman. The suit he was wearing

(Raleigh Haberdasher, $60) had been given him by his mistress. And now he was following her down that long corridor, as cool and clean as that of a hospital. Aldo watched the motion of Ugarte's wife's hips, eyed the chubby back of her neck, the gleaming hair. A strong scent of heliotrope—or was it jonquil?—emanated from her body. Whatever it was, it was sickening. The perfume of his shame, the smell of the liaison that to him was cold and without savor. But the fact remained that in two or three more months he would have enough money to send for his brother. He knew the boy was going to laugh when he told him how he had managed to get those dollars so quickly. "Look, Gino, I sold this body. Like a prostitute." And both would utter great guffaws.

They went into the room, they shut the door. Ninfa clasped the young man to her bosom, rubbed herself against him, uttering moans, and then offered her mouth, her eyes closed. With repugnance Aldo kissed her wet lips, which tasted of lipstick and cigarette smoke. The matron's breasts were like foam rubber. Ninfa had nearly lost human shape. She was a caricature of a woman. Every time he lay down with her, Aldo had the feeling that he was going to be devoured. During the act of love ("love" was not the right word—never!) he closed his eyes and thought of his wife, of her clean, beautiful, firm body.

Ninfa Ugarte began undressing. Aldo took off his coat. He had nothing to say. The fat woman crooned a lullaby from old Spain.

Aldo Borelli undid the knot of his tie reluctantly, and, when he unexpectedly caught a glimpse of his face in a mirror, he lacked the courage to face himself.

After the ambassador left his residence on his way to the chancellery, Michel Michel set out on an inspection tour of the rooms to see whether the cleaning women and maids had done their jobs well. He went down to the kitchen, gave instructions to the chef about the menu for dinner, and finally, heaving a sigh of relief, which was really a symbolic pat on the back he bestowed on himself in congratulations for duty done, he bolted himself in his own room, took up his diary, and wrote in his minute, regular hand:

"I have been observing the new ambassador with an almost scientific interest. *Ce type-là* is indubitably of elementary intellect, but he possesses a mysterious charm. (The personnel of the embassy adore him.) He has no culture, not the slightest notion of literature, painting, or music. But he is undeniably intelligent. He has the intelligence of instinct. In short, a Dionysian. He often fills these salons of the embassy with his loud laughter. (Be it said in passing that, in my opinion, there is nothing in all the world and in life so humorous or witty that it merits laughter of that quality.) But he is odd. From time to time Don G. H. has moments of depression and sits motionless in a chair, huddled up like an Indian, staring fixedly at some point in space in the deepest silence. One such night I was awakened by the sound of footsteps on the upper floor. I slipped on a bathrobe and went up. I found the ambassador, clad in the trousers of his abominable striped pajamas, wandering through the rooms, scratching his head and yawning. He told me that he had been awakened by a nightmare and had got wide awake. He asked me to make him some coffee, he was going to stay up the rest of the night. 'The hours of sleep, Michel, are time that we steal from life.' I took the coffee to him. He invited me courteously to sit down. I accepted. He offered me a cup of coffee. I declined. And then the man told me the story of his life, a mixture of Georges Ohnet and Dumas Père: the poor orphan, the village priest, the revolution. What a novel! (Or can he be a pathological liar?) My eyes were smarting with sleep. I remembered one night, many years ago, when I found Don Alfonso Bustamante wandering like a *revenant* through the rooms of this mansion in the early hours of the morning. But what a difference! Don Alfonso was wearing his elegant silk dressing gown, his hair was neatly combed, and on his feet were *pantoufles à la* Anatole France, as he used to say. We sat up until daybreak discussing philosophical problems. Don Alfonso told me that he was in the habit of waking up in the middle of the night, appalled by the idea of dying, of coming to an end, 'to exist no more.' In our insomniac conversations, he discoursed on the Nothing. *'Qu'est-ce-que-c'est le néant*, Michel?' What could I answer? *'Le néant, c'est le néant*, Monsieur l'Ambassadeur, *c'est tout!'* He shook his head sadly. Poor Don Alfonso! He was obsessed by the fear of dying. Don Gabriel Heliodoro is obsessed by the wish to live."

Seated at his desk in the chancellery of the Embassy of Brazil, Orlando Gonzaga was examining some confidential papers. He summoned his secretary and requested, "Put through an urgent phone call to Brazil. Get me the Secretariat of State."

He re-read the documents. He was astounded. Brazil was going to import beans from the United States! That was the ultimate unthinkable. The purchase was to be effected through the intermediary of an American firm on which the Brazilian Embassy—thanks to his, Gonzaga's, own investigations—had obtained from New York banks the worst references. It was necessary to transmit these data with the utmost urgency to the Secretary of State, to prevent the transaction from being consummated.

Orlando Gonzaga lit a cigarette and sat pensively smoking. He recalled that shortly after the Second World War his country, which had not been economically harmed by it—on the contrary, she had wound up with a credit balance of hundreds of millions of dollars gold in the United States—had had to import potatoes from Holland, that minute country which had been forced to open its dikes and flood its lands to hold back the Nazi invasion, and had had several of its cities and ports razed by the Luftwaffe bombardments.

Gonzaga was going to transmit the information simply to "sweep his own front walk," so that the embassy could not in the future be accused of negligence or complicity. But he had little hope that those bank data would be taken into due consideration. He was beginning to smell chicanery in the bean deal. Sometimes he had the impression that, in Brazil, nearly all the figures responsible for the government had lost their dignity. The so-called elite had failed through omission or commission. The exceptions were extremely few. It was a calamity.

He went over to the window and looked at the embassy garden, then sat down in an armchair, and from the table beside him picked up the copy of a tabloid which had come to him from New York in the morning mail. He leafed through it with vague attention, and finally, by sheer chance, discovered a reference which interested him in the column of one of those famous chroniclers who concern themselves with reporting social gossip—who is going with whom, in what places, and how.

> The flamboyant ambassador of a republic in the Caribbean, a very popular personality even though new in the diplomatic and social circles of Washington, has been seen frequently in several spots of the nation's capital—the Espionage, Pierre's, the Blue Room of the Shoreham—in the company of a dazzling, recently divorced blonde. The aforesaid Latin American diplomat is not only married, he is a grandfather, although he doesn't look it.

Orlando Gonzaga smiled, got up, and telephoned to Ortega.

"*Pablito, qué tal?*"

The other's voice sounded gay. "Well, look, Gonzaga, I woke up without a headache. For me that is almost nirvana!"

"Pablo, I called you because I've just discovered in a New York paper a squib about your ambassador. Listen." He read the passage to which he referred. "What do you think? All that's lacking is to write Don Gabriel Heliodoro's name, letter by letter."

"What do you expect me to do? Our hero seems ready to give concrete proofs of the celebrated Latin virility."

"That's right. He can't get the loan to construct the Trans-Sacramento but it appears that he has already got

Miss Andersen, has scaled her breasts and planted his flag
on those wonderful peaks of snow. Yes, and opened tunnels! What glory for your country, Pablo!"

"Gonzaga, you're a cynic."

"No, what I am is envious!"

In his shirt sleeves, lighted pipe in his mouth, blue
pencil in hand, Bill Godkin was examining two dispatches
,received that morning from the Amalgamated Press correspondent in Cerro Hermoso.

Insistent rumors are current here that President
Carrera is going to rebuild his Cabinet, dismissing all
civilian ministers and filling the vacancies with military men in his confidence. The anticipated crisis is
motivated by the fact that the present Cabinet, with
the single exception of the minister of war, has declared itself opposed to the adoption of an amendment to the Constitution which would permit the
Generalissimo to be re-elected for the second time.
Moreover, the Chamber of Deputies has postponed,
on a variety of pretexts, the discussion of this amendment. It is believed that the majority of the deputies
and senators is seeking by this maneuver to avoid
having the amendment being put to a vote before the
recess of both houses of the Congress next July.

Godkin laced his hands behind his head and sat back,
smoking and thinking. The other dispatch read:

The dinner given last night by the Most Reverend
Don Pánfilo Arango y Aragón in the Archiepiscoal
Palace for Dr. Ignacio Allende, minister of the interior, and the other civilian cabinet ministers, has
aroused much speculation among the exalted circles
of the capital as to the significance of the fact that
Generalissimo Juventino Carrera, an intimate friend
of the archbishop primate, was not invited.

Bill Godkin smiled. The days of Carrera as president
were numbered, unless—well, events in El Sacramento
could unfold in several ways in the coming months. Congress would defeat the amendment demanded by the Gen-

eralissimo and the situation would remain unchanged . . .
but agitation in the country would continue until the date
of the elections, which would be held . . . or not. If they
were, Carrera would present a puppet candidate, who
would be elected or not. If he should be, the Libertador
would continue to rule, pulling the puppet's strings. If he
were not elected, it would be up to the Generalissimo to
pull off a coup d'état in order not to hand over the government to his legal successor, and in that case El Sacramento would once again be under an undisguisable dictatorship.

Bill got up and went over to the window, where he
stood looking vaguely at the traffic in K Street, and at the
pedestrians going and coming on the opposite sidewalk
under the bright sun of the almost summer morning. Ah,
but there were still other possibilities. Carrera could strike
his blow now—maybe he was already doing so—or would
today, or tomorrow, or two or three weeks from now. For
that, however, he needed a good pretext, since the situation in Latin America had changed in the last five years.
Rojas Pinilla, Pérez Jimenez, and Fulgencio Batista had
been overthrown by popular movements and accused of
corruption and other crimes. Public opinion on the American continent was decidedly unfavorable to dictatorships,
either civil or military.

Bill rapped his pipe on the edge of a metal smoking
stand, emptied it, filled it again, and lighted it. What Carrera needed, then, was a good "motive" for the coup d'état.
There was still another possibility. Before that coup and
before the November elections, the revolutionaries would
disembark at several points on the coast of El Sacramento.
Bill was credibly informed that there were contingents of
Sacramentan exiles in Cuba, armed and provisioned, ready
for the invasion. He even knew the name of the leader of
the movement—Miguel Barrios.

If the invasion should materialize, Juventino Carrera
would immediately proclaim a state of war throughout the
country and try to put up the most desperate resistance.
And what chances would the revolutionaries have?

Bill went back to his desk, sat down, and concluded that the odds were all in their favor. The Sacramentan people were tired of Carrera. On walls in the capital phrases were already appearing inciting the people to armed revolution. Clandestine bulletins against the government were circulating. The university, as always, was a "focal point of revolutionary infection," as one of Carrera's newspapers had put it. And what of the National Army? The officers and subalterns who had remained immune to corruption would possibly join the rebels, taking their troops with them.

Godkin heaved a long sigh, together with a cloud of smoke. Ruth, dear Ruth! If you had seen, as I did, over thirty years ago in the Sierra de la Calavera, the young faces, sun- and wind-browned, of Juventino Carrera and Gabriel Heliodoro Alvarado! How much enthusiasm and courage in those hearts! How many ideas of freedom in those heads! What gleams of hope and how many curiosities, appetites, and promises in those two pairs of eyes! They wanted to free their people from tyranny and establish social justice. And yet, my darling, see what they are now. . . . What's the answer, Ruth? Can it be that everything deteriorates with time? Everything?

He glanced over the international political news stories. Gloomy. What did God mean by all this? What's the meaning of this colossal conundrum? If only there were a direct teletype service between the Almighty and the Amalpress. No. Even if there were—Godkin reflected, smiling and putting on his jacket to go down to the drugstore on the ground floor of the building, where he would eat a sandwich—even so, there would be the danger that the agency chief might edit the divine messages every time he considered them harmful to the interests of the great corporations of the United States. Yes, because according to Amalpress policy what was good for the giants of United States industry was necessarily good for God and the universe. That at least was the spirit of the theology which the bishops, archbishops, and cardinals of advertising sought to divulge *urbi et orbi*.

But I mustn't be pessimistic, he decided as he left his office. I'm alive and hungry. And the sun is still shining.

At that hour, sitting in his Impala, parked at the curb, General Hugo Ugarte was waiting for the students to come out of a high school in Arlington. He did this at least twice a week, with the excitement of a boy playing hookey. The entertainment cost him only the gasoline that the car consumed in going there from the chancellery and the ten cents that he put in the parking meter.

His stomach was growling with hunger. Ugarte sat waiting and smoking, his eyes set on the long, one-storied building of bare brick, located at the back of a vast expanse of grass.

Suddenly girls and boys between twelve and fifteen years old came pouring out of its doors. Walking or running, they crossed the grass in noisy jubilance toward the street.

What a sight! The Cerro Hermoso schoolgirls— Ugarte thought nostalgically—wore white blouses and navy-blue skirts of the most varied kinds, and colorful sweaters which accentuated the shapes of their busts. There were girls with women's breasts already, but in others they were barely budding forth—and it was these, from eleven to thirteen years old, that Ugarte most appreciated and desired. A group crossed the street toward the Impala. The general smiled at the ruddy faces, some ugly, others neutral, but many of them pretty—yes, how many there were of these! And, as they drew nearer in greater and greater numbers, he did not know whether he was looking at their faces, their legs, or their busts. Some of the girls were dancing about, others were singing, still others pretended to be quarreling, or acting as if they were on a stage, conscious that they were under the observation of the older people either passing by or standing in line at a bus stop. Oh, the knees!—the general thought, breathing heavily—there was nothing tastier than the thirteen-year-old girls' knees. And how the ankle socks added a piquant grace to their little legs!

His cigarette glued to his lip, Ugarte gazed hard at the schoolgirls, the long stare of a hungry old dog.

At that same instant, a few miles away, Glenda Doremus, sitting at her desk in one of the rooms of the administrative building of the Pan American Union, was eating a sandwich. She had no appetite. She had declined when two of her office mates had invited her just before to lunch with them at Jenny's Pan Asian. If she accepted, she would have to talk to them, and she was not in the mood for that. She had ordered a sandwich and a cup of black coffee. Why the coffee? She drank it without pleasure as one takes a bitter medicine. It was a kind of penance which she set for herself every day. In the late afternoon, whenever any colleague asked, "Want me to bring you a coffee?" she would automatically answer, "Yes, please, without cream or sugar." She would give her colleague a dime and after she received the paper cup she would sit eying the liquid as a suicide on a bridge contemplates the black waters into which he is going to throw himself. She knew that coffee was bad for her and would cause heartburn. But she drank it anyhow, making a point of draining the last drop.

Now she was chewing the sandwich unenthusiastically, feeling the heat of the cup in her hand. She had dropped a little splash of coffee on Pablo's note, which was lying on her desk and which she was reading for the tenth time. Ought she to see him or not? For what purpose? Just because he asked? Wasn't it more sensible to keep on saying no, before it was too late? Too late for what? Why too late? Why, before they fell in love with each other and everything went too fast and she was hurt again, violated and sullied in body and mind!

She took a swallow of coffee. In these last few weeks she had often thought of Pablo with a desire to see him again. The Pablo who appeared in her thoughts was not the man who had locked himself with her in a room of his embassy to tell her of dictators, adulterers, crooks, and thieves. The Pablo who visited her mind was the man whom she had encountered one day in his office, serene, even a little paternal, serious in gesture and word. Which of the two was the real one? Which of the two would she find, if she did accept the invitation to a new encounter?

But she had to reach a decision about her life once and for all. One way or another. Ought she, or oughtn't she, to see Pablo Ortega again?

25

ROSALÍA SWORE TO HERSELF that she would never set foot again in the ambassador's residence. All was over between her and Gabriel Heliodoro. She knew that in the evenings he was being seen at night clubs and restaurants in the company of Frances Andersen. Possibly the two of them went afterward to some hotel, or to the embassy itself, where they spent the night together, while she stayed at home enduring Pancho's whining and pleading. "Rosalía, my dearest, I am going to ask you a serious question, and I want you to answer me with the greatest sincerity. Are you pregnant or not?" She felt like laughing in the idiot's face. "Pregnant? I? If I were, no matter whose child it might be, I'd take poison, so now you know." With the ridiculous clumsiness of a poor actor, Pancho knelt down, laughing, and crying at once, and kissed her hand, babbling, "Thank God! Thank God!" Never in all her life had Rosalía despised her husband more than in that hour. And the wretched fellow spent the rest of the evening in silence, sitting in a corner, doodling his designs with colored pencils and looking at her from time to time with a bovine expression. And how long those hours in their apartment were! Her loneliness increased whenever her husband stayed at home. What to do? Her precarious English kept her from becoming interested in television programs. She had no women

friends. She detested the members of the Sacramentan
colony in Washington. She kept listening for the telephone. Gabriel Heliodoro might call her at any moment.
They had not seen each other for nearly a week. Her body
was hungry for his body, but with her pride wounded she
refused to take the initiative and telephone him. And it
was curious, but Pancho also seemed anxiously awaiting
the ring of the telephone, as if he, too, wanted Gabriel
Heliodoro to take his mistress to bed again.

One evening, watching her eying the phone in anxiety, he could not bear it and asked, "Isn't he ever going to
call you?"

"He? Who?"

"The ambassador."

"Pancho! I don't understand you."

Her husband shrugged. "I don't, either." And he
began rolling his paper cylinder in his fingers, pacing back
and forth, not looking at her. "But if it makes you happy,
I'm not going to be the one to keep you from being with
that man. What I do not want is for you to be sad. Or to
leave me. To keep on living with you I'll put up with
anything. Anything!"

She experienced a sense of nausea. His words had
something coldly viscous about them; they filled the room,
they stuck to the walls, they slid down the furniture like
saliva. They soiled her, outside and in. She felt goose flesh
rising on her back and arms and legs. A kind of weariness
of the head came over her, a dazed sensation as of emptiness in her skull, and her face—mainly her lips and the
skin around her mouth—felt as it did when her dentist
anesthetized her gums.

That evening the telephone remained silent. They got
ready for bed a little after eleven. Pancho, in his hor-
rendous mallow-colored bathrobe over his striped pajamas, came out of the bathroom, and, with a voice reeking
of toothpaste, begged, "May I come to your room?" Oh,
God! If only she could at least take pity on the poor devil!
To shut her eyes, turn off her brain, die for half an hour,
yield up her body to those flabby kisses, to the caress of

those damp hands, listen to the absurd and abject things that her husband said to her. But it was impossible.

"No, Pancho. I have a horrible migraine. Be patient. Tomorrow!"

He bowed his head, resigned. And before saying good night to her, he said softly, "It'll be all right. He'll surely call you tomorrow."

What was to become of her life? In the Sacramentan colony—Ninfa had taken it upon herself to pass on the gossip—she was known as "the ambassador's concubine." Glorious title! A woman of twenty-six who, if she wished, could have at her feet the handsomest young lovers, was a captive, submissive to a man who was old enough to be her father.

She tried to analyze her sentiments toward Gabriel Heliodoro. He had been the first man to succeed in giving her the complete pleasure of an orgasm, the full sensation of being a woman. With him she felt that she was alive all over. The things he said to her gave her the feeling of being important, of really existing. She did not deny that there was an element of fear at the bottom of her physical attraction to the man who reminded her so much of certain figures of Maya idols she had seen in magazines and books when she was a child. How many times had she kissed, in a mixture of fascination and repulsion, the whitened scar that lined his bronzed forehead? And in the delicious agony of the orgasm, when his enormous body was covering her and his muscular arms were holding her close, how many times had she absurdly wished he would kill her, crushing her against his chest? But nearly always, once the spasmodic moment of joy was over, she would burst into tears, would become once more the poor abandoned orphan child who wanted no more of Gabriel Heliodoro than that he stroke her hair, let her nestle into his hot, hard body, and say things to her that had nothing to do with carnal love.

And the ingrate was now deceiving her with the American woman. And he didn't deny it, the cynic.

One day at dusk the telephone rang. Pancho had not yet come home from the chancellery. She jumped and avidly seized the phone. "Hello."

"Rosalía, my dear!" It was his voice.

"Good afternoon, Gabriel Heliodoro."

"What is this indifference, my love? I am missing you damnably. Why don't you come over tonight?"

She remained silent, not knowing what to say. She began to tremble, and with an effort managed to stammer, "I don't know whether I can."

"Of course you can! I'll be waiting for you with a supper as usual."

"I don't know—"

"What don't you know? I'll send Aldo to get you at eight sharp. That's settled."

And so here she was—she who had sworn never to set foot again in the embassy residence—stepping out of the ambassador's Mercedes and pressing the button at the front door. Michel came to open it, and, as usual, made a little bow without looking at her—his duty was not to see, not to identify the evening visitor. *"Bon soir, Madame!"* And once more she was in the lobby. The embassy smells —rugs, the wood of the furniture, the remote scent of pine in a disinfectant—came to her nostrils, joining with erotic memories and a vague shame. And once more she felt that she was back completely and that everything was as before.

Gabriel Heliodoro descended the stairs with open arms. "Rosalía! How good that you have come! How good!" And she let herself be embraced, kissed, and taken upstairs.

Only after they had made love with the fury of a couple possessed did Rosalía speak of Frances Andersen. Both were still in bed.

"After all, darling, the one who should be bothered by that affair is my legitimate wife, not you. The important thing is that I love you and can't live without you."

"Are you telling the truth?"

"What is truth? If you know what truth is, I wish you'd tell me. I don't know. I only know what I feel."

Despite all her efforts, Rosalía could not prevent tears from welling up in her eyes. Gabriel Heliodoro felt them running down among the hairs on his chest.

"What is this, my flower?"

"What is going to become of me?"

"Nothing. I've told you a thousand times, and I'll say it again. Nothing bad can happen to anyone who has your youth and your beauty. Look at me. I've achieved my ends." She was sobbing now. He stroked her head. "If I told you the things that I think when I'm alone in this huge house. . . . Do you by any chance imagine that I have no feelings, that I'm a brute? I wish I were. At the beginning of my life everything and everybody conspired to make me a common bandit, an eternal rebel. But I've beaten all my enemies. Think of the time I went barefoot, ragged, with my stomach aching with hunger. What I have today I owe only to myself and nobody else."

He had an impulse to confess to her, My mother was a whore. I don't know who my father was. I could even say that my engendering cost three lunas. That was the schedule of prices of the *chingada*. They told me there was a special discount on Saturdays for the 5th Infantry soldiers.

"Don't you ever think of your wife," Rosalía asked, "your daughters, your grandchildren?"

"Of course I do, quite a lot. But my family doesn't worry me. My daughters, except the youngest, are all well married. I am a rich man. If anything should happen to me, Francisquita and the girls would be protected. I'm not without a conscience. I think of my family. If the government falls, I'll send them all to Ciudad Trujillo. Afterward they can come to this country, or go to Europe."

"And what about you?"

"I'll go to hell. But not without company. I'll take a lot of people with me."

Rosalía was toying with the little aluminum medal hanging from Gabriel Heliodoro's neck. He smiled and said, "It's the image of Neustra Señora de la Soledad, my patroness. Do you know the story of the image that's in the church in my *pueblo*? No? Well, one day there was a terrible hurricane, it seemed like the end of the world, and the sea threatened to flood the land. The vicar of Soledad del Mar said Mass in the hour of the storm, and prayed to God to have compassion on all those good folk. Throughout the entire night the high wind kept howling, the sea beating on the shore. Those who lived in the lower part of town took refuge in the houses of relatives and friends in the high part. A bolt of lightning fell on the town jail, killed two guards, and all the prisoners fled. I must have been about ten or eleven then. I stayed at the window of my hut a good part of the night, staring at the mountain where Juan Balsa was hiding with his guerrillas. I was praying, begging God to spare the revolutionaries but throw His lightning against the barracks of the 5th Infantry Regiment. When day broke the hurricane had passed, the sky was clear, the sun came out again. And then the fishermen discovered a form lying stretched out on the sand at the edge of the sea. At first they thought it was the corpse of some shipwrecked person. Then they saw that it was the wooden image of some saint, which the waves had cast up on the beach. The parish priest came and had the figure taken to the church. For a long time they tried to find out where the image had come from. Nobody could say. There was no word of any shipwreck. It could only be a miracle. Then the priest ordered the scuplture restored, and Maestro Natalicio came with his oils and painted the saint. And she was prettier than the Virgen de Macarena in the church in Seville, the patron saint of bullfighters. And the archbishop came in person from Cerro Hermoso to Soledad del Mar to consecrate the image, which received the name of Nuestra Señora de la Soledad, was placed in the church, and became the patron saint of the town—and my protector."

Gabriel Heliodoro was silent. Rosalía turned the medal in her fingers. She could not understand this man. But . . . could she understand herself?

26

GLENDA'S NOTE said only "Tomorrow at ten-thirty in the National Gallery of Art, Room 8, in front of Raphael's *Madonna de Alba*." It was Saturday. Pablo arrived first, but did not have to wait more than three minutes. They shook hands and started talking immediately about painting, as if they were picking up a conversation interrupted the evening before. Glenda said that she did not particularly admire Raphael. She thought him too Olympian, his art had the coldness of perfection, he lacked human vibrancy. What did Pablo think? He? Oh! He was in entire agreement.

They began to walk slowly, side by side, from picture to picture. In reality they were paying little attention to the paintings. They were observing each other furtively. Pablo thought Glenda very attractive, dressed in white, her hair loose, with the cool look of having just emerged from her bath.

In front of Botticelli's *Madonna and Child*, doing all he could to speak casually and not appear pedantic, Pablo remarked, "This panel was painted in Florence when Sandro Botticelli was only twenty-six."

"I have never seen in these old pictures a Child Jesus that really looked like a baby," she observed, "one that had an innocent face and limpid eyes."

Pablo agreed with a nod of his head, and cast a more prolonged and personal glance at his companion. "You're looking very well, Glenda."

"Thank you," she said. And she was on the point of adding, Was there any reason she shouldn't? But she restrained herself.

They stopped in silence before Filippino Lippi's

Adoration of the Child, and Pablo was about to remark, It
is said that Filippino was the son of Fra Filippo Lippi by a
nun whom he seduced. But he caught back the words.
Glenda seemed to take any reference to sex badly. She
could very properly reply that she was not interested in
fifteenth-century gossip.

"Ah!" he exclaimed. "Here is one of my favorite pictures."

They approached the canvas. It was the *Portrait of a
Young Man* by Botticelli.

"Don't you think, Glenda, that a whole history is written in the face of this young man? What do you see in
those eyes?"

"A mixture of curiosity, appetite for life, and perplexity—and a little fear, maybe."

Pablo wanted to take the girl's arm, but refrained.
Glenda, on her part, wanted Pablo to do so, but in a way
she liked his not taking the liberty with her so soon. And
thus they went on through the rooms in the west wing of
the museum. Glenda confessed that El Greco did not say
much to her. Pablo replied that with him precisely the
contrary occurred.

They passed, with the stride of the tourist who has
little time at his disposition, through the rooms where canvases of the Flemish painters were aligned, and Glenda
declared that she did think Rembrandt was very good.
And Pablo, who was beginning to feel impatient, felt like
shouting, Well, say so in a good, loud voice, *señorita.* The
self-portrait of Rembrandt is likely to beam out of pure
satisfaction. But he still kept silent.

What did she think of *The Girl in the Red Hat?*
Glenda admitted that when she saw Vermeer's original for
the first time, she had been rather surprised and even disappointed because of its dimensions. But she thought it a
jewel.

They halted under the great central rotunda of the
building next to the fountain, silent before each other.
Suddenly they both broke out laughing.

"What a pair of idiots we are, aren't we, Pablo?"

Then he took her arm and, dropping his formal tone entirely, he said, "Let's go look at the Post-Impressionists, Glenda. You must get used to me. I want to be your friend. It is unpleasant to be always afraid of hurting you with words or gestures." As he spoke, he was leading his friend in the direction of the Gauguins and Van Goghs of his predilection. She smiled without speaking, letting herself be led. And how good it was—Pablo felt and thought—to have that warm, perfumed body beside him. But be careful, *hombre*, be careful. On the package he was handling was an invisible sign: HANDLE WITH CARE. *Fragile*.

"When you get fed up with me," he continued, "you can tell me frankly, you can send me away, O.K.? What do you think of this self-portrait by Gauguin? Would that it were granted me to write . . . yes, and paint, too, as that fellow did. Look at those trees of Van Gogh. Don't they look human in their twisted expression of agony?"

She nodded in agreement. She was not interested in the pictures, which she had seen countless times on previous visits to the museum. She was interested in Pablo, she was positive of that now, although the idea still alarmed her a little. Oh, if they could only go on in that good comradeship, be good friends, meet periodically for long conversations. Perhaps one day she could tell him everything. Everything? No. Impossible! But at least she would have someone with whom she could communicate, although without touching on her most intimate secrets, on the sensitive core of her being, on the poisonous roots of her anguish. Ortega was a man of sensibility. Glenda liked his features, his voice, his presence. There was a nucleus of resistance in her, however, a little citadel which still held out, refusing to surrender.

"Are you tired? We could sit down awhile."

They took seats on a sofa in front of a Manet picture, a bullfighter dead in the arena.

"Pablo," she said, turning to her companion and looking into his eyes, "I must seem a very strange person to you, don't I?"

He hesitated slightly, and then nodded. But he hastened to add, "Who told you that I prefer people who are
not strange?"

"If I ask you a question, do you promise to answer
sincerely?"

"I promise."

"What do you want with me? What do I represent to
you? Can it be that, like the majority of men of your race,
age, and position, you are merely a collector of women?
Do you want to use me as a child uses a toy? What are you
after? Speak frankly. Don't be afraid of wounding or dis-
appointing me."

"Good heavens!" he exclaimed. "You ask me a dozen
questions and want just one answer? I think I might sum-
marize it all this way—I like you, I find your company
very pleasant, and I want to have you with me as frequently as possible. Satisfied?"

"You said that you like me. But isn't that just physically?"

"Well, now! You're not a picture, a melody, an idea.
You are a human being, you have a body. Is there anything wrong in my liking you in your physical, visible,
palpable manifestation?"

"Yes. Because if your interest is only physical, our
destiny is fated to be—what you know already."

He could not suppress a sigh of impatience. "Glenda,
my dear, try to understand me. I look at you, your face,
your features, your body, all that is tangible about you
attracts me. As for the rest, your mind, I still don't know
what it is like, because you keep it locked and double-
locked. You are a touch-me-not, you dodge, you fend me
off, you will not hear of intimacies. I love—there, the word
escaped me, do you see?—I love in you what I can see. As
for your spirit, it cowers behind that wall bristling with
shards of glass which you have erected between us. How
can I love what I don't know? As to what you call our fatal
destiny—I don't see why that has necessarily to be evil or
tragic."

She sat gazing silently at the dead bullfighter in the picture.

Now, for the first time, he could observe Glenda's profile close up, in detail and calmly. He imagined himself painting her portrait with voluptuous care, saw himself drawing the charcoal sketch of the gently rounded forehead, the straight, noble nose, the full lips (Where was the secret?) which were the most sensual note in that face. The girl's flesh was firm over the well-shaped bone structure of her face. Her skin did not have that whiteness, with too open pores, common to some very fair women, which on exposure to the sun takes on blotches that remind one of the bruised spots on fruit. Glenda's complexion suggested, rather, a magnolia petal, not only for its satiny texture but for its light creamy tone. And her eyes, which now expressed a serene melancholy, a kind of nostalgia, were violet in color, in lovely contrast with the deep chestnut of her hair. And Pablo concluded that if those eyes, that forehead, that face, had anything in common with the faces of the many madonnas to be seen in so many of the pictures in the museum, Glenda's lips had nothing angelic about them—they were womanly lips which he had wanted to kiss ever since the first day he had seen them. Yes, he also liked her body, of a deceptively solid slenderness, without excessive flesh, her legs long and well shaped, her hips slim. Once more he verified the fact that Glenda was even more attractive in the flesh than the image of her which he held in his memory. But why was the girl so silent and sad, gazing at the dead bullfighter?

"Listen, Glenda, you must learn not to be afraid of me. Or, rather, you must have confidence in me."

She turned her face toward her friend, who had an impulse to kiss it. "I'm not afraid of you. But I don't trust you, either."

He smiled. "All right. I propose an experiment. Let's meet more often, and talk. Oh, Glenda, really talk, without reserves, without mysteries. If after several days, or weeks, or months, as you prefer, we haven't got along well, you can then send me packing. Agreed?"

She limited herself to a shrug of the shoulders.

Leaning against a doorframe, one of the museum guards was watching them surreptitiously.

Another silence fell. And yet another time Glenda gazed at the dead bullfighter lying in the arena beside his roseate cape and his sword. Gored by a bull. Men were like bulls. They charged down upon women and tore their genital organs, their wombs. And women were left in the position of that bullfigher, lying with legs apart, inert, dead.

To the devil with it all! thought Pablo, taking one of the girl's hands in his. She looked at him with an almost startled expression, but she did not pull away.

"Glenda, my dear, let's have dinner together this evening. I'll come by your apartment to get you. O.K.?" And so that she would not start imagining things, he made it clearer, "You wait for me at the door of the building at seven o'clock sharp. O.K.?"

Glenda Doremus nodded, in an almost imperceptible affirmative. She had her eyes again on the picture. What she was seeing now was not a bullfighter but a Negro boy fallen on the ground, covered with blood, castrated, mutilated. His face had been so pounded, trampled on, that it had completely lost all semblance of a face.

"Glenda, why are you crying? Have I said anything that offended or hurt you?"

They dined that evening at the Rive Gauche. Glenda showed herself more talkative, less inhibited than usual, although she continued to avoid personal subjects. They met on other occasions, on Friday evenings or on Saturdays. One Sunday, a bright, warm day, they went to Glen Echo Park, ate hot dogs, rode on the roller-coaster, and for the first time Pablo heard Glenda laugh, laugh high and clear, like a little girl enjoying herself. And how the laughter brightened her face!

Gradually he succeeded in accustoming her to his ways, that is, to his rather irreverent and critical mental attitudes. Glenda, unlike most American girls he knew, seemed to have no sense of humor.

Now, with the first heat of summer, they found it pleasant to drive through the suburbs with the top down. They took the Mount Vernon Memorial Highway, and went as far as the historic mansion which had been George Washington's. They walked hand in hand around the Tidal Basin, lay on the grass and watched the acrobatics of the squirrels in the trees, and observed the birds. Long, dangerous silences fell between them in which, becoming aware of the solitude about them and of the presence of that young, desirable body at his side, Pablo yielded to erotic fancies which disturbed him, for he was afraid to make any gesture that might wound and put his companion to flight.

Glenda was looking up at the warm blue sky through the foliage of the trees and feeling for the first time in many months a kind of release of tension, both of muscles and of nerves. Pablo was a wonderful companion, and up to now had neither said nor done anything to disappoint her. She had often surprised herself by wishing that he would take her in his arms and kiss her. That was what she hoped and *feared* would happen one day.

But wouldn't it be better to go on as good friends? Till when? Sometimes at home, at night, she would toss and turn in bed, thinking of him, desiring his physical presence, imagining what the sensation of giving herself to him would be like. Pablo couldn't be a brute like other men. He had sensibility, he was an artist, a. . . . She ended by deciding that she had best take a cold bath and think no more about it.

The first real heat came in the last half of June. One evening Glenda and Pablo went out together, parked the car near the Tidal Basin in East Potomac Park, and walked along the river banks as far as Hains Point. They lay down on the grass under a willow and gazed in silence at the stars, and listened to the muted noise of city traffic. The warm breeze reached them, full of summer fragrances. Glenda was doing all she could to thrust out of her mind the memories of that horrible summer in Cedartown, while Pablo was surrendering wholly to memories of the summers of his childhood and adolescence. And the voices, images, and sensations of that time, evoked now by the perfume and the temperature of the night, gradually produced in him a kind of nostalgic torpor. Then, in a low, slow voice, almost as if he were talking to himself, he described to Glenda his paternal home in Cerro Hermoso, the old mansion in Spanish colonial style, full of ancient furniture and odors, with a park of cedars and centenary oaks and sad cypresses that made the boy think of cemeteries. Yes, and also the cool fountain made of tiles from Talavera de la Reina, and the stone statues that bordered the path, paved with flagstones, that led from the fountain to the veranda—the old statues that in a way were living persons out of his infant's world.

"They were the nine Muses, and I was proud of knowing the names of all, and what they stood for. Clio had one of her arms broken off. A piece was out of the mask that Thalia had in her hand. And at the age of twelve I fell madly in love with Erato, whose head was crowned with roses and myrtle, and I wrote her a poem. But when I was at the *liceo* my favorite was Melpomene. Inspired by her, I wrote my 'Greek tragedy' and put myself in the skin of the hero, a sort of Orestes pursued by the Furies."

A silence fell, in which Glenda thought, I wonder where they buried the remains of the lynched Negro? It was said—oh God, why did the summer always bring those memories to mind?—that someone had thrown the boy's genitals to the dogs, who devoured them. And Glenda shook her head from side to side, trying to drive away those black memories.

"It's odd," Pablo went on, with the image of his father now in his mind. "There are scenes of childhood, things sometimes apparently without importance, but which one never forgets. For example, one day at nightfall, it was

rather cold—Cerro Hermoso is around 2600 feet above
sea level, I was about ten or eleven years old, and leaning
out of the window of my room I was watching my father,
who was walking alone in the park, to and fro, with a
shawl over his shoulders, head down, pensive. I don't
know why, I felt enormously sorry for him. Surely because
the boy that I was had an intuition of the profound, hopeless loneliness of that man. I had an impulse to go down,
take him by the hand, and walk beside him, even without
saying a word. My timidity held me back. I never had any
real intimacy with Don Dionisio."

"What is your father like?" Glenda asked.

Pablo hesitated before answering. Did he really know
what his father was like? "A tall, lean, rather stooped man,
gaunt face, with sad eyes, long, *hidalgo* hands, a tired
voice. That, externally. As for the rest, an impenetrable
man, fond of reading, who speaks little and whom all respect. I spent my infancy hearing that I must not annoy
Don Dionisio, make no noise around Don Dionisio, cause
no displeasure to Don Dionisio, because he was very sick.
The family doctor told me one day, 'Your father is still
young enough, but his poor heart is very tired. It is a
thousand years old.' As a boy I took those words literally
and was convinced that my father's heart literally was a
thousand years old."

"And your mother?"

"If my father was, and still is to me, an almost leg-
endary figure—let us say, a shadow in the park among the
statues—my mother, completely different, has a tangible,
strong, dominating presence. A lady of imposing bearing.
She took charge of me with the efficiency of a devoted
governess. Only son, you see. She mingled petting with
demands, kisses with discipline. She even tutored me in
arithmetic. When I got to algebra, she handed me over to
Don Dionisio. I needn't tell you that I don't know any
algebra. The little that I learned has vanished. They made
me take a degree in law only because they thought—the
idea was defended principally by my mother—that a man
must have a doctor's degree, a diploma. But to get back to

Doña Isabel, she is an authoritarian, well-born, with a strong consciousness of her *rank*. (*Ah, you should hear her talk about the genealogical tree of the Ortega y Murat family!*) My mother has always been the bridge between her husband, a lonely island, and the continent of the world. A kind of interpreter. It was as though she had his power of attorney to deal with life for him. Thanks to her, the Ortega y Murat affairs prospered. And, mind you, all this in a starkly patriarchal country."

"What was your father doing while all this was happening?"

"I suspect that he was living, and still lives, nourishing fancies and repudiating reality, in a world which does not correspond to his dreams. I am convinced that Don Dionisio has a mind for the monastic vocation. He would be happy in a convent as a lay brother."

Pablo was lying on his back, his hands linked between his head and the grass. As Glenda was still silent, he went on:

"It is essential to take into account the fact that Don Dionisio since his youth has been obsessed by two terrors. One is fear of dying, and that led him to the Church. He knows theology perhaps as well as the archbishop primate. The other terror is that a Communist revolution may confiscate his property and deprive him of the freedom of worship and the other freedoms without which he could not live. But he is a profoundly good man, Glenda, believe me. He has made attempts, touching despite their disastrous failure, to communicate with me."

"And you, how did you react to those attempts?"

"Well, when I was a boy, I felt for him an affection mingled with respect and compassion. When I became a man, I rebelled. The rebellion culminated in my gesture of the Tragic Night, of which I have told you. I think I saved Gris's life not only out of friendship for my old professor, but also *against* my father and my mother, whose world was threatened by the ideas of Gris, the agnostic and socialist. Of course, I understood that only much later."

"Ah, Pablo," Glenda sighed. "How complicated life is!"

"When I was fifteen, during a vacation at Soledad del Mar, where the Ortega y Murat family has a country house and plantations, I fell in love with the daughter of a peon. She must have been my age and her name was Pía. We would wander into the cane fields, lie among the plants, eat fruits, and laugh and swap stories. And the inevitable happened, since we were living beings. One afternoon we made love in the clumsiest manner you can imagine. It was Pía who took the initiative. And then . . . we fell deeply in love with one another. We continued to meet secretly that summer, sometimes we would love in the thickets on the edge of the river and then, quite naked, we would dive into the water to swim. Odd . . . even today when I smell the odor of molasses, of green things, of earth warm from the sun, I still remember Pía. Well. One day I was discovered and informed on, and the world came crashing about me. You may imagine the reaction of Doña Isabel Ortega y Murat. Her son, flesh of her flesh, blood of her blood, misbehaving in the cane fields with the daughter of a peon! I was expelled from the Garden of Eden. My mother wept, anathematized me, and at last, wiping her eyes, she asked, 'Do you want to kill your father? Don't you know that his heart cannot bear these hurts?' She decided not to tell him of his son's 'crime.' The scandal was suppressed. Pía's father, dismissed, had to go off to another plantation with his whole family. As for me, they sent me to a Jesuit boarding school, where I learned religion and was threatened with hell fire. I believe that the two years I spent in that school laid the foundation for my agnosticism. I found religion a very sad thing, and God too severe a father. My mother's ideal was to keep me virgin until an early marriage to a girl of my class, out of which would come many children to perpetuate and assume, time out of mind, the name, the lands, and the lordliness of the Ortega y Murat family. At eighteen, when I entered the university, she had already made a list of the candidates. There were three or four, girls of great families of Cerro Hermoso. I rebelled again. With no vocation whatever for a marriage of expediency, without love, and moreover without the slightest inclination for chastity, I have had many women, not all necessarily prostitutes. But all this nauseates you, doesn't it, Glenda?"

She did not answer immediately. For an instant she had the notion that she had another mutilated man beside her. "No, Pablo. Why should it? It saddens me. I can't resign myself to the gratuitousness of life."

"The year that I was to receive my diploma in law, I had to abandon El Sacramento for the reasons you know about. And now here I am, trying to do nothing that can wound Don Dionisio's heart or Doña Isabel's pride."

He stopped. He lay looking up at the lights of a plane passing low overhead, bound for the airport, and he concluded, positively now, that Glenda had something about her physically that reminded him of Pía. The mouth, perhaps. The long legs. And yet there was a great difference in the tone of the skin. Pía was a brunette. And her eyes— what color were they? He could not remember.

"In spite of everything, you like your father more than your mother, don't you, Pablo?"

"It's curious, but I try not to think of that. It is true that I have clashes with my mother when we meet and even when we correspond. And my impatience with her causes in me a certain guilty feeling. I have always had more tenderness (*Or was it only pity?*) for my father. One of the regrets that I carry with me is that since I became an adult I never seriously attempted a more intimate communication with him."

Shapes passed under the trees. Lights twinkled on the other side of the river. Over the city rose a kind of luminous halo of yellow tinged with red.

"And do you want to go back home?" Glenda asked, feeling that the question was not addressed to Pablo alone but also to herself.

"I do and I don't. I am afraid. I think my world is very different from theirs. Or perhaps I am afraid of discovering that at heart I am like them, which would leave me disappointed in myself. It's a hellish complication."

"Some day your father has to die," Glenda murmured after some hesitancy.

"And that day my mother will discover some other type of blackmail with which she will seek to continue her dominance of my life. My father's heart will have ceased beating, his body will be in the eternal resting place of the Ortegas, and then Doña Isabel will begin to exploit the memory of Don Dionisio, which I shall have the sacred obligation to honor. Then she will tell me all the things that the old man expected of me, that is, the maintenance of the family properties, the acceptance of the economic and social system of which he was one of the strongest props . . . a system which I personally find cruel, unjust, and absurd."

"Are you a socialist, Pablo?"

"Funny how you Americans are afraid of the word socialism. And it's only of the word, because I don't know of any other country on earth more prepared for socialism than this one. In a way forms of socialism already exist here. Well, I'm going to answer your question. Label me socialist, if you will. Utopian socialist, liberal with socialist tendencies, humanist. The name doesn't interest me. What preoccupies me is the establishment of social justice. My country has nearly two million inhabitants, and, in the final analysis, it is dominated by some thirty rich families and two powerful American companies. The rest is not just silence, but misery, hunger, disease, premature death, misfortune. Do you think I can go back to El Sacramento and help maintain that state of things?"

"What other alternative is there?"

He rolled over, and lay propped on his elbows, head back. "That's what I'm trying to find out."

27

ICHEL MICHEL withdrew to his apartments and made another small entry in his personal diary:

"8:20 P.M. This afternoon G.H., winking in a manner that once more revealed his lack of breeding, ordered a special supper for two to be served at ten o'clock, after he comes down from his room with his mistress.

"When I heard the bell ring a few minutes ago and went to open the door, I had a surprise. Instead of seeing Mme. V., as I expected, I found Mlle. F. A., the beautiful blonde American, who was smiling her toothpaste advertisement smile. *Bon Dieu!* The two are now up there, possibly already stripped and rolling in the Isabeline bed—the statue of white marble and the faun of copper. Exquisite contrast! I should like to witness the scene, half through scientific interest and half in a spirit of lewdness. *Hélas!*"

Before she took off her clothes, Rosalía always demanded that Gabriel Heliodoro turn out all the lights in the room, consenting only to leaving one blue lamp burning in a corner. Frances Andersen, however, had undressed with naturalness in a tranquil striptease in the light of both the bedside lamps and the ambassador, with only a light silk bathrobe covering his body, was contemplating her from the bathroom door, foretasting the pleasure to be given him by the white, white woman. Taking into consideration his impatience, his eagerness, and his desire, his "campaign" had been a long one, and there had been moments when he had to make a strenuous effort not to explode. How many visits to caberets and restaurants, how many words murmured into each other's ears, while they danced, how many promises unfulfilled, how many feints, advances, retreats! He had given Miss Andersen several presents, jewels with semiprecious and precious stones from his country; he had had a great black pearl, found in the Gulf of Mexico, set in a platinum ring, which she was now wearing.

Frances Andersen lay on the bed completely naked, eyes closed, her breasts rising and descending in time with a breathing that to Gabriel Heliodoro seemed normal. White, so white and clean. He had never in all his life had a woman who gave him such an impression of purity, of something distant and unattainable.

He slowly approached the bed. He had nothing to say. They could make love in silence. Only the language of moans would they speak.

He sat down on the bed. Frances smiled, sensing the man's proximity. Her eyes, however, remained closed. Gabriel Heliodoro leaned over and deposited a light kiss on each of her breasts. She gave a slight shiver and automatically crossed her thighs. He stripped off his bathrobe and threw it on the floor. He spread his hand flat on the woman's belly, and enjoyed the contrast of the two skins. His hand drifted downward, but Frances kept her legs crossed, protecting her sex. He sought her mouth, but she denied it to him. He kissed her hair, her temple, her cheek, her chin, her neck, her breasts again, her belly, and then, opening herself to him, she seized his hair, moaning, with both hands as if she wished to tear it out. Then he lay down beside her, his breath coming faster, his nostrils palpitating; he embraced her, clasped her to his chest. Again he attempted to kiss her mouth, but did not succeed, for Frances threw her head back, and, nettled, he felt like biting her neck.

Can she find me repugnant? he thought. I'll teach you, you little proud white bitch. I'll tame you. And he had a ferocious desire to degrade that body, to defile it. And while he was thinking this, he was pressing her closer and closer, wholly, against his body.

"Take it easy, Gabriel Heliodoro," Frances murmured in his ear. "Don't be in such a hurry. Are you thinking about the clock? We have eternity before us. Let me breathe a little."

He released her suddenly, and turned on his back beside her. The room was air-conditioned, but he was beginning to feel his body growing moist with sweat. Frances smiled, her head turned toward him, her eyes open now.

"What did you feel when you killed your first man?"

He was almost shocked by the unexpected question. "Who told you I ever killed anyone?"

"Now, Gabriel Heliodoro, I am familiar with the story of your life. Tell me what you felt. Did you kill in cold blood, or was it in passion, in a blaze of anger?"

"I never killed anyone in cold blood."

"That's hard to believe."

"Why?"

"Because you have taken part in more than one revolution. A guerrilla usually attacks at night, by surprise. He prefers to kill sentries with a knife, noiselessly. Come, tell me what you felt."

"I don't remember the first time I killed. I have a lousy memory. I detest the past."

"But what does one feel when he kills?"

"In battle? Joy. It's almost a game. The object is to send the enemy to hell before he can do the same to you."

"And afterward? Do you feel remorse?"

"Why do you want to know these things? Do you think that, if I say I am a murderer, you are going to find more pleasure with me?"

"Who knows? I'm tired of sleeping with half men, with handsome, healthy boys who treat me as if I were half mistress and half mother. They are always so pure, innocent, and nice that they make me lose desire."

"I'm no son of yours, but neither am I your father, even if I am old enough for that. I think it's time to stop this talk."

Once more he sought Frances' mouth, but she turned away. "How many men have you killed in your life, Gabriel Heliodoro?" she asked. "How many?"

He caressed her body in all the ways he knew, but Frances remained unexcited, refusing to yield herself to him. "How many?" she repeated. "Ten, twenty, fifty?"

"I never counted!" he shouted, with an impulse to slap her.

"Well, what does one feel?"

"When I had a machine gun in my hand I squeezed the trigger, fanning out the bullets. The bodies of the ones who fell dead or wounded by my bullets were not men, but enemies. They were faceless and nameless."

"But how many?"

"Fifty, a hundred, two hundred—what does it matter?"

"And you would be capable of killing me if I refused to give myself to you now?"

"No. I don't want to kill you, I want to give you, more than you ever felt it, the feeling that you are really alive."

"But I can tell you're a murderer, Gabriel Heliodoro. Why deny it? You must have killed someone not with grenades or machine guns but your own hands. Tell me, come, tell me!"

He did not want to remember. He had buried his corpses in the graveyard of memory, in a common grave. They had no epitaphs. They deserved none. Burning with desire, he seized Frances, again crushed her against his chest, the bed creaked, and suddenly he rememberd.

"All right. I was twenty-one, and was on the run from the dictator's police, because I had taken part in a conspiracy, a frustrated attempt to throw a bomb into President Chamorro's car."

"And you were the one to throw the bomb? With your own hands, at the risk of your life?"

"There were four of us. We hadn't yet cast lots to see who would sacrifice himself. Somebody gave us away, the police raided the house where we used to meet, and my three companions were arrested, but I managed to get away."

"And if you had drawn the lot, would you have accepted the mission to kill the president and be blown to pieces by the same bomb?"

"No! I hated the dictator. His soldiers had murdered friends of mine, a lot of innocent peasants in the town where I was born. But I was very young, I wanted to live. To live, in order to go on hating. The dead can't hate."

She smiled. "Mightn't it have been you who betrayed your companions, to rid yourself of the responsibility?"

Gabriel Heliodoro again had an impulse to smash Frances' face, but he held himself in. "Your question is an insult and doesn't even deserve answering."

She now ran her hand down her lover's spine. She breathed into his ear, "Go on. You fled. Where did you find refuge?"

"In the room of a prostitute, a friend of mine. Her name was Elvira."

"What was she like? Pretty? Young?"

"Neither pretty nor ugly. Bleached hair. But she was over forty. At that time I considered her almost an old woman."

"Was she crazy about you?"

"I don't know. She liked me."

"How did she hide you?"

"In a little rented room in an old house in the red-light zone in Cerro Hermoso. The room was poor and had the smell of her body, of her cheap perfumes, of the sweat of the men who used her."

"What did you do when a customer came in?"

"Elvira used to lean over the windowsill, on the lookout for men passing on the sidewalk. Before the customer came in, I would climb up into the attic and lie hidden there among rats and spiders."

"And could you hear or see what was going on in the room while the men were in bed with your friend?"

"I tried not to. I would lie there sweating, dying of the

heat. But the ceiling was low, and there were gaps—I couldn't help hearing. The little room was like a kind of theater through which the queerest persons passed. Sexual perverts. Boys who were having a woman for the first time. Well. After the man left, I would come down and wait for the next one. By early morning, when Elvira locked her door, I was dead tired and then I could sleep in peace."

"With her?"

"There was just one bed."

"How long did this go on?"

"Two weeks, fifteen or twenty days, I don't recall. Elvira brought me food, cigarettes, even clothes. But I had to get out of the city."

"Now tell me about the man you killed."

Gabriel Heliodoro hesitated an instant.

"I don't know for sure that I did kill him."

"You said you had. Come on!"

"It could have been a dream, a nightmare."

Frances laughed. "Tell me your nightmare, then."

"One night, lying in the prostitute's bed, I felt sick, burning with fever, shaking as if from malarial chills, but I said nothing to Elvira. She was leaning out of the window. I could hear footsteps in the street. Men would stop and talk to her, they would discuss prices, and then go on their way. Then, some time later, one of them decided to come in. Elvira signaled to me. With great difficulty I climbed up into the attic, and lay down on top of one of the beams. My body ached all over, I was dazed, with chills, I think I was beginning to be delirious . . . or I went to sleep and dreamed. The customer came in. From his voice I judged him to be middle-aged. He undressed, and demanded that Elvira get completely naked. I heard the bed groan. The man started talking. He wanted Elvira to ask him something."

"What?"

" 'Make me a son.' She answered, 'Don't be silly. Get on with it.' But the man insisted, 'I'll give you two lunas more if you'll tell me you want me to make a son on you.' She asked, 'But why?' And he, 'It's just make-believe. I get a bigger kick out of it that way. Five lunas more! Say, "Make me a son, make me a son." ' Very awkwardly, she began to repeat his words. A hatred hit me all of a sudden, a loathing of that man, or, rather, of that voice. 'Say it again, "Make me a son!" Again! Ay!' And Elvira would say it again, and laugh, and say it again. And the man was grunting like an animal."

Gabriel Heliodoro picked up the tip of the sheet and wiped his forehead. "I don't recall rightly what happened then. Everything was confused. It seems I jumped down from the attic, fell on the man who was on top of Elvira, and buried the blade of my knife in his back. He screamed, Elvira screamed. I saw I was lost, my only hope was to flee. I ran to the door, out to the sidewalk, headed for the first alley, and went away from there."

"Do you think it really was a nightmare?"

"I don't know. I don't know. When day broke I was in the outskirts of the city, minus my fever, sweating, my forehead cool. I had some money in my pocket. I took a train and went to Soledad del Mar. I jumped off before the train reached the station, hid in the woods, waited until night to enter the town, where everyone knew me, and went to Padre Catalino's house because he was my friend."

"Did you tell the priest that you had murdered a man?"

"I did. It was he who told me that it might have all been the product of my delirium."

"Why?"

"Because I had no bloodstain whatever on my clothes or on my hands. And because I couldn't remember carrying a knife on me."

Gabriel Heliodoro got up, went to the bathroom, snatched up a towel, wiped his armpits and torso with it, put some deodorant under his arms, and returned to the bed.

"I stayed hidden in the church belfry two days. Padre Catalino brought me the Cerro Hermoso papers of the last three days. None of them printed the news of any crime in the red-light district. One night I managed to get out of town, climbed the Sierra, and joined Juventino Carrera's guerrillas."

The American woman smiled. "Let's suppose it was just a dream, or a delirium. Even so, what did you feel when you knifed that man?"

"It's curious. I felt something just like the joy that I got with the first woman I ever had in my life. Only quicker, more violent."

Suddenly, Frances threw herself upon Gabriel Heliodoro, kissed his lips voraciously, her tongue slithered like a reptile inside his mouth, and both wallowed on the bed, eager, panting, in a kind of wrestling match.

At that hour Pancho Vivanco was walking up and down the sidewalk on Massachusetts Avenue in front of the embassy. The heat was sultry, the air was still, a hot, humid breath was rising from the stones and asphalt. Rosalía's husband felt his shirt, soaked in sweat, sticking to his body unpleasantly. He mopped his face frequently with his handkerchief, but he did not stop walking, his eyes steadily on the ambassador's residence, his attention concentrated principally on the light in those two windows on the upper floor. There, in that room, was Gabriel Heliodoro with his American mistress, while Rosalía, the poor child, was suffering at home, her eyes swollen and red with so much weeping, sitting by the telephone waiting for a call that never came.

Vivanco halted, half panting, leaned against the trunk of a tree, and stood watching the embassy guard, who at that moment was crossing the park on his night patrol.

He imagined what was going on in the ambassador's suite at that moment. He felt an exquisitely voluptuous pleasure in thinking not only of the American woman's nudity but of Gabriel Heliodoro's. And there was an instant when he put himself in the ambassador's body and possessed the *gringa,* and at the same time, confusedly, he was the woman, and could feel the embrace of the huge man, and he was sticking a knife into his neck and bleeding him like a pig. (*Morcillas de Páramo!* See the blood

sausages from Páramo. Two *lunas* apiece. *Morcillas de Páramo!*) And when the pig was grunting and his blood was
draining away and he was turning white on the bed, he,
Francisco Vivanco, would tell him, "That's to pay you
back for all the wrong you've done us!"

He wiped his face again. The handkerchief was
soaked. His throat was burning. No. The best way would
be bullets. He would put five bullets in the monster's body.
He would be arrested and taken to El Sacramento, where
he would be tried and inevitably condemned to thirty
years in prison. Gabriel Heliodoro was a bosom friend of
the president. No jury would have the nerve to acquit his
murderer. Thirty years in a filthy penitentiary. They might
find a way to poison him. Or kill him with excruciating
tortures. No. The only way out would be suicide. He had
lost Rosalía for good. A bullet in his head? Too brutal. He
could throw himself from one of the viaducts—he could
hear the noise of his own skull striking the concrete pavement and bursting. He was enormously sorry for himself.
The best way was to take an overdose of barbiturates and
enter death through the doors of sleep.

Slowly Vivanco went up the street to Wisconsin Avenue, where he had left the car. He was thirsty. He found a
drugstore that was still open. He went in and took a seat at
the counter. He ordered a lemonade, which he drained
without stopping for breath, and then asked for a vanilla
ice cream.

"With fudge or without?" the waitress asked.

The doctor had forbidden fattening things, but Vivanco liked fudge very much. He must lose ten or twelve
pounds, at least. But what did that matter now, if he was
going to commit suicide?

"With fudge," he said resolutely.

The girl picked up a ladle and poured the hot chocolate sauce over the ice cream. Pancho began to eat it with
a boyish greediness.

Clad in his Franciscan habit, Jorge Molina was
stretched out on the floor of his bedroom, his head resting

on a pillow. The lights were out, the room temperature was springlike, and the only sound that could be heard was the humming of the air-conditioner.

It had been a fruitful evening for work, thought the minister-counselor, his eyes shut, a grand evening! After many doubts and arguments with himself, he had reached a final decision about the orientation he would follow in the composition of his biography of the archbishop primate of El Sacramento. Faithful to his original plan, he would make Don Pánfilo the hero of the story. Padre Catalino would be kept in his obscure status as a village priest, or might even not be mentioned in the book. After all, the admirable permanence of the Church in history was due to its princes, bishops, archbishops, and cardinals, men who not only knew theology but were endowed with political skill and shrewdness, a sense of history, and common sense —men who thought, spoke, and acted in the shadow, or, rather, in the light of the immense figure of the Pope. If the Church's administration were handed over to sentimental, ignorant, or innocent priests like the vicar of Soledad del Mar—and in that specific case political innocence was a mortal sin—Catholicism would slip gradually toward the left and inevitably fall into the voracious, insatiable mouth of the communist dragon.

Lying exactly in the position recommended by the yogis for putting the body into the ideal state of relaxation and repose in which it ceases to be a burden to the spirit, Molina was seeking to view, in his mind, the figures and scenes of the first chapter of his biography. He was determined not to follow a strictly chronological order. He would use the technique of certain novels, with discretion. Thus, he would write, It is nearly ten o'clock of a bright May morning in 1915. (Describe Cerro Hermoso, its colonial roofs, the towers of the churches, etc., etc. Don't forget the lake, the thin air of the plateau.) The festive pealing of the bells is heard. It is time for Mass, and a multitude fills the cathedral in the Plaza de Armas. (Describe the façade of the plateresque temple and give a rapid outline of its history.) One feels that something extraordinary is going to happen. (Perhaps I ought to put in a dialogue between two elderly gentlemen at the door of the cathedral. "You didn't know? Why, today young Father Pánfilo Arango y Aragón is to preach his first sermon." And the other, surprised, "The son of Don Ramiro?" No, no, no! Better avoid such cheap devices. The author must say in his own words what is going to take place.)

Molina *sees* the scene. More than that, he hears all the sounds, breathes all the smells that fill the cathedral. The baroque altars laminated with gold. The light of the candles in the candelabrum. The sculpturing of the inside columns of the temple. The ancient images—some of them two or three centuries old—in their niches. The smoke and the odor of incense. The sound of the organ swelling in the cathedral. *Cathédrale Engloutie.* (Curious how some words are inevitably associated with certain others in our mind.) The Mass begins. Then comes the moment awaited by all, when young Padre Pánfilo mounts to the pulpit. A stifled murmur goes around the congregation. Someone coughs. A bench creaks. Another cough. Then silence. Padre Pánfilo, splendid in his chasuble embroidered with gold thread (a present from Doña Rafaela Chamorro), looks out over his audience. He lifts his arm in a dramatic gesture, and his deep, masculine voice fills the interior of the cathedral. (See exact text of his first sermon. Found in first volume of his *Sermons and Pastorals*.) Show the reaction of the faithful, describe the expression on some of the faces seen from Don Pánfilo's viewpoint. Analyze the sensations of the young priest as he pronounces his famous sermon against war and violence, condemning Juan Balsa and his bandits.

What about the second chapter? It would be interesting for the author to jump backward in time and take the reader to the Arango mansion (1890), where the wail of a newborn infant can be heard.

But the house that the minister-counselor now has in mind is not the mansion of old Don Ramiro, but his own home. A newborn baby's cry is heard, and with it the sobs of a man. That man is his own father.

Jorge Molina surrendered wholly to a thought from which he always sought to flee—his mother had died in giving birth to him.

28

I N THAT LAST half of June, smothered by a heat wave that lasted nearly two weeks, Washington was like a lighted oven. It was a massive heat, humid, sticky and implacable, which reached its highest temperatures around four o'clock in the afternoon and continued on into the night without the slightest relief, and retained the same intensity the next day.

Gabriel Heliodoro fled to one of the beaches in Virginia and took Frances Andersen with him.

Rosalía Vivanco, grown thin, spent her days alone, shut in her home, lying on the bed looking at magazines with vague attention, alternating crises of carnal desire with crises of weeping. When her husband came back from the chancellery, she would bolt herself into the bedroom and refuse to see him. Pancho would then pace back and forth in the living room, in torture. At times he would sally out into the night, dine alone in a restaurant, and then walk along the banks of the Potomac, thinking of throwing himself into its waters and letting himself drown. When he returned home and his wife again repulsed him, he would whimper for some minutes before her locked door, and then go examine the revolver he had bought recently, and once more would imagine the scene in which he murdered Gabriel Heliodoro. There were nights, though, when his sexual desire was so intense that he masturbated, eyes closed, lying on the sofa, thinking of Rosalía naked in the arms of the ambassador.

Molina hardly felt the heat. He continued the routine of his lonely life, and now was particularly happy, for he had succeeded in writing three chapters of his biography of Don Pánfilo to his own satisfaction.

On Sundays he went to Mass in the Church of St. Thomas in Georgetown. He would kneel, pray, strive with all his senses to penetrate the mystery of the Mass, and think how good it would be if he could only seek out a priest, confess to him, cleanse his head and his heart, and then enjoy the privilege of communion. Why did God refuse to exist in his brain as an idea, if He existed as a sentiment in his heart?

The Ugartes also took refuge at a beach, where the general easily found partners for chats and poker, *gente de habla española*. Meanwhile Ninfa, exhibiting her fat in a bathing costume she had bought at a sale at Woodward & Lothrop's, gazed at the sea, sighed with longing for Aldo Borelli, and tried—though without any success—to catch the fancy of the young, athletic lifeguards.

Titito, now, remained in Washington, full of a nimble gaiety and squirrel-like mischievousness. He told his friend Clare Ogilvy that he was making ready to give at his apartment, decorated in pink and black, a party that would be famous in the annals of Washington. "Just for men," he explained, half shutting his eyes and smiling meaningly. "And do you know who the guest of honor is? Guess." Miss Ogilvy shook her head; she could not imagine. Titito then, exalted, tossed his bombshell. "Vic Troy!" She knew that this was one of the most popular movie stars of the moment, a "big boy," six feet, six inches tall, broad-shouldered, with blond hair and rather feminine features. Women were crazy about him. When they met him they assaulted him hysterically, tore his clothes, cut off his tie and even locks of his hair; they wanted souvenirs of their idol, of that marvel of the human species. So Vic Troy, whom Titito had met shortly before at an intimate party in New York, had accepted the invitation to come to

Washington early that fall to take part in Mr. Villalba's party. Wasn't he a love? La Ogilvita shrugged. She felt jaded. She could see her plans going down the drain; she had hoped to make her vacation coincide with the music festival at Aspen, Colorado. Merceditas and the other stenographers were out of town, in the mountains. The chancellery was as silent as a tomb—and a tomb in the middle of the Sahara Desert. "Oh, Titito, how I envy your enthusiasm. To be thinking of a party in this heat!" But the second secretary was not discouraged. "It's going to be a kind of *bal masqué*, transvestite, you understand?" Did she understand!

Orlando Gonzaga had left Washington to spend his vacation in Brazil. It was very convenient for him—he told Pablo—to flee that inferno on the banks of the Potomac to enjoy the amenities of the *inverno,* using his Portuguese for the pun, of Rio de Janeiro.

Godkin was leading his usual life. Sometimes he would meet Pablo for lunch or dinner. To Godkin, the young man seemed preoccupied. One evening he put his finger directly in the wound.

"The affair with Glenda's not going well, eh?"

"Word of honor, Bill, the more I see of that girl, the less I understand her. There are times when she seems to have fallen for me, ready for anything. And suddenly she acts as if she hates me."

"Aren't you afraid . . ." the newspaperman hesitated. "Excuse my butting into your private affairs, but aren't you afraid of complicating your life by getting involved with a—ah, ah—neurotic?"

"Yes, a little. But I'm going to get involved, or, rather, I am already. I feel an almost obsessive physical attraction for that girl."

"Do you think she—well, I mean—has already had some sexual experience?"

"If she has, it was something quite disastrous, which brought about a trauma that she hasn't yet recovered from."

"These women of ours from the South are more complicated, let's put it, than those from the West or the Midwest. I believe the presence of the Negro—"

Pablo quickly interrupted his friend. "Don't you think that Glenda's problem has a lot to do with her hatred of the Negro? One day I commented on a newspaper article about a children's book that an Alabama state senator demanded be burned just because in one of its stories a white bunny marries a black bunny. Naturally I said I thought it was absurd, ridiculous. Glenda looked at me with a furious expression and cried, 'Are you a nigger-lover, too?' "

Godkin shook his head slowly.

"The other day," Ortega went on, "we were walking along, hand in hand, looking at the victoria regias, the hyacinths, and water lilies in Kenilworth Gardens, when suddenly I took Glenda in my arms, kissed her, and waited for the worst sort of reaction from her, a slap, an insult. . . . But no. The girl accepted the kiss, and in an active way, you understand? My blood was up, my body throbbing with desire. I've told you before, Bill, that the color green combined with the blue of the sky and the smell of grass, of plants, fruits, of nature, in short, are things that excite me sexually. Glenda, feeling my desire in what might be called tangible form, thrust me away. Sometimes I think that what frightens her in me is the color of my skin. She must surely imagine that I have Negro blood in my veins."

"Poppycock. You have Spain written on your face."

The heat wave had been oppressive for several days, and according to the papers it already had been the cause of more than ten deaths.

One afternoon, sitting at the steering wheel of his car, his shirt soaked with sweat, his eyes clouded, his skull bursting with pain, Pablo Ortega was waiting at a corner for the traffic policeman's signal when he saw the officer fall, the victim of a sunstroke. He returned home with the feeling that he was going to faint. He lay down to sleep dressed as he was, had obsessive, feverish dreams, and did not wake until the following morning, his head and chest relieved. He found that a torrential rain had fallen during the night and the air was now clean, cool, and light, and the city and the world seemed relieved of an infernal nightmare.

To celebrate his reconciliation with the summer season, Pablo composed a *haikai* and sent it to Kimiko Hirota.

SUMMER
Bright green fly,
Ripe fruit on the ground . . .
Oh, honey of life!

Glenda Doremus, however, persisted in giving him gall instead of honey. There were times when her stomach acid seemed to infect her ideas and words. Pablo's headaches were aggravated now when he was with the Georgia girl. On their walks together they frequently went into a drugstore, she to take an Alka-Seltzer and he, one or two aspirin. Once Ortega muttered, depressed, "Sometimes I try to imagine what would result from a cross of your stomach-aches and my headaches." To his amazement and delight, Glenda burst out laughing.

The next day, late in the afternoon, they were driving along Connecticut Avenue bound for the Chinese restaurant where they had decided to dine, when Pablo stopped the car at the curb in front of his apartment house. He unexpectedly embraced Glenda, kissed her voraciously, and felt desire in the way she responded to his kiss. Then he dared to say, "Shall we go up to my apartment?" She lowered her eyes and nodded. Pablo at first could not believe his eyes. But Glenda jumped out of the car to the sidewalk and headed straight for the door of the building. In the elevator they kept silent. They did not even look at each other. She lit a cigarette with shaking hands. He felt the hammering of his blood in his temples in a desperate desire for the girl.

They entered the apartment.

"Make yourself at home," Pablo said, closing the door. But he himself did not feel at ease. To be doing something, he began to show Glenda his books, confusedly, and his pictures, his records, his figures from the hand of Maestro Natalicio. Did she like Vivaldi? They could listen to a record. . . .

In saying these things he heard his voice becoming thicker than usual. It was a good thing Glenda was keeping her back turned to him, because his desire had now taken on a grotesque, visible shape, like a deformity.

Suddenly Glenda turned around and exclaimed, "Please, Pablo, let's not pretend to each other that we don't know why we came here!"

Without saying another word, Pablo crushed her to his chest, kissed her lips, and then, lifting her in his arms, carried her to the bedroom and placed her on the bed. She lay there motionless, eyes closed, in the half-light. He sat down beside her, and lightly and repeatedly kissed her eyelids, her cheeks, and then, with more force, her lips, in a long kiss. Glenda's arms, which until then had been lying inert along her body, rose, and she caught Pablo's head in both hands.

"I can't stand it any longer," she moaned softly. "I must get rid of this doubt . . . or I'll go crazy."

"Take it easy, darling, take it easy," he whispered.

"Don't treat me as if I were a child. I am a woman."

She opened her eyes, dimmed now by a lustrous cloud of desire. Pablo then began to undress her. He took off her shoes, then her stockings, and was about to unbutton her blouse when Glenda pushed him away with a gesture and said, "Go out of the room a few minutes. I'll undress myself."

He obeyed. When he came back he found her naked, huddled under the sheet. He lay down, also nude, beside the warm, quivering body. It all seemed unreal to him. The semidarkness of the room, the continuous humming of the air-conditioner, the picture of Doña Isabel on a bedside table ("A son of mine committing immoral acts in the cane fields with the daughter of a peon! Do you want to kill your father?"). Glenda was doubled up, her back toward him, with her hands between her thighs. Pablo took

the same posture, pulled the girl's body into the concave
formed by his own body, and kissed the back of her neck,
the lobe of her ear, caressed her breasts, and then tried to
get her to straighten out. Glenda, however, remained as
she was.

"Please . . ." he whispered.

She said plaintively, "Be patient, Pablo. I'm scared."

He continued to kiss her—shoulders, arms, back—
while his hands slid down along the girl's thighs, and his
fingers sought the spot which she continued to shield.

From outside came the sound of automobiles rolling
down the avenue, and from time to time the snorting of
the pneumatic doors of the buses as they opened and shut
at the bus stop on the next corner.

Suddenly, Glenda turned over and embraced Pablo,
not as a lover who surrenders but like a little girl begging
for protection. And with a different voice she exclaimed,
"You've got to understand! A horrible thing happened to
me when I was a child."

He stroked her hair.

"All right, Glenda, whatever it was, I'll understand.
Tell me."

He felt against his chest the accelerated beating of
that poor lonely heart. Glenda opened her mouth to speak,
but for a moment her jaws locked as if paralyzed, her lips
trembled in a nervous stutter, and not the slightest sound
came out. Suddenly she recovered her voice and exploded.

"I was raped by a Negro!"

A fraction of a second before Glenda began the sentence, Pablo had already divined it. (Or had it been an
illusion?) He continued to stroke the girl's head, murmuring, "Tell me, tell me all about it." She rested her scalding
hot face on his chest, and went on.

"I must have been about thirteen."

She fell silent. Pablo felt that he might encourage her
with a casual question.

"Was it in your home town?"

"Yes. In Cedartown. A hired hand, a boy, a Negro,
worked at our house. His body smelled bad, his thoughts

were dirty, his eyes were mean, they undressed me, followed me, soiled me."

"Yes, Glenda, and then?"

"One day I was playing by myself in the backyard in a kind of barn, and he suddenly appeared. He came toward me, saying nasty things, making horrible gestures. I tried to scream, but couldn't. I tried to run, but I was paralyzed. The Negro pushed me down, lifted my dress, and . . . and . . . I don't know what he did to me, I fainted with terror."

Pablo kissed her hair, holding her close in his arms. She seemed to be burning with fever.

"When my father found me lying on the ground, I don't know how long afterward, I told him that I had been attacked. I had heard of cases like that, things that happened to other girls. My father was like a man possessed, blind with hate. He gathered relatives, neighbors, friends, and they all went out hunting the Negro all through the city."

Suddenly Glenda pulled away from Pablo's arms, whirled over and lay face down, her face against the pillow.

"It was frightful," she said in a smothered voice. "They found the Negro hidden in an abandoned house, and they castrated him. They broke his arms, his legs, they beat him so hard with clubs, and kicked him in the face so much he was unrecognizable."

She stopped, gave vent to a flood of tears, and her body was shaken with sobs.

Pablo felt a strange, sudden inhibition, as if that revelation had made Glenda's body untouchable.

"How many years ago did this happen?"

"Fifteen."

"Glenda, darling. Try to forget all the things that happened so long ago. Think this way, *'I wasn't to blame!'* You can't spend the rest of your life enslaved to that terrible past. Shake it off."

Persuasive, he succeeded in getting Glenda to turn on her back, with her face uncovered. Her eyes were closed, however, and tears were running down her cheeks.

"Do you want a cigarette?" he asked.

"No."

"Open your eyes. Face up to life. You were absolutely not to blame for what happened."

She pulled the tip of the sheet up to her forehead, but he bared her face again.

"Pablo, try to understand."

"I understand. It's you who don't *want* to understand. Your body is young, you can't keep on denying the pleasure that it demands. Don't be ashamed of your flesh, Glenda. What's past is past. Imagine that you have just now been born, this instant. You just can't imagine how much I love you!"

As he spoke these words, he seized the tip of the sheet covering her, snatched it away, and threw it on the floor. Glenda remained still, her breasts erect, her belly smooth, her waist slender, her thighs long and rounded. Pablo felt desire flood back into him in a wave so violent that he had to make an effort not to throw himself on the woman like an animal.

He then began to excite her with caresses, and when he felt that she was ready to receive him, he covered her. Glenda resisted for a few seconds, but at last, biting her lips, her eyes still shut, she surrendered. Even so, when he began to penetrate her she cried out, "No!" and tried to thrust him away from her, but he seemed now desirous of transfixing her in a kind of punitive fury, and she continued to moan, "No, no, no!" as her nails lacerated Pablo's back, and just at the moment when he sensed the oncoming of the orgasm, she managed to free herself, jumped out of bed, wrapped herself in the sheet, ran to a corner of the room, and huddled there, crouching, trembling like a frightened child, while the man spilled the sap of his love on the sheet, spasmodically, face down, panting, exasperated by the woman's behavior and at the same time feeling the ridiculousness of the whole affair. And when, moments later, dazed and frustrated, he sat up in bed, he had a shock on seeing an unmistakable bloodstain on the sheet.

"Glenda, you were a virgin!"

She neither spoke nor made the slightest movement.

"Why, I don't understand," he muttered, at the same time that a horrible suspicion burst in his mind.

He rose, and finding himself ridiculous in his nudity, donned the bathrobe which he had left at the foot of the bed. His back burned as if it had been scorched.

"But didn't you say . . ." he began.

Glenda picked up her garments in silence, went into the bathroom, and closed the door. Pablo sat down in a chair, confused and shaken, lit a cigarette, and began to smoke and coordinate his thoughts, afraid of what he might discover. Could it be possible, what he was imagining?

He heard the noise of the shower. He got up, went to the window and stood there gazing out. The city lights were already on, but there was still a vague ruddy glow on the horizon.

When, minutes later, Glenda emerged from the bathroom completely dressed, and started toward the living room, he followed her.

"You are not leaving here without giving me an explanation."

"You men are all alike! You all want the same thing from a woman. Pigs!"

"Glenda, that nastiness can be only in your mind."

"What?"

"In your imagination. You were never raped."

Now in her face was an expression of terror mixed with alarm. She sat down on the sofa and continued to regard Pablo with a lost look.

"Come, Glenda, tell me the truth."

She hid her face in her hands.

"Please, Pablo, don't torture me."

"I only want to help you rid yourself of a nightmare. You have been the captive of a hallucination, of a lie!"

"Well, he was a filthy Negro. He kept spying on me. Stole my underwear, took them to his room. He was an animal. The stink of him kept after me night and day, day and night."

Pablo went to her, seized her forcibly by the shoulders, shook her, and made her look at him. "But he never *touched* you. Tell the truth!"

"He was a nasty Negro, he thought and did dirty things. He stank up the whole house."

"But he didn't touch you!"

"Stop that, Pablo, for the love of God!"

"Confess, it was all a fantasy of yours."

"I don't know, I don't know, leave me alone, I don't know."

"You don't *want* to know, but you've got to face the facts. Confess that the boy didn't even touch your body."

"How do I know? I was a little thirteen-year-old girl."

"Why didn't you stop your father and the others from going after that boy?"

"I didn't know they were going to kill the Negro!"

Pablo could not control himself. "You knew!" he roared. "You knew and wanted it to happen!"

She stretched out on the sofa and burst into tears again. He was pacing back and forth in the room, from one side to the other. What to do? What to do? Continue torturing Glenda with his questions? Send her away, leave her alone?

He sat down beside her, again stroked her hair with his hand, making every effort to speak in a paternal tone.

"Now it's best to tell everything, to unburden yourself of this weight you have on your conscience. Tell me one thing. After that . . . that deed . . . weren't you examined by a doctor?"

She hesitated for some seconds and at last assented, with eyes closed, "Yes."

"And he verified the fact that you hadn't even been touched, didn't he?"

She did not reply. She kept on crying, now in convulsive sobs.

"Did he, or not?"

Suddenly Glenda turned her contorted face to him and cried, "Yes! It's true! Everybody found out the whole story. My father and the others were brought to trial, and were acquitted. But we had to leave Cedartown. That ruined our lives for all of us, my father's, my mother's, mine. Are you satisfied? Are you satisfied?"

"Glenda, I've already told you, all I want is to help you."

"Nobody can help me. Not even God."

"Don't say such a thing. I feel responsible for you. Now more than ever."

"If you talk to me about marriage, because . . . of what happened, I'll laugh in your face."

Glenda rose, caught up her purse, stood for an instant looking from side to side as if stunned.

Once more he lost his self-control. "When all is said and done, you have realized the secret desire of your childhood—you have been violated by a sordid fellow with a dark skin. Now I am the one to ask whether you are satisfied."

"But who can assure me that what occurred just now in your room wasn't another fantasy of mine?"

"Glenda, be reasonable. Let me help you."

She gazed at him in silence for some moments and then said in a rage that could be sensed in the way she bit off her words, "You may have helped me more than you think. You have convinced me that, in reality, I don't feel as much remorse as I thought, for what they did to that other Negro."

She stalked to the door. He made no gesture to detain her.

29

PABLO ORTEGA had no recollection of ever having passed a more unpleasant week in his whole life than the one that followed his incident with Glenda Doremus. When he woke in the mornings, after a sleep disturbed by confused and troubled dreams, his head ached dully. In the chancellery he avoided talking with his colleagues and spent minutes on end staring at the telephone, both wishing and not wishing to call Glenda. He thought, If I do call, what am I going to say? And was there any more to say after all that had occurred? Wouldn't it be better, both for him and for her, if they ceased seeing each other?

He could not concentrate on his work. At times he would spend entire hours filling up his memo pad with designs: Glenda's profile, just as he had seen it that day in the National Gallery; a narrow, tortuous street going down to the beach (Soledad del Mar); Maestro Natalicio's face; the figure of a bent man under cypresses; Glenda again, her eyes and her mouth, especially her mouth.

Frequently he stuck an aspirin tablet in his mouth. Now and then he would close his eyes, lean back in his swivel chair, listen to the air-conditioner humming, and recall that late afternoon. He felt the need of unburdening himself to someone. But to whom? And would he have the courage to tell *everything*, no matter to whom? Gonzaga was still out of the country, but even if he could see him within the hour, he would not have the nerve to confess to him, for he knew that his Brazilian friend would certainly end by laughing at his problems. ("Oh, Pablo, you complicate the simplest things. The whole mystery of women lies more in the timid minds of men than in feminine hearts.") Godkin? Ortega admired and respected the journalist, but he could foresee his reaction to the terrible story. Bill would listen attentively, placidly smoking his pipe, and then would grumble something affectionate but neutral. Gris! Yes, Gris was the man. He could lay himself bare with his old professor as to a father. Father?

One morning he asked the operator for an outside line and dialed the number of the exile's apartment, but got no answer. He called the office at the university, and a feminine voice informed him that Dr. Leonardo Gris at that hour must be at home, for he had classes only in the afternoon.

Pablo left his office and went out along the hall, head down, lost in thought. When he returned to consciousness he was in Clare Ogilvy's office.

"Pablo Ortega y Murat!"

"Is the ambassador in?"

"No. He went to the Pan American Union with the minister-counselor. That Nicaragua case still . . ."

Pablo sat down beside his friend's desk, and she offered him a cigarette. He declined with a shake of the head.

"You can fool the others," she said, "but not me. I've been watching you for days. What's your problem?"

"There's no problem," Pablo muttered, hoping that she would insist on the question, *forcing* him to tell her everything.

"Glenda Doremus?"

He nodded, and immediately poured out the whole story, omitting no detail, even the most scabrous. He ended his narrative with a question. "Do you think I did wrong?"

La Ogilvita raised her eyebrows, looked at him with her water-gray eyes, and gradually her equine features softened. "You acted like a normal man. Glenda reacted like a neurotic. Moreover, as far as Negroes are concerned, more than half the white population of this country enter- tains fantasies either identical or similar, or distantly re- lated, to this girl's imaginings. Now if you want to be the Lamb of God and take up all the world's sins on your shoulders . . . well, don't count on me to chant the *miserere nobis.*"

"But what should I do now?"

"Nothing. Let time solve the problem."

"But I consider myself responsible for Glenda."

"If it's on account of that anatomical detail of vir- ginity, rest your mind, boy, for in this country that's not taken as seriously as in the so-called Latin world. And if you want me to carry my frankness further, I'll add that no woman in her right mind and with all her apparatus functioning normally would refuse your love, Pablo, my impossible passion."

She laughed. But he started shaking his legs nervously.

"Stop that St. Vitus dance, man!"

Pablo obeyed. Then he growled, "I'd like to know how and where Glenda is. I'm afraid she may do something crazy."

"Wait," La Ogilvita said, reaching for the telephone and giving a number to the embassy operator. Waiting for the ring to be answered, the receiver to her ear, she winked at Pablo now and then as if she were about to play a prank.

"Hello. Pan American Union? I'd like to speak to Miss Glenda Doremus." A pause. "Yes." Another, longer pause. "When? Ah! Many thanks." Clare replaced the phone in its cradle and looked at her friend.

"Miss Doremus resigned her job irrevocably more than a week ago and three days ago returned to her parents' home in Atlanta."

"Now what?"

"Do you really want a piece of advice? Take a vacation. Take a few books—nothing serious, just detective stories, science fiction—and go to the mountains or the seashore. Walk, paint, write verses, and forget that girl."

Pablo Ortega easily obtained leave to enjoy two weeks of vacation. The ambassador was most cordial. "Why, sure, man! All the time you want! Two weeks, or even three. Go get some rest."

Pablo packed his bags, threw in a few books, his paints, brushes, canvases, and old notebooks with charcoal and pencil sketches. He set out in his Thunderbird without definite destination, and finally stopped at a quiet motel near the Skyline Drive in Virginia, overlooking the Shenandoah Valley. There were many tourists there, whom Pablo avoided, reluctantly noting that since Glenda had called him a Negro, he felt rather ill at ease in the company of Americans, especially southerners, with their easily recognized accent. What idiocy! He knew non-Negro Americans with skin darker than his.

In the little motel he led his own life. He had a room with windows overlooking the valley. In the mornings he took long walks, and before lunch he swam in the pool. In the early afternoon he read or slept, and when the sun was starting downward he would climb a mountain to watch the sunset from the top.

One day he decided to paint. He set up his easel, prepared his palette, and thought about reproducing on canvas the immense valley, unfolding its enormous space before his eyes with so many tones of green, blue, brown, and red meeting in a kind of chromatic congress, in which the day's light always had the last word.

At first he was inhibited, as if someone caught his hand and prevented it from putting brush to canvas. He thought of his first paintings—tempera and watercolor—made during summer vacations on the family plantations in Soledad del Mar. His favorite subject was the town and its inhabitants—the whitewashed houses on the slope of the hill, its narrow, tortuous streets through which he had so often seen religious or funeral processions filing past. They were scenes in which the picturesque and decorative predominated—the whitewashed walls of yards and houses, the blue of the sky, the purplish shadows, the women in black, the men in white, the children barefoot and ragged, and here and there the scarlet, pink, or yellow of a flower, a rug, or a sheet. Later, in his Paris "exile," he had forgotten Soledad del Mar, the cane fields, the Sierra de la Calavera on the horizon, and gradually the human figures disappeared from his pictures—yes, and from his verses, too, which formerly had followed the same theme as his canvases—and he had entered his abstract phase. Then he had only colors to cope with, and his paintings, as a critic had reminded him, looked like labyrinths, while "in his poems the theme of the maze was repeated in arid and tortuous verbal corridors, in a kind of chaos of sound, without the remotest hope of a way out into the open air of the human dimension."

Now what to paint? Pablo asked of his blank canvas. He consulted his book of sketches made on his last visit to Soledad del Mar. In it he found several faces—Padre Catalino's, Maestro Natalicio's, the artist's children. . . . Also in the sketchbook were many other children's faces, and only now did Pablo see how gaunt they were, how sad and how sickly they looked. He had used those faces as decorative elements in several pictures of his early phase—*Children Playing Ball, The Little Girl and the Flower, Blind-Man's Buff.*

He selected a charcoal stick and began drawing on the canvas. In the foreground he sketched the face of a boy and in the background the perspective of a street down which came a funeral procession of poor people accompanying a little coffin of rough wood. The sketch completed, Pablo began painting without conscious plan, and what resulted from half an hour's work left him startled. As he painted the eyes of the foreground face, he had remembered the children suffering from trachoma whom he had so often encountered as a boy on his strolls around Soledad del Mar. On those occasions, more sickened than pitying, he would turn his face away and close his eyes so as not to look at the sorry, unpleasant picture. And hadn't that always been his attitude when confronted by all the miseries of his land—close his eyes and turn his head away? And now, as he painted the first human image in the last seven years, what emerged from his brush was the yellowish face of a child whose hypertrophied eyelids, of a granular texture, looked like horrible purulent raspberries. And those eyes were now gazing steadily at him, and Pablo felt that he was a prisoner, no longer of his literary and esthetic labyrinths, but of those pupils dulled by pus. He painted a fly on one of the raspberries and two more on the emaciated cheek. (He and Pía used to eat raspberries in the forests of the Garden of Eden, while green horseflies flitted about their naked bodies.) In a kind of frenzy Pablo set himself to painting the background faces, a procession of tragic countenances—men, women, and children, all with their ulcerated eyes accusingly focused on the man who was painting them.

One of the vacationists from the motel, seeing Pablo at his easel, approached, eager, perhaps imagining that he was painting the tranquil Shenandoah Valley, but when she saw the boy's face in the picture, her face wrinkled in a grimace of repugnance, she uttered an exclamation of distaste, turned her back, and went off.

That night Pablo dreamed that he was walking blindly through the narrow, twisted streets of a nocturnal city in which he recognized now Soledad del Mar, now the cemetery of Cerro Hermoso. He was carrying in his arms a sick child burning with fever, and the child was at one and the same time himself and the boy in the picture. He stumbled at every step, he was lost in a blind labyrinth, he sought in vain for a light, the warmth of a human presence, he beat his aching head at doors, which opened to emit figures of faceless men whom he silently asked where the doctor was, because he needed a doctor to save the child, and the faceless men shrugged their shoulders and shook their heads negatively, for none seemed interested in saving the sick child's life.

He awoke early. His head ached, his eyelids were heavy, his vision was clouded, and he could not clearly make out his own image in the mirror. Still dazed with sleep, he felt that he was going blind. Almost alarmed, he washed his eyelids with cold water and then put some drops of collyrium in his eyes, blinked for a little, and felt reassured only when he verified that his vision was still normal.

Then he tried to fish up from his memory—vague and evasive fishes—details of the night's dream. He remembered that whenever a door opened, the name he pronounced was Dr. Ashy. Why that? Of course! The doctor he sought, Dr. Ashy, was Dr. Gris—Dr. Gray, in his dream-name Dr. Ashy. He smiled at the discovery.

At the cafeteria table he cast his net deeper, and

brought up another fish. Dr. Martínez, the old doctor for
the Ortega y Murat family—dead nearly twenty years—
whenever he was summoned to diagnose some indisposi-
tion of the child Pablo, used to sit down on his bed, order
him to open his mouth wide, and say "Ah!"; take his pulse,
stick the thermometer under his armpit, and when his
medical functions were finished he would tell the boy stories. Pablo's favorite one was *Cinderella*; hence the mental
link of cinder-ash, ashy-gray, gray, Dr. Gris. Pablo used to
attribute to Dr. Martínez the faculties of a magician. His
mere presence in the room made him feel better; it was
like the company of Leonardo Gris for the adult Pablo.
And was it not Gris, as it happened, who was thinking of a
"remedy" to save the children and the fathers of the children of all El Sacramento? Perhaps that interpretation of
the dream was wrong, but the truth was that he *wanted* to
accept it as valid.

That morning he did not even glance at the canvas
painted the day before. He went out walking, and took
with him a little book which Kimiko Hirota had given him,
A Chinese Garden of Serenity, the reflections of a Zen
Buddhist. He climbed the slope of a hill, sat down under a
tree, sat for a moment contemplating the valley, and then
opened the book at random and read: "When the wind
blows in the sparse patches of bamboo, the canes do not
retain the sound of the wind. When the wild geese fly over
a cold lake, the water does not hold the shadow of the
birds that have passed. So the mind of the superior man
begins to function only when something happens; and it
becomes a vacuum when the event ends." Pablo raised his
eyes and thought of Glenda. What could she be doing at
that exact instant? He lowered his head again: "In every
human heart [he heard Kimiko's tiny voice reading those
same words] exists a Book of Truth bound with worn-out
strings and torn bamboo papers. In every human heart
there also exists a Nature Symphony smothered by sensual
songs and voluptuous dances. A man must sweep out all
that is external and search his innermost self in order to
find happiness."

He closed the book impatiently. How could anyone sit with legs crossed like a Zen Buddhist, making that mystical dive into his inner lake, completely alien to the misfortunes and injustices of the so-called external world? And if he, Pablo, shut his eyes now and dived into his own well, what would he find there? The pearl of wisdom, the very heart of truth, or merely the purulent eyes of the children of Soledad del Mar?

The luminous, tranquil spaciousness of the valley augmented his feeling of loneliness. He closed the book, got up, and returned to the motel.

In the central foyer, sitting around a radio, several guests were listening to the ten o'clock news. Pablo, who had not read a newspaper since his arrival several days before, took no interest in what the announcer's deep, well-modulated voice was saying. At the desk he asked for his key, and was already on his way to the stairs when the sound of a name—Leonardo Gris—caught his ear, stopping and holding him like a lasso, forcing him to pay attention to the voice.

". . . exiled politician of El Sacramento who for several years has been professor of Latin American history and literature at American University in Washington, D. C., is still missing. Professor Gris, who in numerous articles and lectures has strongly accused that Caribbean republic's present government of corruption, was seen for the last time five days ago by the girl at the desk of the building where he has his apartment. The police, notified of the fact, started investigating to discover the whereabouts of Dr. Gris. The theory that the ex-secretary of education of El Sacramento may have been the victim of an accident seems definitely out as being probable. The theory has been put forward that Dr. Gris has left the country of his own volition, but this also appears quite unlikely. Some papers are beginning to ask whether it may not be a new Galíndez case. As our hearers are doubtless aware, Dr. Jesús Galíndez, a professor at Columbia University, disappeared mysteriously on the eve of the publication of his work in which he made highly compromising accusations against the government of the Dominican Republic. Later, the police of the United States discovered clues that Dr. Galíndez had been kidnapped and taken out of the country, and possibly murdered, by agents in the pay of General Leonidas Trujillo. The ambassador of El Sacramento in Washington wrote a letter to the paper protesting the insinuation, which he considers absurd as well as insulting."

Pablo was stunned. In a certain prescient fashion he was expecting this to happen. He started slowly up the stairs, his throat contracted, his mouth dry. He no longer had any doubts. Gris had been kidnapped and now was possibly dead. He thought of the man in the light raincoat who used to trail the professor. It must have all been the work of Ugarte, the scoundrel!

He calculated that he could reach Bill Godkin at that hour at his office. He put in a call for Amalgamated Press. Within a few minutes he had his friend on the other end of the wire.

"Bill? Pablo Ortega. I have just heard over the radio the news of Dr. Gris's disappearance. Tell me what happened, will you? Is there any hope?"

"Pablo, old man, it looks pretty bad to me. At first it was thought that there might have been an accident—but if it was, the body would have been found, one way or another. Five days—you understand."

"Have the police searched Dr. Gris's apartment?"

"Naturally. They found everything in order. No sign of violence. His suits are in his closet, with the luggage— the underwear and so on in the drawers. His reading glasses were on his desk."

"And what does the embassy say?"

"It alleges that it knows absolutely nothing. And that Dr. Gris was not even registered as a member of the Sacramentan colony in Washington."

"Don't you think it may be a case like that of Dr. Galíndez?"

Godkin seemed to hesitate. "Well . . . it's what we think here at Amalpress."

"Ugarte, that ruffian, must have been the mastermind of the kidnapping."

"The general has been out of town for more than two weeks."

"Of course! To avoid suspicion. He's a dirty louse."

"Pablo, don't get excited. It'll get you nowhere. Try to rest and let the FBI handle the affair."

"Rest? I'm coming back to Washington this very day."

"All right, but listen. Promise me one thing. Don't do or say anything in haste. If you really want to help your friend, keep a clear, cool head."

"But those murderers deserve to be denounced!"

"Obviously, man, but to denounce them we need concrete proof. To prove there was really a murder, the first thing we have to show is a corpse."

"By this time Gris's corpse must be at the bottom of the sea."

"That's a theory. But there are others, too. Take it easy. What time do you expect to get here?"

Pablo consulted his watch. "It's ten-thirty. At noon I'll be in Washington."

"Don't do any speeding. Drive carefully. . . . Oh! Promise me you will come talk to me before you go to the chancellery."

"All right."

30

THAT AFTERNOON General Hugo Ugarte came back from the beach, more tanned than usual, and phlegmatically entered the chancellery. He noticed immediately that the atmosphere was charged. Merceditas cast a glance full of fearful expectancy at him. Molina, whom he met in the hall, found a pretext not to speak to him. Ernesto Villalba, however, skipped up to him and asked, "So you know about the Gris affair?"

"That's why I'm here. The ambassador urgently called me back. If it were not for that, I'd be vacationing until the end of the month. This heat in Washington is enough to fry one."

Ugarte entered Miss Ogilvy's office. She was so upset that it did not even occur to her to greet the recent arrival. "The ambassador is expecting you. You may go in."

Juventino Carrera's ex-chief of police entered and closed the door behind him. Gabriel Heliodoro, seated behind his desk, got up and charged upon him as if he were going to attack him. "Stupid! Bungler! Where do you think you are? In Nigeria? In Cochinchina?"

Ugarte did not lose his calm. He was expecting the verbal explosion. He sat down, lit a cigarette, emitted a puff of smoke, looked at the ambassador with a froglike expression, and said, "Now explain why you are throwing all those compliments in my face?"

"What have you done with Dr. Gris?"

"I? Nothing."

"Don't lie. You people kidnapped the professor and probably took him out of the country to kill him."

There was an expression of rancor on Gabriel Heliodoro's face. His scar was inflamed. "Didn't I tell you," he went on through clenched teeth, "that I did not endorse violence? Dr. Gris was an expatriate, a traitor, but he was an inoffensive creature at heart. Why did you go and pull an uncivilized stunt like that?"

"I've told you we didn't do a thing. I've spent the whole time lying on the sand at the beach, belly up."

"I don't believe it."

The general shrugged. The ambassador had his fists clenched in an urge to punch the other man.

"Where is Dr. Galíndez?" he demanded.

"Who?"

"I mean, where is Dr. Gris?"

Ugarte stood up, and with the cigarette stuck in the corner of his mouth spoke confidentially. "Whoever did the job, it wasn't us."

"Who was it, then?"

"You remember the confidential communication from the Ministry of War? Right. I replied saying that the operation was risky, it could compromise the embassy, and I gave it as my opinion that the best thing would be for them to hire others for the job without telling us who or how. I washed my hands, too."

"Why didn't you notify me of that?"

"Because you yourself told me you wanted to know nothing more about the matter, no matter what."

Gabriel Heliodoro went over to the window and stared at the solid, tranquil chimneys of the British Embassy. He turned then to the military attaché, and they faced each other squarely.

"But what did they do with Gris?"

"I haven't the slightest idea."

"It was our people, I mean, compatriots of ours, that . . . that . . . you know what I mean."

Ugarte bit on the cigarette and, with a reflective air, squinted his eyes. "I suspect they hired some gringo specialists in such matters. I don't know rightly, and I don't want to know. I'm tired of taking the blame for everything rotten that's done, just to protect the others."

Gabriel Heliodoro dropped his whole weight on the sofa. His *compadre* Carrera was a man who held grudges, and would not forgive Gris the insults which the latter had addressed to him in articles and lectures.

"Have you read the papers, Hugo? They are beginning to accuse us of murder. This can do us tremendous harm. How am I going to look my American friends and my OAS colleagues in the face? What I've accomplished up to now, with my hands and my head, your minister has undone with his ass's hoofs!"

Ugarte slipped a hand into his trouser pocket and scratched his groin. The cigarette ash dropped on his tie. "What now?" he inquired.

"I'm going to write a frank letter to *compadre* Carrera telling him what I think of this whole filthy affair."

Ugarte looked at the calendar on the desk. "This is the end of July. No word on that amendment. If we don't strike that blow before November, we're cooked."

Gabriel Heliodoro shrugged his shoulders indifferently.

Pablo Ortega spent a good part of that evening in Bill Godkin's apartment, where they studied the Gris disappearance from all possible angles. The *Star* that day printed an item, already cut down, on the Gris case. (How quickly news aged. How little value was placed on a man's life!) The FBI informed the press that the search was continuing throughout the country. No air or steamship line had had the name of Leonardo Gris on its passenger lists during the past week. No travel agency had made any reservation for him. The Potomac was dragged from Washington to Chesapeake Bay. Pictures of Gris were sent to the police in hundreds of American cities.

The morning after his return to the capital, Pablo went to the building in which Gris had his apartment and talked with the girl at the desk, whom he knew. She repeated the story already published by the papers. A week before, more or less, Dr. Gris had gone out at six-thirty for dinner at one of the Georgetown restaurants. She remembered the fact because he, as was his custom, had stopped at her desk to chat briefly with her, had spoken of the heat, said the temperature in the capital of his country was always pleasant, and that he did not intend leaving Washington that summer.

"Did he seem worried?"

"No . . . not that I recall."

"And you are positive you didn't see him again?"

"Yes, because the next day he didn't come by my desk on his way to the university. And he didn't come back late that afternoon. We thought he was sick. We knocked at his apartment door, but got no answer. Next day Dr. Gris's department head at the university notified the police."

Pablo talked with other people in the building. No one remembered having seen any suspicious-looking persons around there during the last several days.

He covered several restaurants in Georgetown where Gris was in the habit of dining. In none of them could he gather the slightest useful information. He walked repeatedly around Wisconsin Avenue and adjacent streets for several days in the hope—which he himself felt absurd—of glimpsing the man in the light raincoat. How was it possible to go around in a raincoat on hot, sunshiny days like these? Nevertheless, he had faith in his good memory; he remembered perfectly the features and the voice of the man who had trailed Gris. He must have been a private detective. The Federal Bureau of Investigation must have the dossiers of all Americans in that occupation. He spent a whole afternoon in one of the sections of the FBI examining hundreds of photographs, but with no positive result.

At dusk he telephoned Clare Ogilvy.

"Pablo, you in town?" she said, surprised.

"I came back three days ago on account of the matter of Dr. Gris."

"I didn't want to send word to you so as not to upset your vacation. I trust the FBI. But, *chico*, how are you?"

"You can imagine. Gris was my friend."

"Don't be pessimistic. Say *is*, not *was*."

"I'm beginning to lose hope that he is still alive."

"When are you coming to the chancellery?"

"Tomorrow."

La Ogilvita cleared her throat significantly. She lowered her voice. "Pablo, my love, take a tranquilizer. The atmosphere here is—how shall I say it?—funereal."

"That chancellery is a tomb. You're the only living person in it, Clare."

"Thanks. But my case is different. Be good. Don't lose your head."

"I can't stand any more. I think I'm going to explode."

"Don't. Remember Don Dionisio."

"The hell with Don Dionisio! There's a limit to everything."

"Pablo, dear, take *two* tablets before you come here."

Next morning Ortega entered the chancellery, shook hands with Merceditas and the other stenographers, went into the minister-counselor's room, greeted him coldly, and, without beating around the bush, bluntly asked, "In your opinion, what did happen to Dr. Gris?"

"I cannot imagine. Why?"

"I believe he was kidnapped, taken out of the country, and murdered by men in the pay of that scum Ugarte."

Jorge Molina joined the tips of the fingers of both hands as if he were going to pray, laid both index fingers on lips and chin, and gazed placidly at the first secretary.

"One cannot accuse a citizen without concrete proofs. There are several other possibilities in the Gris case besides kidnapping and murder."

"Dr. Molina, I should like to have your serenity, your peace of mind, and that cold love of logic. But the fact is, I haven't. Every time I come into this building I feel demeaned, soiled, ashamed of myself."

Molina looked like a yogi in profound communion with the cosmos. After a pause he retorted, "I hope that you are not accusing me of having participated in that— kidnapping—young man!"

"No, Dr. Molina. You are absolutely innocent. I'll go further. You are perhaps the most innocent person I have ever encountered in all my life!" He turned his back on the minister-counselor and left.

Clare Ogilvy, advised by Merceditas of Pablo's presence in the chancellery, was waiting for him in the corridor. "Come to my office," she invited, alarmed for fear Pablo might encounter Ugarte, whose figure she had seen far down the hall.

Pablo let himself be led.

"The ambassador hasn't arrived yet. Sit down. And pay close attention to what I am going to say. Yesterday I eavesdropped on the conversation between Don Gabriel

Heliodoro and the general. It is not, and never has been, my habit to do that, and if I did it, it was for your sake."

"What did you discover?"

"The ambassador is furious. He thought that Ugarte had been the person responsible for what happened to Dr. Gris."

She related the rest of the dialogue. Pablo listened in a moody silence. "Couldn't all that have been something staged for you to hear and tell others afterward?"

She shook her head in a decided negative. Pablo ran his fingers through his hair, muttering, "I don't know . . . I don't know. . . ." And getting up suddenly he exclaimed, "I can't keep on serving this government of murderers!"

La Ogilvita sniffed loudly, twisting her mouth and wrinkling her nose. "Are you going to write to your parents?"

"Maybe."

"And won't this attitude of yours make it impossible for you to return to El Sacramento?"

"The world is large."

"Think of your old folks."

"I've been thinking a lot lately of other old folk, and young people and children."

He told her the story of the picture he had painted during his vacation.

Clare was pensive, and after a pause said, "Trachoma was completely eliminated from El Sacramento more than ten years ago by the World Health Organization. You are using material gathered in your adolescence."

"Ah, Clare! Don't be so statistical, so . . . so American."

"All right. The eyes of those poor sickly children, with or without trachoma, are following you. But do you think that by resigning your position as secretary *now* you are going to save those kids?"

"At least it's the beginning of something. A form of protest. I'll be free to denounce the filthy gang which took over the government by force in my country."

"And take the place of Dr. Gris?"

"Exactly, even though minus his qualities and authority."

The ambassador's secretary, a cigarette in the corner of her mouth, started to walk around the chair in which her friend was seated. "All right," she said at last, stopping behind Pablo and laying her large, brown-mottled hands on his shoulders. "If that's what you think you must do, do it. But not today. Go home now. Your leave is not up yet. Don't see anyone else. Sleep on all those resolves, distrusts, guilty feelings, and so on."

"Why leave until tomorrow what I can do today?"

"I'll be more explicit. Won't it be easier for you to discover something about Dr. Gris's whereabouts if you keep on working in this chancellery?"

"I don't see why. And besides, Clare, I'm beginning to be ashamed of my own face when I see it every morning in the mirror."

"For reasons different from yours"—she smiled—"I, too, used to be ashamed of myself when I saw my face in the mirror. But one gets used to anything. Don't think I'm advising you to accommodate yourself to the situation. But nobody ought to sacrifice himself for nothing. Sell your resignation, dear. Find material to destroy that government."

Pablo was pensive for a moment. "I don't know, I don't know, I don't know."

"O.K. But go now before the ambassador gets here. He, too, is depressed and worried. The situation in El Sacramento is not good—I mean, for the government. If you two should meet today, two things could happen, both undesirable."

"What do you mean by that?"

"You insult him and both of you engage in physical combat. And I don't know whether you, despite the difference in age, would have the advantage. Or else Don Gabriel Heliodoro grabs you in an *abrazo,* overwhelms you with his charm, and you go out of here worse defeated than when you came in."

31

IN THE EVENING of the same day, around eleven o'clock, Pancho Vivanco was walking up and down the sidewalk in front of the embassy residence. For more than an hour he had been pacing there, eying the lights in the windows of the ambassador's suite, which contained the famous Isabeline room which he knew from the descriptions he had succeeded in prying out of Rosalía, bit by bit. Quite soon now the Mercedes would emerge from the back of the park and stop in front of the mansion. The door would open; Gabriel Heliodoro and Frances Andersen, arm in arm, would come down the steps of the portico and exchange a long kiss before she got into the car.

Pancho fondled the butt of the revolver in his jacket pocket. The heat was stifling, sweat ran streaming down his forehead and into his eyes, blurring his vision. The consul thought about his calamitous situation, which had worsened in the past week. On some days he was tormented by the fear that Rosalía might commit suicide by swallowing the Seconal tablets from the three bottles she kept hidden somewhere; and sitting at his desk in the chancellery, incapable of working, looking irresolutely at the papers to be dispatched, he would sit scribbling unenthusiastically with his colored pencils on his note pad. If the telephone rang, it startled him, the rhythm of his heart accelerated, his throat closed up, and he began to tremble, hesitating to pick up the phone, horrified at the notion that someone was going to inform him that his wife had been found dead.

The evening before, at twilight, the telephone in his apartment had rung. He hurried to answer, but perceived that Rosalía had already lifted the receiver of the bedroom extension, where as usual she was locked in. Curiosity pricked him. Who could be calling? He thought of taking up the telephone, but an invincible inhibition prevented him. The conversation lasted several minutes. Vivanco began to suspect that the call was from Gabriel Heliodoro. He started pacing impatiently back and forth. At last a click announced that the connection had been cut off. He waited. He felt that something was going to happen. Half an hour later, Rosalía came out of her room wearing a gray-green dress, cut very low. She was excessively made up, he noticed, and had sprayed perfume lavishly.

"I'm dining out," she said without looking at him.

"Do you want me to take you in the car?"

"No. You still have to take your bath. I've left cold chicken and salad in the refrigerator. I don't think I'll be out very late, but don't stay up for me."

He nodded in submissive agreement. Her eyes were sparkling. Her hands were shaking. With abrupt movements she snatched up her cigarette case and lighter, thrust them into her purse, and went out.

He approached the window and looked down to the sidewalk; he saw Rosalía go to the curb and look up and down the street. She raised an arm, and a yellow taxi stopped in front of her. She got into the car, which drove off down the avenue toward the center of town.

Pancho looked at his watch. Seven-five. From here to Dupont Circle, he thought, the taxi takes about five minutes. From the circle to the embassy residence, some eight or ten—let's say, in all, fifteen or twenty.

He left the window, turned on the television set, sat down on the sofa before it, and waited. For what? He was a little out of breath, with the feeling of a vacuum in the pit of his stomach, a tingling on his skin. It was as if he had made an appointment with his mistress and was now waiting in excitement for her knock at the door. He watched and listened with no real interest to the images and sounds on the television screen. A mulatto woman with a warm, oily voice was singing a blues song. He stuck a hand into his pocket and began rolling the paper cylinder between his fingers. Every other instant he looked at his watch. Rosalía must be happy. She was making it up with her lover. She would come home in a gayer mood. Of course. The affair between Gabriel Heliodoro and the American woman was ending. The society columnists had already announced that Miss Andersen would soon marry a Chicago millionaire, who was also divorced. He closed his eyes and inhaled the perfume that his wife had left in the air. Again he looked at his watch. Seven-thirty. Rosalía must be going into the embassy. Gabriel Heliodoro himself was opening the door. They were embracing, kissing lingeringly. She was crying, her head on her lover's shoulder.

On the television screen a mixed quartet was singing a jingle, enumerating the qualities of a famous brand of cigarettes, king size. Gabriel Heliodoro was a king-size man. He had his arm around Rosalía's waist, and they were ascending the stairs of the mansion together, were going into the room, turning on the blue lamp. Rosalía now is starting to take off her clothes, Gabriel Heliodoro comes up behind her, clasps both her breasts in his hands and kisses the nape of her neck, her shoulders. The thrill she feels transmits itself to him, Vivanco, who writhes on the sofa. Now the two, naked, are on the great bed, where they lie entwined.

He covered his face with shaking hands. He must be sick, very sick. He snapped off the television, turned out the light in the room, lay down on the sofa, and remained there in a torpor that was neither sleep nor waking, but a kind of cataleptic state which held him motionless, incapable of moving a finger but with his brain working incessantly around two or three images. He awoke completely only when the light was turned on in the room. He stood up, eyes blinking, and saw Rosalía in the doorway, her face dissolved, her eyes swollen as from long crying. He looked at her with a pathetic glance. "What's the matter?" He went to her. "Have you been with the ambassador?" She nodded. Suddenly her eyes flashed and she exclaimed, "That man is a monster."

She ran to the bathroom, went in, and locked the door. He followed and stood listening, excited, to all the sounds that came from inside. He felt a ferocious desire to possess his wife physically that night. He stood in ambush at the bathroom door for long minutes, like a famished wild beast awaiting its prey. When Rosalía emerged, he seized her.

"Let me alone, Pancho!"

"Just this time, darling," he panted, "just tonight."

She managed to shake him off. "One pig an evening is enough!" she cried.

And then, possessed, he gave her a slap that caught her full on the mouth.

Now, now on the embassy residence sidewalk, in a mixture of horror and shame, Vivanco was turning it all over in his mind. He had left home in the morning, but he had lacked the nerve to enter the chancellery. He had wandered aimlessly around the city, then had crossed the Potomac toward the airport, but on the way he had stopped his car along the river and tried to get his mind on other things by watching the planes taking off or landing. Later he had gone on to Alexandria, where he ate a sandwich in a drugstore. In the afternoon he had gone to a movie, without ceasing to think of Rosalía. How could he face her after his stupid gesture of violence? Never in all his life had he struck a woman. He came out of the theater, dazed. He thought of telephoning Ninfa Ugarte to ask her to go see Rosalía, stay with her to prevent the poor child from doing something rash, but could not bring himself to make the call. He continued walking aimlessly through the business streets of Alexandria, looking in the shop windows. He went into a stationery store and was examining some office supplies when a name, in black letters on a multicolored background, caught his eye and at the same time caused a strange sensation in his chest, as if invisible fingers had touched his heart lightly. Colorolas. It was like suddenly finding Sidney and his childhood again. He picked up the box of wax crayons with tender, delighted fingers, opened it, smelled it, examined the figure on the outside . . . what a pity! It was no longer the Wild West scene, Indians chasing buffaloes, but the color photograph of Yellowstone Park in autumn. But what the devil!—they were Colorolas. He bought the box and stuck it in his pocket.

Now, on the sidewalk of Massachusetts Avenue, again he fondled "Sidney's crayons" with his fingertips. Ah, but what did those sticks of wax matter in comparison with his trouble?

What to do? Ideas, in confusion, passed through the consul's mind. Ought he to climb the portico steps, put a bullet in his brain, and fall at the embassy door, so that, on coming out with his mistress, Gabriel Heliodoro would step on his corpse? No. It would be a suicide without that supreme sacrifice being useful to anyone. He should first write a letter to the newspapers denouncing Gabriel Heliodoro as responsible for the kidnapping and murder of Leonardo Gris. Another letter to Doña Francisca, telling her about her husband's adulteries. Yes, and another to Rosalía, begging her forgiveness for everything. Tomorrow he would write all those letters.

With his right hand he gripped the butt of the revolver while he ran the fingers of his left over the tips of the Colorolas.

He saw the lights go out in the windows of the ambassador's suite. Several minutes passed. Pancho looked at his watch in the light of a street lamp. Nearly midnight. He saw the shape of the Mercedes come out from the back of the park and stop, as black as a hearse, at the portico. He went into the park, walked toward the embassy residence, and hid behind a tree, a few yards from the house, and stood there waiting. Noises in the foyer. A woman's laugh. The door opened. Aldo Borelli jumped out of the car and stood at attention beside it, cap in hand. And then, in the light of the lamp over the door, Pancho Vivanco saw his ambassador, clad in a dark dressing gown, bringing the American blonde by the arm. "Scum," he muttered. "Treacherous dog." A sudden access of rage shook him.

On the bottom step Gabriel Heliodoro kissed Frances Andersen on the mouth. Then she got into the car, which started off. The ambassador stayed where he was for several minutes, waving to his mistress until the Mercedes disappeared. Pancho Vivanco was shaking from head to foot. He was only a few steps from the cause of all his misfortunes. That man deserved to be punished so that he would not continue to trample on other people. He saw him now going up the stairs, returning to the comfort of his home—gigantic, broad-shouldered, master of life, playing with the destinies of others as one juggles balls. In a sort of trance, Pancho Vivanco came out of his hiding place and followed the steps of Gabriel Heliodoro, who was now ready to close the door. He called to him with a choked voice, "Ambassador!"

Gabriel Heliodoro's brows drew together. "Vivanco," he muttered, with an air of surprise. He even sketched a smile, but when he saw that Rosalía's husband had a revolver in his hand, he recoiled, exclaiming, "Are you mad? Give me that gun!" Pancho, in reality, was not there with gun in hand; he was really dreaming the whole thing, and therefore was not responsible for anything—dreaming that he was going to kill the lover for whom his wife was deceiving him—he was an avenging angel at that moment. With tremulous hand he aimed the revolver at Gabriel Heliodoro Alvarado's genitals and pulled the trigger. The explosion resounded in the entrance hall. The ambassador, his face contorted with fury, advanced toward him. "Madman! *Loco!*"

"Five bullets," Vivanco thought, retreating, "five bullets in his balls." Five stones were needed to knock over the giant Goliath. He was about to pull the trigger again when, simultaneously with another shot, he felt on the left side of his throat an impact that knocked him down. He dropped his revolver. His glasses fell off. He rolled on the ground, half rose, crawled for brief seconds babbling incoherently—*crayola . . . caray . . . canalla . . . no va . . . no va crayolanalla . . . colorolaslolas . . . lolas.* He made an effort to get to his feet, but in vain. Something had broken inside him, an enormous internal wave engulfed his chest, rose up into his throat, and ice began to invade his whole body. He babbled another half-dozen incomprehensible words, managed to reach for his glasses and touch them with his fingers as if he wished to put them back on. Everything was turning dark around him, and at last Pancho Vivanco fell stiffly backward, his eyes already glassy, and the last image that reached his retina was that of a great shining light—the eye of God pendant from the firmament.

The ambassador was now looking at the door, beside which the night watchman stood with the still smoking revolver in his hand. "I saw that man come in, Mr. Ambassador," he mumbled in his precarious Spanish, his voice uncertain.

Michel entered the foyer and stood staring at the scene, with an expression of shock on his pale face. Gabriel Heliodoro went to the body of his consul, knelt beside it, and tried to find the pulse. He thought that it was no longer beating. He put his hand under Vivanco's jacket on the left side of the chest; he could feel no heartbeat. For an instant he stared at the reflection of the great chandelier in the dead man's pupils. One thing puzzled him—no trace of blood could be seen. He sought the wound and finally discovered that the bullet had entered the thorax through the axillary region. It must have cut the aorta. He knew of cases like that. He rose to his feet. The butler asked whether a doctor should be summoned. Gabriel Heliodoro answered that it would be useless. The consul was *jodido*.

"Is Your Excellency wounded, Señor Ambassador?" Michel inquired.

"No. The man had a wretched aim."

"What do we do now?" the watchman wanted to know.

"Nothing. Wait. Let no one leave the house." He looked at the revolver lying a little distance from the corpse. "Let no one touch that gun."

He felt as though he were back in the Sierra de la

Calavera. He was leader of a guerrilla patrol. He had to think quickly and clearly, and carry out the plan without waste of time. He looked around, seeking something. Vivanco's bullet, he ascertained, had passed very close by his left hip, actually piercing the dressing gown. He discovered afterward that the bullet had lodged in the wood of the second step of the central stairway.

"Michel! Telephone General Ugarte and tell him to come *immediately,* that something *very serious* has happened. But don't tell him what it is. Understand? Quickly!"

The butler left the entrance hall almost running. Gabriel Heliodoro looked at the guard.

"Ask Michel to give you a stiff drink of whiskey."

"Thank you, Mr. Ambassador."

"I'm the one to be thanking you. But go, and don't leave this house or communicate with anyone without my authorization."

Alone with the corpse, Gabriel Heliodoro cast it a glance of cold pity. Poor bungling devil!

He lighted a cigarette and began striding up and down, muttering, "This was all I needed after that Gris scandal. The last straw." But it would not be hard to prove that there had really been an attempt on his life. The newspapers could not doubt its genuineness. The night watchman's statement would clinch it. There was Michel's testimony, besides. But—what about Rosalía? The thought occurred to him suddenly. He stopped short. He made a gesture of annoyance. How could he tell her the story?

He looked down again at the dead man. In death Pancho Vivanco was no more attractive than he had been in life. His unshaven beard was creating a greenish-looking shadow on the waxy cheeks. Voices from infancy echoed in Gabriel Heliodoro's memory, and he bent down to close the dead man's eyes.

Michel reappeared bringing a glass of straight whiskey on a tray. "The general will not be long, Mr. Ambassador."

"Thanks, Michel," Gabriel Heliodoro said, seizing the

glass and taking a long swallow. "Prepare a lot of coffee, make it strong. I shall have to be up all night. You may retire for the present. I will call you when I need you."

The butler bowed and withdrew. Now, glass in hand, the ambassador again walked around the corpse. He could have expected anything from Vivanco except an act of aggression. Well, a man never really knows what people are. At all events it had been the gesture of almost a real man. Why had the wretched fellow's hand trembled at the instant of firing? How could anyone miss a target of his size from so short a distance?

General Hugo Ugarte arrived a few minutes later. When he caught sight of the corpse, he stood with mouth agape in astonishment. Gabriel Heliodoro summarized the affair:

"This dog tried to shoot me down, but the night watchman got here in time and stopped him."

"Now what?"

Gabriel Heliodoro smiled. "Use your head, man. Don't you get the story yet?"

"What story? Jealousy?"

"Tommyrot! Think. Don't you see that it was a carefully prepared attempt to eliminate me?"

"Prepared by whom?"

"Hugo, you're still not awake. Want a strong coffee?"

The general gazed in perplexity at the deceased. Gabriel Heliodoro took another swallow and said, "There's the opportunity we were hoping for. Vivanco was party to a leftist conspiracy. My assassination would be the signal to begin acts of terrorism and sabotage in El Sacramento, understand?"

"And what about proof?"

"The proof, old boy, we—you and I—are going to fabricate now. Telephone to one of your lieutenants who can type—and whom you trust to the fullest."

Without taking his eyes off the dead man, Ugarte slowly wagged his head.

"We'll prepare documents that will prove the connection of Francisco Vivanco with the revolutionaries. We must not forget that the American police *must* find in this fellow's pocket a letter in which someone informs someone (*Invent names, that's your specialty.*) that Dr. Gris left the United States secretly, of his own free will, and is already with the Sacramentan exiles in Cuba. We need a long list of names of persons from El Sacramento implicated in the movement, so that our police can start arrests." He laid a hand on the shoulder of the military attaché. "Don't you see that we are going to offer my *compadre* Juventino Carrera on a golden tray the pretext that he is waiting for to justify a new *Movimiento de Salvación Nacional* in the eyes of the world?"

Ugarte was beaming now, comprehending the whole plan.

Gabriel Heliodoro squatted down beside Vivanco's corpse and ransacked his pockets. He pulled out a damp, soiled handkerchief, a dollar bill rolled like a cigarette, and a box of colored crayons. He raised his eyes to his accomplice and smiled. "I don't think these proofs are sufficient." He stood up again.

"After we have all the documents ready, we'll put the letter about Gris in the dead man's pocket and tuck away the other compromising papers in a drawer of his desk in the chancellery. But mind you, it's necessary that the key of that drawer be found in this character's pocket, too." As he spoke, he pointed to the corpse with his foot.

He raised his glass. "When the operation is over," he continued, clicking his tongue, "we'll notify the police, whatever the hour may be. And tomorrow morning I'll send a note on the subject to the Department of State, and call the newspapers for a press conference. Want a drink?"

Ugarte replied that he preferred coffee. When he added that he was going to call one of his aides, Gabriel Heliodoro stopped him with a gesture.

"Another thing. Ask Ninfa to break the news to Rosalía, but not now, tomorrow morning, understand? Ah! Molina and the others must not suspect our trick. The secret will be mine, yours, and the lieutenant's, whichever one does the paper work."

Ugarte assented with a nod of his head, and withdrew. Gabriel Heliodoro once more began to walk around the dead man with his eyes steadily on him. "For the first time in your miserable life," he remarked *sotto voce,* "you are going to be of some use to your country."

32

A LITTLE BEFORE daybreak, the ambassador, sleepy, put through a telephone call to Cerro Hermoso, got hold of his president, and told him, in a few words, what had happened. The documents proving the conspiracy would follow in the diplomatic pouch on that day's plane. His *compadre* uttered a satisfied laugh, comprehending the game immediately.

"Thanks, old man," he exulted. "But you are not really wounded?"

Gabriel Heliodoro answered, "I don't believe Vivanco had ever fired a gun in all his life. Ah, *compadre!* Telephone to Francisquita and say that I'm perfectly all right, and that I'm going to write her a letter this very day telling her everything, in full detail."

It was nearly noon when the Washington police finished their investigation in the entrance hall of the embassy. They also took the statements of the ambassador, the night watchman, and the butler. Before being taken to the morgue, where it would be subjected to an autopsy, the corpse of Francisco Vivanco was photographed from several angles.

Ninfa Ugarte had transmitted to Rosalía the news of her husband's death, which the young woman received with a pathological indifference. Did she want to take the body for burial in the Cerro Hermoso cemetery? she was asked. "I don't care," she answered, shutting herself within a stony silence.

Ernesto Villalba, alternating moments of sincere consternation with the flighty excitement that swept over him whenever there was trouble, scandal, and spicy tidbits around him, was charged by the ambassador with the funeral ceremonies for Vivanco—everything, naturally, at the embassy's expense. And on hearing this last detail Titito could not resist the temptation to comment, "*Noblesse oblige.*" But the story of the conspiracy failed utterly to convince him. He kept quiet, however, because to doubt it would mean deadly peril for him.

Molina was extremely nervous. He did not want to be involved in the sordid story. Gabriel Heliodoro had instructed him to write the note in which the ambassador of El Sacramento would officially communicate "the dramatic incident" to the Department of State. He had spent a good part of the morning doing that with the aid of Clare Ogilvy. There were already four versions of the note, and none of them satisfied the minister-counselor. He felt that his lack of conviction in the veracity of the facts narrated to him by the ambassador was infecting the composition of the note.

He was now dictating the fifth version, watching the secretary and fearing lest she might suddenly ask him whether he believed the tale. La Ogilvita, who had lined herself with tranquilizers, was thinking of Pablo more than of any other person or institution. Where was he? How had he reacted to the news of Vivanco's death? What was he going to *do* now? She had attempted several times to communicate with her friend by telephone that morning, but in vain.

Merceditas's eyes were bloodshot from so much weeping. Vivanco had always mistreated her, made a scapegoat of her. He had seemed to derive a certain pleasure in torturing her with insolence, verbal insults, and all sorts of minute perversities. She, however, had never hated him.

She was even rather sorry for him. And now, from one minute to another, she would murmur, "Poor thing, poor thing!"

At ten o'clock Gabriel Heliodoro, scowling, burst into the chancellery, and spoke to no one. He met Miss Ogilvy on her way back to her post. "Is the communication for the Department of State ready?"

"Yes, Mr. Ambassador. It is on your desk, with the translation in Spanish."

Gabriel Heliodoro sat down, read the note, found it satisfactory, and signed it, while his secretary, standing beside him, awaited orders.

"Who would have thought it, eh, Clare?"

She sniffed loudly and twisted her mouth and nose to one side, but remained silent.

"What are they saying in the chancellery?" he asked.

"I don't know, Mr. Ambassador. I pay no attention to gossip."

"But you don't doubt that Vivanco really did try to kill me, do you?"

"No, Mr. Ambassador. Besides your word, we have the conclusions of the police experts, which corroborate you."

"And you know that we found some highly compromising documents on the body and in his desk drawers here?"

La Ogilvita looked steadily at her chief, her lips compressed, her face expressionless. Gabriel Heliodoro could not withstand the expression of honesty in those light eyes, which seemed to read his mind. He lowered his head.

"Well, where is Pablo?"

"He has not arrived yet."

"What? At this hour? Telephone his apartment."

"I have already tried several times. No one answers."

"What time are the gentlemen of the press due?"

"In twenty minutes."

"I want Pablo to be my interpreter."

"If the ambassador will permit a suggestion from me, Pablo is not the best person for that service."

"Why?"

"For a reason which he himself is going to explain to you today, tomorrow, or later."

Gabriel Heliodoro sat staring steadily at the portrait of Don Alfonso Bustamante. "All right. Then you'll do the interpreting."

"In your opinion, what should I tell the journalists?"

"Tell exactly what occurred. And the fewer commentaries you make on the fact, the better."

Gabriel Heliodoro shook his head slowly, picked up the ivory paper knife, and began rapping a tattoo with it on the glass cover of his desk. "Do you think the press people are going to ask to see those documents? I mean, the proofs of Vivanco's participation in the plot?"

"Without the slightest doubt."

"But the papers are already in the diplomatic pouch on the way to Cerro Hermoso! We have no photostatic copies."

"Then say so to the reporters, Mr. Ambassador."

"Clare, what's the matter with you today?"

"Nothing, Mr. Ambassador."

"All right, when the boys from the press come, have them go into the meeting room. And have some coffee sent in—some whiskey—or arsenic!"

The secretary withdrew. Gabriel Heliodoro sensed someone looking at him. He raised his head and encountered the austere gaze of Don Alfonso Bustamante. He hurled the paper knife at the portrait.

The American newspapers gave prominence to the story of the tragedy in the Embassy of El Sacramento. The *Post*, the *Star*, and the *News* gave the case greater attention than did the dailies in other cities. The ambassador's interview was, in general, reproduced with no comment, but a New York tabloid printed a skeptical editorial on the subject under the title of "Another Dark Day in El Sacramento Embassy." And, as was to be expected, the disappearance of Gris was brought up and related to the killing of Vivanco.

It was Bill Godkin who carried the news of the tragedy to Pablo. They went to have their breakfast in the coffee shop of the Hotel Statler. After telling the waiter what they wanted, they sat staring at each other in silence. It was the American who spoke first.

"What do you think about all this?"

"I think it's a pretty thin story. And you?"

"Agreed, but there are certain facts which were clearly proved by the local police. In actual fact there was an attempt at murder committed against the person of Gabriel Heliodoro, the revolver did belong to Vivanco and bore his fingerprints on the butt, and the bullet fired from that gun was found embedded in a step of the stairs. The bullet that killed Vivanco did come from the night watchman's gun. More important than all that is the unequivocal statement of the night watchman himself, which was corroborated by the ambassador's and the butler's statements. There were no discrepancies, nor were any doubts remaining."

"But the tale of the conspiracy is false. It was forged by Gabriel Heliodoro and his military attaché, who is an expert in such matters. The letter referring to Gris's flight is utterly ridiculous. The man would not have the slightest need to *flee* the country. He could travel normally to Cuba or anywhere else, if he wished. And how is it explained that his name is not to be found on any passenger list of any airline or maritime company in the last two or three weeks? And does anyone travel of his own free will leaving behind his clothes, his books, his business affairs, and even his reading glasses? A man like Gris would not leave the country without having paid his rent and other bills. And without at least informing the head of his university department. Yes, and without saying good-by to me, if only over the telephone."

The waiter had brought the things ordered: black coffee, with dry toast for Pablo, and a complete breakfast —scrambled eggs, sausage, cereal, toast, butter—for Godkin, who set about his food with appetite.

"I agree with you," he said.

A spot of egg yolk was staining his chin. He wiped it with his napkin. Pablo was drinking his coffee but did not touch his toast.

"I spent a damnable night, sleepless, thinking what I must do. I wrote a long letter to my parents, explaining the situation to them and telling them plainly why I am going to resign my job."

"Have you sent the letter?"

"I went down early in the morning and shoved the envelope in a mailbox before I changed my mind. When we leave here, I'll send a cable to the foreign minister, making my resignation formal."

Godkin spread jelly on a piece of toast. "And afterward?"

"Tomorrow I'll go to the chancellery to confront the ambassador."

"And what do you think Gabriel Heliodoro's reaction will be?"

"It doesn't interest me."

"How do you imagine that El Libertador is going to use those famous 'subversive documents'?"

"It's obvious that they were the pretext Carrera was waiting for to cancel the November elections and take the first steps to perpetuate himself in office."

"I'll bet we'll have news from your country this very evening, Pablo. And I could compose, here and now, without fear of error or exaggeration, the news of what's going to happen."

On the following day the newspapers carried sensational headlines about a new coup d'état in the Republic of El Sacramento. Generalissimo Juventino Carrera had dissolved his Cabinet, closed both houses of Congress, and decreed a state of siege throughout the country. Individuals involved in the "leftist conspiracy aiming at the overthrow of the government by force" were arrested by the hundreds all over the nation. In the federal university alone more than two hundred persons, including professors and students, had already been detained and held incommunicado. In a speech broadcast over a radio network the president had explained the reasons for the measures taken and asked the people to support him and to have full confidence in him. His desire to be just would not prevent him from showing himself "inflexible toward the traitors threatening the public order, the democratic system, and the Christian traditions of our fatherland."

La Ogilvita read the news in the *Post,* wrinkled her nose, sniffed spectacularly, and then heaved a sigh that came from the marrow of her being. Another coup d'état!

The ambassador put in a good part of the morning telephoning to his colleagues of the OAS. He urgently requested the convoking of an extraordinary session of the council so that he could explain the political situation in his country.

Molina was crushed. He had read in one of the papers the news that Don Pánfilo Arango y Aragón had already declared himself publicly on Carrera's coup d'état, and had appealed to the Catholics to support the president unhesitatingly in the dramatic hour of his struggle against Bolshevism.

Another chapter for the biography, thought the minister-counselor. What worried him most, however, was not that, but the consequences of the situation. He had the presentiment that something very grave was yet to happen. The island would be invaded at any moment by an army of exiles; and in the interior of the country a fifth column, possibly well trained and well armed, was awaiting the signal for the revolution to break out.

If the revolution wins, what is going to become of me? he thought. Carrera was a common, ambitious fellow, a dishonest man with no greatness in him, but his government was preferable to a dictatorship of the left. Molina was thinking now, with horror, of the shootings in Cuba, and could feel over his head the shadow of the firing squad wall. He had no fear of death. Life sometimes frightened him more than death. He was determined not to go back to his country, in the event of a victory by the rebels. He

preferred dying by his own hand to being subjected to the
outrages and indignities of a trial by a revolutionary popular tribunal, to the sordidness of a jail, to the sarcasm and
the vituperation of his enemies. A thousand times death! A
swift, clean, dignified death.

Where was God? he asked himself. Where was God?
And where was Gris? God. Gris. God. Gris. God. Gris.

Clare Ogilvy entered her chief's office and returned a
minute later, telling Pablo, who was waiting for her in the
next room, "You can go in. But be careful."

Ortega went in and came to a halt before the ambassador's desk.

"Sit down, Pablo."

"Thank you. I shall stand."

Gabriel Heliodoro did not insist. He picked up the
paper knife in both hands and inquired in a lackluster
voice, "What is it?"

"I have to inform you that I have just telegraphed to
the Foreign Ministry, resigning my post in the diplomatic
service—irrevocably."

The ambassador was still for an instant in silence,
pensive, gazing at his own hands. Then he asked, "Why?"

"Do you really want to know?"

"Of course I do."

Pablo swallowed, clenched his fists, and replied, "It is
because I cannot continue to serve a government of murderers and thieves."

He expected a violent reaction from the other man.
He even took a look at the paperweight on the desk, which
he could use as a weapon in case of necessity. He was
surprised by the tranquil, glum silence of Gabriel Heliodoro, who kept his eyes down.

"Have you thought it over carefully, what you are
doing? Have you thought of your father, your mother?
Have you thought, too, that the news of your resignation
can only aggravate my situation here in Washington, a
situation already so bad after . . . after all the other
events?"

"I am not interested in your situation."

"All right. But try to understand this difficult moment for our country."

"It was you who created *this* moment and gave a pretext to your *compadre* for the coup d'état which will maintain him in power as a dictator."

"Then you don't believe in the documents which we discovered in Vivanco's possession?"

"It is not exactly that. I don't believe that subversive documents have really been found in the possession of that poor man."

Pablo was startled at Gabriel Heliodoro's apathy. He had come prepared for a violent reaction on the other's part, and yet the ambassador was sunk into his chair as though diminished in stature, gripping the paper knife with such force that the joints of his hands had whitened. And the look that he was bending on him now was so humble (the Indian, the barefoot Indian, the downtrodden Indian, gazing at the son of the rich plantation owner!) that Ortega, reluctantly, felt a touch of pity for the man whom he did not like, but could not manage to hate.

Gabriel Heliodoro was shaking his head in a slow gesture. "All right, Pablo, all right. Do what you think best. I don't dislike you for it. If you prefer not to come back to the chancellery, don't return. Wait at home for the Foreign Ministry's decision. But don't forget one thing. I've tried to be your friend. You have rejected my friendship. You may go. Be happy."

The ambassador's eyes were wet. Pablo left the office without saying a word. Clare Ogilvy was awaiting him in the next room. She took his arm and led him out in the hall. Pablo described the scene which had just taken place. Then the secretary told him, "A few minutes ago they notified Don Gabriel Heliodoro that Rosalía Vivanco tried to commit suicide by taking barbiturates."

"Will she die?"

"I don't know. She is in a coma and her condition is grave."

Pablo went into his own office to open drawers and

destroy papers. He found on the desk a letter from his mother, which he tore up without reading, and another from Miss Hirota, which he stuck in his pocket.

La Ogilvita accompanied him to the street door. "Now what, Pablo?"

He smiled. "Do you want to know something? I'm feeling fine. My headache hasn't appeared since yesterday. And I never felt less burdened in all my life. It's as if I had taken a bath inside."

"God bless you, boy."

They said good-by. He went away, feeling somehow uplifted, out through the park. Then he remembered the blue envelope that he had stuck in his pocket. He opened it. A fragrance of jasmine evoked the face of Kimiko. The blue paper contained only a *haikai*:

> Drop of morning dew
> In a lily corolla:
> Jewel of time.

IV

The Mountain

33

O NE HOT, stifling day in the first week of August
the newspapers announced that "mercenary
forces, possibly coming from Cuba," under the
command of one Miguel Barrios, had landed in El Sacramento in the environs of Soledad del Mar, where they
counted on the federal garrison's joining them. As the
latter had offered unexpected resistance, the invaders had
been obliged to seek refuge in the Sierra de la Calavera,
from which, it was presumed, they would initiate the usual
guerrilla action. Unconfirmed rumors had it that landings
had also taken place in the southern provinces of the
island.

Before daybreak Gabriel Heliodoro Alvarado was already aware of these events. President Carrera in person
had telephoned him from Cerro Hermoso at five o'clock,
catching him in bed. Sleep-dulled, the ambassador took
several seconds to absorb the news, but when he perceived
the gravity of the situation, he uttered his habitual ana-
lytic interjection:

"How many men have landed at Soledad del Mar,
compadre?"

"Some seven or eight hundred, maybe a thousand, I
don't know, and well armed."

"Was that the only landing?"

"Unfortunately there were two others, at Oro Verde
and San Fernando. I am not informed of the rebel's effec-
tiveness in the south. The news is confused. I am sending
my air force to bombard and strafe the enemy positions."

Gabriel Heliodoro noted that the president's voice
betrayed a certain tension.

"*Compadre,* listen, I'm thinking of taking off for home right away."

"Don't do that!"

"Listen, Mr. President, I know the Sierra like the palm of my hand. I'm still in fine physical shape. I can command guerrillas. Our experience showed us that only guerrillas can effectively fight against guerrillas. We must not fall into the error made by Chamorro's generals—remember?"

"Stay there for the time being, Gabriel Heliodoro. I need you there for a very important job. We have proof that Barrios and his mercenaries were transported in Cuban ships. You must convoke an extraordinary session of the OAS Council and accuse Cuba of aggression. . . . Hello! Another thing, *compadre.* Talk with the Undersecretary of State and reveal the situation to him frankly. The munitions at our disposal cannot last more than two or three months. If the United States doesn't help us, we can't hold out for long. Remind them of the Batista case. It's still fresh in their minds. It was the embargo on the sale of arms to the government of Cuba that gave the victory to her leader. I have confidence in your skill, *compadre.* Don't fail me!"

Gabriel Heliodoro was breathing hard, and a great thirst was beginning to burn his throat and chest.

"How is the situation there in the capital?"

There was some hesitation on the president's part. "*Bueno,* it's not good. The usual thing. Subversive bulletins turn up in the streets and houses without its being known who is distributing them. Walls tarred with words insulting my person. A clandestine radio station which never ceases attacking my government and inciting the people to revolt." A pause, then, "Hello! The students last night stoned two soldiers of the military police, who responded with bullets, killing two or three boys and wounding half a dozen—or a dozen, I can't recall. It's the very devil—but there was no help for it. If we show weakness, we're sunk."

"Of course, of course. Look, *compadre.* Keep me informed of how things are going, either by telephone or

cablegram. Oh, I have a favor to ask. Have one of your
secretaries telephone to Francisquita, saying that I'm fine,
that everything is all right—I mean, here."

"Gabriel Heliodoro, open the game with the undersecretary. Get me automatic weapons and munitions. Otherwise we're lost."

The ambassador went into the bathroom and shaved
with such haste that he gashed his cheek. He took a cold
bath, then hurriedly drank his coffee. At seven he telephoned to the minister-counselor and to the military attaché, summoning them urgently to his office.

At nine, as usual, the other functionaries arrived at
the chancellery. All faces were shadowed. Merceditas,
huddled in her corner, could not get any work done; fear
paralyzed her fingers on the typewriter. Titito Villalba had
a nervous attack. Miss Ogilvy shoved two tablets of her
favorite tranquilizer down his throat and made the "boy"
lie down on a sofa. The officers in General Ugarte's office
displayed the most varied reactions. Two of them—the
youngest—requested leave to return to their country immediately; they wanted to take up arms against the invaders. The colonel sat at his desk, mute, stunned, repeatedly drinking swallows of water, and when he felt better
tried to ascertain his balance in the Chase Manhattan
Bank. The major had a nervous dysentery which kept him
running to the toilet for a good part of the morning.

"Dr. Molina!" Gabriel Heliodoro exclaimed, as he
paced up and down his office, as intractable as a recently
caged wild beast. "Telephone to the Department of State
and make an urgent appointment for me with the undersecretary. The OAS Council is in recess, but we must get a
special session called immediately and request convoca-
tion of the Meeting of Consultation. I am going to denounce Cuba as an aggressor nation."

Sitting on the sofa, depressed, Ugarte was staring at
the toes of his shoes. The dark brown of his face had taken
on the purplish color of an eggplant. ("It's that damned
asthma," he had explained on arriving at the chancellery.)
The only thing to do now, he reflected, the only way out

was to flee to Switzerland. If Carrera fell—and everything indicated that the situation was extremely grave—Hugo Ugarte would be extradited and shot. Yes, Switzerland had no extradition treaty with El Sacramento. The mob won't catch me, he thought. He loosened his tie, unbuttoned his collar. He looked at the ambassador. But I'm not saying a word to Gabriel Heliodoro, he decided. And Ninfa is going to find out about the plan only on the eve of the trip. A woman can't keep a secret.

"Ugarte!" shouted the ambassador. "Do something!"

"Man alive, what can I do?"

"At the first meeting of the Committee of Defense, reveal the situation to your colleagues and walk all over the representative from Cuba. Give it to him good! We have to get the deal going, stir up public opinion in the Americas. We must denounce the Cuban aggression to the world. This is not a revolution—it's undeclared war between two countries!"

He glanced rancorously at the portrait of Dr. Bustamante, so calm in his world of canvas, paint, and varnish. Then he turned to the minister-counselor.

"Dr. Molina, call together the newspaper correspondents for a news conference here in the chancellery as soon as possible. Prepare a written statement to distribute to the news agencies. If the revolution of that fellow Barrios wins out, the Russians will have two unsinkable aircraft carriers in the Caribbean from which they will be able to fire atomic projectiles against United States territory."

The minister-counselor started for the door, but the ambassador stopped him. "Another thing, Doctor. Inform the press that Barrios is a man of bad character, sought by the police for the crime of . . . of swindling . . . or rape . . . or anything!"

"But . . ." Molina began, knowing that this was all lies.

"Invent something, Doctor, use your imagination. Any weapon is valid in this hour, when the nation is in danger." He went to the minister, caught his lapels, and, with nostrils dilated, eyes half shut, he said between his teeth, "Not only the nation, Doctor, but our skin. If the revolutionaries win, they'll stand us up against the wall and stitch us up with bullets."

Four days later, in the late afternoon, Gabriel Heliodoro felt so alone in the silence of his office that he resolved to make company for himself, and burst into song, loudly singing some pornographic verses he had learned among the riffraff when he was an adolescent. In the adjoining room Clare Ogilvy was startled, bent her ear, and listened, vaguely alarmed.

The ambassador was thinking of the events of the day before. In the extraordinary session of the OAS Council he had made a direct, smashing attack on Cuba, accusing her of having aided in the invasion of El Sacramento. At one point, unable to control his tongue, he launched personal insults at members of the Cuban government. The representative of Cuba rose in fury to retort to the attack, and in the heat of the wrangle shouted, "Scoundrel! Liar!" Gabriel Heliodoro then lost his head completely and threw himself on the Cuban with the intention of beating him up. He was seized and held by three of his colleagues. The session had adjourned with no positive action.

That same day Gabriel Heliodoro had had an interview with the Undersecretary of State, and set forth frankly the situation in El Sacramento. "If my government is not aided by the United States with arms and munitions, *immediately*, we shall not be responsible for the future. I believe that you understand what it will mean for us to have one more Caribbean country in the hands of the enemies of democracy."

The American listened to him in silence, seated in his chair, his long legs crossed, his hands linked across his lean belly. His face, which made one think of a Protestant missionary, revealed not the least emotion. At last he gave an indefinite response. He would study the matter carefully and consult the Secretary of State. And he said good-by with a social smile, as if he had received a simple courtesy visit.

Remembering these things now, Gabriel Heliodoro

grew impatient. What else could he do? Almost daily telephone calls from the Foreign Ministry of El Sacramento
kept him up to date on events. There was street fighting in
Oro Verde. In the Province of San Fernando a loyalist
regiment had joined the revolutionaries, who were preparing an offensive against Soledad del Mar. It was said, too,
though without confirmation, that a landing had been
made in the region of Cañaverales, on the western flank of
the island. God in Heaven! Where could Barrios have
managed to recruit so many for the invasion? Beyond all
doubt, his files held names of hundreds of mercenaries
from other Central and South American countries.

Gabriel Heliodoro lighted a cigar and smoked it
absent-mindedly, gazing steadily at the portrait of Don
Alfonso. He thought of Rosalía. The doctors had succeeded in saving her life, and now—poor little thing!—she
was in a psychiatric clinic. After she was released he
would send her back to Cerro Hermoso, where she would
be in the care of the old aunt who had raised her.

He thought of Frances Andersen. The American
woman had left Washington two weeks earlier to marry a
millionaire. "And me alone here—and that damned revolution on top of everything else!"

For some seconds he was still, watching the smoke
from his cigar and thinking of his women. He had them in
his memory and in his imagination; he performed erotic
acrobatics with both on the Isabeline bed. And the ruminating on past pleasures—kisses, savorings, fragrances,
murmurings, moans, refinements—enhanced his sensation
of abandonment and solitude. These last weeks he had
received, at night in the embassy, the women that Titito
had arranged for him. But those healthy Americans did
not satisfy him. He found them too inexperienced, still
with an academic fustiness—yes, even a touch of Sunday
school—about them. They made love with the studious
application of girls who were preparing a school theme,
hoping to get a good grade. Or as one plays a game of
tennis, with rules and scoring of points.

He heaved a sigh, and looked at his desk, quite bare

of papers. He thought of Pablo, the ingrate who had rejected his friendship and insulted him. What had become
of him? It occurred to him that the boy might now decide
to join the revolutionaries. Hardly! Intellectuals of Ortega's stamp never got further than theories. They lived in
a false world of dreams and books. They had as much
horror of blood and violence as small children have of dark
rooms.

He rose and went to the window, leaned his forehead
on the pane, and gazed at the trees in the park. Familiar
images flitted rapidly through his mind: his daughters, his
grandchildren, a bit of the garden at his home in Cerro
Hermoso. . . . He sat down and asked his secretary to
telephone to the Ambassador of Nicaragua.

"Hello, old friend!" he exclaimed. "How goes it? . . .
No. . . . Very well. . . . Naturally. . . . Well, now, I'm the
one to apologize. I just lost my temper completely. But one
thing I tell you, my dear Ambassador, if we don't take
some serious steps, these fellows will wind up setting the
whole Caribbean on fire!"

He listened to the other's cooler judgment for some
moments, and then suggested, "We must get the council to
set up the Meeting of Consultation with the greatest urgency and send a committee to Soledad del Mar to verify
on the spot the truth of my accusations. The ships which
transported Barrios' troops were photographed at the moment they dropped anchor in a small bay some twenty-odd
kilometers from the town. There are scores of eyewitnesses
of the fact. The soldiers of the 5th Infantry captured two
wounded revolutionaries, left behind by their companions,
and got signed confessions from them proving the participation of the Cuban government in the invasion of El
Sacramento. . . . Of course, old friend. *Bueno*, I'll be seeing
you."

Still later that same afternoon he got into his Mercedes and asked Aldo Borelli to take him to the Lincoln
Memorial. In his hours of sadness or loneliness he was in
the habit of visiting the patriarch. He slowly climbed the

steps of the monument. He went in, stopped at the foot of
the crystalline marble figure, and gazed long into the illuminated face. He then strolled slowly around the statue,
thoughtful, hands in pockets, head down. And his steps
echoed—*pock, pock, pock*—in the enclosed space, empty
but for him at that hour.

Abraham Lincoln seemed to contemplate serenely the
cupola of the Capitol, shining white in the distance beyond the Mall. Gabriel Heliodoro remained for a little,
leaning against one of the columns at the entrance to the
memorial, looking at the long pool in which the fiery colors
of the setting sun and the severe bulk of the obelisk were
reflected. His heart ached with a profound, tremulous
yearning, for what or whom he did not know.

Before going to bed that night, Michel Michel wrote
in his diary:

"12 August. Wednesday. Another revolution. *Bon
Dieu!* This is the end of Juventino Carrera, and I do not
feel brave or strong enough to face another ambassador. I
have decided to resign my position as butler of this embassy and return to my own country. I have enough dollar
savings in the bank to permit me to live comfortably the
rest of my life. I am thinking of opening, in Avignon, a
restaurant of typical Latin American dishes. I may even
marry some lady of middle age, not too ugly, economical,
hardworking, and with the flesh not very demanding.
Speaking of flesh, I have the recipe for the famous
empanadas sacramenteñas. I shall give the restaurant an
exotic name, like 'Páramo' or 'Cerro Hermoso,' or else the
obvious 'Chez Michel.' In Avignon I shall write my
memoirs. And wait for Death. *'Entrez, chère Madame.
Vous êtes en retard!'* "

In the small hours of the night Michel was awakened
by shouts. He recognized his employer's voice, leaped out
of bed, slipped on his bathrobe, and went upstairs. He
found Gabriel Heliodoro walking down the hall barefoot,
wearing only the trousers of his pajamas. He was gesticulating and shouting, "Sons of bitches! Cowards! Don't run

—throw those grenades back at the enemy!" He halted and was silent when he saw the butler.

"Do you wish anything, Mr. Ambassador?"

"Who called you?"

"Well, Your Excellency, I thought . . ." Michel murmured, bowing his head and starting to withdraw.

"Wait. Let's go downstairs."

The Sacramentan caught the Frenchman's arm in an intimacy he had not shown him until then, and both went down the stairs side by side. Michel was ill at ease, not knowing what to say, and the other's bare torso, hot and damp with sweat, so close beside him made him strangely uncomfortable.

They went into the library. The butler turned on the lights. Gabriel Heliodoro paced back and forth in the room for several minutes, as though in a somnambulistic state, and at last, turning to the butler, he requested, "Bring me the bottle of cognac and two glasses. And make me some very strong coffee. Quick!"

Minutes later the two were seated in leather armchairs facing each other. Michel once again felt his profound scorn for this uncouth fellow who invited his *valet de chambre* to sit down with him and share a bottle of cognac. Don Alfonso was different. He could do these things with finesse.

"I had a dream, Michel. I was in the Sierra de la Calavera, in the thick of a battle, and my soldiers were deserting, abandoning me and running down the mountain, dropping their hand grenades and their pistols on the ground. A bunch of capons! Then I started yelling. I woke up, jumped out of bed, and to get it off my chest I kept on yelling. When all's said and done, I am in my own house."

He drank the rest of his cognac, upending the glass. Michel served him a cup of coffee. "Do you think I look very old?"

"Why, Mr. Ambassador, I would take you at most for forty-four or forty-five."

"That's right. Look at these hands. They are a young man's hands. You can't see those dark blotches on them that appear on old men's hands. See? You can't. Miss Andersen told me that she had never slept with a man like me. Turn on the air conditioner. It's too hot in here."

The butler obeyed.

"Well, Michel, you're looking at a man who's on the wrong side in this war. I've always been against the government. Life has taken so many turns that now I'm left on the side of legality. Imagine me, me, on the side of the 5th Infantry! I, Gabriel Heliodoro Alvarado, am going to have to fight the rebels. Isn't that an irony of fate?"

Michel shook his head repeatedly like an automaton. The ambassador rose and started walking around the chairs and sofa, talking all the time, but in a tone of one who is talking to himself.

"It was a paradise up there on top of the Sierra. The air thin and transparent, like crystal. Nothing grander exists than the break of day seen from up there. It seems as though the womb of the sea is opening up to give birth to the sun. The peaks are golden. But sit down, Michel, don't be formal. Tonight I am not your boss. I am a boy from Soledad del Mar, one Gabriel Heliodoro, *hijo de una chingada*. My home was the regimental latrine. Put that in your memoirs! But everything up there on the mountains was clean. Even Ugarte! I've never forgotten the day that we shot down a government fighter plane that was flying low over the mountain to strafe our positions. Hidden among the rocks, we fired our automatic weapons at it. *Br-r-r-r-á!* I saw the plane explode in the air and fall in flames. A sight to swell the chest. Ah, and how good it was to lie watching the flight of the condors over the peaks! That was living. A world without walls or protocol. And here I am in this air-conditioned tomb, in this city of perpetual resting places, in this huge cemetery along the Potomac. Why, Michel? Why?" A pause. "What time is it? Three? Do you know what bothers me? There are no dogs barking at night in Washington. Or cocks crowing at dawn. Make a note of this: I'm going to be shot at five o'clock some morning. Don't ask me the day. I only know the hour.

Now go to sleep, Michel. These problems are mine, mine alone. Forget what I've said. I never got to know my legitimate mother. My adoptive one is the *Virgen de la Soledad*, who is in the little church in my home town. The vicar is Padre Catalino Sender, my friend."

He stopped, pensive for an instant, and then added, "Who at this moment is surely in the Sierra looking after the living and the dead. Go and sleep, Michel. Thanks. Good night."

"Good night, Mr. Ambassador."

At that hour the lights were out in the Ugarte house on a quiet street of Bethesda, but in the couple's bedroom, which was redolent of heliotrope and human perspiration, there was a half-light, for the darkness was lessened by the glow from the street lamps through the windows.

Ninfa Ugarte had not yet managed to get to sleep. She tossed and turned, restlessly, thinking of the unexpected trip. *Ay!* From the hour when her husband had informed her of his decision to leave in two days for Switzerland— since Carrera's downfall had become inevitable—she had begun to feel an oppression in her chest with palpitations. *Dios mío!* What a sorry life! Rosalía had lost her mind. El Sacramento had been invaded by Communist bandits. Switzerland must be a monotonous green postcard, with mountains, valleys, chalets, cheeses, and cows. Luckily, it was the land of good chocolates. But she was going to lose Aldo Borelli. And her lovely Pyrex dishes. And all those pretty things she had bought in Washington and sent back to her house in Cerro Hermoso.

Ninfa heaved a long shuddering sigh, which shook her breasts. Tears began to roll down her cream-coated cheeks. At her side, her husband was sleeping uneasily, at intervals uttering groans of distress. The respiration of the fat old tomcat was a continuous panting wheeze. She cast a glance full of resentment and laden with complaint at the general's form.

The ex-chief of police at one point began to groan

louder, while his body shivered in epileptoid convulsions. Ninfa shook him by the shoulders. "Hugo, Hugo! Wake up!" He awoke, sat up in bed, stared around him, turned on the light, and stayed motionless for an instant with his head dropped on his laboring chest.

"What was it?"

He took some time to reply. "A nightmare. Horrible. I was on the heights of the Sierra, downed in battle . . . couldn't help it. I threw myself . . . down the slope . . . a huge stone, rolling after me . . . going to crush me . . . I felt a heavy weight . . . on my legs . . . couldn't run any more. That was when you woke me up."

"You were sleeping on your back, belly up. Lie on your side."

He obeyed. She turned out the light and closed her eyes. Against the dark background of her lids, as on a movie screen, she watched figures passing. Aldo Borelli naked in a motel room. The Pyrex dishes like a multicolored flight of birds. Aldo in the bed beside her. Look what a lovely plate, Doña Francisquita, red with white trim. Yes, I bought it in Washington. No, it's not at all cheap. *Ay, Aldo! Adiós, mi vida!* Are you going to forget me, darling? But look at this green one, too, Señora Presidenta. And you can put them on the fire without harming them. *Ay, Aldo!* My uterus is on fire, I want a son by you! Yes, neighbor, the blue ones are very delicate—I could have made a fortune with them if it hadn't been for that *mierda* of a revolution, if you'll excuse my language. Aldo, would you be capable of abandoning everything, wife, children, your brother, everything, to go with me on this trip to Switzerland? Don't answer. I know it's impossible. The Pyrex dishes! You don't love me. You exploit me. You do it all for money. Oh, how wretched I am!

She turned over in the bed, seeking a more comfortable position. She came face to face with her husband, whose acid breath blew gently on her cheek. Suddenly she was filled with such a hatred of the man asleep by her side that she had an impulse to crush his withered, useless scrotum with her knee.

Next day Gabriel Heliodoro was late. The president had not telephoned him for two days. The morning papers carried the news that Oro Verde and San Fernando were definitely in the hands of the revolutionaries, but that an attempt at landing in the vicinity of Puerto Esmerelda had been repulsed by troops faithful to the government.

The ambassador summoned Titito to his office. "Any message from the Department of State?"

"None, Excellency."

"Idiots! They are going to lose the leadership of the Western world through sheer lack of diplomatic skill. They ought to hire an English statesman as soon as possible to run the foreign policy of this country."

"Have you seen your interview in the papers?"

"No. Did it all come out right?"

"They cut more than half of your statements. The whole thing was left rather vague. The sad truth, Mr. Ambassador, is that our country's affairs are not considered important by the American press. Newspapers that day gave more space to the invention of stainless-steel dentures for cows than to your interview."

Gabriel Heliodoro smiled, made a resigned gesture, and said, "All right, Titito. If there is any new development, inform me."

In his office, sitting at his desk, Dr. Jorge Molina was writing on a sheet of paper with a pencil.

SITUATION IN EL SACRAMENTO:

1. The whole southern part of the island in rebel hands.

2. Barrios' troops descend periodically from the Sierra in paralyzing commando raids. Their ranks are swelled daily by scores of volunteers.

3. Landings of rebel forces (unconfirmed) in Cañaverales.

4. At Puerto Esmeralda a whole battalion revolted, but, failing to win over the rest of the federal garrison, abandoned the city and headed for the *cordillera*. (Possibly.)

5. The embargo on arms for the island continues.

6. The revolution is spreading like an oil slick.

7. Public opinion in the Americas seems to lean toward the revolutionary cause.

The minister-counselor closed his eyes. His government's situation was critical. How many more months could Carrera resist? Two? Three? Four? He recalled his thoughts and feelings of the night before in his apartment. He had put on his monkish robe to write, trying to concentrate his whole attention on the personality of Don Pánfilo. Vain effort. The figure of Padre Catalino persisted in shadowing his mind like a tatterdemalion phantom, a black shape against the bluish, distant slope of the Sierra. He had felt then a kind of envy of that village priest who was now, in all probability, repeating his exploits of thirty-four years ago, going up and down the slopes of the mountain range on his burro to give spiritual aid to the revolutionaries. Padre Catalino could face God, if God did exist, with clear and dauntless eyes. If God did not exist, the parish priest of Soledad del Mar was at least ready to contemplate other men and history without blinking, his face and heart serene. And his faith and his goodness now seemed to Molina so great that they might even constrain God to exist.

The ex-seminarian traced on the paper, with his pencil, a line as sinuous as the profile of a *cordillera*. He thought of his youth. From the window of his room in the Seminario Mayor in Páramo, on days of transparent atmosphere, he could see in the distance the bulk of the Cordillera de los Indios. For the mountains he had always felt a certain fascination tinged with fear. As a boy he had imagined that the lightning and the thunder came out of the Sierra; it was in the mountains that the winds dwelt. More than once in his moments of doubt about the existence of God—this with his ordination less than a year away—he sent mute questions to the spurs of the Sierra, and sensed that his queries came back to him unanswered, and, hard as basalt, beat again upon his heart.

The minister-counselor felt a sharp pain in his shoulder. Was it worth while to go on living? Could he go back to El Sacramento if Carrera should be thrown out of office? No. Never. Furthermore, he found himself without the courage to begin a new life, no matter where. He had no strong motive to live on. He loved no one. He was loved by none.

Then and there, alone in his cold, impersonal office, Jorge Molina came to a decision. Up to the last moment (the best form of suicide was the one chosen by Señora de Vivanco) he would seek to watch events with an objective, even cynical, eye. He would amuse himself a little with the situation. Would it be asking too much of life to give him, as a kind of meager dividend for his long stay on earth, the bitter gray pleasure of witnessing that downfall? He wanted to observe the reactions of his embassy colleagues to the events in El Sacramento. He would savor the tragi-comedy scene by scene. Mainly he was curious to see what Gabriel Heliodoro's attitude would be. Would he have the dignity to return to Cerro Hermoso to help defend his *compadre* and chief? Certainly not. He was a man without nobility, a common adventurer. He would quite certainly fly to Switzerland as Ugarte had just done.

I also want to observe my own reactions, Molina thought. Shall I have the fortitude for the definitive gesture? Or am I perhaps a cowardly, compliant egoist like the others?

34

WHEN PABLO ORTEGA read in the papers the news of the first landing of rebel troops in the environs of Soledad del Mar, he saw that a new door was opening to him, and that his destiny was now plain. He had no other alternative than to join the forces of Miguel

Barrios. Several images and voices in his mind were pointing out to him the path of the revolution.

He determined to think no more of the state of his father's heart, and he began to make ready for his departure. He studied the surest paths to reach the Sierra. And all his preparations—canceling the apartment lease, paying his bills, tearing up and burning his papers—produced in him the excitement of a boy on the eve of a long vacation. His headaches disappeared, and he was on the verge of reconciliation with the fellow who faced him every morning in the mirror as he shaved.

But a letter from his mother arrived about that time that left him perturbed for a while.

"My son: Your ill-timed decision to leave the diplomatic service has surprised and shocked us deeply. First I thought I would conceal it from your father, since lately he has been having palpitations, pains in his chest, and some shortness of breath. I saw, however, that sooner or later some unwary friend or a newspaper item would reveal it to him, and that would make the shock much worse. So I have told him the story piecemeal in the gentlest way possible. You cannot imagine how hurt and sad your gesture has left him.

"No matter how I try, I cannot understand why you did not have the delicacy at least to consult us before taking that step, which is going to make your return to your country and your home so difficult.

"I beg you for the love of God, at least give us some idea of what you intend to do now. We miss you very much. Were it not for the state of your father's health, we should both go to Washington immediately to visit you, even though I no longer believe you really want to see us again.

"The old saying is quite true—misfortunes never come singly. We are extremely disturbed also by the news of our country's invasion by mercenary troops coming from Cuba. It is a calamity. The churches here are full of the faithful at all hours, praying and making promises, begging God not to allow the victory of the Communists.

Your father says he prefers death to falling into the hands of those barbarians.

"Getting back to your case, it would be very sad if Dionisio should die without seeing you again. Perhaps we can get His Reverence the Archbishop to intervene with the president and obtain his consent to your return, without your being molested by the authorities.

"Your father sends you his blessing and your mother does the same, for in spite of everything she loves you and sends affectionate kisses.

Isabel"

"In spite of everything"? Pablo put the letter in his pocket with a brusque, irritated gesture, and sought to forget his mother's words—something he achieved with a facility that surprised him. The fact was that the kidnapping and probable liquidation of Dr. Gris, plus the sordid intrigue of the killing of Vivanco, the pretext for Juventino Carrera to deliver his coup d'état and unleash a fresh series of outrages and violence—all these things had acted upon his mind like a kind of vaccine that made him immune to the virus of the maternal blackmail.

One evening he invited Orlando Gonzaga to come to his apartment. As he usually did on entering, the Brazilian diplomat went over to the mantel above the fireplace, on which were aligned several groups of the painted clay figures by Maestro Natalicio representing the Stations of the Cross. Every time he examined them, Gonzaga discovered a detail that before had escaped him. Natalicio had modeled the figurines with modern clothing, and among them —as Pablo had explained—it was possible to recognize some individuals of Sacramentan politics of 1915. The figure of Jesus Christ was Juan Balsa himself, whom Chamorro's soldiers had martyred. Pablo's usual name for the whole collection was "The Passion According to San Natalicio."

As he prepared the drinks, Ortega was smiling, glancing up from time to time at his friend. "I have some good news for you. You've always coveted those pieces. Once you went so far as to offer me five hundred dollars for them, remember? Well, now the good news—you are going to get the entire group as a gift."

Gonzaga whirled around. "Are you joking?" But in the very instant he pronounced the words he had an intuition of what Pablo was about to say to him.

"I've decided to go to the Sierra."

"I had some suspicion of it already."

"Why?"

"Oh, certain things you've been saying or asking these last few days. Your silences, your air of misgiving. It's all as clear as water."

"And what do you think of the notion?"

The Brazilian shrugged, accepted the glass of whiskey handed to him, sat down, and said, "It's a matter that only you can decide. At first I imagined you were going to Paris."

"That would be merely flight, a simple change of scene. My problem is not geographical. The little drama would go on. And I'd only be taking to the Rive Gauche and to the Champs Élysées this guilty feeling of mine like a kind of bad smell."

Gonzaga looked pensively into his glass. He hesitated a few seconds before inquiring, "What about Don Dionisio?"

Pablo pulled out of his pocket the letter he had received from his mother and handed it to his friend, who read it attentively.

"What do you say to that?" Ortega asked, when he returned the paper to him.

"The sweet maternal blackmail."

"Sweet? That has been embittering my life for many years."

Gonzaga let out a dry laugh. "You think your parents castrated you, Pablo. The operation began with your adventure with—what was her name? Pía. And now, ever since that revolution broke out, you've got the idea into your head—a bit confused, barely semiconscious—that your genital organs are up on the Pico de la Calavera, and that you have to scale the mountain through hardship and peril to recover your sex and your male dignity. Am I right?"

"It's not all that simple."

Ortega was drinking, too, but with a rather absent-minded air. He wanted to put his friend abreast of his plans, but to do so in a natural way, without melodrama. He feared the other's wry humor . . . and his own, for that matter.

A long silence fell, in which the Brazilian stared at Natalicio's figures without seeing them. He was thinking of Pablo's decision, and could see him in a khaki uniform, grasping a submachine gun, his cartridge belt over his shoulder.

"Pablo, I'm going to be frank with you. You have such a horror of violence that I can't imagine you shooting and killing people. Have you thought of that?"

"Of course. I've gone sleepless many a night reflecting on all these things."

"In the heat of battle, our animal side comes to the surface and killing must be relatively easy. But think of the following day, when the warrior's gun and head cool off. Think of the hangover from the combat."

Orlando got up, lit a cigarette, stroked with his fingertips the "bloody" back of Juan Balsa, who was bent under the weight of the cross, while a centurion was cudgeling him.

"Think of the victory, too, which is another problem. All those passions let loose . . . the vengeances . . . the *paredón* and the firing squads . . . injustice inextricably mixed with justice . . . the popular tribunals. . . . Do you think you've got the stomach to endure all that?"

Pablo also stood up, impatient. "And do you think I have the stomach and the head to bear all *this*? And besides, Gonzaga, a decision such as I have taken cannot be analyzed coldly, as if it were a question of a problem in mathematics. The unknown quantities are many, I know. But if I wish to embark rationally on this adventure, with all doubts satisfied, all guarantees assured . . . well, I'll wind up apathetic, cowed, immobilized here in Washington. And I shall not respect myself for it. On the contrary."

"You're a masochist, Pablo."

"Nonsense. You know I'm not. I like the good life as well as you do."

"Has the thought ever passed through your head that I, too, have a problem similar to yours? Do you think, by any chance, that I feel happy in this iridescent soap bubble of a diplomatic world, while in my country millions and millions of fellow countrymen are living more like animals than like people? But as it happens, I also think of the dangers of a civil war in a country the size of Brazil. You'll say that I'm self-indulgent, compliant. I am, I can't deny it. But I don't hate myself for that. I tried once to despise myself, but I wasn't at all successful. I like myself very much. I have an unlimited tolerance for my frailties and defects. Besides, I know that if I got into an armed movement and were forced to kill, I'd go crazy. Maybe the thought of being dead is less disagreeable even than that. No! No! Not that either, I don't know. You may say I'm a coward. Perhaps. But I am not without sensibilities. I sometimes look at the map of Brazil, the sleeping giant, I think of her problems, her eternal, sordid, crooked politics, and I ask myself, What to do? With whom? How? In what direction? And I conclude that it would be madness to meddle in a revolutionary conspiracy just to satisfy my feeling of responsibility—if I really have one. The important thing is to save Brazil, not Orlando Gonzaga. And as you can see, this line of reasoning doesn't get me anywhere, either."

"I didn't invite you here to accuse you, but to discuss my problems with you. I am determined to join the Barrios forces without regard for consequences. And now I'll answer the question you asked just now. To all intents and purposes I have *already* murdered my father."

"And how do you feel?"

"For the moment, I feel nothing. I am anesthetized. And I must stay that way until the end of the revolution."

"When do you intend to set off?"

"As soon as possible. Within two or three days. Or even before."

"How do you expect to reach the Sierra?"

"I see two possible ways. First, to take an international airline from New York to Puerto Esmeralda, and there get a national plane that will take me to Soledad del Mar."

Gonzaga made a pessimistic grimace. "Suppose they arrest you when you get off at the jewel of the Caribbean? And suppose the commercial flights to Soledad del Mar are canceled because of the revolution?"

"Well, I can also fly from New York to Jamaica and there charter a plane that can land on my father's estate."

"That plan strikes me as being the safer. And then?"

"The Ortega y Murat cane fields extend from the vicinity of Soledad del Mar to the skirts of the Sierra. I am certain that Padre Catalino will help me to find Barrios and his soldiers."

"As he helped Gabriel Heliodoro to find Carrera thirty-four years ago?"

"Exactly." Pablo smiled, throwing himself on the sofa, where he lay prone.

Gonzaga did not seem satisfied. "And suppose the air taxi falls into the sea?"

"That would itself be one solution."

Ortega immediately saw the negative sense of what he had just said. In that case, was he going in search of a penance or a punishment, and not just to win a better life for his people? He was alarmed.

After a short silence Orlando inquired, "Who else knows of your decision?"

"Only two persons, you and Bill Godkin."

"What about Clare Ogilvy? And the Japanese doll?"

"I'll say good-by to both just as soon as I can. I'll tell them I'm leaving for Europe. Or even for Cerro Hermoso. It doesn't matter. But now I must discuss with you some matters of a practical nature. You will be not only one of my heirs but also my executor."

"You're not dead yet, man! I hope you'll be very much alive the day that Carrera and his bandits bite the dust."

"So I hope and desire. But I must act as if I were never going to return. Anything can happen." He made a broad gesture that took in the whole room. "Choose some books and records for yourself and give the rest to Godkin." He pointed to the mantel. " 'The Passion According to San Natalicio' is yours. You can take it away tonight."

"I'll act only as the repository of it."

"No. It's yours. Definitely. And no more arguing. The hi-fi is for Miss Hirota, with some books of poetry that I'll leave separately. The furniture of this apartment that belongs to me, two or three items, I'll give to Merceditas. To Clare I leave my Thunderbird. I'll leave a complete list of my possessions so that you can divide them up."

"Shut up, will you!"

Much against his will, Gonzaga was beginning to feel touched. To dissimulate, he started whistling a samba through his teeth.

"I've made out checks to pay all my debts."

"Do you want to make me cry."

Pablo rose, putting an end to the discussion of the "matters of a practical nature."

"Funny," he said, "when I last saw Gris I complained of a headache. You know what he said? 'The mountain air will cure those headaches.' Yes, those were his very words. I'm not dreaming them up."

"Do you believe, then—"

"Yes. Gris knew that shortly there would be revolutionaries in the Sierra de la Calavera. And what's more, he was certain that I would be with them."

Pablo turned on the hi-fi. He pulled a record off the shelf at random. It was one of the Brandenburg Concertos. The two sat listening in silence.

"You won't have Bach in the Sierra," Gonzaga remarked softly after a few minutes, "only the explosion of grenades and the rat-tat-tat of machine guns."

"I'm suspicious of you. You must be a secret agent of Carrera's under orders to dishearten me."

"Hardly. I find that I'm envious of you."

Pablo measured his friend with his eyes. "Too bad you're shorter and fatter than I am."

"Why?"

"If you weren't, you could inherit my suits, too."

"Oh, go to . . ." Gonzaga caught back the word, and then, pitching his voice theatrically, he declaimed, "You will have no difficulty in finding the path to the Sierra even on the darkest night, oh heroic youth! Because your genitals will be shining like a lighthouse on the heights of the Pico de la Calavera!"

35

NEXT MORNING, at his desk in the Amalgamated Press office, Bill Godkin was looking over the latest news. The victorious landing of revolutionary contingents in the Province of Cañaverales was confirmed. Oro Verde and San Fernando were definitely in the hands of the invaders, whose march on Soledad del Mar was nevertheless proceeding very slowly, not only on account of the poor conditions of the roads and the difficulties of supplying the troops, but also because the loyalist fighter planes repeatedly strafed the rebel columns in low-flying sweeps.

Miguel Barrios, now confirmed as supreme chief of the revolution, had installed his general headquarters in the Sierra de la Calavera. Soledad del Mar, however, was still in the power of the federals. The taking of the town was of vital importance for the revolutionaries, for the 5th Infantry Regiment, reinforced now by a regiment of artillery, dominated the narrow strip of seashore that offered the easiest and safest passage to the north of the island, bypassing the *cordillera*.

Godkin reread the confidential letter which he had

just received from the Amalpress correspondent in Cerro Hermoso and which, to evade the implacable censorship of Carrera's police, had been sent through the good offices of the United States Embassy by way of the diplomatic pouch. The letter reported that it was getting harder and harder to find out what was really happening in the rest of the country, because the Sacramentan government prohibited foreign correspondents' leaving the capital, while at the same time it censored their dispatches. There were rumors of agitation in the streets of Puerto Esmeralda and Páramo. Cerro Hermoso, the correspondent continued, looked like a besieged city. Its inhabitants were obliged to retire to their homes after 8 P.M. Gatherings both public and private had been strictly forbidden. The university had been closed, and the same was true of all cafés, clubs, theaters, and movie houses in the capital. At night, in the deserted street, only stray dogs and army patrols with loaded weapons were to be seen. Arrests of "suspect elements" continued. There was talk about summary executions, tortures inflicted on political prisoners—dark stories that no newspaper dared publish. The conservative classes were in panic, and there were rumors that some members of the Congress dissolved by Carrera were already seeking to reach an understanding with Barrios' agents. The end of the letter ran, "It would be overoptimistic to count on Carrera's complete defeat in the next few weeks or even the next month. The whole air force is still loyal to the government, as are the powerful garrisons of Cerro Hermoso and Puerto Esmeralda. But there is one problem beginning to perturb the dictator and his generals seriously —the growing scarcity of arms and munitions, aggravated by the embargo imposed by the United States on the sale of matériel to either side. This being so, it cannot be an exaggeration to state that El Libertador will not be able to celebrate next Christmas in the Palace of Government. He will have to do it in exile or in hell."

Godkin looked up, linked his fingers behind his head, and sat smoking, his eyes fixed on the window. If the United States maintained the arms embargo, it was be-

cause the Department of State was no longer interested in
the continuation of Juventino Carrera and his gang in
power. On the other hand, it also seemed clear that,
Miguel Barrios still being a politically unknown quantity,
it was not at all safe to help him take over. The ideal
solution for North American interests would, then, be an
agreement—signed on Carrera's corpse—between the rebels and the wealthy elements of El Sacramento. It was
possible that the American ambassador in Cerro Hermoso
was already working to that end, aided by the archbishop
primate and the members of the former Cabinet of the
Generalissimo.

Godkin was aware of a sense of discomfort, a vague
anxiety, a kind of "white fear." He always felt this whenever the time was drawing near for doing something
dangerous, difficult, or merely unpleasant. Suddenly he
realized the cause. In a little while he would have to take
Pablo Ortega to the airport to leave for New York, there to
change to a plane for Jamaica, final destination the Sierra
de la Calavera.

Poor Pablo! He was violating his nature, opposed to
violence, because his feeling of guilt for not doing something to save his people from misery and oppression had
become unbearable. Godkin rapped the bowl of his pipe
on the edge of the ashtray. Could there be any man in this
world completely free of a guilty conscience? he asked
himself.

Why at this moment should he feel responsible for
Ruth's death? There was not a thing that he or any other
mortal could have done to save her. The disease was incurable. And yet he had felt that the simple fact of having
survived her was a treachery to his wife.

The three friends were rolling down Constitution
Avenue in Gonzaga's car en route to the airport. Sitting
beside his Brazilian friend, Pablo Ortega was gazing out
unseeingly, feeling in the pit of his stomach the same dizzy
sensation that a man teetering high on a trapeze with nothing but the ground beneath him must feel. Slumped on the

back seat, Bill Godkin vainly hunted about in his mind for something to say.

It had rained the night before, and the sky, like the air, was limpid. The morning light lent a new luster to the greens of the trees and the lawns. When the car passed the Administration Building of the Pan American Union, the tormented shade of Glenda Doremus obtruded itself for a few seconds in Ortega's mind.

To the left rose the Lincoln Memorial. The image of the ambassador extinguished that of the girl from Georgia. That morning last April, the President smiling at the top of the steps at the entrance to the White House, and Gabriel Heliodoro, eyes shining, face like a sun, climbing the steps with hand already extended.

The car was now crossing Memorial Bridge. The Potomac waters were a clouded rose. Toward Georgetown, above a clump of trees, appeared the slate-colored roofs of the Jesuit university. Pablo recalled the lecture delivered by Gris in one of those buildings the autumn before. His subject was the Spanish poet Góngora, and the professor was having one of his great evenings. He paced up and down before his audience—students of Spanish literature —with the easy freedom of a consummate actor, reciting the Fábula de Polifemo y Galatea. Pablo murmured to himself:

> *infame turba de nocturnas aves*
> *gimiendo tristes y volando graves.*
> (wretched flock of night birds
> moaning sadly and flying gravely.)

"Eh?" Gonzaga looked around at him.

"Nothing. Just recalling a poem."

"Oh."

The car was now going along the other side of the river. As he caught sight of the monument erected by the American government to the memory of all men lost at sea—a brief, light *haikai* in greenish bronze—a flight of gulls on the crest of a breaking wave—Ortega thought of Kimiko. They had met the evening before at their usual

tea house. He had told the little Japanese girl that this was
good-by. She had replied serenely that she knew the sad
hour would have to come sooner or later. He told her that
he was going back to his own land. And she said, " 'Land'
is a very large word, Pablo. 'Land' means cities, fields,
rivers, valleys—and also mountains." And then he realized
that she had divined his real destination; he could not
deceive her. They said good-by in front of the building in
which Kimiko had her apartment. He took his little friend
in his arms and kissed her forehead. She pushed away from
him and went straight to the front door, almost running
and not looking back.

Nor was it possible to deceive Clare Ogilvy. "To me
you've always been as transparent as glass, Pablo. Well, so
you're off to Paris, eh? Well, I don't believe it. You're going
to the Sierra." She sniffed, twisting her face in a grimace,
her eyes wet.

"Clare, I want you to have my Thunderbird."

"I can take care of it during your absence."

"No! I'm giving you the car as a present."

Shock on the secretary's face. "Are you *chiflado*? How
can I accept a present like that?"

He smiled. "Clare, my dear, you Americans are past
masters at the art of giving, but you need to learn to cultivate the art of receiving. The thought of leaving my car
with you as a souvenir is very pleasant to me. So take it
without asking ethical or technical questions." And the experienced, mature, efficient woman, like a child, burst into
tears.

At the airport, after Pablo presented his tickets at the
Pan American Airways window, where he also checked his
bags, the three friends, with nowhere to go and nothing to
say, wandered back and forth, an odd trio performing an
unsynchronized sonata of throat clearings, whistling, pipe
puffing, forced coughs. . . . Ortega went to a newsstand
and bought a detective story in a pocket edition to read on
the plane. To kill time was easy. The hard thing would be
to kill human beings. Even his worst enemies. Best not

to think of that. He must keep one idea in mind—to get to the Sierra. He would concentrate on it. He would erect a wall to hide the past and another to shut off the future. And in the limited but living, urgent, elastic space of the present he would move on implacably toward his objective.

From time to time the three friends would glance furtively at the great clock or discreetly consult their watches. When the voice over the loudspeakers announced the departure of a flight, all three would grow tense.

At last Gonzaga spoke. "May I ask you a question of a personal nature, Pablo?"

"Of course."

"Up yonder in the Sierra, do you intend to grow a beard like Fidel Castro?"

Ortega gave a short, nervous laugh. Godkin's eyes also laughed behind the curtain of his pipe smoke. At last the departure of Pablo's flight was announced. The three walked toward the gate. Godkin shook Pablo's hand for some time, muttering, "Take care of yourself, boy." Gonzaga gave him the Latin embrace without saying a word. And hardly had Pablo vanished down the corridor leading to his plane when his companions, still silent, returned to the car.

36

O NE NIGHT toward the end of September Godkin had a dream that perturbed him. He was scaling a high mountain, experiencing a strange sensation, a mixture of joy and fear. He was endeavoring to reach, at all costs, the highest point of the mountain, even though he was certain that death awaited him up there. "If I know that," he asked himself, "why am I continuing the climb?" And he answered himself, "Because I must. Because I must. Because I must." He was drawing farther and farther away from the world of men, without sorrow and without regrets. He did not want to look down. He did not want to get dizzy. He felt clean, light, nimble. The air of the heights was a cold crystal. The stars were in reach of his hands. But suddenly he saw his own cadaver toppled over a flat rock and covered with black vultures eating his flesh. He understood why he was climbing the mountain. He had made a date with Ruth on the Pico de la Calavera. How could he have forgotten so important and definitive an appointment? Ruth and death were one and the same.

He awoke in the middle of the night, and sat awhile on the bed, trying to reconstruct the dream and feeling more than ever the mystery and wonder of life.

He left the bed early next morning and, while he was shaving, his mind seized once more on the first verse of a poem of Auden's that Pablo had been in the habit of reciting with an almost obsessive frequency in the last week before departing: "I know a retired dentist who only paints mountains."

Sitting at the kitchen table drinking coffee, he became aware of an idea taking shape in his mind. On reaching the Amalpress office he had already made a decision that gave him a sense of newness and sudden rejuvenation. He went straight to the office of the agency director.

"Fred, I've got an idea."

"Good morning anyway, Bill."

"Excuse me, Fred, good morning. You must know that I started my career as a correspondent by interviewing the present President Juventino Carrera in the days when he was in the Sierra trying to overthrow the dictator Chammorro."

"Sure, that's history now."

"O.K. The time for my retirement is getting close. I thought it would be interesting to close the circle of my professional life by interviewing now, in the same mountains, the man who wants to overthrow the dictator Carrera."

Fred looked at him with a noncommittal expression on his brick-dust red face. "A man of your age climbing mountains? You're nuts."

"Now, first of all, it's not as tough as it may seem. There are still burros in Soledad del Mar. Padre Catalino is still in his parish. God's in His heaven. And I'm not as old as you think."

"But how do you expect to reach the Sierra? I'm not talking about the physical difficulties but the bureaucratic ones. You know what I mean."

"Our embassy in Cerro Hermoso can help."

Fred shook his head pessimistically. "I don't believe the Department of State wants to meddle. The situation is very delicate. Don't forget that we have a correspondent in the capital of El Sacramento and he can't get permission from the authorities to leave the city."

"I know all that. But even so I think it's worth the effort to try."

"Bill, what are you trying to prove?"

The newspaper man was as pensive for an instant. "I don't know yet. It's an idea that just occurred to me today, and I like it."

"Don't count on my *official* approval for your adventure. But you can be sure that I'll do nothing to hinder you. Go on your own, at your own risk. But I suspect that the difficulties will start right here in Washington. Don Gabriel Heliodoro will not authorize a visa for your passport."

Days later the newspapers announced that Miguel Barrios had come down from the Sierra with his forces and, aided by the revolutionary columns coming up from the south, had laid siege to the city of Soledad del Mar, whose garrison had surrendered after a short resistance. The road to the north was now open to the insurgents. Announcement was also made of successful landings of revolutionary contingents on the west coast of the island with the purpose of taking the city of Páramo, obligatory passageway to the capital.

Godkin now listened every night to the news broadcast from the radio station which the revolutionaries had set up in Soledad del Mar. By this means he came to learn, among many other things, that Miguel Barrios had established his headquarters in the plantation house of the Ortega y Murat family, and that Pablo Ortega was with him, serving as secretary to the column. One night he had the pleasant surprise of hearing his friend's voice reading a communiqué from the Revolutionary Command. Now, he reflected, he could easily get his interview with Barrios. He made ready for the trip.

October came in with its amber and violet placidity. One afternoon Kimiko Hirota approached the window of her office in the Embassy of Japan and stood contemplating the garden, where squirrels were running over the lawn and up the trees, whose leaves were now the color of gold or rusty red. She thought of Pablo, and mentally sent him a *haikai*.

AUTUMN
Woods copper-hued,
Yellow butterfly,
Tawny squirrel.

Sadly she turned back to her desk, sat down and began deciphering a code dispatch which had arrived from Tokyo just before.

At the window of his office in the chancellery Gabriel Heliodoro Alvarado was looking at the dry leaves that the wind was dragging about on the park grass. He was depressed. He had talked that morning to President Carrera. His *compadre* had informed him that the situation was very grave, although not yet desperate. But Gabriel Heliodoro had no illusions. He knew that the victory of the revolutionaries was only a matter of time.

He cast an envious, almost resentful, glance at the chimneys of the British Embassy. He felt defeated. Despite all his efforts, he had not succeeded in having the OAS Council declare Cuba an aggressor nation. Nor had he been able to convince the Department of State to lift the embargo on the shipment of arms to his government. . . . He turned and looked at the portrait of Don Alfonso Bustamante with a desire to spit on that imbecilic face. He called Miss Ogilvy.

"Tell Dr. Molina to come here immediately."

Minutes later, the minister-counselor entered. Gabriel Heliodoro looked squarely at him. "No sooner did they sense that the ship was beginning to founder, the rats fled from the hold. The first to escape was Ugarte, who took off to Switzerland with his wife. And he didn't even say 'So long!' to me. The blackguard! The coward! Did you know anything about it?"

"I give you my word, I knew nothing. The general and I have always been on very formal footing."

"That Titito has fled to Paris is not surprising, because that little ninny is not even a man." He looked his minister-counselor straight in the eye. "And you, when are you going?"

"Where?"

"How do I know? You should know." He turned around, his back to his interlocutor, as if the latter's face annoyed him. "Michel left me last week too. He only waited for his monthly check. He didn't have the nerve to face me. Said good-by in a letter. And in French!"

Now that Ugarte had deserted and his aides had been called back to El Sacramento, on active duty, the chancellery was almost deserted. The ambassador felt that he had been betrayed and abandoned.

"Have you read the latest news?" he asked.

"Yes," the minister-counselor replied, savoring the moment. He did not want to miss a word, a gesture, any expression of that vain and overbearing man whose downfall had begun.

"And what is your opinion?"

"I think the situation is desperate for our government."

"That's what I think, too. And the devil of it is that I have nothing more to do here. Why don't you sit down, Dr. Molina?"

Gabriel Heliodoro took his seat, and his features suddenly fell apart like a wax mask melting. The Indian in him became visible, his eyes dull, sad, spiritless, his shoulders bowed. Abruptly he straightened up, however, his face composed itself once more, and his eyes glinted again.

"Clare! Clare!" he shouted. And when his secretary appeared, he ordered, "Telephone Pan American and reserve me a seat. One way only."

"Where to?" La Ogilvita asked.

"I take that question as an insult. To Cerro Hermoso, of course. See whether you can get me a seat on tomorrow's flight."

Clare withdrew. The minister-counselor's forehead was wrinkled in a frown. This scene did not belong in his version of the farce.

"Dr. Molina, as of this moment you are the chargé d'affaires of the Republic of El Sacramento in Washington. Inform the Department of State of the fact. Tell them I've been urgently summoned by my president. And tell those gringos to go to hell, with my compliments."

Molina was stupefied.

"Did you hear what I told you?"

"Perfectly, Mr. Ambassador. But—may I ask what you intend to do in El Sacramento?"

Before answering, Gabriel Heliodoro ran his hand over his face in a gesture of weariness. "By this time my whole family is safe, wife, daughters, sons-in-law, grandchildren. But I—I'm going to join my *compadre* to resist to the end. And to die at his side, if necessary."

For the first time Jorge Molina looked at his chief with the ghost of a feeling of admiration and respect.

37

BILL GODKIN had to wait three days in Havana to get on a plane that would take him to Soledad del Mar. And when the plane was maneuvering for a landing, first circling over the city and then approaching the spurs of the mountain range, finally to descend at the airport, Bill pondered the mystery of life and of time, and sought in the landscape and in himself the man of twenty-five he had been on his first and only trip to these regions.

The sea was a faded blue with violet tones, stained here and there with broad patches of jade green. Its waves broke gently on the light sand. The houses of the city, white, small, gave the impression of a flock of sheep motionless on the green slopes of the hill.

"Ruth, Ruth! Here I am again, and I still haven't managed to read the message. I'm still illiterate, beloved." And he gazed at the *cordillera* with the absurd, but nonetheless disturbing, impression that his wife was expecting him on the heights of the Sierra.

Pablo Ortega was awaiting him at the airport. He was dressed in a khaki field uniform—blouse, trousers, ankle-high boots—and wore a beret on his head. He dashed toward his friend and hugged him.

"Bill, old man! What a pleasure! How is everything with you? How was the trip? How is Gonzaga? And Clare? How many bags have you? Where are your baggage checks?"

The journalist took quite a while ransacking his pockets before he found the yellow stubs. Ten minutes later they were off in a jeep driven by a Negro soldier with a gay and attractive face. Bill was smoking, looking at his friend at intervals. Pablo was sunburned, a little leaner, but the old expression of ill-disguised anxiety still marked his face.

The jeep rolled along a narrow strip of asphalt between fields of cane swaying in the breeze. From time to time a mansion gleamed white among the trees. Pablo mentioned the name of the family to whom the property belonged. Or, again, it was a sugar mill, and a warm, sweet smell of molasses saturated the air.

For several minutes Pablo was very loquacious, but absolutely impersonal. He spoke Spanish, calling Bill's attention to the color of the soil, to the shape of some tree or other, to the configuration of the little bay, or to some human figure they were passing. Bill listened, contemplated the landscape, and steeped himself in its ample, luminous beauty. The cool sea breeze lessened the heat of the sun.

Abruptly, Ortega fell silent. Godkin gave him an oblique glance and asked in English, "What's the matter with you?"

"We'll talk later."

They finally came to the plantation. An avenue bordered with plantains led to the two-centuries-old mansion of colonial style, with walls as thick as those of a fortress and constructed around an inner patio. It had a restful, patriarchal air about it, and its façade, bone-white, displayed with dignity the marks of time and weather.

Two soldiers armed with submachine guns stood guard at the door. As he went in, Bill Godkin heard the clicking of typewriters and noted a going and coming of uniformed men and women from one room to another, all with an air of efficiency and a strictly military manner.

Pablo led him to his quarters. "There's the bathroom. Unpack, take a shower, that is, if you want one, of course, then we'll lunch together, and at four o'clock you'll see the chief."

A little before that hour, equipped with camera and tape recorder, Bill Godkin was taken to a spacious room where there was dark, heavy furniture, many books on plain shelving, and a huge fireplace of medieval aspect. He was received by Roberto Valencia in person. They shook hands. Godkin looked at Barrios' chief of staff with a photographic and appraising eye. Valencia could not be much more than forty. He was a man of medium stature, strongly built, but the impression of power and authority he gave—or so the journalist reflected—came not only from the broad chest and the solidity of the biceps but from something centered in the brown face, thin in proportion to the rest of his body, with a hooked nose and stubborn mouth. In his keen eyes a flameless passion seemed to burn, as slow and enduring as the fire in a live coal. Without quite knowing why, Bill concluded that Valencia must be of Basque descent. In reality the man's face was not unpleasing, but for some mysterious reason it set off alarm bells in the reporter.

"Mr. Godkin," the chief of staff of the Revolutionary Column said, General Barrios will grant you exactly fifty minutes. Not a second more. I see you have a recorder. Excellent. The interview will be recorded on tape. You will be free to ask what you wish. The chief will answer if and as he wishes. As for the photographs, we shall have to limit them to three. But we can see to these details afterward."

Godkin nodded, assenting, and the other continued.

"The interview over, you will want to transcribe your notes. We require that you show us the story in its final version so that we can study it, and approve it or not. We shall keep the tape until the interview is published, as proof. At the close of the conversation you are to state into the microphone that nothing more was said or asked beyond what has been recorded on the tape. The dialogue will thus be authenticated."

Godkin smiled. "I see you don't trust me."

"I don't trust anyone, sir," Valencia replied. "Sometimes not even myself."

At four o'clock sharp, Miguel Barrios entered the room. The officers present rose, came to attention, and withdrew. Regarding the chief, tall and lean as Don Quixote, his long black beard in accentuated contrast with the unhealthy yellow of his forehead and cheekbones, Godkin wondered why the *caudillos* of Latin America, when they did not imitate Simón Bolívar, sought to resemble Jesus Christ.

Barrios extended his hand. Godkin clasped it, mumbling the usual formula of courtesy. The head of the revolution sat down in an easy chair, crossed his legs, and folded his arms, and with his didactic manner of speech he opened the conversation.

"I understand that there is a questionnaire containing your questions."

Valencia glanced at the American, who hastened to reply, "I bring no written questions, General. I thought the interview would go better if it had a casual air of improvisation. Of course, I know what I am going to ask you."

Barrios replied, "And you can believe that I know what I am going to answer. We can begin."

Godkin connected the recorder, tested it, and finally set its reels turning.

"This is William Godkin speaking, of the Amalgamated Press. I am at the headquarters of the Revolutionary Forces of El Sacramento, in Soledad del Mar, and I am about to interview their leader, General Miguel Barrios. It is 4:01 P.M., October 18, 1959." He placed the microphone on a small table equidistant from himself and the general. "General Barrios, what is the objective of this revolution?"

"I suppose that is a rhetorical question, señor journalist. But I am going to answer it. Our objective is as clear as noonday—to overthrow the present government and institute a popular administration capable of lifting this republic to social justice and progress."

"Does the revolutionary government intend to follow Cuba's example?"

"We consider the Cubans our friends and allies, but we shall be independent of Cuba as well as of any other nation in the world. We seek genuine self-determination for our fatherland, a status which it has never enjoyed."

"You hope, then, to re-establish democracy in this island. . . ."

Barrios put his long, pale hands together in an attitude of prayer and replied, " 'Re-establish' is not the exact
word, Mr. Godkin. One cannot re-establish what has never
been established."

"Very well, I'll replace the verb. Let's say, *establish*
democracy."

"Yes, we want for El Sacramento the democracy of
which Lincoln spoke—of the people, by the people, and
for the people. But I must warn the press of America and
the rest of the world that we are not interested in verbal
and academic definitions of the term democracy. We shall
endeavor primarily to achieve economic democracy, without which the social and political democracy cannot exist."

The spools whirled on. Valencia was smoking, emit-
ting clouds of smoke toward the ceiling with the bored
look of the man who considers such verbiage a sheer waste
of time. Sitting beside Godkin, Pablo Ortega was doodling
on a sheet of paper with the stub of a pencil.

"What will be the revolutionary government's attitude
toward the American companies?" the newspaperman
asked.

Barrios cleared his throat. Valencia was suddenly
tense. Pablo lifted his head.

"They and the world will learn in due time," the chief
replied.

"Will the revolutionary government immediately take
up the problem of agrarian reform?"

"Obviously."

"On what basis?"

"We are not interested in a literary definition of such
reform, either. We shall seek the one that will give
quicker, more positive results for the country. In short, we
shall do what we deem best for the people."

"Can you tell me what you mean by 'the people'?"

Barrios straightened up, glanced quickly at Valencia,
and then replied, "I consider your question futile and frivolous. I shall not waste time on it."

Godkin could not resist the temptation to glance at

Pablo out of the corner of his eye, but his friend's face remained impassive. He went on to other questions: Did the revolutionary government expect prompt recognition from the other nations of the Americas? How, in his view, could the disappearance of Dr. Leonardo Gris be explained?

Barrios replied to these queries with the preciseness of a pedantic schoolmaster. At one point, when he hesitated a fraction of a second in choosing a word, Pablo attempted to help. Valencia brusquely intervened, "The chief can do without tutors."

"So can I," Ortega retorted.

Godkin inquired whether the leadership of the revolution would accept an agreement with the ruling class to avoid more bloodshed—an agreement, he specified, based on the immediate resignation of Juventino Carrera.

"My dear journalist," Barrios answered, "the reply is simply *no*. We have victory in sight. We shall make no pacts with anyone. Within a few weeks or even days we shall enter Cerro Hermoso. The country is almost wholly in our hands."

"Do you expect to continue the Good Neighbor policy with the United States?"

"Not only with the United States but with all the nations of the world, both occidental and oriental."

"Do you wish to send through us any message to the Americas?"

Barrios looked at his watch first, then at the revolving spool, and suddenly got up, saying, "This is not the time for messages, señor journalist. We are still engaged in combat. In good time the Revolutionary Command will declare itself."

He posed, a trifle fidgety, for three photographs (Valencia declined to appear in them), and then with a dry "Good-by" he turned his back on Godkin and went out.

"When do you expect to have your article transcribed?" Valencia asked.

"At dusk. I want to send it to Washington by tomorrow's plane. But first I should like to send a cablegram to Amalgamated with a summary of the talk."

"Compose your dispatch, Mr. Godkin, and I shall take it on myself to expedite it. I shall be in my office until nightfall."

38

BILL GODKIN spent the next two hours hammering on the typewriter in his room. At seven sharp he handed Valencia the transcription, together with the tape on which it had been recorded.

"Before ten tonight you will have these papers back," the revolutionary assured him.

Ortega suggested to Godkin that they stroll around the streets of Soledad del Mar while there was still a remnant of sunlight. Afterward they could have dinner in one of the local taverns.

They climbed into the jeep. This time Pablo took the wheel. It seemed to Godkin that he drove in a rather nervous way, speeding unnecessarily. But he said nothing. They talked little on the road between the Ortega y Murat property and the city.

The fiery disk of the sun was slowly going down over the *cordillera*, the profile of which was taking on a purplish tone. Nodding toward the ocean, Pablo remarked, "The wine-dark sea of Homer."

They left the car parked near the town's central plaza at the crown of its principal hill, and set off on foot, slowly. In the quiet air there was a late afternoon languor redolent of sun-warmed stone and earth.

"How peaceful!" Godkin exclaimed, gazing at the dark women with sad faces who were leaning out of their windows. "It's as though time has stopped here."

An old woman dressed all in black, sitting in a doorway, held a rosary of large wooden beads in her livid, cracked hands. A naked infant was playing with a broken doll in the gutter. Beside his door, seated on a bench, a shoemaker was hammering on a sole. Barefoot men in white cotton and with straw hats on their heads were walking in the street. They looked at Pablo and Godkin with shy curiosity, and respectfully stepped off the narrow sidewalk to let them pass.

Godkin found that the Plaza de la Madre de Dios had not changed at all in the past thirty-odd years. There was the *pila* still, where the *comadres* used to come for water and talk, and still did. And the ancient street lamps. And the Café de los Pescadores, with its dull pine tables on the sidewalk surrounded by rustic chairs with straw seats. And the fruit vendors' stalls, where flies and bees swarmed around the mangoes, the pineapples, and the *sapotes*. The old church, which dated from the time of the conquistadores, had a quarter of its façade covered by a bougainvillea loaded with crimson flowers.

"It's too bad that Padre Catalino is not in town," Pablo said. "He was summoned to Cerro Hermoso by the archbishop."

"For another reprimand?"

"No. This time His Reverence, it seems, is going to use the priest as his emissary to sound out Barrios on his attitude toward an agreement with the bourgeoisie."

"And how is Padre Sender?"

"Oh, cultivating his ulcer—and taking care of other people's ulcers, particularly the spiritual ones. Up yonder in the Sierra we held some conversations that have been very profitable to me. He's a strange man."

"Strange?"

"Maybe that's not the word. He is . . . an unusual . . . an extraordinary man. In his presence I feel my defects and frailties more keenly than ever."

They sat down on a bench and watched the coming and going in the plaza: small boys playing ball; a cat, tense on a wall, eyeing two shining green parakeets in a cage; women carrying kerosene cans full of water on their heads, walking down the streets radiating out from the plaza to the bay.

"What about your headaches?" Godkin inquired.

"They've disappeared. But let's walk on."

They moved off toward the beginning of a long street that would come out on the beach. A skinny, mangy mongrel followed them, smelling at Pablo's boots and Godkin's shoes. From one of the nearby houses came the wail of a child. The two friends walked in silence for a little.

"Bill, have you heard about . . . my father?"

"No. What happened?"

"He died."

"When?"

"Two weeks ago. I was still 'up yonder on top.'" Pablo jerked his head in the direction of the Sierra.

"How did you come to find out?"

"We listened regularly to the official station in Cerro Hermoso, which reported falsified news about us every evening. They also reported other kinds. They made a great to-do about Don Dionisio's death from a heart attack. They bluntly stated that he was a victim of his grief at seeing me with 'the revolutionary rabble.' My mother was interviewed. They had her make a recording in which she confirmed the cause of her husband's death, called me a murderer, and declared that she never wanted to see me again."

"Was it really her voice?"

"Not the slightest doubt about it. Of course the radio station man made the most of the opportunity to call me a traitor, expatriate, and parricide."

"And you . . . how did you feel?"

Pablo shrugged. "Not as bad as might have been expected. There is some sort of magic up in the mountains. It must be the rarefied air. Things are just different. One looks at the world from a unique angle—gets a new perspective on life and on men. But—naturally—I did regret my father's death."

"I hope you won't admit the blame they want to put

on you. As you told me, your father already had an ailing heart when you were still in short pants. Imagine a man of Don Dionisio's moral fiber compelled, through fear of communism, to support a criminal, corrupt administration like Carrera's against his will. In my opinion, it was that contradiction gnawing at him from inside that finally killed him. They want to make a scapegoat of you. Don't accept the role."

Godkin noticed that now and then Pablo turned his head to look covertly behind him. They stopped in front of a shop window in which cheap plastic dolls were displayed.

Pablo spoke low. "Look to your right. See that fellow in a khaki uniform? He has been trailing us ever since we got out of the jeep."

"Why?"

"Probably on orders from Valencia, who wants to know where we go, what we do, and if possible what we talk about."

"Then you mean he distrusts you, too?"

"Exactly. I'll explain my situation later. Let's set a trap for our stool pigeon."

They turned the first corner. Pablo caught his friend by the arm and made him stop and wait as he did, flat against the wall. Godkin was enjoying this. They heard steps on the sidewalk, and finally the man who was following them appeared—a squat, Indian type. At sight of Pablo he gave a start which suddenly and audibly cut off his breath.

"Why are you following us?" Ortega shouted, approaching the soldier as if he were about to attack. "On whose order?"

The man came to attention. "Why señor capitán!" he stammered. "I'm just strolling around."

Pablo's nostrils were quivering as he looked the mestizo up and down. "Tell whoever ordered you to trail me that he's wasting his time. Now get out of my sight!"

The other saluted, abashed, and went off down the street at a faster pace. Godkin grinned. Pablo was still serious, but after a glance at his companion's face he suddenly burst out laughing.

"Look, Bill, you are positively forbidden to mention this scene in your articles. I have a lot more to tell you, but only on one condition. You'll give me your word to consider everything I tell you from here on as strictly confidential, not for publication."

"You have my word."

"Then let's go find something to eat. I know a tavern where seafood is the specialty. It's down yonder almost at the end of the street. A poor place, but at all events it's clean and you'll find a little relief from the monotony of American drugstores and cafeterias with their Formica, plastic, chrome, metal and fluorescent lights. And speaking of light, our electricity is rationed. We'll have to eat by candlelight."

"Excellent, excellent!"

In the pale sky of dusk the evening star twinkled above the Pico de la Calavera. From some yard came a smokiness that turned the air blue, filling it with the fragrance of burned molasses.

"That smell recalls my childhood on the Kansas prairies," Godkin said, breathing deep, remembering his home, the figure of his mother frying doughnuts in the kitchen, and his father in a rocking chair on the porch, reading the Emporia *Gazette*.

"It's smoke from burning *jacaranda*. The scent reminds me of Pía and our afternoons in the Garden of Eden."

They came to the tavern, the name of which, La Sirena Pensativa, was painted in great green letters on the whitewashed wall under the eaves. Entering, they went to sit at a table in one of the angles of the little room near a window overlooking the bay. Godkin looked around him. The walls, like the floor, were covered with grass mats. From the beams of the ceiling hung fishermen's nets and huge empty wine bottles. Hanging over the door to the kitchen was an oil painting, a fat siren with golden scales and rosy breasts was reclining on a deserted beach, her eyes closed—the work of a local primitive artist, Pablo explained.

There was no one else in the shadowy room. A fat man, graying and with tanned skin, with great mustachios like a Turk, came to ask what the gentlemen would have. Recognizing Pablo, he shook hands and noisily demonstrated how glad he was to see him there.

"Bill, this is my old friend Macario, owner of the tavern. Macario, shake hands with Mr. Godkin. He's a gringo and a journalist. He interviewed the chief today."

"What'll you eat?" the tavernkeeper asked.

"We'll leave that to you," Pablo said. "Bring us some shrimp first, the way you fix them, and then a good fish of your own selection. With wine, bread, and cheese, of course."

Godkin approved the menu. He gazed out at the piers of the bay, to which several fishing boats were moored. The sea now looked like pure wine.

Pablo pointed to a white house at the end of the street, near the sand of the beach. "That's where Maestro Natalicio lived."

"Lived?" the other repeated in surprise.

"Yes. He died last week, on the occasion of our last assault on the town."

"How?"

"A stray bullet. He was sitting in his doorway, shaping a figurine. The battle didn't disturb him. We'll never know where the bullet came from that killed him."

"Where are the children?"

"With us. All good soldiers."

Godkin continued to gaze at the bay. "I'm eager to hear your story, Pablo," he said after a brief silence.

At that moment two men came into the tavern and sat down at one of the tables near the street door. They looked like fishermen.

"You must promise me once more to keep secret everything that I am going to tell you."

"I repeat—my word of honor."

"Well, as you know, I didn't have much trouble in

reaching the Barrios troops. I landed at nightfall in an air taxi on the plantation landing field. That same night I made my way through the cane fields and climbed the slope, guided by a peon, taking with me all the weapons and munitions I could lay hands on."

"How did Barrios receive you?"

"At first with a certain distrust. But there was no help for it. He had to accept me. He made me secretary of the brigade with the rank of captain. That has its comic side, I recognize—Captain Ortega!"

"It sounds nice."

"But it doesn't mean anything."

"And why should it? Get on with it."

They decided it would be better to speak English. The room was gradually filling up with customers, among whom were some men in uniform. A loud voice demanded light. The tavernkeeper began lighting the candles stuck in the necks of bottles on the tables.

"From the Sierra," Pablo went on, "the revolutionaries went out in commando groups to attack both the towns in the vicinity and the federal patrols. They did so almost always at night. I stayed with the chief, and my job was not only to make out the orders of the day but also to maintain a kind of diary of the brigade. As you may imagine, I didn't feel very good in the comfortable job of amanuensis. I was safe up there in a cabin while my companions were going down the mountain and risking their lives. Many of them didn't come back."

"After all," Godkin interrupted, "you didn't come here expressly to die. Or did you?"

"Of course not."

"What's the trouble between you and Valencia?"

"Oh, as I'm an intellectual, son of a landowner, and an ex-diplomat on top of that, from the first day I was under suspicion from Valencia. And his ill will toward me was revealed in the least little things."

Night had fallen completely. Stars were gleaming over the town, the mountains, and the sea.

"What sort of man is this Barrios?"

"A charismatic figure, without the shadow of a doubt. I have abundant proof of his sincerity to the cause, of his physical courage and tenacity. What intrigues me is the fact that not even in his highest moments of prophetic transport or in those of great military decisions, does he ever neglect his grammar and rhetoric." Pablo gripped his friend's arm for an instant. "Once more, Bill, all this I'm telling you now is strictly confidential."

The newspaperman nodded in mute agreement. "And Valencia?"

"Ah! That one is the ideologist, the real brain of the revolution. I needn't tell you he is a Marxist. Trained in Moscow. Past master at guerrilla warfare. An extremely able organizer, with a cool head. He knows and he gets what he wants . . . and without regard for the means."

"What is his attitude toward the chief?"

"Of course he sees in Barrios the figurehead of the ship of the revolution. But the man at the helm is Valencia, who uses the chief to attain his ends."

"And what are his ends?" Godkin asked, out of sheer professional habit, for he already knew the answer.

"First, to overthrow the government, and then lead the revolution to the left, as close as possible to communism."

"Do you think Barrios will follow that direction?"

Pablo shrugged. "He will get all screwed up. On the one hand we have the skill and cunning of Roberto Valencia, and on the other the proverbial lack of skill and cunning of your Department of State. Furthermore, Barrios respects and admires Valencia, listens to his advice, follows it. . . . Valencia, like a sculptor, has taken care to model an ideal image—the savior of the people, the predestined man—and has symbolically offered it to the chief, who is now seeking to live in accord with it. I watched Barrios gradually become transformed up there in the Sierra. The change could be noted in his words, his attitudes, his opinions."

The tavernkeeper brought a steaming platter on which shrimp were immersed in a rich olive-oil sauce,

orange-yellow, and set it on the table together with a bottle of wine and a dish with slices of goat's-milk cheese and
homemade bread. The two friends began to eat and
drink.

"Valencia still needs Barrios," Ortega continued. "The
peasants worship him. The most remarkable thing is that
in these short months of revolution a whole mythology has
grown up around the figure of the chief. The humble folk
tell tales of miracles performed by Barrios. It is said that
the mere touch of his fingers on a sick man's forehead is
sufficient to cure him. Once the story spread that Miguel
Barrios had been seen in three places, quite distant from
each other, at the same time—the Sierra, Oro Verde, and
Páramo. What helps him greatly, Bill, is that with his
black beard he has an extraordinary likeness to Juan Balsa,
the saint of the island people's martyrology."

Godkin was watching the lantern shining from the
bow of a boat entering the bay from the open sea. "When
did you and Valencia start to clash?"

"As I told you, ever since my arrival he has eyed me
with a mixture of distrust and scorn. The situation
worsened the day that one of our patrols caught a peasant
who had ventured too near our camp at night. They swore
he was a soldier of the 5th Infantry—this was never
proved—with the express mission of assassinating Barrios."

"Was he armed?"

"He had a machete on him, but that's common among
our peasants. Valencia decided to shoot him immediately.
I protested and demanded a trial. Then Valencia called me
a 'sentimental *petit bourgeois*' and declared before the
other officers that men like me were neither physically nor
psychologically ready for revolutionary action."

Macario brought the fish in a steaming clay vessel
redolent of garlic and sweet marjoram.

"And afterward?" Godkin asked.

"I insisted on the trial. Barrios, to my surprise, supported me. I took charge of the prisoner's defense. My
argument was simple. Why not believe him when he de-

clared that he had come to join the revolutionaries? But Valencia replied, 'Why then did he do so at night, crawling in and attempting to elude our sentries?' To sum it all up, a jury of seven officers found the man 'a risk.' If we sent him off, he might reveal our positions and security arrangements to the federals. If we held him alive, he would be a permanent danger, for he could treacherously kill one of our officers or even Barrios himself."

"So the man was condemned to death."

"What was one life? As we could not afford to waste ammunition on that Indian, one of our soldiers cut his throat. But let's get on with the fish."

Godkin helped himself from the platter. Pablo did likewise. There was a silence.

"From then on," Ortega said, resuming his narrative, "my relations with Roberto Valencia deteriorated completely. We spoke to each other only as was necessary, on service affairs. Once I overheard him refer to me, in a group, as 'our bookkeeper poet.' I felt like hurling my mug of coffee, which I had in my hand at the time, right in his face. He kept insulting me. One day I asked Barrios to let me get into action."

"And . . . ?"

"I volunteered to lead one of our night commandos against this town. It was a very special operation, and one of the most daring. There were twenty of us in all. Eight specialists in the use of the machete were to go in front to kill the sentries without making any fuss, and thus open the way for the rest of the group. The others, under my command, had orders to approach the 5th Infantry barracks wall that faces west, machine-gun the windows, and throw the greatest possible number of grenades into the rooms. There were twelve windows. There were exactly twelve of us. I drew the last, or rather the first window counting from the north end of the barracks."

Fork poised, forgetting his fish, Godkin listened attentively. Pablo was rolling a bit of soft bread in his fingers, making a little ball. The image of Pancho Vivanco shot through his mind for the fraction of a second.

"Well, we chose a night of new moon and went down. One of Maestro Natalicio's sons served as guide. I know it's grotesque—Pablo Ortega, apprentice hero, on an expedition against the 5th Infantry. All right. The men in front did their job well, and we succeeded in getting close to the barracks without being discovered. We got so close that we could hear the sounds of voices and laughter inside. We held still for several seconds, lying flat on our bellies on the ground. Natalicio's son, stretched out by my side, whispered in my ear, 'Do you hear it?' I said, 'Hear what?' And he told me, 'The river running under the ground.' I laid my ear on the ground and could hear nothing but the beating of my heart. My mouth was dry, my throat constricted, my chest oppressed. But my head was clear. I had to carry out that mission at any cost. Suddenly it occurred to me that I was at war not against the federals but against Roberto Valencia. It was against *him* that I was leading that night attack."

A stentorian guffaw exploded in the tavern. Macario passed by with another platter of fish. The strum of a guitar, coming from the beach, reached their ears.

"I gave the order to advance," Pablo went on. "Each man went to his window at quickstep, all of them bent over. It was arranged that I would be the first to fire. I broke the glass in my window with a burst of machine-gun fire—I heard the other eleven bursts—and immediately I pulled the pin of a hand grenade and tossed it inside the barracks and threw myself on the ground. I heard its explosion followed by others. I threw my second and third grenades. Then I blew my whistle, the signal for the withdrawal."

"It's fantastic!"

"I'm not surprised you think so. I find I'm telling you the story as if it were a dream—or a lie."

"Was there any reaction from the barracks?"

"When we heard bugle calls and the crackle of the federal machine guns, we were already on the way up the Sierra and meeting our own patrols. We managed to get back without the loss of a man. Got back to the camp at daybreak."

"What did Valencia say?"

"Nothing. He didn't even look at me. Naturally, he thought I had done no more than my duty. And he was right in that."

"What did you feel after the affair was over?"

"I couldn't sleep. I thought, how many men, I wonder, were in the room where I threw my grenades? How many did I kill? And I was amazed at not being *very* deeply affected by it. I repeat, up there on top things look different. Only after taking Soledad del Mar did I find out that our commandos had killed at least twenty soldiers that night, wounding perhaps twice that number. Since I came down, I've been thinking about a lot of things. And you know what the worst is? I can't square that act of mine—I mean the throwing of grenades against unarmed soldiers caught off guard—I can't harmonize it with the context of my revolutionary action. I volunteered for the mission because I wanted to prove to myself, to the others, and principally to Valencia, that I am not a coward. And the price of that proof was the lives of several men. But what shocks me most is the idea that I acted as if I were going to kill abstractions, symbols, and not human beings."

"Those human beings, for their part, were also defending other abstractions—legality, the government, the honor of the regiment, etc."

"Right. Isn't it terrible?"

"*C'est la guerre,* as our ineffable Michel Michel would say."

"It's funny, Godkin. My mother was badly upset at my losing my innocence with Pía in the cane fields. But a man really loses his innocence not when he knows his first woman but when he kills for the first time."

One of the soldiers was singing. Another gestured in friendly fashion at Pablo, lifting his glass. Ortega responded in like manner, smiling.

"Now what?" Godkin wanted to know.

"Victory is in sight. It's a matter of weeks, or even days. I confess I'm more afraid of it than of the revolutionary fighting. Must we pay the price of the change that Valencia desires? Will it be worth while? Or, rather, isn't there some other path to social justice?"

He looked out at the bay, over which a gasoline-powered boat was sailing with a red lantern at the prow.

"When we installed ourselves in our—I mean, in the Ortega y Murat hacienda—Valencia and I had an altercation in Barrios' presence one day. He accused me of being irresolute, an intellectual seeking an impossible middle-of-the-road, obsessed by a sense of guilt more mythical than real. 'After all,' he asked, 'do you wish to free your people from tyranny and misery or do you merely want to pacify your individual conscience?' I was furious, because that devil of a man had touched on the very quick of my problem. He tried to convince me that the golden mean leads nowhere, for history has always proved that only violence can give birth to great social changes. I retorted that if an ideology is not kept within certain limits of morality, it will end by becoming dehumanized. It ceases to be a means and becomes an end in itself. We would have gone further if Barrios, with one of his Olympian phrases, had not ordered us to stop the argument."

"And what do you intend to do now?"

"To continue. To go on to the end. I intend to be a thorn in Colonel Roberto Valencia's side. *But always faithful to the revolution.*"

Godkin made a pessimistic grimace and clicked his tongue.

"I'm afraid that sooner or later you'll be crushed. I can visualize you already as a refugee in Miami. Or—"

"Arrested? Shot?"

"*Quién sabe?*"

39

FROM THE NOTES of William B. Godkin:

"22 October. I am now *persona grata* with the Supreme Revolutionary Command. Valencia has approved the text of my talk with Barrios without cutting out even a comma. Amalpress, to my surprise, also distributed it without mutilating. I have with me a copy of the Washington *Post* which published my interview with Barrios in full, a three-column spread with a picture of the hero. In it I present the bearded leader in a very favorable light, and appeal to the nations of America to lend their moral support to the rebels. In short, I am doing my penance for having in the past, to the extent of my abilities, contributed to putting Juventino Carrera in power.

"Professor Leonardo Gris was right when he said that the so-called men of conscience are at heart chronic penitents.

"23 October. Good news. The federal garrison of Puerto Esmeralda has revolted as one man, joining the rebel cause. By order of the Revolutionary Command, the garrison has marched on Los Plátanos, whose fall is imminent.

"We are preparing (here I go, using the first person plural) for the final offensive against Cerro Hermoso, 'to batter the monster on the head,' as Barrios puts it.

"For five minutes this morning (pure chance) I 'monopolized' Valencia's attention and sounded him out discreetly in an attempt to gain confirmation of his ideological purposes. The man is cunning, as slippery as an eel. He gave me only oblique answers and cut short the dialogue—'This is no time to be discussing ideologies. The revolutionary war is not over yet. The revolution itself, properly speaking, will come later.'

"Pablo Ortega is working incessantly on the final composition of the communiqués and manifestoes which Barrios dictates to him. They argue heatedly over questions of grammar and style. The chief treats his secretary as a professor would treat an industrious but self-willed student. He magnanimously makes small concessions here and there, but in the majority of cases he demands that his words, sentences, commas, and ideas be left strictly intact. Valencia abstains from the literary arguments, but nothing is published without his final approval.

"24 October. All automobiles and trucks in the town and on the plantations and at the mills in the surrounding countryside have been requisitioned for transporting the revolutionary forces encamped at Soledad del Mar. The march on Cerro Hermoso starts today. Rebel contingents from practically all parts of the country will converge on the capital in accord with a plan set up by Barrios' general staff.

"At 5 A.M. the first patrol set out. Then the advance guard leaves. I obtain permission to accompany the forces, as close as possible to Barrios. I install myself with my skimpy baggage in the jeep that carries Pablo Ortega, his papers, his typewriter, and his files. The driver is the same likable Negro who brought us from the airport to headquarters.

"It is a sunny day, and I feel twenty years younger. I suggest to Ortega that Fra Angelico must have been busy coloring this Antillean sky with the aid of his angels. My friend only looked indifferently at the firmament and made a vague motion of his head. He looks worried to me. I think the prospect of victory is making him apprehensive.

"Before taking the main highway, Miguel Barrios insists on parading through the streets of Soledad del Mar. He stands in his car and with august gestures acknowledges the people's demonstrations—men, women, and children are waving to him with hands, handkerchiefs, and flags, from windows, doors, and sidewalks. The 'enthusiasm' of these mestizos and Indians is singular. They confine themselves to timid gestures. From their mouths comes not the slightest sound. It all looks like an underwater scene in spite of the dehydrated aspect of these poor folk. The only sound to be heard is the rolling of the vehicles over the irregular stones of the streets. I take color snapshots of the crowds, and, considering the quality of this light, I am sure they will come out clear. I am thinking of doing a series of illustrated stories about this campaign.

"The column halts at nightfall in a place called Refugio de los Angeles. The officers occupy all the rooms of the only hotel here. In the light of the troops' campfires inscrutable Indian faces come into view only to vanish instantly.

"Pablo and I share a room. It is a night of full moon. The tepid breeze blowing from the northeast brings the scent of aromatic herbs and grasses. Mosquitoes play their tiny violins dangerously close to our ears.

"Ortega calls me over to the window and shows me two forms pacing back and forth together in the hotel garden. I identify Barrios and Valencia. It is the latter who does most of the talking. The other limits himself to listening. Pablo remarks softly, 'The commissar is polishing his image.'

"25 October. We leave again shortly before dawn. We pass through villages, towns, and cities where Barrios is received with great enthusiasm. The people of this region seem to have more Spain in their blood. It is as though the 'silent film' of our march has taken on a sound track. One hears cheers and hurrahs. Men and women approach the hero to kiss his hand or simply to touch his clothes. I photograph the demonstrators from every possible angle. On the roll of color film in my camera are recorded the most varied human masks, expressing joy, mystical ecstasy, pride, hope, and, in the case of an occasional woman, a kind of sacred orgasm.

"I hold lightning interviews with members of the common people. One old woman assures me that Barrios is Jesus Christ. An octogenarian affirms that the chief is a reincarnation of Juan Balsa, beside whom he himself fought in the Sierra between 1914 and 1915. Mothers bring their children in their arms for the chief of the revolution to lay his hands on the little ones' heads.

"Miguel Barrios, who never smiles, seems to be convinced of his function as a prophet. He is undeniably impressive—tall, lean, his long hair and beard waving in the breeze, his eyes fixed on a horizon that seems to be rather in time than in space.

"The Revolutionary Column is gradually swelled by not only youths but middle-aged men and even old men who want to march with it. They ask for weapons, and look glum when refused. I interviewed a peasant who expressed to me his unshakable certainty that the life of the poor people is going to get better now, because Barrios will give the rural people not only lands for planting but also plows and seeds, and everyone will have food. A mulatto of superb carriage, who used to work on the machines of one of these sugar mills, assures me that, with the victorious revolution, the plantations and the mills will be taken away from the rich and distributed among the workers.

"We find not the slightest resistance by the enemy along the way. Some detachments of federals surrender without fighting. Bridges are intact, and the tracks of the railway are in place. The government planes have vanished from the sky.

"Behind us is the region of the *littoral,* made up of rain forests, the zone of the cane fields, banana plantations and cacao—the land known as *tierra caliente.* We climb toward the *tierra templada,* the plateau where the capital lies and whose average altitude is 2600 feet above sea level. The temperature starts down, the days are warm and the nights cool, almost cold.

"Today is Sunday. Barrios orders the column to halt at ten o'clock in the hamlet of Manzanares so that he can attend Mass in the little chapel of the village. Two or three officers go with him. Valencia remains outside the chapel, walking back and forth with an impatient air, glancing now and then at his wristwatch.

"I keep observing three men with special attention: Barrios, Valencia, and Pablo. The first seems constantly to be in a permanent state of mystic trance. When we arrive at dusk at Santa María de la Sierra, foreign correspondents come to meet him, to photograph and interview him. Valencia keeps in the background when cameras and contacts with the press are in the offing. He continues to be only a kind of shadow of Barrios, but a shadow with much more substance than the object which projects it. He is a squid hiding in its own ink. But there is no possible doubt that he is still the real architect of this revolution, or, rather its real 'manager.' He never leaves the chief's side. He intervenes when necessary, but he does so in a discreet way. He limits the time of the interviews between the chief and the journalists, supervises his poses for pictures, and exercises an iron censorship over everything that is written about the revolution and its commanders.

"Pablo Ortega is getting more and more depressed the closer we come to Cerro Hermoso. Today I ask him whether he thinks the capital is going to resist. He says no. 'It will be an idle stroll from here to the Palace of Government,' he says. 'We have just had word that there is fighting in the streets of the city and that several government battalions have joined our side.' What worries Ortega, I understand, is that in Cerro Hermoso he will find his mother, his home, his friends, his past—and the corpse of his father.

"26 October. We are barely thirty kilometers from Cerro Hermoso, on an elevation of the terrain from which we can distinguish the capital, its mass of white buildings gleaming in the green valley At 10 A.M. Barrios receives a delegation of revolutionaries, most of them bearded and dirty, their clothing bloody. They come to inform him that the capital has just fallen into the hands of the popular forces. They are men of the people, and students. They report that the battle, which lasted two days and two nights, was terrible, and that there are many dead and wounded on both sides. Barrios listens in silence. Valencia asks, 'What about Carrera?' The head of the delegation replies, 'Unfortunately he succeeded in escaping from the palace to the airport, where he took off in his private plane for Ciudad Trujillo.' Barrios made an irritated gesture. Valencia lashed out at them, 'Didn't it pass through the head of any of you gentlemen that one of the first things to do in such a case is to attack and take the airport?' 'We made several attempts to do so, but we were thrown back with heavy losses.' Valencia wanted more information. 'Do you know who got away, along with the dictator?' The others exchanged glances and finally one answered, 'Members of his family and maybe some of his generals.' Valencia reflected for an instant. 'How was the flight possible,' he inquired, 'if the Palace of Government was surrounded?' 'Carrera fled in a helicopter. At the airport a detachment of loyalist soldiers protected his retreat, and held out until the minute the plane took off. We didn't have any planes to follow them.'

Valencia was thoughtful for an instant. Then he asked, 'Who commanded the defense of the airport? Colonel Zabala?' One of the students shook his head and replied, 'Don Gabriel Heliodoro Alvarado. He was the one who commanded the resistance in the city, too. Zabala surrendered the first day.' Valencia asked further, 'Was Gabriel Heliodoro killed?' One of the students elaborated, 'He fell wounded in the airport fighting and was taken by our soldiers.' Valencia's eyes shone. 'Take good care of that man and of Zabala! Don't ill-treat them, don't let them die. We want no martyrs. Those two scoundrels and all the other criminals will have to be tried by a popular tribunal. Their monstrous crimes will be disclosed to the eyes of the world, and they will be shot like the bandits they are, not like victims!'

"Pablo Ortega was puzzled. 'Incredible!' he told me when we were left alone. 'I imagined Gabriel Heliodoro in Europe. I never deemed him capable of such a gesture of loyalty to his friend. What's the explanation?' (What's the

answer, Ruth? I think to myself.) And I say 'I'm a newspaperman. I report facts. I suspect that my superiors don't
like it much when I try to interpret them.'

"Miguel Barrios summons Pablo, to dictate to him the
first proclamation to the country and to the world, at the
moment of installing himself as the chief of the People's
Revolutionary Government in the Republic of El Sacramento. They stay working for two hours in the building
where the column's general staff members are billeted.
Roberto Valencia, as usual, is present and continues to
exert his right of veto, making opportune comments. 'That
is too literary.' 'No. That is a subject to be avoided for the
present.' 'We must not alarm, nor must we soothe, any
country or economic group. It is well to leave them in
suspense for the time being.' 'In my opinion that proclamation should not contain more than two hundred words.'

"The same afternoon officers arrive representing the
brigades that had converged on Cerro Hermoso from
Puerto Esmeralda, Los Plátanos, and Páramo, to lay siege
to the capital. They all gather together and study the best
means of consolidating their hold on the capital, of estab-
lishing a strict security plan, and of preparing the atmosphere for the entrance of Barrios and his forces the next
day.

"That same evening Roberto Valencia goes on to
Cerro Hermoso with the members of the delegation of students and men of the people, as well as with the officers of
the other revolutionary units.

"27 October. Before daybreak a sleepless Roberto
Valencia comes to find Miguel Barrios, who is no better off
than Valencia in the matter of sleep.

"The entrance of the liberating forces into Cerro
Hermoso is set for ten o'clock this morning. The column
gets under way at seven-thirty, slowly, in perfect order.
Another bright day. (These deep, velvety greens remind
me of Virginia.) We come across gracious white homes
along the way, with porticos on the verandas, many of
them covered with bougainvillea, with flowers running
from magenta to scarlet. In the hamlets near Cerro

Hermoso the inhabitants carpet the road where the new Libertador is to pass, covering it with leaves and flowers and branches of trees. A little amateur band, touchingly out of tune but full of a tremendous civic enthusiasm, plays marches in a little square in which I see a multitude of anxious heads, arms waving with colorful handkerchiefs, flowers, and banners. From atop his jeep Barrios waves to the demonstrators. Skyrockets hiss, rise into the sky, and burst in the air. One citizen attempts to make a speech but he finally desists because the shouting and the skyrocket explosions smother his voice.

"At the gates of the city our procession halts in another plaza. Beside a colonial fountain I see a solemn black limousine standing, very shiny and well kept. A priest steps out of the car and approaches the chief's jeep, bows, and says something to him. Barrios exchanges a glance and a couple of words with Valencia, and then waves affirmatively to the priest, who returns to the limousine. The door of the car opens, and Don Pánfilo Arango y Aragón gets out. (I believe I am going to witness a historic scene that may provide me with material for a fine piece of reporting.) Barrios leaps out of the jeep, but remains beside it— he does not take a step toward the prince of the Church. The latter comes smiling to meet him, in his impeccable priestly vestments. The crowd is now watching the scene in silence. Don Pánfilo is carrying, on a cushion, the symbolic key of the city. I draw nearer. I want to witness the great moment. I begin taking a series of color photographs from the moment the two men are five paces apart. The archbishop primate lifts his hand as though expecting Miguel Barrios to kiss his ring, but the revolutionary merely grasps the tips of his fingers quickly.

"I don't want to miss a single word of the dialogue. Other persons come up, too, forming a circle in the center of which stand the two principal personages of the scene.

"At seventy the archbishop primate is still a handsome man of erect posture, pink cheeks, and noble, extremely attractive features. The smile with which he emerged from his car has been gradually fading from his lips and eyes, confronted with the chill indifference which he notes in the faces of Barrios and his officers.

"Presenting the gilded key to the chief of the revolution, the prelate says, 'I have the honor to give you welcome, General, and to deliver to you the symbolic key of our beloved capital.'

"Barrios replies dryly, 'Your Reverence must agree that it has come a little late. The key can be of no use whatever to us, now that we have already knocked down the gates of Cerro Hermoso with our bodies, our blood, our lives.'

"For some seconds Don Pánfilo seems disconcerted. He clears his throat, looks around, recovers his aplomb, and says, 'I trust that at least you will understand my gesture of courtesy.'

"'We have not come here seeking courtesy, but a better life for our people.'

"The archbishop's lips tremble and his voice turns opaque when he replies, 'So be it. But in the name of Christian principles and for the sake of all you hold dear, I beg of you not to permit further bloodshed in this poor city, not to allow outrages to be committed once more, or human lives degraded and destroyed!'

"'Archbishop,' Barrios smiled, 'for years men, women, and even children have been debased and treated unjustly, have died of hunger, of diseases, or tortured by the dictator's police, without any of this seeming to have impressed Your Reverence very much, with all of your Christian sentiments.'

"The archbishop turned pale. Before he could speak again, Barrios added, 'There is one thing I can promise you honestly. Justice!'

"'Don't forget, Commander, that above the imperfect justice of men exists the definitive and infallible justice of God. It may be slow, but it never fails.'

"'Well, Archbishop, until the divine infallible justice shows itself, we shall have to be content with our imperfect justice. A good day to you.'

"The two face each other for an instant. Don Pánfilo

makes a slight bow and immediately turns, sees Pablo Ortega, recognizes him, approaches him, and holds a rapid, low-voiced dialogue, the substance of which I learn only next day, thanks to Ortega himself.

" 'It was I myself who administered the last sacraments to Don Dionisio. The last word your father pronounced was your name, Pablo. You dealt him a mortal wound with your act of rebellion.'

"Ortega faced him squarely. 'Is Your Reverence telling me this to provoke a sense of guilt in me? Do you think, too, like my mother, that I was to blame for my father's death?'

"The archbishop seemed to hesitate for a moment, but he could not resist the temptation to deliver a 'great phrase.' 'Every man who rebels against the established moral, social, and economic order, my son, kills his own father symbolically—and sometimes biologically as well. May God have mercy on your soul!'

"It was obvious that Don Pánfilo was revenging himself on Pablo for the humiliation to which Barrios had subjected him. But the young man smiled, bowed ironically, and murmured, 'I am most grateful to Your Reverence for these words, so full of the purest sentiment of Christian charity.'

"His head erect, the prelate walked with firm steps back to his black automobile."

40

O N THE FOLLOWING DAY in his office in the chancellery in Washington, Dr. Jorge Molina read in a morning paper about the triumphal entrance of Miguel Barrios and his troops into Cerro Hermoso. The story, under the by-line of William B. Godkin, had been distributed by Amalpress. It was an objective piece of reporting, sparing of adjectives, but it gave a clear and plain idea of what the spectacle had been like—the parade through the streets and avenues, the bands, the popular acclaim—the bells of all the churches had remained silent. Nearly fifty thousand people crowded into the Plaza de Armas when Barrios emerged on the balcony of the Palace of Government. Godkin stressed the fact that, thanks to the action of the Revolutionary Central Committee, there had been no outrages, no sacking, no personal vengeance, or any other manifestations of violence. The policing of the capital had been strict and efficient from the first hour.

Besides the former members of Juventino Carrera's Cabinet, several of his generals, agents, hired thugs, and, principally, individuals of his police, had been arrested and were awaiting trial. Everything indicated, Godkin went on, that the two "star criminals"—since Juventino Carrera had succeeded in making his getaway—would be Pedro Zabala, the chief of police, hated by the people for his brutality, and Gabriel Heliodoro Alvarado, who seemed to symbolize, more than anyone, all that his friend and *compadre* Juventino Carrera represented in regard to administrative corruption, despotism, and self-enrichment at the expense of the people. In the opinion of the Amalgamated Press correspondent, the Revolutionary Central Committee attached a very particular importance to the trial of these two men.

Molina rose and began to walk up and down the office. There was a great silence in the chancellery. That morning he had sent Merceditas home, the other stenographers, and the lesser functionaries.

He had spent more than an hour destroying papers. It was the end. He had already made his decision. He would not await the ambassador of the new government to hand over the post to him.

He pressed the button summoning Clare Ogilvy. He saw that the secretary's eyes were red with weeping, but he said nothing.

"May I smoke, Doctor?"

"Do what you wish. Sit down, please."

She obeyed. She lit a cigarette and blew out a cloud of smoke in a convulsive puff, like a sob. The chargé d'affaires turned to her.

"Miss Ogilvy, you are of course aware of the situation in El Sacramento. I want to ask one last favor of you. Since from this moment I regard myself as automatically severed from the diplomatic service, I beg of you to take charge of the embassy residence and its servants—the chauffeur, the gardener, the cooks, and maids, etc. Yes, and of those boys and girls I sent home today. And the chancellery, of course."

La Ogilvita confined herself to an affirmative bow.

"Believe it or not," Molina continued, "you are now the representative *de facto,* if not *de jure,* of the Republic of El Sacramento in Washington."

He spoke these words without the least humorous intent. "And you, sir, where are you going? If I ask it is because I need your next address to forward your correspondence."

Molina expressed his indifference with a frown. "I am not interested in corresponding with anyone." Unless with God, he thought, but I still cannot find out the number of His post-office box. But how to explain to an American that some person in the world may *not* have a definite address?

"Well, I shall write to you at the opportune time, telling you where I am."

He felt a kind of morbid voluptuousness in thinking of himself as a man about to die. He had devoted most of the morning to his most important plans. One thing, however, horrified him—the idea of lying decomposing on a bed and being discovered only through the stench of his rotting flesh. He had always respected his own body—and his chastity, was that not his respect carried to its ultimate extreme?—and he had a horror of the notion that he might stink. It must be—the thought occurred to him now—because his own father had smelled. His breath stank of rum when he came home drunk. And from his body, sweaty and unwashed, habitually emanated a sour smell which the boy Molina had detested.

"Very good, Miss Ogilvy. I need another favor of you. A most special one. I want you to go, without fail, tomorrow at noon exactly, to my apartment." He stopped, reddened, because it sounded to his own ears like an invitation. "I mean, I shall not be there, but I am going to give you the key. You will go in, pick up four or five letters which you will find on top of the writing desk—all duly stamped—and will be so kind as to mail them for me. Oh, and one of them will be addressed to you, with instructions."

"To me?"

"Exactly. I repeat, it is important that you arrive at my apartment at noon sharp. Open the door. Here is the key."

Miss Ogilvy accepted the key as he handed it to her. Molina imagined the shock to the secretary when she saw him lying on the bed, livid and motionless as a wax doll. Then she would comprehend everything.

"Yes, Mr. Minister."

"I am no longer a minister, miss."

"Very well, Dr. Molina. I'll do what you ask. You can trust me." Clare stubbed out her cigarette in the ashtray. Then she said, "I read about the ambassador."

"Ex-ambassador."

"Yes. Don Gabriel Heliodoro. Do you think they are going to shoot him?"

"In all probability."

"Have you any news of Pablo Ortega?"

"Direct? None."

"Can he be . . .?"

Molina shook his head. "Be at ease. Nothing bad has happened to him. In his latest story, published today, Mr. Godkin relates that he was at Ortega's side when Barrios spoke to the people from the balcony of the palace."

Jorge Molina put on his gabardine overcoat, picked up his leather dispatch case and his Homburg, and looked around the room as in a formal leave-taking.

"Good-by Miss Ogilvy. I don't know how to thank you for all that you have done and are still going to do for me.

But it is most important that you go to my apartment to-morrow at noon sharp. Most important! I am certain that you will not fail me in this critical situation, for you have never failed me in working hours."

Jorge Molina extended his hand to Clare, who clasped it and felt it as cold as that of a corpse. Could the poor man be sick? What could he have meant by "critical situation"? But the ex-minister-counselor quickly drew his hand away, turned toward the door, and the secretary remained where she was, listening to the steps of the singular creature resounding in the deserted hall as though under the vault of a catacomb.

In front of the chancellery Molina gazed long at the park and the embassy residence. For an instant he was absorbed in following the movements of the squirrels as they whisked about, running up and down the trees. One of them came so close that it all but touched Molina's highly polished shoes, and he had a sudden impulse to squat down and stroke the little animal's fur. But he restrained himself—it might bite him or scratch his fingers—and remained erect, repeatedly clearing his throat, with a cold sensation of emptiness in his chest. Again his father's face came to his mind. "God does not exist!" the old man exclaimed. "If He did, there would be justice and goodness on earth, and your mother would not have died stupidly in giving birth to you." A fine excuse for drinking, for yielding himself up to despair, for running away from the struggle, he thought. Yes, and for not taking baths, for not brushing his teeth, for keeping the same clothes on his body for weeks.

At the corner of Massachusetts and 34th Street he signaled to a yellow taxi cruising by, empty.

From noon until three o'clock Jorge Molina, locked in his study alone, was occupied in making out and signing checks (apartment rent, light and gas, last installments on the Encyclopedia Britannica, etc.), and writing letters. He addressed the first to Jenkins & Jenkins, Morticians, whose brochure he had previously examined with the most

scrupulous care. He informed the funeral home that, as he
wanted a modest service, he had selected Number 3-A,
which included cremation. He made one special stipulation: "I earnestly ask that you do not put the usual makeup
on my face, which would be useless as well as ridiculous.
There will be no viewing of the body, for I have neither
friends nor relatives. My body is to be cremated as soon as
the legal formalities are complied with. My ex-secretary,
Miss Clare W. Ogilvy, bearer of this letter, will take
charge of disposing of my ashes. I enclose a check in
favor of your firm to cover all expenses, in accord with
the prices stated in the aforementioned brochure. With
thanks in advance. . . ."

The next letter was addressed to Miss Ogilvy:

"Forgive me for the shock which I may have caused
you. I realize that to enter an apartment and find a dead
body on the bed must not be a very pleasant experience.
However, as I do not believe that you have the slightest
sentiment of affection for me, I know that the shock will
not be great, and this thought relieves to some extent the
constraint I feel now.

"I shall not even attempt an explanation of my motives for committing suicide. It would be too complicated
and boring, and my reasons would sound false to you in
any case. The main thing is to make it quite clear that no
one but myself is responsible for this act of mine, which is
not even one of despair. I am in full possession of my
mental faculties.

"Accept the *fait accompli*, therefore, and do not ask
questions of yourself or of others about it. And please do
not hate me for the inconvenience which I am causing
you.

"I beg you to accept the little present enclosed in the
form of a check for one thousand dollars. And please mail
the letters I am leaving on this desk, among them one addressed to the police authorities of Washington.

"As for funeral arrangements, I have taken measures
on that score in the letter addressed to Jenkins & Jenkins,
Morticians, which I ask you to deliver in person to the

addressees after you have read it. (I hereby authorize you
to do so.) And now we come to the problem of my ashes. I
consider it unnecessary to bury them or to keep them
anywhere. They mean nothing to anyone. Find a discreet,
practical way to dispose of them. I suggest that you throw
them into the Potomac or on the first rubbish heap you
come across. Why not in your garbage pail? Believe me, I
make this suggestion without the least bitterness. I have
always respected my body while it was alive, but I have
not the slightest interest in its ashes.

"Thank you, Miss Ogilvy, thank you for everything.
Believe me when I say that I have always had the greatest
respect and admiration for you.

Sincerely yours
Jorge Molina"

He verified the state of his bank account with the
greatest care and calculated what was left after subtract-
ing the amounts of the checks he had made out and signed.
His balance was slightly over $30,000. He wrote a check
for that sum in favor of Padre Catalino Sender and put it
in an envelope with a letter which read, "My dear Father
Sender, You probably do not remember me. We have seen
each other only two or three times. Here are some dollars
for your works of charity." Before signing the message, he
sat with the pen in the air, a bitter smile on his pale lips,
for it had occurred to him to add, "I hope that you do not
have to use this money in the near future for the aid of a
revolutionary movement against the administration of
Miguel Barrios." But he restrained himself and added
only, "Pray for me." And he signed his name.

He rose and looked around. Everything was ready. He
glanced at his watch. Several minutes past three. If he
took the barbiturates before four, and Miss Ogilvy entered the apartment at twelve noon the next day, they
would not have time to take him to a hospital and use
a stomach pump on him. It would be atrocious, it would
be ridiculous if they saved his life.

He went into the bathroom, undressed, took a warm
bath, shaved, donned his monk's habit, and returned to the

living room. But he did not return alone. Two forms, his
father's and Padre Catalino's, disputed precedence in his
thoughts. Old Molina exclaimed, "Didn't I tell you? God
does not exist." Padre Sender did not shout, but his low
voice was more audible than the drunken man's loud one.
"I do not want your money, my son. I want your soul."
"What soul?" old Molina yelled. And the ex-minister-
counselor could actually smell the sour odor of the old
man's body, the effluvium of rum, and the fermentation
from his mouth, full of rotting teeth. "What soul?" Then
Jorge Molina came to realize that he had entered the
seminary in protest against his father. He had to prove to
him that God did exist and that His mercy was so great
that it far surpassed the understanding of men. But now he
could not help recognizing that the old drunkard had finally won out. "No," the image of Padre Sender said. "The
persistence of your father's figure in your memory is proof
that God does exist."

Molina sat down again at his writing desk, removed
the sheets of his biography of Don Pánfilo Arango y
Aragón from a drawer, and began ripping them across,
page by page. And as he destroyed the work of more than
three years, he thought about the archbishop primate. Gris
was right. Don Pánfilo was the personification of a colossal
fraud. How shameful! How humiliating! A prince of the
Church demeaning himself before a man like Miguel Barrios! Running to meet the revolutionaries when he ought
to have had the decency to stay locked in the Archiepis-
copal Palace, resigned to a political ostracism that could
only add to his dignity. Let others, if they wished, seek
him out later. Either to beg his moral support or to shoot
him. And as he thought these things, Molina went on tearing up papers in a growing fury.

Without any doubt whatever, Padre Catalino was the
one who represented the real Church of Christ, the one
nearest to the heart of the common folk, to the rawness of
man's suffering and to life. The Church could survive with
dignity only by refusing to allow itself to be contaminated
by the glories, honors, and vanities of temporal power.

Beads of sweat ran down his face, wetting his hands with a cold damp that suggested the chill of death. And yet in his heart there was still the remnant of a flame—of the stump of a candle before some remote altar of his childhood?

Suddenly the silence and loneliness of the apartment startled him. He looked at his watch. He would take the contents of two bottles of Seconal and lie down on the bed. But—suppose Clare did not come? If she did not, he would be left rotting on his bed, and the neighbors, who had never cared much for him anyway, would come to hate him not only because the stench of his putrefied corpse would permeate their apartments and their nostrils, but also because the reminder that a man has the power to put an end to his own life would poison their minds and disturb them for hours, perhaps for days. No. Clare was the embodiment of efficiency. She could not fail. She was the *deus ex machina.*

He wiped the cold sweat from the palms of his hands with a handkerchief. Taking his pulse, he noted that it was considerably accelerated. There was a slight constriction of the throat, his respiration was short, he was panting a little, and he felt a weakness in his legs and arms. Fear? Ridiculous. He was not going to suffer any pain. He would enter gently into the Great Sleep.

He reviewed all the measures he had taken during these last hours. Remembering his library now, he added in a postscript to Miss Ogilvy, "Give all my books, including the encyclopedias, to the library of the Catholic University. And my clothes to some institution of charity that you select."

He went to the kitchenette. Padre Catalino followed him, bent, his cassock brushing the red earth of Soledad del Mar. "Reflect, my son. You are going to kill a man. You are committing a premeditated murder." "He killed his mother already!" old Molina exclaimed. The ex-seminarian turned on the faucet at the sink in the tiny kitchen, filled a glass, returned to his bedroom, and sat down on the bed.

Padre Catalino spoke again. "Don't forget that your mother carried you for nine months in her womb, with discomfort but with joy and hope. She gave her life to bring you into the world, not through any fault of yours, Jorge, but because it was God's will. You have no right to destroy by your own hand the man your mother conceived and loved. It will be not only a homicide but a fratricide."

Jorge Molina gazed long at his mother's portrait beside his bed, and tears came into his eyes. How man years since he had wept? Twenty? Thirty?

He picked up the two little bottles of barbiturates standing by the picture and spilled their contents out on the bedside table.

If God exists, he reflected, He must be laughing at me now. Or can He be suffering? But if He feels the need to laugh or has the capacity to suffer, He is not God. And if an idea in His mind is sufficient to save me, why doesn't He form that idea? And Padre Sender responded, "The mere fact that He gave you the faculty to formulate your questions, my son, is the beginning of salvation."

Molina put a tablet on his tongue, took a sip of water, and swallowed the first installment of his death. He recalled his first communion, and how hard it had been for him to swallow the wafer without crunching it. His aunt's voice: "Don't chew it, my boy, that's a sin, because the body and the blood of Christ are in the wafer." He remembered the sensation of inward peace and purity he had felt after that first communion. And the bag of candy his aunt had given him.

He felt a sudden need of prayer. He knelt beside the bed, folded his hands, looked at his mother's picture, then closed his eyes and murmured, "*Salve Regina, mater misericordiae; vita, dulcedo et spes nostra, salve.*" But his father thrust his way into the prayer, gesticulating, "If God does not exist, why should the Virgin Mary? And what's the use of praying? To whom? "*Ad te clamamus exsules filii Hevae. Ad te suspiramus gementes et fluentes in hoc lacrimarum valle. Eia ergo, advocata nostra, illos*

tuos misericordes oculos ad nos converte. Et Jesum, bene-
dictum fructum ventris tui, nobis post hoc exsilium os-
tende." He had been the cursed fruit. *"O clemens, o pia, o*
dulcis Virgo Maria!" Cursed fruit. Acid. Putrid. Amen!

He got up. His knees hurt. His stomach ached. He
had eaten nothing since the day before. He felt slightly
dizzy. He looked at his watch. Twenty to four? His vision
was somewhat clouded. The pills were on the table. The
bridge across to the other side. Odd, this habit of viewing
death in terms of space. The beyond. The other side. Why
not the other time? It occurred to him then that God, being
an inhabitant of eternity, was in no hurry, and being God
could not get impatient. But he, Jorge Molina, now had
only a few minutes at his disposal to make the final gesture. He looked at the tablets again. He remembered a
picnic in his boyhood. He had crossed a river on stepping-
stones without wetting his feet. Those tablets there could
take him dryshod to the other side of the river which separates life from death. Those miserable tablets, mass-
produced in a laboratory, industrially. . . . He thought of
the price he had paid for them. Ridiculous! Those things
could be bought in pharmacies, along with Coca-Cola,
sandwiches, magazines, toys, Mickey Mouse stories—those
insignificant, shiny, colored tablets could put an end to his
life. "Think it over, my son," Padre Sender was now whispering to him, "instead of going to a church to seek the
solution of your problems you go and buy it in a drugstore."

"That is part of the absurdity of life," Molina said
aloud. "God has abandoned me."

Padre Catalino smiled. "No," he said gently, "God has
sent the humblest and mangiest of his dogs to bark at your
feet, warning you of the dangers of the forest. Don't cross
the river. Stay on this bank and wait. God will come to
your aid one day."

Jorge Molina sat on the bed. Was suicide a paranoiac
action? A man decides to take his own fate in his own
hands, like a god. His father had once called him a cow-

ard. Maybe he was right. He was a coward. He had never had the courage to face up to life. Worse than that. He was an egotist. His notion of not being loved, accepted, he realized it now, came from his own incapacity for loving, tolerating, accepting others. His revolt against God—had it not been a revolt against his father? And had he ever attempted a gesture of understanding, love, and forgiveness toward his father? His admiration for the archbishop primate—was it not less for the creature of God that dwelt in him than for his power and his glory as a prince of the Church?

Yes, an egotist! Nothing more. So egotistical that he had all but reached the conclusion that the world, life, all men were in a conspiracy against him. He had not understood—stupid that he was!—that God could exist in the universe atomized in His creatures, and that his incapacity to love God was nothing more nor less than an incapacity to love the things which He had created. Idiot! Idiot! Idiot! He had spent his life seeking a God that would be exclusively his, as logical as a mathematical formula, as luminous as a sun, a God always visible and at his disposition, a God who stretched out His arms to him and said, "Come, my dearly beloved son, and sit beside me."

Jorge Molina was thinking these things while gazing steadily at the tablets. His passage from this life to the other side of the mystery depended on a gesture that any innocent infant or any mental weakling could make—put the tablets in your mouth and swallow them one by one as in a kind of inconsequential game.

The ex-seminarian abruptly got to his feet. He had suddenly experienced an intense desire to go on living. He swept the tablets together into the hollow of his hands, ran to the bathroom, poured them into the toilet, and flushed them down the drain.

And now what? Now what? he thought, excitedly. He changed his clothes, went down in the elevator, entered a public telephone booth, and dialed the chancellery number.

"Miss Ogilvy? This is Molina speaking. . . . Yes, Jorge Molina. Listen carefully to what I say, *Don't* come to my apartment tomorrow as I asked you to. Understand? *Don't* come. I have changed my plans. It is all right now. And many thanks. Don't come. Thank you. God bless you."

He hung up before the secretary could ask questions. He went back to his apartment. Now what he had to do was destroy the letters he had written. He would spare only those containing the checks to pay his bills.

He took his passport from a drawer. Next he set about packing his bags in a disorderly, furious haste. Yes. Spain! He remembered an afternoon in the dark cathedral of the Barrio Gótico in Barcelona. There was no better spot in the world for a secret meeting with God. He would buy plane tickets for Madrid that very afternoon. *Las Meninas,* of Velázquez. The mad works of Hieronymus Bosch. Thirty thousand dollars and a bit over was enough money. He could easily obtain a place as professor in the University of Salamanca. Spain! To live again! Another life. Another man!

He whistled, he hummed, he made absolutely absurd motions. The sweat was running down his torso. But it was the sweat of life, not of death. Suddenly he realized that he was hungry. Naturally. He had put nothing in his stomach for nearly twenty-four hours.

He went into the kitchen, opened the refrigerator, took out the milk bottle, then two lettuce leaves, a slice of cheese and one of ham, and put the materials for a sandwich between two slices of bread and began to eat and drink with a happy voracity. He would put some bread crumbs in his pocket to give to the first squirrels he encountered. . . . Were there squirrels in the parks of Madrid?

Yes, to sally forth into the world in a new search for God! Now, more than ever, he felt that God could be anywhere in the universe. Even in a refrigerator.

41

A T THAT SAME INSTANT, sitting at his desk in a third-floor room of the Palace of Government, Pablo Ortega was also eating a sandwich and drinking a glass of milk. But he was not thinking of God. He was thinking, as a matter of fact, about Roberto Valencia, who after a fashion was seeking to play the role of an omnipotent, omnipresent god in the revolution. His omnipresence was guaranteed by the four telephones he had on his desk and by the powerful radio station installed in the palace, by means of which he kept in communication with all sectors of the country, transmitting orders, receiving information and consultations.

His omnipotence arose from the fact that, beside exerting complete dominion over Miguel Barrios, he had taken care to appoint trustworthy men to govern the provinces and to occupy the key posts in the Revolutionary Central Committee.

The image which appeared in the newspapers and magazines of a good part of the world, as a symbol of the revolution, was that of Miguel Barrios. But Roberto Valencia, who made no speeches, gave no interviews and never allowed himself to be photographed, was the man who really governed the country in his post as secretary-general of the central committee.

He had extraordinary physical stamina, an exceptional head, and a will of steel. He worked at least fifteen hours a day. He slept four or five at most. He lunched frugally at his desk without stepping out of his office, which adjoined that of Barrios and in which every morning a barber shaved him while he was dictating letters to his stenographers, conferring with his aides, and making and answering telephone calls. He it was who had com-

posed the first decrees signed by Miguel Barrios—dissolv-
ing political parties, closing down newspapers, setting up
investigating committees not only to ascertain cases of corruption among members of the deposed administration but
to examine the books of national and foreign companies. A
financial expert in his full confidence was now occupying
the position of governor of the Federal Bank, which was
known to be the source of the grossest, most disreputable
exchange frauds of Juventino Carrera's government.

Valencia was also preoccupied with the idea of
founding, without delay, a Revolutionary Popular Party,
which would be the only one legally existent in the country. He himself had composed an outline of the program
and the by-laws for the new political organization, charging a committee of specialists with the final editing of both
documents. (Ortega knew that Valencia regarded only
orthodox Marxists as "specialists.") He was already studying the draft of a new constitution for El Sacramento, and
the work was in the hands of a group of jurists—nearly all
of them men who had remained outside the country, in
exile, during Carrera's administration, or else had rotted in
the depths of the humid dungeons of the federal police.
Another problem now occupying the attention of the secretary-general was the immediate organization of trade
unions. He received, in his office, delegations of peasants,
workmen, and representatives of the liberal professions.
He roundly refused to see reporters and correspondents of
foreign newspapers and news agencies, to which he sent
laconic notes: "Our actions and the facts speak for themselves. As for the future, I am no prophet. Let the newspapermen wait." It mattered little to him whether he was
liked and popular among the men of the press.

Ortega could not help admiring (Was "admiring" the
right word?) that sober, objective, stubborn man who
wasted neither words nor gestures, and who seemed not to
have the slightest need of music, poetry, or even love. As
to his personal life, the only positive knowledge was that
his wife had been tortured and murdered by agents of the
dictator's police, in the time when Ugarte was the chief of

Carrera's police. He had never remarried. If he had mistresses, neither their names nor their faces were known.

Pablo Ortega finished his sandwich, drank the rest of the milk in the glass, wiped his hands with the paper napkin, and went to a window overlooking the plaza, where men, women, and children were now in movement, converging on the front of the palace. Pablo smiled. In a little while, when the group swelled and became a crowd, it would begin to chant in chorus, "*Ba*-rrios! *Ba*-rrios! *Ba*-rrios!" And the chief would be compelled to step out on the balcony where, standing before a microphone connected with dozens of loudspeakers placed at different points around the plaza and the adjacent streets, he would finally improvise a little speech. Such things as this happened almost daily around 5 P.M. And the image which Valencia continued to polish daily, with the care of a connoisseur, would gleam in that late October sun with a brighter and fresher brilliance than that of the bronze equestrian statue of Simón Bolívar which reared up in the middle of the plaza, in a circle bordered with tall palms.

Ten days before, at dawn, Pedro Zabala and his accomplices had been shot in the inner courtyard of the barracks of the 2d Infantry Regiment on the outskirts of Cerro Hermoso. Hundreds of people were at the barracks gates bellowing their demands to be allowed to enter and witness the execution. When their demands went unheeded, they began howling and throwing stones at the windows of the buildings.

This had convinced Roberto Valencia that the long-suffering, vengeance-thirsty common people had every right, not only to appease their fury, but also to witness the executions and see that revolutionary justice was not failing them. Yes, the shooting of the criminals should be turned into a kind of national public show. Where? In the Gran Plaza de Toros, the bullring. Yes, under the eyes of more than thirty thousand persons. Pablo Ortega regarded the notion as sinister and dangerously compromising for the revolution. He told Valencia so, plainly.

"Captain Ortega," retorted Valencia, "your duty is to

advise the Department of Propaganda and Information. Look after your own tasks. The central committee knows what it is doing."

Pablo refused to appear at the public executions, which were carried out in the same fashion as bullfights, with band music and trumpet calls. It nauseated him even to think of the spectacle, of which he had seen pictures in the daily *Revolución*, the official organ of the new government, the only newspaper now existing in the whole national territory. After being killed, the condemned were dragged out of the arena by horses, like fallen bulls. And the crowd laughed, shouted, applauded, and sang. *Olé! Olé! Olé!* It was said that some waggish fellows bellowed requests for "the ears of the bull."

In the following weeks there were nearly four hundred executions in the Gran Plaza de Toros. They always began with the men of minor political importance. The "big bulls," the Miuras among the condemned, were reserved for the final spot on the program.

Ortega one day obtained an audience with Barrios. "Chief, this macabre pantomine ought to stop. Read what the foreign newspapers have to say about it. It is giving the world a wrong idea about our revolution."

Barrios gave him a long stare with an appraising eye, and said, "Tell me one thing, Captain Ortega. Were those men condemned to death only after a fair trial, or not?"

"In a general way, yes."

"Were they guilty or not?"

"They were."

"The rest, Captain, is irrelevant. In France it is the guillotine. In England, the gallows. In the United States, the electric chair. The shootings here will continue to be carried out in public. The people deserve the show. Our upper class needs a painful lesson." He dropped his pompous tone to assume a paternal air, as he added, "Would it not be much worse if we let the mob take justice into its own hands, lynching people in the streets, breaking into the homes of our delicate aristocracy and violating their wives and daughters?"

Pablo Ortega saluted, which he had always thought ridiculous, and was about to withdraw when Barrios stopped him with a gesture.

"Yesterday the auxiliary bishop asked me for an audience. I granted it, but limited it to fifteen minutes. He brought a message from the archbishop primate, who earnestly begged me to put an end to the shootings." Barrios paused, threw back his head and uttered a dry, short laugh. "Do you know his reason? In His Reverence's opinion, a revolutionary tribunal operates too hastily, under the influence of unquenchable passions, and in a way pressured by the hatred of the audience attending the sessions and shouting its demands for the condemnation of the criminals."

Miguel Barrios got up and began striding up and down the room, his hands linked behind him.

"Do you know what I replied? I said, 'Tell His Reverence the Archbishop that the Revolutionary Popular Tribunal is no more hasty, impassioned or "pressured" than the tribunals of the Holy Inquisition were in the past. And don't forget, my dear Bishop, that we are more merciful than the inquisitors. We kill the condemned quickly, with a volley from the firing squad—we never burn them slowly on a bonfire.' "

He gave another little laugh. Going over to Pablo, he laid a hand on his shoulder. He had had a visit from the United States ambassador in person a few minutes before.

"The fellow came to me with certain demands," he said. "Naturally I rejected them. He informed me that he is to fly to Washington tomorrow for consultation. He had the nerve to hint that if the executions continue, and if we carry out our threat to nationalize the American companies without a 'fair compensation in dollars,' he was sure that the Department of State would not recognize the new government. I replied, 'The United States is a free and sovereign nation. That is what El Sacramento desires to be. A very good day to you, Ambassador.' "

Looking now out at the square, Pablo Ortega was recalling these events of the past two weeks. His headaches had returned, he slept little and poorly, and the only person with whom he could unburden himself frankly was Bill Godkin, who was still in Cerro Hermoso writing news stories for the Amalgamated Press.

More than once he had tried to see his mother, but she remained inflexible in her determination not to permit him to enter his paternal home. Sometimes he would pass in front of the mansion with Godkin and, through the iron grillwork, stand gazing at the old residence of the Ortega y Murat family, rising beyond the park with its sad, grave look, its walls covered with ivy, its windows shut.

Since his arrival he had several times encountered old friends and acquaintances on the street, people of his class and generation, and had noted that they pretended not to see him, or, when that was not possible, merely stared indifferently at him as if they did not know him.

Once a certain lady, an old friend of his family, the matriarch of a prolific and traditional clan (chicle, ba-nanas, and sisal) had got out of her car, marched up to him as he stood on a corner, and, finger stiffly leveled at him, almost touching the tip of his nose, had exclaimed, "Pablo Ortega, you should be ashamed to wear that uni-form and go around with that revolutionary rabble. Aren't you satisfied with killing Don Dionisio? Do you want to kill Doña Isabel, too?" And before he could say a word, she had whirled around and re-entered her car. And he, far from feeling shocked at such an attack, had regarded it as a scene out of a cheap *zarzuela*.

He telephoned one day to Dr. Mora, his family's doc-tor, identified himself, and asked for news of Doña Isabel. The doctor replied laconically, "She is as well as can be, after the death of her husband and all her other misfor-tunes." And he hung up without another word.

Hearing the sound of steps, Pablo turned around. One of Roberto Valencia's aides had come into the office.

"Captain, the chief wishes to see you immediately."

Ortega knew who was meant, but irritated by the

"immediately," he inquired, "Which chief? Barrios or Valencia?"

"Colonel Valencia."

"Very well, Tell him that I am coming."

The aide withdrew, and Pablo stood fiddling with some papers, pretending to himself that he was doing something important. He knew that, when either of the chiefs called, those who worked in the government building responded on the double. Pablo detested the Prussian discipline which Valencia was attempting to establish among the functionaries of the Palace of Government. It might be necessary, but even so it was obnoxious. He deliberately waited five minutes, timed by his watch, before going down to the secretary-general's office. He found him alone, sitting at his desk in front of piles of paper. Valencia did not invite him to sit down. Ortega expected that, but sat down anyway. The other went on writing as if he had not noticed Pablo's entrance. The silence lasted several minutes. At last the secretary-general lifted his eyes.

"Captain Ortega, I have been studying your notes on our draft of the new law of the press."

Pablo watched him silently. Valencia went on, "Your remarks are ingenuous, erroneous, ridiculous."

"That is your personal opinion."

"That is also Barrios' opinion and the opinion of the other comrades. In sum, it is the opinion of the Revolutionary Central Committee. I'll tell you one thing, Pablo Ortega, you are not the right man for the position you occupy."

"Why?"

"Because, among other things, you have an obsession about liberty. To you bourgeois liberals' freedom is something that can exist outside the context of life and the well-being of the people. A false jewel in my opinion. Useless."

"Have you thought, Valencia, that Chamorro and Carrera perhaps had that same concept of liberty?"

"Don't be ridiculous! Learn to reason dialectically, if that is not too much to ask of a literary man." He picked up the papers in front of him, raised them to the height of his chest, and then dropped them on the desk in a gesture alien to his habitual calm. "Do you really think it is possible for us to carry out our revolutionary program in this island without first eliminating those commercial newspapers which have always been the mouthpieces of the oligarchy and of the foreign companies? Do you think we are going to allow these sensation-mongering rags to keep on poisoning the public mind with lies that serve only the interests of the rich and privileged classes? Use your head, Ortega! Liberty cannot be an end in itself. It is a *means* to provide a better life for the majority. If it does not attain that objective, it is worth nothing."

"Are we to have our *Pravda,* then, the word of the government, the supreme truth, one and infallible?"

"And why not? Did you want us to ask UNIPLANCO and the Sugar Emporium every day about what and how we ought to compose our editorials? Reactionism has as many lives as a cat. If we are not very careful, it will infiltrate through the slightest chink we leave open in our walls of defense. And if they take over the country again, have no illusions about it, they will liquidate us without mercy. Do you remember Moreno? He was innocent enough to think that he could carry out his program of social reform while allowing freedom to that indecent capitalistic press, which attacked and slandered him from the day he entered the Palace of Government, and which finally destroyed him."

He picked up the papers again, shuffled them into order, and handed them to Pablo. "Here. Examine the draft again. Get into the spirit of the revolution. I am giving you this extra chance."

"I've read that pile of paper more than ten times, Valencia. My opinion of the draft is expressed in those marginal notes. That law of the press has an unmistakable totalitarian smell."

Roberto Valencia smiled, lit a cigarette, blew out a cloud of smoke through his nostrils, and looked steadily at Ortego. "Liberty!" the secretary-general exclaimed.

"Liberty! You intellectuals find pleasure in words as children amuse themselves with toys. Liberty! In the name of that myth you bourgeois writers have been churning out literature completely divorced from the class struggle, from social reality for centuries."

"Your famous *engagement!*" Pablo exclaimed. "Why must the artist or the writer be *engagé* necessarily to the Communist Party, as if it were the bearer of the one absolute truth? Why not let him take his stand on the totality of man? Why not a total commitment to life and all its riches and ambiguities, its countless doors, paths, labyrinths, and mysteries? You Communists, who boast so about your socialist realism, give yourselves up to a dialectic juggling with two abstract balls—history and humanity. And in that juggling you permit yourselves the luxury of ignoring the human person. You think it right to kill a man to save humanity. So death for you ends by turning into an abstraction, too."

Roberto Valencia thought for an instant before replying. Then he spoke in a colorless voice. "Pablo Ortega, literary men of your ilk commit themselves only to themselves. They are onanists who masturbate before a mirror."

"And Marxists like you, Valencia, masturbate staring at the portraits of Marx and Lenin, now that the Kremlin has declared that Stalin must no longer provoke an orgasm in any Communist worthy of the name."

The secretary-general seemed to be finding pleasure in the argument. A slight smile softened the severe cut of his mouth for a second. "One day *up there*," he murmured, "you told me that you considered yourself a humanist. Well, at the time I was too busy with a commando operation to waste time on academic arguments. But now I can tell you that terms like humanist and liberal are nothing more than things as mythical as the new clothes of the emperor in the legend, who was really naked. You intellectuals wrap yourselves up in those labels, seeking thus to free yourselves from the hard responsibility of taking a decisive combat position beside the people."

"You think I haven't taken that position already?"

"You have, but reluctantly and without the necessary psychological preparation to carry your gesture to its ultimate consequences."

"And what do you call 'ultimate consequences'? The legitimation of murder? The adoption of violence as the norm? The acceptance of a totalitarian system of government? No, Valencia, don't count on me for that!"

"To be frank with you, Ortega, I don't count on you for anything. I've never been deluded about you. I know your kind. I've told you once, and I repeat it now, you are more interested in saving yourself than our people. You may deny it, but the Jesuit school has left in your mind a terrain ready for the germination of sentiments of guilt and desires of expiation. Men like you can never further social happiness."

Pablo Ortega rose, but Valencia went on.

"Like a good literary man you continue to play with words. And like all those of your breed, at the first drop of blood you shrink back, you feel sick at your stomach, you run away from the struggle. You are the sensitive plants of the human species." He stretched out his arm and pointed an accusing finger at the other man. "I'll lay a bet that within a few more weeks you will be going around grumbling—if you're not already—that this is not the revolution you dreamed of. And you will wind up by taking advantage of the first opportunity to escape to Miami, where you'll lie getting a nice tan under the warm sun, frequenting casinos, and writing articles against the revolutionary government of El Sacramento and poems about the enslavement of our people under 'the Communist boot.' And all the while, of course, you will don a discreet air of martyrdom, which will give you great prestige among the American old women interested in the salvation of the 'banana republics.' And you will be paid quite well by the Yankee press for your articles against us."

"Then you are roundly deceived, Valencia. *I am not leaving.* I am going to stay to see that all the promises made by the revolution to the people are carried out. I have that right."

"I don't deny your right. But I doubt that you've got the guts for it."

"Then wait and see."

Valencia got up, opened a thermos bottle, poured out a little of its contents into a glass, took a tablet from a metal box, gulped it down, and then took a swallow of water. Under his armpits dark patches of sweat were widening on his khaki shirt. The fan hummed. The telephone rang on the secretary-general's desk, and he picked up the receiver.

"Yes? Valencia. What is it? . . . Who? . . . Not now. Have him come in in five minutes."

He replaced the receiver, sat down on the edge of his desk, and folded his arms.

"Listen, Pablo Ortega. Your friend Gris used to say that there was one kind of violence that he could accept, even though with repugnance. It was the violence of the righteous, employed to combat the violence of the bandits. We have some gigantic tasks before us. We cannot waste time on trifles."

"If you consider a human life a trifle, I haven't much hope for the future of this revolution."

"Don't worry about that. We real revolutionaries will deal with that future, in which we have unshakable confidence."

Days later Ortega was strolling in the evening through the streets of Cerro Hermoso with Godkin, with whom he had just dined, when the loudspeakers blared out into the streets the news that Gabriel Heliodoro Alvarado had that day been discharged from the hospital where he had been held and would be tried in a week by the Revolutionary Popular Tribunal.

"Did you know?" Bill asked.

"Since yesterday afternoon. The news circulated in the palace. I've been thinking a good deal about his case."

"Can it be that you are going to try to prove you are responsible for that man's fate, too?"

They went into a bar. Pablo bought two tokens at the

cashier's desk and they approached the counter in front of an espresso machine.

"I've made a decision, Bill. I'm going to offer to defend Gabriel Heliodoro."

Godkin lighted his pipe, blew out a puff of smoke, looked at his friend with his clear eyes, and inquired, "Why?"

"I don't know. A gesture."

"I understand. A symbolic gesture. But symbolic of what?"

Pablo shrugged. The waitress, a dark girl with large eyes and blue-shadowed eyelids, smiled coquettishly at Pablo and poured coffee into the cups before the two friends.

Pablo took a single sip of the scalding coffee and made a face because he had forgotten to put in sugar. "What do you think of my idea?"

"It can be suicide. Especially after your rows with Valencia."

"Let it! Drink your coffee and let's go to a movie."

The next morning Pablo managed to see Barrios and inform him of his decision to defend Gabriel Heliodoro.

The chief of the revolution heard him out and then gravely said, "Have you thought how prejudicial this gesture may be for you?"

"I have."

"It is a repugnant and thankless job to defend in public a scoundrel of the calibre of Gabriel Heliodoro. I am surprised at your volunteering for so sordid a task." He was thoughtful for an instant, and then added, "No one will understand your action."

"I know."

"Your position in the movement can be considerably weakened by this attitude of yours."

"I am not interested in positions."

"All right, but I hope that you are interested in the revolution, at least."

"Obviously I am."

"And you think that defending Gabriel Heliodoro can aid our cause?"

Pablo Ortega lost patience. "Commander, tell me one thing, does Gabriel Heliodoro have the right to a lawyer or not?"

"He has, even though the braggart does not deserve it. We were appointing a professional for the task, but since you insist—if you do insist."

"I do."

"I trust that you are not going to allege later that we forced you to play this embarrassing role."

"Why should I?"

"Another thing. Do you know who is going to act as public prosecutor this time?"

"No."

"Roberto Valencia in person. Have no illusions. The secretary-general will be implacable. And it is possible that, when you complete your defense, the prosecutor will request a rebuttal, and may destroy not only the prisoner but you also. He will be merciless."

"May I be frank, General? Of a man like Roberto Valencia I expect many things—intelligence, courage, tenacity—never mercy."

"Am I to take that as a criticism of our comrade?"

"I wish to believe that we have not yet reached the point of deifying the chiefs of this revolution to such an extent that they are immune to criticism."

"Have you pondered the dangers of that kind of reasoning?"

"Yes. But I cannot think otherwise."

Miguel Barrios gazed steadily at him with eyes which expressed now gentleness, now a kind of delirium. "Very well. I shall tell the president of the tribunal that I concur in your defending your friend Gabriel Heliodoro Alvarado."

"I want to make it quite clear that Gabriel Heliodoro is *not* my friend."

Miguel Barrios waved this away impatiently. "Whatever he is, Captain! You may go."

That same day Pablo Ortega obtained permission to interview his client in one of the rooms of the 2d Infantry barracks where the ex-ambassador was held prisoner. Beside the door of the room two guards armed with submachine guns were posted. The room was square, and larger and better-lighted than Pablo expected. The dirty light of the cloudy, humid, hot afternoon entered through two barred windows which overlooked the inner quadrangle of the barracks.

As he went in Pablo Ortega was greeted by a voice which was making an effort to be jovial. "Come in, Mr. First Secretary."

Gabriel Heliodoro lifted himself on his elbow on the iron cot where he was lying and stretched out his hand to the recent arrival. Pablo hesitated for a fraction of a second before clasping his ex-chief's hand.

"Pay no attention, Pablo. I'm stinking. I haven't had a bath or changed clothes for nearly a week. The barber has not put in an appearance for three days." He ran the palms of his hands over his cheeks, which were covered with a grayish stubble. He gave a short, hoarse laugh, which was more like a death rattle. "Do you remember that April morning when I handed my credentials to the President? You said I had sprayed cologne with too heavy a hand." He spread a palm on the breast of his sweaty shirt, of a soiled white, showed his khaki drill trousers all wrinkled and full of creases, and went on, "As you can see, things have changed. But it doesn't matter. Life is like that. Sit down."

Pablo pulled a chair up to the bed and sat down. And while the ex-ambassador talked of things of little importance—the poor quality of the food they were serving him, the behavior of the guards, who were forbidden to say a word to him, the heat, the trumpet and drum calls, which irritated him so much—Ortega examined the man whose life he was going to attempt to save.

Gabriel Heliodoro was unrecognizable. He had grown very gaunt. His puffy eyes, the pupils of which had lost their old gleam, suggested nights of broken slumber or of complete insomnia. His voice had lost its insolent timbre, and the clean copper of the Mayan idol's face was now stained with the verdigris of fatigue, worry, and suffering. What struck him most was that the man's hair had turned almost completely white. Pablo Ortega was looking at a man who appeared to be seventy years old.

"Say nothing, Pablo. I know what you are thinking. I have aged twenty years in these last weeks. I saw my face in a mirror when I was in the hospital. I didn't recognize myself. But it's of no matter, I'm going to get better. When they shave me and cut my hair and give me a decent suit to wear, I'll be a different man. I want to face that shitty tribunal with my head erect. If they think I'm going to beg for mercy, or melt into tears, they're wrong."

He sat up in the bed, pulled up a trouser leg, and displayed the soiled bandage covering the wound in his knee. "They'd nearly cut off my leg. It still hurts a lot. But I think it's better now. Oh, another thing. When is the trial?"

"Next Friday. And that is what brings me here."

Pablo rose, went to the window, and stared out at the patio, where some soldiers were playing soccer. "I've come to ask you to accept me as your lawyer," he said without looking at the prisoner.

"You?"

"Does it seem absurd to you?"

Gabriel Heliodoro smiled. "No. You always did like me, Pablo, even though against your will. I always liked you, as the son I wanted and God denied me. Nothing hurt me more than the things you said to me the day you came into my office to present your resignation. Had it been anyone else, I would have kicked him out. But I didn't expect—word of honor—that you might be interested in my defense. I confess I'm glad of it—as a good intention, of course."

Silence fell. It suddenly occurred to Pablo that there might be a microphone planted somewhere in the room to record his conversation with the prisoner. He began a surreptitious hunt for it. He looked under the bed, climbed on the chair to inspect the light fixture. It was not easy to conceal a microphone in a room so bare of furniture; there was only the iron cot, a bedside table, two chairs, and a lavatory—an iron stand supporting a tin basin and a crockery pitcher.

"I know what you're looking for, Pablo. I think it's a waste of time. You won't find a microphone. I've already thought of that and made my own search. Your comrades must not be very interested in what we talk about, since they know that I'll be condemned to death, no matter what."

"But will you accept me as your lawyer?"

"Since it's a mere formality, Pablo, I accept your offer, but only out of my regard for you. I have no illusions. I know I'm sunk. They are going to make a big show of my trial. Have you a cigarette? Mine have run out."

Pablo handed him a full package. "Keep it. I'll send you more."

Pablo held his lighter to the prisoner's cigarette. For a little while Gabriel Heliodoro smoked with a pensive air. Then he half smiled. "What an idea, to shoot the condemned in a bullring! That never occurred to my *compadre* Carrera."

"I find the spectacle depressing," Pablo said as he sat down again. "Now. I want to tell you exactly what I intend to do. My main objective will be to keep them from sentencing you to death."

Gabriel Heliodoro laughed; a poor, wan imitation of his famous metallic, cascading guffaws. "Why should they spare me? In me they are not trying just a man but a whole situation, an entire regime."

"The evidence accumulated against you is overwhelming."

"Evidence of what?"

"Of misappropriation of funds, speculation, illicit self-enrichment, nepotism, crimes against the National Treasury, abuse of economic power—"

"Since when are those *crimes* punishable with death?"

"You are also accused of coresponsibility for the kidnapping and murder of Dr. Leonardo Gris."

Gabriel Heliodoro stiffened. "I had nothing to do with that business! It must have been the work of that ass Zabala. And besides, Pablo, accuse a man of a capital crime without presenting at least the corpse of the victim? Don Leonardo Gris may still be alive!"

"You will be accused also of complicity, by commission or omission, in all the murders and tortures committed by the Federal Police under both Ugarte and Zabala."

"I have never killed anybody except in battle or a duel. I swear it by the Virgen de la Soledad, by the life of my wife and my daughters and grandchildren!"

He caught Pablo by the shoulders with both hands. "You do believe me, don't you?"

The heat had increased. The man's disagreeable smell struck Pablo's nostrils, reminding him of the peons on his father's hacienda when they were working in the sun on the plantation.

"Do you believe me?" Gabriel Heliodoro repeated.

Pablo freed himself from the prisoner's dirty-nailed hands and the sticky proximity of his body. "I believe you. But what we have to do is to make the jury believe it, too. It won't be easy. Thousands of people will be there demanding your death."

Gabriel Heliodoro began to hobble around the room like a huge, wounded animal. He approached the window, gripped the bars with both hands, and stared out, breathing hard from his effort. "One thing I ask of you right now, Pablo Ortega. Do what you think best. Say what you think best. But one thing I beg of you—I *demand* of you. Don't speak of my mother, you understand? Don't say that I am a poor *hijo de una chingada*. I forbid it, you hear? And another thing. Don't ask the jury for mercy. Don't use the word. Don't put me in the position of being a poor repentant devil who's wetting his pants out of fear of dying. Hear me? I don't want anybody's pity. If they can't like me, it's better that they hate me. Promise! Promise! Promise!"

"I promise," Pablo muttered, feeling his khaki shirt glued to his back by his sweat.

Limping and groaning, Gabriel Heliodoro went to the washstand and started bathing his face in the water, already used many times over, in the basin. He soaked his hair, his arms, and then turned to the other man. He seemed to have recovered his spirits. He was less stooped, his eyes had lost a little of their opacity.

"Pablo, go away! Don't defend me. It's useless. Save your skin. You are going to be a marked man to your comrades."

The heat in the room seemed to increase. Ortega's head was throbbing with pain. His mouth was dry with thirst and he had a desperate desire to flee to the open air. He could go away now, forget all this. He recalled Godkin's words from the day before: "You accuse Valencia of wishing to play God, but in a way you, Pablo, are trying to imitate Jesus Christ. Gabriel Heliodoro does not deserve that sacrifice. You are going to act out a sorry parody of the tragedy of Golgotha—you will be crucified along with the wicked thief."

"Go, Pablo," the prisoner repeated. "And don't think of me any more."

Ortega unbuttoned his shirt and passed his handkerchief over his face, his neck, his chest. He faced the other.

"I am your attorney now, Gabriel Heliodoro. That is decided. I shall not turn back. But now I want to talk to you man to man. I had every reason to hate you and to wish you out of the way."

"But you don't hate me, Pablo, you don't. And you know why? You know why? It's because I am and I do a lot of things that you would like to be and do, but you aren't and don't on account of that poppycock you call principles. Own up! You don't know whether your way is any more right than mine."

Pablo was trying to put his thoughts in order. Valencia had made it quite plain that this would be his first and last interview with Gabriel Heliodoro, whom he would see again only on the day of the trial.

The prisoner stretched out on the bed, face up, panting from the effort he had made. He continued to smoke. The ash from the cigarette fell on his chest, momentarily staining the little medal with the effigy of the Virgin.

"Speak, Pablo. Ask what you want to. I have only a week of life left."

Where to begin? There were so many questions he had to ask. "There are some aspects of your character that puzzle me."

"What aspects, *chico?*"

His eyes half closed, the prisoner now seemed calmer.

"You came up from the bottom, you were a poor boy, barefoot, ragged, hungry, wretched. You saw your friends shot and tortured by Chamorro's soldiers. At twenty-one you joined Carrera's revolutionaries and risked your life to destroy the dictator. You promised the people of your country justice and a better life, but you wound up forgetting your promises completely. You made a rich marriage, and became a big man in the republic, acted unscrupulously, and ended by being Carrera's best friend, and he turned into a dictator worse than Chamorro. Why?"

"Don't ask me. Ask God. But God is the great mute. Nobody has yet found out what He wishes. I know only one thing. I had a body, and that body demanded things that I did not deny it. No one, nothing is closer to a man than his own body. From the hour he is born until the hour he dies."

"But haven't you ever felt remorse at having betrayed your friends?"

" 'Betrayed?' Life is a constant betrayal. The ones who are alive are betraying the dead by that very fact. A man betrays others in act or thought, whether he will or not, from the time he gets out of bed in the morning until the hour he goes to bed again. We are all selfish. The only difference is that some have the courage to be what they are, right to the end, and others are cowed, complaining of life, justifying their cowardice or their impotence with fake philosophies. To me only one important thing existed —the present moment. I have tamed my memory and it has learned to forget the past, everything it doesn't suit me to remember. What mattered to me was living."

"But now you are going to die."

"I've lived a hundred lives. How many men can say as much?"

There is one thing that bothers me," Pablo said after a short silence. "Your conscience. Hasn't it ever disturbed you? You became the lover of Vivanco's wife, you made that poor man's life a torment, and you were finally the indirect cause of his death."

"Vivanco was a worm. He didn't deserve even getting born." He laughed. "I hope they're not accusing me of murdering Vivanco."

"No, Gabriel Heliodoro, you are evading my question. Can it be that, never, at any time of day or night, your conscience has not accused you of anything, even if it were for no more than a minute, a second, a fraction of a second? You cannot be so different from other men."

He watched the man whose days were numbered. And yet he was smoking, smiling, apparently tranquil. Pablo was not sure just what he felt toward him. He was cynical, brutal, egocentric, exasperating, but even so he could not hate him.

"Another thing," he continued, "another thing that puzzles me, perturbs me because it is so incomprehensible, unexpected, inexplicable—"

"Speak up, *chico.*"

"You knew that Carrera was ruined. You sent your family to take refuge in the Dominican Republic. Didn't you?"

"Right."

"You were in Washington, you could have requested asylum of the American government, or flown to Ciudad Trujillo or to Switzerland, like, Ugarte, like the others. Why didn't you?"

"Do I need to explain?"

"Of course! Wasn't it to be expected that, loving life as you say you do, you would want to live longer?"

For an instant the prisoner remained silent. Then, making a catapult of his forefinger, he snapped the cigarette butt against the ceiling. "The man who loves life," he replied, "cannot be afraid of death. One thing cannot exist without the other. They are two sides of the same coin." He turned his face toward Pablo. "Nice, eh, Pablo? You can use the phrase as your own. I don't know whether it's my own or I read it somewhere. The man who loves life greatly, in a certain way loves death, too."

"It's just a phrase, Gabriel Heliodoro. It's just a phrase."

"All right. A man has his male pride. And you, Pablo, would you be more tranquil—or happy—if I had fled to Switzerland like that cuckold Ugarte, instead of coming to defend my chief and *compadre*?"

"Of course not, but—"

"You see? The man who knows how to live must also know how to die."

He raised himself to a sitting position, swung his legs off the bed, lighted another cigarette, and looked at his visitor.

"Only one thing disturbs me. It's the idea of dying in the arena, in a bullring, tied up like a pig for the slaughter . . . and in front of an audience that's going to enjoy the spectacle of my death."

Pablo Ortega stubbornly shook his head, meaning that Gabriel Heliodoro's explanations did not satisfy him.

"Pablo, you want to know something? I may be ignorant, but I'm not stupid. I know life and I know men. You think you came here only because you are worried about me, but the truth is you came because you are worried about yourself. The fact is that you don't yet know whether that revolution of yours is really going to save the people from misery as your chiefs claim. How many of the last administration have been shot these last few weeks? Three hundred? Four hundred? There you are. The

slaughter will go on for a long time. You can't stomach it.
You must have killed with your own hands, in combat, and
that thing you call conscience must be hurting you. Now
you want to be assured that all the violence and all the
massacre were really necessary. And as my execution will
be one more death on your conscience, you are going to try
to save my life."

He got up. "When I was in the hospital," he proceeded, "the nurses gave me issues of that revolutionary
paper—what's the name of that filthy rag? *Revolución!*
And I read its lines, and between the lines. Miguel Barrios
is nothing but a puppet. The one who pulls the strings is
that fellow Roberto Valencia. Am I right or not?"

"Of course you are right."

"Very well. Listen to what I am telling you, Pablo.
Nobody has told me a thing, but I can swear you don't like
Valencia and he doesn't like you. In reality you are anti-
Valencia. But take note of one thing. He's the one who's
right, not you!"

Pablo quickly lifted his head. "Why?"

"Try to understand me. Even though that fellow
wants my head, I can't help admiring him. He knows what
he wants. He doesn't stop at sacrifices, and he doesn't care
about the means, to achieve his ends. He's a man. And a
real revolution can be carried out with men of that mettle.
Don't ever forget, Pablo, that right is always on the side of
the conquerors."

"I disagree."

"That'll get you nowhere. The facts are there. You'll
be shot one day in the bullring, if you don't succeed in
getting out of the country. It's a simple question of time."

"I refuse to accept those alternatives. The revolution
is not, cannot, and must not be the property of Valencia or
of the Communist Party. It is ours, the people's."

Pablo clasped his aching head in his hands. A bugle
call sounded, harsh and strident, in the barracks quadrangle. Gabriel Heliodoro had resumed his moving around
the room, dragging his wounded leg.

Suddenly the image of Leonardo Gris rose up in

Pablo's mind. "I want you to be perfectly frank with me," he said. "I have to satisfy my curiosity, blot out a doubt. It's about the *Noche Trágica*. You people made the world believe that President Moreno committed suicide with a bullet in his head. What is the truth?"

Gabriel Heliodoro seized the water pitcher and drank a long swallow, noisily, letting the liquid run out of the corners of his mouth, down his neck, and over his chest. He wiped his lips with the back of his hand and looked at the other man. "Dr. Moreno did not commit suicide."

"Ah, that was what Gris thought. You killed him, then."

The other shook his head in denial. "I don't give a damn whether the jurors believe my deposition or not. But I want *you*, Pablo, to know the truth. Why should I lie to you, if I know that it's all up with me whatever happens?"

He paused briefly, breathed deeply, and then resumed. "Dr. Julio Moreno died of a heart attack. He had already had two since he took over the government. You must recall that the newspapers published that fact. I was the first to enter his office on the *Noche Trágica*. I found him alone, fallen face down over his desk, dead. I swear by the Virgen de la Soledad that I am telling the truth. A physician examined him and determined the cause of death. The rest was invented by my *compadre* Carrera and his chief of police without my knowledge."

Ortega went up to Gabriel Heliodoro and pointed to the medal of the saint hanging from his neck. "That medal —your devotion to the Virgin. It's an absurd, contradictory type of religion that I can't figure out."

"I can't, either. Isn't it the priests themselves who say that religion is not a matter of logic, but of faith?"

"But even faith—" the other began.

"Do you believe in God?" Gabriel Heliodoro interrupted.

"I am an agnostic. I neither affirm nor deny His existence."

"Well, I believe in the Supreme Being. Funny! I'm the believer and act like an unbeliever. You, the unbeliever,

408] HIS EXCELLENCY, THE AMBASSADOR

are the moralist. Life has no coherence, Pablo Ortega y Murat."

The visitor prepared to leave. His eyes were blurred and his head ached with a more and more blinding intensity. "We have an understanding, haven't we? I'll defend you. My aim will be to prevent your being sentenced to death."

"You'll be wasting your breath. But if that pacifies your conscience, I shall not oppose it. But I repeat what I said just now. Don't ask for mercy. Don't mention my mother. Let me spend this final week of my life with the dignity of a man. And note, Pablo, that I say dignity of a man and not of an angel or a saint."

Gabriel Heliodoro held out his hand. "Don't be afraid to shake that hand. Lack of character is not a contagious disease. If it were, there would be an insuperable, chronic epidemic in the world."

Ortega grasped it. "We'll see each other at the tribunal."

"Ah! I'm going to ask you for several things. Get them to send me decent clothes and let me take a bath, and have a barber shave me on the day of the trial. Another thing, Pablo, don't make too much of an effort. Don't risk your neck. Remember what I told you about Roberto Valencia. He's a dangerous man. My sentence may very well be yours."

"I know."

"If you know, why insist on defending me?"

For his only response Pablo Ortega turned his back and walked to the door.

"In his sermons," Gabriel Heliodoro said in an almost jovial voice, "our Padre Catalino used to quote that Bible verse 'Blessed are the meek, for they shall inherit the earth.' I never did believe that. The meek may inherit heaven. The earth, Pablo—that's for the masterful."

Ortega knocked on the door, which one of the guards opened. He cast a last glance at the ex-ambassador, and then went out along the corridor.

42

EVEN IN THE KNOWLEDGE that Amalgamated Press would cut at least two-thirds of his story of the trial of Gabriel Heliodoro Alvarado, Bill Godkin decided to record the most sensational moments of the verbal duel about to begin between Roberto Valencia and Pablo Ortega.

Seated on the bench reserved for representatives of the press, he opened his story with a description of the scene.

"Imagine more than five thousand human bodies in full combustion crowded into a hall with a zinc roof, which as the sun climbs is getting as hot as an incandescent sheet of metal. I do not believe that the world contains a language that lends itself better than Caribbean Spanish to the creation of oral pandemonium in great popular assemblies.

"Hundreds of persons entered this hall at 7 A.M. in order to get a good place. They brought their victuals: chicken, roast beef, sandwiches, pastries, tongue, ham, cheese. Fearing the audience's bellicosity, the authorities prohibited the bringing in of bottles or other blunt objects that might serve as missiles when simple verbal aggression needed a solid complement. The people who did not find seats are standing in the corridors or are sitting on the floor against the walls—men, women, and even children—a rich collection of faces shining with sweat, most of them swarthy and with black, quick eyes. And until the "show" starts, they are talking, eating, singing, smoking, spitting, chewing chicle, whistling, shouting *vivas* or *mueras*, breaking out into sudden jeering or applause, the objects of which I fail to discover, but mostly they stamp their feet, demanding that the show begin. The heat seems to make the air thick and greasy, and the numerous fans whirring and buzzing in this vast hall are only mixing up all these smells—a barbarous potpourri of human sweat, fried foods, garlic, onion, and tobacco.

"Outside, a multitude estimated at nearly thirty thousand is yelling and whistling, indignant because it cannot get into the building. It is going to listen to the trial over the loudspeakers placed in the center and at the angles of the four sides of the building, which is surrounded by a strong contingent of revolutionary militia, armed with machine guns and tear gas bombs. I was told a few minutes ago that there was the beginning of a riot when a group attempted to force an entrance into the Sports Palace in spite of the announcement over the loudspeakers that 'there was not room for another pin inside.'"

According to the Cerro Hermoso weather bureau, the temperature that Friday, November 13, was a little over ninety-one degrees, and the humidity was 80 percent. The single television station in the country, now nationalized and placed exclusively at the service of the revolution, had set up its cameras and lights strategically in the hall. When the lights were turned on, illuminating the platform where the jurors were sitting at a long table, the heat was raised infernally. Members of the jury blinked, dazzled; the president of the tribunal—an old man of benign aspect —made a gesture of irritability and protected his eyes with his hand. Miguel Barrios, who was occupying the seat of honor between the members of the sentencing council, remained impassive, certainly conscious that his image was now being reproduced on thousands of television sets in the city and suburbs. Photographers and movie cameramen immediately went into action. The members of the jury fanned themselves or shooed away the flies with palm-leaf fans or with the cardboard folders enclosing the photocopies of the numerous documents entered in evidence for the prosecution. In the area assigned to the press more than forty foreign representatives of newspapers, magazines, and news agencies were taking notes, using

telephones, talking with one another, drinking countless
glasses of cold lemonade, and wiping faces and necks with
handkerchiefs which gradually got soaking wet.

The president of the tribunal rang his bell, calling for
a silence which he obtained only minutes later, and then in
rather precarious fashion despite the declaration by a
voice of metallic gravity over the loudspeaker that His
Excellency required of the audience the most absolute
composure and complete silence during the session.

At nine-twenty, flanked by four guards armed with
submachine guns, Gabriel Heliodoro Alvarado was led
into the hall. His hands were manacled and he was in shirt
sleeves, but with clean shirt and trousers. The pallor of
illness discolored his freshly shaven face. His eyes were
glazed by the delirious gleam of fever, and at intervals he
licked his cracked, dry lips. Nevertheless, he walked with
head erect, looking straight ahead and upward. Perceiving
that the ex-ambassador was limping, Bill Godkin could not
banish a feeling of commiseration, a detail which he did
not record in his notes, since a reporter must remain impersonal.

At sight of the prisoner the multitude broke out in
shouts and insults, a swollen sound which to many was
reminiscent of the soccer field on days when the city
championship game was played. The uproar lasted several
minutes, in spite of the president of the tribunal banging
his bell repeatedly and the voice of the loudspeaker demanding silence, or His Excellency would be obliged to
empty the courtroom.

Bill Godkin saw expressions of loathing and hatred in
most faces. The epithets continued. Thief! Murderer!
Scoundrel! Bandit! Depraved! Swine!

Seated on his backless bench, his body erect, Gabriel
Heliodoro Alvarado was apparently seeking not to focus
his eyes on any one spot.

Someone sitting in one of the front rows hurled a
rotten egg at him which smashed against his face, and its
fetid contents ran down his cheek and onto his shirt, with
a dirty, mustard-yellow stain. A sergeant dashed over to

the place from which the egg had been thrown to discover who the culprit was. A melee of short duration followed. Gabriel Heliodoro, however, remained motionless, without making the least attempt to wipe his face. Names more rotten than the egg were hurled at him. He continued imperturbable. But when a strong voice of a man, standing out from the rest, yelled *"Hijo de una chingada!"* Bill Godkin saw that Gabriel Heliodoro's countenance suffered a slight contraction, and the scar on his forehead flamed red.

From that moment the Amalpress correspondent decided to forget his impartial objectivity and started jotting down in hasty shorthand not only what was being said and done in the hall but also his own emotions. At some time in the future he could use all this material for a book into which the editors at his agency would have no right to stick either their noses or their mutilating blue pencils.

"The president recognized Roberto Valencia, who wasted no time on courteous phrases or greetings, but launched into the attack. 'We are gathered here to try not only a man but an entire regime, a historic epoch, a black situation which for long years stained our land with shame and blood, destroyed our economy and made our people wretched.' He enumerated minutely and methodically the crimes of which the prisoner was accused: abuse of economic power, illicit self-enrichment, black market operations, embezzlement of public funds, usury, complicity in all the cruelties and outrages committed by the Federal Police, direct and active participation in the great swindle in the construction of the new Palace of Government, and enjoyment of official favors and privileges harmful to the National Treasury. He analyzed the private life of the accused, principally his sexual orgies in his famous country house not far from Cerro Hermoso.

"For two solid hours he presented abundant proof of the accuracy of his accusations (some of them vague, in my opinion, but others irrefutable). He called scores of persons to give their oral testimony and called the jurors'

attention to the photocopies of the documents supporting his accusations, which they already had in their cardboard folders.

"Gabriel Heliodoro Alvarado is sunk, I thought. Valencia could stop, for he had already won the game. And yet he continued. He proved that 'this human pustule' had been one of the main authors of the 'mythological conspiracy' attributed to Communists, and which had furnished Juventino Carrera the pretext needed by the tyrant to remain in power—the famous Movimiento de Salvación Nacional, in which so many innocents had been arrested, tortured, and killed. 'It was this same fellow who commanded the Fifth Column which operated in this capital on the occasion of the usurper's return from exile in 1951, aided by the American companies, the United Plantations Company and the Caribbean Sugar Emporium. It was this miscreant also who, with his mercenaries, burst into the Palace of Government and shot President Moreno to death!'

"At this point a kind of collective howl rose from the crowd, ending in a rhythmic, angry chant: 'Plaza de Toros! Plaza de Toros! Plaza de Toros!' The chorus lasted several minutes. Pablo Ortega, seated at his table, was now taking notes, now playing nervously with his pencil or wiping his face and neck with his handkerchief. He was sweating profusely, and I had the impression that I could actually see his head aching under the dull pounding of the blood in his temples.

"When order was restored, Valencia resumed. 'Not only of being a thief and murderer do I accuse Gabriel Heliodoro Alvarado. Besides being directly guilty of the death of Dr. Julio Moreno, he is also indirectly responsible for the kidnapping and murder of Dr. Leonardo Gris, who, in Washington, was drugged by agents of Carrera under orders from his embassy, put into a private plane, and, as in the revolting case of Professor Jesús Galíndez, thrown into the sea!' At this point the prisoner frowned and tried to catch his attorney's eye. Pablo Ortega, however, had his head down, studying his notes. 'It was likewise this sensual, dissolute person,' the prosecutor continued, 'who was responsible for the killing of a secretary of embassy of El Sacramento in Washington, Francisco Vivanco, whose wife was his mistress. Not satisfied with having contributed to the elimination of the man whom he betrayed and rendered unhappy, he did not hesitate to stain his memory by falsely implicating him in a pseudo conspiracy which supplied Juventino Carrera with the pretext he needed for his last coup d'état.' Here, nearly the entire audience stood up and resumed the chant: 'Plaza de Toros! Plaza de Toros!' The president rang his bell in vain. Guards charged against the first rows of seats, bayonets fixed; there were exchanges of shoves and insults; a sergeant got a blow on the head; and at last the commander of the detachment policing the palace ordered his soldiers to fire in the air. This brought on a hint of panic, and order was restored only after some fifteen or twenty minutes, and silence returned to this little branch of hell. Roberto Valencia pronounced these final words: 'Gentlemen of the jury, I have nothing more to say but to ask this council, in the name of revolutionary justice, which is the justice of the people, to mete out to Gabriel Heliodoro Alvarado, the symbol of the dictatorship and of corruption, the punishment he merits—the penalty of death!' The applause and yells that followed, interspersed by hisses and insults addressed to the prisoner, gave me the impression that the explosive fervor and intensity of their reverberations might even smash out the walls and blow the roof off."

43

THE PRESIDENT of the Tribunal recognized the attorney for the defense. Pablo Ortega rose slowly. His khaki blouse was already completely soaked with sweat. He took two steps in front of his table, bowed toward the president and Miguel Barrios, and approached the microphone. His first words were interrupted by a jeering in which—it seemed to me—all the persons in the upper tiers of seats joined. I could make out cries of 'Shut your mouth, traitor!' 'Out with the fascist!' 'Take him to the Plaza de Toros, too!' The soldiers had to intervene again to restore order. The president of the tribunal made a little speech reminding the audience that the law grants to 'any criminal' the right to have a defense attorney.

"Pablo Ortega waited, his legs apart in the military 'at ease' position, his hands clasped behind his back. I got the impression that he was calmer than I expected, and that, at heart, the bullying attitude of the public stimulated rather than terrorized him.

"In a firm, clear voice he began his defense of the prisoner. He stated that he would not even attempt to answer the accusations and the proofs presented by the prosecutor, as far as the acts of dishonesty and the sexual life of his client were concerned, but he rejected strongly the accusations of murder which the prosecutor had made with more passion than logic, with more hatred than convincing proof. 'There is not even an eyewitness,' he declared, 'to say that Gabriel Heliodoro Alvarado has been the instigator or the agent in the murder of Dr. Julio Moreno. As for Professor Leonardo Gris, how can murder be mentioned when it is not even certain that he has died? Who has seen his body?'

"At this point, a swarthy fat woman, with heavy down on her face, who was sitting in the front row, almost ran up the three steps separating the main floor from the platform, and before the soldiers became aware of her action, she approached Pablo Ortega and spat in his face to almost general applause. Two soldiers immediately seized her and took her out of the hall in the midst of a fresh tumult. Meantime, Pablo Ortega wiped his face with apparent serenity, and for the first time since the trial had begun, I saw an expression of revolt on the face of the prisoner, who wriggled on his bench and even moved as though to rise, an act prevented by two of the soldiers mounting guard over him.

"From the middle of the audience rose a man's voice, clear but tremulous with indignation. 'You are an ingrate! Dr. Gris was your professor and friend.' I noted an expression of sadness on Pablo Ortega's face when he replied, without rancor, "I loved Dr. Gris as a father. If I were convinced that Gabriel Heliodoro Alvarado had the slightest responsibility for his disappearance, I should not be here to defend him but to accuse him.' These simple words provoked a new, aggressive, verbal explosion from the crowd, after which Pablo spoke for several minutes, seeking to prove that it was absurd to try Gabriel Heliodoro for the crimes of Carrera, Ugarte, Zabala, and the other villains of the overthrown government. The prisoner was not a 'symbol' but a man, and as such he should be tried for his own crimes. He could not continue, because the sinister chant commenced again. 'Plaza de Toros! Plaza de Toros! Plaza de Toros!' Pablo Ortega abruptly turned to the president of the tribunal and said heatedly, 'Mr. President, I propose that the present trial be transferred to another day and another locale, for this body of jurors is in no condition to pass a serene judgment, as it is undergoing strong pressure from the public, with its demands for the defendant's death sentence.'

"Valencia rose and shouted, 'I protest! We have no time to waste on juridical hairsplitting. The people have the right to manifest their opinions and emotions, because this is now a democracy and no longer a dictatorship. And the jurors are men of courage and dignity, and therefore capable of judging the criminal conscientiously in the light of the irrefutable proofs which the prosecution has offered in evidence against him!'

"New applause and frenzied cries. A television camera moved toward the defense attorney to catch the expression on his face in a close-up. Pablo Ortega faced Roberto Valencia and shouted, 'This revolution was made to establish social justice and pure and simple justice definitively in this land, not to carry out personal revenge! The learned

prosecutor and the Central Committee seem more bent on
providing the public with another bloody spectacle in the
Plaza de Toros than in really doing justice. I declare my
client guilty of a series of crimes which justify his imprisonment, his segregation for the remainder of his life as a
dangerous and prejudicial element in society. Sentence
this man to life imprisonment, but spare his life! The eyes
of the world are upon us. The barbaric spectacle of executions in the Plaza de Toros is giving other nations a wrong
idea of our revolution!' He thrust his hand into a pocket
and drew out a newspaper clipping. Turning to Miguel
Barrios he said, 'Interviewed day before yesterday by foreign correspondents who wished to learn how many more
were to be shot, General Barrios replied, and now I am
going to read his own words, "Don't worry. Our cleaning-
out operation is drawing to a close. With the shooting next
Sunday of Gabriel Heliodoro Alvarado, one of the major
criminals of the past regime, we shall put a stop to the
executions. If you gentlemen of the press are interested in
statistics, I have the pleasure to inform you that Alvarado
will be execution number five hundred." '

"Barrios at this point seemed to me to be disturbed.
He half rose from his chair and cast a glance at Valencia as
if to ask his help. Pablo Ortega turned to the audience.
'Ladies and gentlemen, the statement by the chief of the
revolution which I have just read, that prejudgment of
Gabriel Heliodoro Alvarado, turns the present trial into a
tragic farce.' He stuck the clipping back into his pocket,
made a little bow to the bench, and said, 'Mr. President of
the Revolutionary Tribunal, the defense rests.' And he went
back to his seat amid clamorous jeering.

"Roberto Valencia got up and asked for recognition.
The president made an affirmative sign with his head and
the prosecutor went to the microphone, raised both hands,
smiling, requesting that the applause cease, and obtained
quiet. He spoke for nearly twenty minutes, but he confined
himself to attacking Pablo Ortega personally and directly,
saying, 'Ever since this young man turned up at our camp
in the Sierra de la Calavera, to join our forces, I have

realized that he was more interested in solving his personal problems than in saving our people from the dictatorship and from misery. The son, grandson, and great-grandson of landowners, Pablo Ortega y Murat is the most representative type I know of the intellectual, the slave of fallacious abstractions, the kind that wants and at the same time doesn't want the revolution, that desires and yet fears the change in the socio-economic structure of his country.' Pablo listened to his enemy's words with his head down, scribbling on his memorandum pad. 'Types like Pablo Ortega,' Valencia went on, 'are the germs of infection that all revolutions carry inevitably in their organisms, individuals who some day will become deserters, saboteurs, and counterrevolutionaries.' He pointed toward my friend, who was now facing him squarely, arms folded, face hard, and continued, 'That young man with smooth hands, good manners and good intentions [general laughter] for several years—make a note of this—for several years drew more than a thousand dollars a month from Juventino Carrera's administration, first as secretary of embassy of El Sacramento in Paris, and then in Washington, before he felt those pricks of conscience that led him to climb the Sierra de la Calavera. While many of us were undergoing tortures and hardships in the prisons of Ugarte and Zabala, while our wives, daughters, and sisters were being cruelly handled, violated, and murdered by the police of the dictatorship, this young diplomat was driving his Thunderbird around the avenues of the capital of the United States, having a good time at receptions and dinners, writing poems in his idle moments—which evidently were numerous. I now ask, Why did he take so long to become ashamed of his situation and seek to redeem himself? All this, ladies and gentlemen, is why I do not concede Pablo Ortega the right to criticize our chief and this tribunal. I renew my appeal to the jurors: Death to the criminal Gabriel Heliodoro Alvarado! Do not let yourselves be moved by that delicate poet who has such a horror of blood, which he is seeing now close up for the first time, having shared in the responsibility for its shedding.'

"As he ended these words Roberto Valencia returned to his seat under a rain of applause and bravos. Pablo Ortega quickly got up and went to the microphone. The president of the tribunal banged his bell repeatedly and exclaimed, 'The arguments are closed. The jury will go into recess to make its final decision.'

"Ortega turned to the old judge and said, 'Mr. President, I have just been made the target of grave accusations, and therefore have the right to defend myself. I beg you to let me speak for ten more minutes.'

"The judge leaned toward Miguel Barrios, murmured something into his ear, and the chief nodded.

" 'Very well,' the magistrate said aloud. 'Captain Ortega will have ten minutes, not a second more, to defend himself, to use his own expression.'

"Ortega looked at Roberto Valencia, who was in his seat with arms folded, an ineffable smile giving his face the aspect of an archaic sculpture.

" 'The secretary-general has managed to do what he has long desired. He has placed me also in the dock with the criminals and he chose an admirable occasion on which more than six thousand persons are seeing and hearing inside this hall, and hundreds of thousands of other compatriots of ours are listening to us over the radio and hearing and watching us on their television sets.'

"He paused briefly, again glanced at the secretary-general and shouted, 'And I wish to take this opportunity to accuse him publicly of perverting the aims of our revolution! We have not yet succeeded in calculating the total number of Sacramentans who lost their lives or were wounded or mutilated in the struggle against Carrera's dictatorship. Be that as it may, we today are the warrantors of all those heroes and martyrs. We have the obligation to destroy, root and branch, the semifeudal oligarchic system which has caused so much wretchedness for so many years. Social justice will someday be established in this island. Our people must be really protected, rescued from misery, from disease, from illiteracy, from the most ignominious peonage and brought to a level of happiness, prosperity, and dignity. It is shameful, it is absurd that any country can be governed arbitrarily by a group of privileged families and two or three foreign companies!'

"While Pablo was speaking, an unexpected silence had fallen in the chamber. During his pauses it was possible to hear the buzz of a fly. I looked at my watch—1:15 P.M. Hunger was beginning to bore holes in my stomach.

" 'Among the evils of the dictatorship which we are fighting, one of those that caused the greatest indignation in thinking men was the lack of freedom of speech, of the free exchange of ideas.' Pablo Ortega again extended his arm in the direction of the secretary-general and, raising his voice and enunciating every syllable clearly, said, 'I accuse Colonel Roberto Valencia of already engendering for our new regime laws and political arrangements tending to eliminate free speech!'

"Valencia lifted himself in his chair, and I thought he was going to pull his revolver from its holster and put a bullet in Pablo Ortega. However, he resumed his former position and his smile, which he had assumed from the beginning of the other's speech.

" 'Indeed,' Ortega proceeded, 'Roberto Valencia is organizing the foundations of a totalitarian state in which we shall all run the risk of ceasing to be human beings and turn into statistical and bureaucratic elements, in short, into abstractions!'

"Valencia could not contain himself and exclaimed, 'Shut your mouth, idiot!'

"Pablo Ortega smiled and retorted immediately, his face turned toward the audience, 'It is just as I stated. The secretary-general prefers insult to argument.'

"The president hammered his bell. Ortega turned to him, looked at his watch, and said, 'Excellency, I still have seven minutes.'

"Valencia got up and shouted, 'If Captain Ortega really wants a debate, I'll give him the response he deserves. A revolution is not made with poets, artists, and literary men who have a horror of blood and violence. A country is not built by innocent dreamers, but by men who, when necessary, shoot first and ask questions afterward. Before us we have a formidable enemy, protected by one of the most powerful imperialist nations in the world. If I can be accused of anything, it is of knowing exactly what I want, and of being sheltered by an ideology.' And he sat down. Applause broke out all over the hall.

" 'Ideology!' Ortega repeated. 'It is good that the brave colonel should have used that word. In my opinion, 'ideology' is a word of elastic meaning which can be stretched or shrunk according to the needs of political realism, whether communist, fascist, or even of our famous liberal democracy. If an ideology is not strictly confined within certain limits of morality and ethics, it will end by becoming dehumanized, and tyranny will be set up in its name. Colonel Valencia says that a revolution is made with men who shoot first and ask questions later. I have a name for that type of man: fanatic. In my life I have seen fanatics in black cassocks, in commissars' blouses— or in shirt sleeves, in a bullring, demanding in loud bellows the blood of the bull, of the bullfighter, or of both!'

"A tremendous uproar of hoots and jeers burst out at that moment. Pablo merely looked at his watch and timed the duration. When silence was restored, he continued.

" 'To conclude, I wish to notify not only Colonel Valencia but all who are listening to me, that I do not intend to desert, or to perform acts of sabotage, and much less to take part in a counterrevolution. Because this revolution belongs to us all. It is not Washington's, but neither is it Moscow's. It is ours, our people's.' He turned to the secretary-general again. 'After all that I have said here today, I do not know what plans the Revolutionary Central Committee may have with respect to my physical and juridical person. But whatever they may be, I want my final words to be a warning. If we find that for the foundations of the new Sacramento we are going to build, the best mortar is the flesh and blood of our enemies, or of

those who disagree with us, we shall be running the grave
risk of repeating the same old sorry, tragic history of the
Latin American dictatorships. Because, if in the base of
that great and beautiful edifice which is our fatherland of
tomorrow, besides our labor, our intelligence, our honesty,
our tireless vigilance, there is not also an element of tolerance and love, we shall have built our house upon the
sand!'

"Pablo Ortega returned to his seat. The president of
the tribunal announced that the sentencing council would
recess to judge the case.

"Valencia sat with arms still folded. The smile had
vanished from his face."

44

THE STORY published next day in the Washington
Post under the headline "Ex-Ambassador to Washington Condemned to Death" ran thus:

Cerro Hermoso, Nov. 14. By William B. Godkin,
Amalpress. Gabriel Heliodoro Alvarado, who until
September of this year served in Washington as ambassador of the Republic of El Sacramento, was tried
yesterday and condemned to death by the popular
tribunal set up by the revolutionary forces which
recently took over the government in this island,
expelling the dictator Juventino Carrera.

Colonel Roberto Valencia, secretary-general of
the provisional government, acted as public prosecutor, and the prisoner's defense was in the hands of
Captain Pablo Ortega, who for nearly two years performed the functions of first secretary in his country's embassy to the White House and to the OAS.

Gabriel Heliodoro Alvarado will be shot tomorrow
at ten o'clock in the great bullring of this capital.

"That execution in an arena is repulsive!" Clare Ogilvy exclaimed, throwing the paper down on the table. And Orlando Gonzaga, who had been with her for several minutes in the bar on Connecticut Avenue where he used to meet Godkin and Ortega shook his head and took a sip of his manhattan. They were both on their third cocktail and, from the moment they had sat down at the table, had been talking about Pablo with nostalgia and affection.

Clare sniffed loudly, twisting her whole face to one side, opened her purse, took out a bunch of keys, and tossed it on the paper. "The keys to the embassy residence and to the chancellery," she murmured, propping her elbows on the table and putting her hands to her cheeks.

"Just see what turns life takes, Gonzaga. I, Clare W. Ogilvy, American citizen, chargé d'affaires of the Republic of El Sacramento—until the ambassador of the new government arrives."

Gonzaga shook his head. "He won't get here soon. I'll bet the Department of State is going to make Miguel Barrios cool his heels for a while."

"Sometimes I go to the chancellery," La Ogilvita said dreamily, "I open the windows to let in the sun and the air, and, shivering with cold, because the heat is turned off, I walk alone through the rooms, remembering faces, voices, smells. It's like visiting a cemetery. There is Dr. Jorge Molina's tomb. Farther on, General Ugarte's. I go into Don Gabriel Heliodoro's office and I can still smell the scent of his Havana and—with a little imagination—breathe the perfumes he overdid. Suddenly I encounter Don Alfonso Bustamante in his picture, and the old man seems to be calling me to account for the affairs of his country. In the corridors I meet the ghosts of those lieutenants, captains, and majors with lewd eyes who liked so much to gaze at the breasts, legs, and behinds of the stenographers— except Merceditas', of course. Suddenly Titito passes, as ethereal as a sylph. The little paper birds that Vivanco used to sail through the air—they cross the air in front of me like the specters of birds. Or—who knows?—like notes the poor man is trying to send me from the beyond. And, alas, when I go into the office that was Pablo's, my heart closes up and I break into tears, and then I sniffle a while, wind up sneezing, and conclude that the chill is giving me a cold; then I shut the windows and go back home. Waiter! Another manhattan, please. Gonzaga, what's the news with you? Are things not going well with you, either?"

"No, they are not. Clare, I'm a louse. Pablo is the one who acted like a man. He reached a man's decision. But I am a parasite like my father, who, like the majority of the great merchants and industrialists of Brazil, cheats on his income tax and with the money buys dollars, which he deposits in a bank in Switzerland in a numbered account, or in banks in Manhattan. Hey, waiter! Another Swiss bank—I mean another manhattan."

Clare, however, made a negative sign to the waiter and called for the check. "Let's go, Orlando."

"The check is on me."

When the waiter returned, he took the bill from his hands. Clare Ogilvy looked at her watch and sighed.

"Nearly seven. Have you thought that this is Gabriel Heliodoro's last night? Can you imagine what he feels in his cell, waiting for the hour of his death?"

"That's another case. Don Gabriel Heliodoro. He joined his thumb and forefinger, put them up to his head, and made a motion as if turning a key. "For today I am stopping my thinking machine. Will you dine with me? . . . No? Got a date? . . . Patience. I'll dine alone. Afterward I'll drop in at a movie to watch one of those colored imbecilities fabricated in Hollywood on a wide screen and with stereophonic sound. Probably I'll go out of the movie before the end of the film, get in my car, and drive the streets in search of a woman to sleep with."

"Which is no solution, either."

"Which is no solution, I agree, but it does solve, at least for one night, another kind of problem."

They rose. Gonzaga paid the bill, leaving a royal tip which made the waiter display an ordinarily invisible gold tooth. On the way to the door the Brazilian asked, "Clare, what is the answer, the great answer to all this?"

Grasping her friend's arm, La Ogilvita answered with a story. "They say that on her deathbed, a few minutes before she died, Gertrude Stein turned to her devoted companion, Miss Toklas, and asked, 'What is the answer?' And before the other had time to open her mouth, Miss Stein added, 'But what is the question?' "

The two went out into the cold November evening.

45

ON THAT SAME SATURDAY evening Pablo Ortega and Bill Godkin, who had dined together, were walking side by side along the sidewalks of the Paseo de Bolívar in Cerro Hermoso. All the colored neon signs were dark, for the new administration had decided to ration electricity. But all the street lights, in lamps of colonial style, were shining on the tops of the posts lining the sidewalks and the central flower beds, furnishing enough light to give a festive air to the principal avenue of the capital. Many people were on the promenades. The cafes, movie theaters, restaurants, and bars were open and filled. Many men were wearing the uniform of the Revolutionary Militia. In almost every face there was an expression of relief, joy, and hopeful expectancy. Some of the soldiers were walking arm in arm with girls, talking, singing, or laughing, and going into or coming out of public places. Sitting on one of the benches aligned beside the central flower beds of the promenade, a boy and a girl were glued together in an embrace, with the immobility of a statue. Pablo Ortega smiled, thought of Glenda Doremus, then of Kimiko Hirota, and finally of Pía. Pía what? He could remember no more. Perhaps he had never known the family name of his companion in Eden.

The evening before, exhausted from the defense of Gabriel Heliodoro Alvarado, he had found relief in physical love. He had taken to his third-class hotel room one of the stenographers who worked in his office in the Palace of Government, a brunette with almond eyes, whose features reminded him a little of Miss Hirota's, and he had asked her to spend the night with him. He felt, as he had never before felt in his life, the need of a feminine presence.

"I fell asleep with her in my arms," he was now telling Godkin. "I awoke early and found her no longer in bed. I heard a noise, a crackle—I turned my head and saw the girl searching first the papers in my writing desk, then the drawers of the bureau, and finally the pockets of my clothes. I pretended I was still asleep and saw nothing. At last she came back to bed and put her arms around me again."

"A spy of Valencia's?"

"Probably."

"Now look at that fellow in the white suit, with the Panama on his head. He was in the restaurant while we were eating and didn't take his eyes off our table. He has been following us ever since we came out."

Godkin and Ortega left the central streets of the city, which, in the newspaperman's opinion, were losing their national character and becoming gradually Americanized by the skyscrapers, the drugstores, and the cafeterias. They headed for the old part—which was Pablo's favorite, too—with its narrow streets paved with cobblestones, its houses with tile façades, its colonial eaves and gates and roofs. From inside some of the houses floated familiar smells: fried oil, burned sugar, lavender, honeysuckle, attic mustiness, braziers, and melted wax from the candles of the household chapels.

Now and then the two friends would stop to look in at some patio. Bill Godkin let Pablo lead the way, and was not long in perceiving where he was heading. After some twenty minutes' walk they arrived in front of the residence of the Ortega y Murat family. Pablo went up to the iron gate, seized its bars in both hands, and stood a long time gazing in silence at his home. (A curious kind of prisoner, Godkin reflected.) The great house in the depths of the park continued to keep its windows shut. Godkin knew that, even though she was ill, Doña Isabel, with her Castilian pride, refused not only to see her son but to answer his telephone calls.

At last the two friends resumed their stroll. When Bill stopped under a street lamp to fill and light his pipe, Pablo, out of the corner of his eye, saw that the man in the Panama hat was still following them.

"Do you think, Bill, my mother watched the trial on television?"

"It's probable. Would you like her to have watched it?"

"I don't know. Maybe. I don't know. It's all still very confused."

In an ill-lighted street the two suddenly found the night in an almost pure state, a broad, charcoal-blue sky in which stars were twinkling.

They were on their way back to the center of town when the newspaperman remarked with a casual air, "Oh, I was forgetting to say that I have passage on tomorrow's plane to New York. I think my professional job in El Sacramento is over."

"What time do you leave?"

The other shook his head. "No, don't go to the airport. I don't like good-bys. I prefer to say 'so long' at the door of your hotel. O.K?"

"O.K."

"Have you anything special to ask me to do?"

"Tell Gonzaga and Clare that I always think of them with nostalgia. And you, when you have time, write me a few lines."

They were passing a cafe. Pablo caught Godkin's arm and led him inside. "Let's have something cold. And I'll take the opportunity to write a little note, which you will do me the favor of delivering to Miss Hirota."

They took seats at a table. They ordered sherbet.

Cigarette smoke was hovering in the air, touched by the violet light from the television. The cafe was almost full, and all were watching the screen, on which a news analyst was commenting on the trial of Gabriel Heliodoro. Godkin perceived Pablo's uneasiness; he must be fearing the possibility of being recognized as the "reprobate" who had defended the criminal. But no one seemed interested in the recent arrivals. Ortega took a notebook out of his pocket, tore out a sheet, and wrote on it with a ballpoint pen:

FOOLISH GARDENER
He spent his life
Cultivating, unaware,
The flower of death.

The image of Valencia flashed through his mind, smiling disdainfully. Pablo, irritated, crushed the paper and put it in his pocket. "I've changed my mind." He began eating the sherbet, which the waiter had brought. "Telephone Miss Hirota, Bill, and tell her that I sometimes think of her. No. Don't say anything. Washington is not a real world for me now. Like the other worlds I lived in before that."

The television commentator was describing what the "show," the execution of the "notorious Gabriel Heliodoro," would be like next day. The central committee had announced to the country and to the world that with the execution of "Carrera's accomplice" the punitive phase of the revolution was over. He announced also that there were no more tickets available for the "fiesta," but that the public could follow, at home or in public places, all the phases of the execution, "thanks to the cameras of our powerful station."

"Let's go," Pablo murmured, leaving five lunas on the marble of the table. "That story is turning my stomach."

They went out. After the heat and the smoke of the interior of the cafe, it was good to breathe again the pure, cool air of the night. The man in the Panama was standing at the corner.

"Now what, Pablo?"

"As I've told you, Bill, I'm staying. I will not be cowed. I shall try to influence the central committee. I am not alone. Many comrades in arms hunted me up this morning to tell me they think as I do, that they are not ready to accept Valencia's dictatorship."

"They're not spies of Valencia's?"

"Suppose they are! I'm not planning any counterrevolution. I *am* trying to establish a dialogue—I simply want Barrios and the other leaders to fulfill all the promises of their manifestoes and speeches—social justice, a democratic government, with all the freedoms—except, of course, the freedom to deprive others of freedom. This poor nation cannot, must not, be duped again."

For some minutes they walked on in silence. The man in white continued to follow them at some thirty yards' distance.

"As you see," Pablo smiled, "Valencia insists on my knowing that I am being watched. He wants to frighten me. It's ridiculous."

"Pablo, don't underestimate Valencia. He is a terrible man."

"But he is a man. His terribleness doesn't scare me. I am determined to face up to him. I have invested practically all I have in this revolution. I am going to collect my dividends, not in positions of command, or in personal profits, but in benefits that can be distributed among the majority of this suffering people. I don't intend to exile myself, nor put a bullet in my head. I am staying. I am harder-headed than I myself imagined. If this revolution had served no other purpose, it would have achieved the useful end of making me know myself better. I confess that my season in hell yesterday was not entirely unpleasant for me."

Godkin shook his head. They were in front of the Cerro Hermoso Hilton. They looked at each other in silence for some time. At last they shook hands.

"Good-by, Pablo. It's been a privilege to know you."

"Thanks for everything, Bill. I won't say good-by but only . . . I'll be seeing you." He smiled. "Make the most of the occasion and throw away that awful bile-colored tie. I'm going to send you another as a present."

The American silently wagged his head (Ruth! Ruth! Ruth!), turned and went into the hotel. Pablo Ortega lighted a cigarette, thought about Gabriel Heliodoro, and immediately tried to forget him. He had done all he could to save him. He was at peace with his conscience. His head felt limpid, lucid, without an ache.

He set off toward his hotel. The man in white followed.

46

AFTER HIS TRIAL Gabriel Heliodoro was removed from his prison in the 2d Infantry barracks to a cell in the basement of the old Central Police Building, where he was to await the hour of his execution.

In the early morning of that Saturday he spent some time limping back and forth, dragging his leg, which ached and throbbed intensely. There was no electric light in the dungeon, which was illuminated only by a candle stuck in a tin holder on a rough table. Beside the table an old priest was sitting, his hoary head dropped on his chest, his arms folded. Padre Catalino Sender had come from Soledad del Mar expressly to attend the condemned man in his last hours. The light of the candle accentuated the yellowness of his wrinkled face and his gaunt cheeks.

"Stop walking, Gabriel Heliodoro," he requested in his weak voice, hoarsened by chronic throat-clearing.

"But I'm positive!" the condemned man exclaimed. "Absolutely certain. It was in this same cell that I was imprisoned for two months, exactly thirty-six years ago. There were five of us boys, all more or less the same age. Chamorro's police caught us writing revolutionary phrases in tar on the walls of the city. I remember perfectly. One day I wrote here on one of these walls, somewhere, some words—Down with the dictatorship! *Viva la Libertad!* I signed my name beneath. I remember perfectly. The date —the date must have been November or December of 1923. I was sure I was going to be shot."

He looked at his hands. "As I had neither pencil nor charcoal, I engraved the words with my fingernails."

He limped to the table, picked up the candlestick, and prowled along the walls, stained with damp and mold, in search of his inscription, talking low to himself. He knelt in a corner for several minutes. Then he got up again with a groan. His whole body was shaking, aching, weakened with fever.

"Padre, lend me your glasses, please. I can't make out anything rightly."

The priest rose, took the glasses from their leather case, and handed them to Gabriel Heliodoro, who adjusted them as best he could to his own eyes and continued his search. The padre returned to his seat and began to pray. His withered lips moved, giving a vague shape to the words of the prayer. He was sad. Gabriel Heliodoro had refused to confess, saying, "God knows me. He knows my good qualities and my defects. He is a judge without political party. He will know how to do justice. If I am a criminal, He will condemn me. Don't insist, padre. I will not confess. I repent of nothing."

Gabriel Heliodoro brought the flame of the candle close to the walls and with difficulty read the inscriptions of several generations of innocent and guilty men. There were also pornographic sketches, rough representations of male and female genital organs. Phrases half extinguished —"Oh, Marieta, if you'd only give me your . . ." "The chief of police is a *maricón*," "Chamorro is a horned cuckold," "*Viva la patria!*" "Good-by, dear mother, I die thinking of you," "A real man dies standing up," "I swear to God I am innocent," "My name is Antonio Pérez and my destination is hell."

I remember, Gabriel Heliodoro thought. I wrote kneeling down in a corner. Maybe on the other side.

He dragged himself to the opposite wall and sat down in another corner, panting. The wax from the candle dripped on his fingers. A sharp pain lanced through his wound. He lifted his hand to his scalding forehead. He put the candle close to the wall again. He had engraved in capital letters. As he finished the last digit of the year, his nails were broken and his fingers bleeding. Ah! Yes, and he had painted a heart with his own blood, just under his name.

He rose with difficulty and continued his search, from one side to the other, in a kind of delirium. The priest got up, put his skinny arm around his waist, and managed to get him back close to the table and make him sit down.

"Quiet down, Gabriel Heliodoro. That was thirty-six years ago. In that time these walls must have been painted many times."

"No, padre, no! No chief of police of any government ever thought of painting jails like this. They were always full of the riffraff of the streets. One time there were fifty persons in this room. They defecated and urinated on the floor. The stink was unbearable. There were people of all sorts. Political prisoners, pickpockets, perverts, drunks. But I must find what I wrote, I must!"

"Why, my son?"

"I want to have a souvenir of the *other* man that I was. The Gabriel Heliodoro of twenty. The revolutionary. The enemy of the dictator."

"Very well. I understand. But finding that inscription is not going to restore your youth to you."

"I know, I know, but that's the only thing left to me now, padre. The only one."

The priest only laid his hand on the condemned man's forehead. "You must have a very high fever. I asked the prison warden more than once to send you a doctor. Until now no one has come."

"Doctor? What for, if they are going to kill me tomorrow? The gangrene works slower than a firing squad."

Gabriel Heliodoro stared fixedly at the candle flame.

Suddenly he exclaimed, "This damned windowless dungeon! One can't see night or day. You never wore a watch, padre. And mine, one of these bailiffs stole from me. We don't know whether day is already breaking."

"Why not write a letter to your family? I have pencil and paper here."

"No. I might let some complaint, some phrase of martyrdom escape to the page. You write it afterward, padre. Say that I thought about them a great deal this last night of mine. Tell them to forgive me. I've been a bad husband, a bad father, a bad grandfather. Tell them not to worry about me. To die is not the worst thing that can happen to a man."

Padre Catalino clasped his folded arms across his stomach.

"Is your ulcer hurting?"

"A little. But it's nothing. I'm used to it."

"Go now, father. You're a sick man. You can't spend a night like this, sleepless."

"Let me see the wound on your leg. And as for that fever—if you could sweat a little. Take an aspirin. Some tablet to relieve your pain."

"Don't bother. I've always borne any pain well. But father, why did you come so far?"

The priest shrugged and smiled in sadness. "I thought I might help a little on this lonely night."

Gabriel Heliodoro picked up the porous clay jug standing beside the candlestick, put it to his mouth, and took a long swallow. He stood up again and recommenced his prowling, candlestick in hand. "Courageous, that *chico* was," he murmured.

"Who?"

"Pablo Ortega. He stood up to Valencia and the thousands of barbarians that wanted to lynch me. He did what he promised. He didn't ask for mercy, he didn't demean me. And he didn't talk about my mother. If there's a thing I can't stand it's other people's pity. Hatred hurts me less than commiseration." He suddenly looked at the priest, as though suspicious. "Padre, did you come to help me through compassion?"

The other shook his head and said, "Compassion? No, my son. The correct word is love."

Gabriel Heliodoro stretched out on the cot. "I thought I was going to die at five in the morning, against a cemetery wall. With five bullets in my chest. Like Juan Balsa."

He ran his shaking hands through his hair. "In a bull-ring—at ten o'clock. With a band, *pasodobles*. A fiesta. At ten in the morning. Padre, why don't you sleep a little?"

The priest of Soledad del Mar shook his head. "No, my friend, a man of my age doesn't need sleep. You are the one who ought to try to sleep. Close your eyes and I'll tell you a story."

"I'm no baby."

"You are, Gabriel Heliodoro. To me you are and always have been the boy who served me as acolyte in the church at Soledad del Mar. Come, try to sleep."

"Within a few hours they are going to put me to sleep forever."

"Forever?" The priest shook his head. "You will awaken in a better world than this, my son."

"In hell?"

"We must never despair of the mercy of God."

Catalino Sender took the bottle of milk he had by his chair and poured a little of its contents into a tin cup. "I am going to nourish my ulcer. Excuse me."

He began sipping the milk without taking his eyes off the condemned man, who was squirming on the bed. A long silence followed. The candle gradually burned lower. The long howl of a dog came to their ears, seeming to come from a remote past, from one of those warm mornings of Soledad del Mar when the boy Gabriel Heliodoro was wandering through the streets, ashamed to return home.

"Padre, you remember my mother, of course."

"I do, indeed."

"She made her confession to you."

"At times. Very few, unfortunately."

"Did she ever tell you who my father was?"

"No. Never. And if she had, I could not break the seal of the confessional."

"Well, anyway, nothing matters now."

A new silence. For a moment Padre Sender had the impression that Gabriel Heliodoro was sleeping. He stood up and covered him with a campaign blanket which gave off a fetid smell like that of a wet dog.

"It must be somewhere," the condemned man muttered.

"What are you talking about, my son?"

"The phrase I wrote with my fingernails. I was twenty years old. Do you remember the day you took me up to the top of the Sierra? I told you I wanted to die for freedom. What am I going to die for now? For nothing. A useless death."

"God writes straight through crooked lines. And the fingers of God sometimes bleed, my son."

Gabriel Heliodoro closed his eyes. His body was shaking from head to foot. And for a moment of delirium—how long had it lasted?—he went wandering over the mountain —young and free, close to the sky and the condors. At last he lifted himself on an elbow and inquired, "What time will they come for me?"

"I don't know, my friend. Perhaps at nine, or nine-thirty."

"Padre, I'm going to ask you a favor. You have some influence with Barrios. Ask him—but in your own name, not mine, understand?—not to let them tie my hands or bandage my eyes. I want to die like a man, not an animal. And I want to look death in the face."

"Your will shall be done. I give you my word."

Gabriel Heliodoro became quiet. He began rubbing between thumb and forefinger the medal of the Virgin which he wore hanging from his neck, like a child who needs a placebo to go to sleep.

47

ACCORDING TO THE political reporter of *Revolución*, the execution of Gabriel Heliodoro Alvarado on that Sunday morning, November 15, 1959, would endure as "a spectacle unforgettable for its symbolic and historic significance." The federal weather bureau had predicted, the evening before, that the weather would remain good for the next twenty-four hours; the temperature would vary between seventy-three and seventy-nine degrees; the relative humidity would not rise above 60 percent, and the winds would be easterly, gentle and cool.

It was common gossip that never in all its history had the Gran Plaza de Toros harbored an audience so numerous, unless perhaps at a certain memorable *corrida* one Sunday in 1943, when Manolete, the famous Spanish matador, had appeared there.

The Sunday sky was an innocent and limpid blue, and a gleaming sun, so clear that it looked more silver than gold, shone down on the velvety greens of the hill and the parks, as well as on the roofs of the old capital of El Sacramento.

Hundreds of persons, fearful of not finding places in spite of holding tickets—for there were reserved seats only for the authorities and the representatives of the press—began arriving at the Plaza de Toros at seven in the morning.

At close to nine o'clock, seeing that the Plaza was already completely filled, the authorities ordered all the gates shut. Police brigades were obliged to go into action several times, and twice had to use tear-gas bombs to hold back the multitude besieging the ring and charging against the police barrier or against the gates, protesting their right to witness the spectacle.

The *Revolución* reporter later wrote:

> It was a pleasure to see the people, persons of all the social strata (except, obviously, members of our decadent oligarchy and the representatives of the so-called upper classes) seated in the amphitheater of the Gran Plaza in the most touching fraternization, singing and dancing to the sound of *pasodobles, boleros,* and marches played by the excellent band of the spirited Corps of Firemen. When the observer looked at the tiers of seats, especially at those on the sunny side, the incessant movement of shirts, banners, handkerchiefs, *rebozos,* and dresses in the richest and most varied colors, gave the effect of a gigantic kaleidoscope in constant, rich mutations. The sun lent changing tints of copper to the arena.
>
> When General Miguel Barrios, president of the Revolutionary Central Committee, entered the box of honor accompanied by other members of his administration, the crowd, estimated at more than 30,000 persons, rose as one, bursting into an ovation for the chief which lasted for more than ten minutes. The National Hymn was then sung.

The producer of the television program which was to broadcast the spectacle "live" had promised since the eve of this day a "dramatic, realistic covering of the execution." He would give the TV viewers the opportunity to see, on the same screen divided in half, the pictures from two cameras. One would show a long shot of the firing squad at the precise instant of discharging their rifles, and the other, thanks to a telescopic lens, would give a close-up of the face of the condemned man in the exact moment when the bullets penetrated his body.

At twelve minutes past 10 A.M. Gabriel Heliodoro entered the arena, surrounded by armed soldiers. He was limping, moving with difficulty, his leg wound throbbing and aching with such intensity that he had to bite his lips to keep from crying out. He walked, however, as erectly as he could, and with head up.